I Am Nero

Samuel Collins

07702 331427
SAM.CADE@GMAIL.COM

ISBN 978-1-84799-935-1

Printed in The United States Of America and in the United Kingdom.

Typeset in Bookman Old Style.

www.iamnero.com
www.lulu.com/content/1002664
www.samuelcollins.com

For my family on both sides;

This is a warning from the Others.

1

It's usually dark when I wake up. The first thing I do when I realise I'm awake is go out of the apartment and check the barricades. I am rich. I am a millionaire. I own the top floors of the tower on Russian Hill Island. I command the twenty below, too, for I blew out the bottom floors with explosive made from gasoline and plastic cups. I used a lot of my fuel up doing it.

There used to be others in the building, on the floors below me and on the two floors above. When the troubles began the rich families on my floor and the penthouse packed up and fled to New York. By this time oil prices were astronomical – rising two or three thousand percent a month, and it was only the rich that could afford to travel – they were the only ones who had somewhere to go.

The two floors of the penthouse were occupied by a Spanish-Filipino banker whose family was old money – old conquistador gold I had the feeling. Michael. He was single, he worked late and, as he had both floors to himself and concierge service, I never saw him in the hallways. Sometimes we crossed paths in the lobby; sometimes I heard him moving above.

One day as I lay listening to the food riots and the sirens and the burning, I heard his phone. It was amazing, for by this time the phones had been completely down in the city for two months, and they had been unreliable for years before – since the waters had begun to rise and flood SoMa, Fisherman's Wharf and Lower Market.

I sat up and listened to the faint electronic ringing of a telephone, quite amazed, and it seemed I wasn't the only one, for the telephone rang for some time before thunderous footsteps ran into the room above mine to retrieve it. Michael's voice was shaking as he answered and that's all I cared to listen to. I could guess what would be happening in New York and the rest of the country. Presently the footsteps and the voice receded, and I realised it must have been a cell phone, if such things still worked, or possibly a satellite phone.

I heard much commotion from above for the rest of that day and much of the night, and it was silent after that. He was gone. That evening Mrs. Leibowitz from the other apartment on my floor knocked on my door, bearing a large cage covered by a cloth.

"Hello?"

"Hello. Oh!" She was nervous and shaken, and we had never really gotten on. Whenever she had passed me on the way to her door or shared an elevator with me, she had treated me with an air of suspicion, but now it seemed she had something to say to me.

"Yes?"

"I – that is – we're leaving, and I was wondering if you would take care of him?" Mrs. Leibowitz held up the cage awkwardly, it swung into my doorframe and banged. Something inside jumped. I knew what it was – it was a rat. I must have looked aghast.

"Oh – you don't have to! Only I promised David I'd ask and we're in such a rush."

"But Mrs. Leibowitz, what will I feed him?" I asked slowly. The woman stared at me and shrugged.

"S... Scraps?"

I almost laughed that, when for months scraps had been all anyone had had to eat, they should be saved for a pet. A pet rat no less.

"I'm sure he would survive if you were to just let him go."

"I see. Of course. I'll tell David. It's just that he wanted to know that he – that he'd be all right."

I could hear the fires and the protests on the island below.

"My dear, I'm afraid none of us will be all right."

At this the woman's face crumpled and she turned, bent as if I had winded her, hit her in the chest with a baseball bat. In that moment I felt as if I had just confirmed all of the woman's worst fears about me.

"Wait." I held out my hand. Mrs. Leibowitz looked at me and handed me the cage. I was now the proud owner of another living thing. I think I must have looked down at the brass handle in my hand for some moments before asking quietly, "Where will you go?"

"New York. Mr. Marquis flew out this morning. He says there are fewer looters left there, and my parents may be... My parents live there."

"But how will you get there? Fly?"

She shook her head. "We don't know when there will be another plane, so we're taking a boat to the interior and then hopefully a convoy, or a – or a bus."

I lowered my voice again. "Mrs Leibowitz, I think it may be very dangerous to cross the continent by land. There may be roving bandits and you have a young family. I think you should wait for another plane if you really think New York will be better. And there will be ice..."

She looked from side to side and shook like a frightened animal, her voice rising in pitch. "The city is burning, we have no food, our ration stamps aren't worth a damn, the police are hijacking supplies so they can run the black market, and in a month we will not be able to afford food, fuel or travel. What do you suggest we do?"

I was about to reply but I could see the woman was desperate and they had decided to run regardless of rhyme or reason. I said simply, "Wait here."

I put down the cage, closed the door, for I did not want her to see my modest stockpiles, and I retrieved a six-pack of bottled water and a small chamois bundle. When I returned with the water her eyes bugged out. It was a small amount to me, but as much as I wanted to part with.

"Take this. Trade it if you have to, but try and save it for yourselves. At least you'll have something safe to drink. It won't last the journey for the three of you so use it only when there's nothing else. And save the bottles and lids – they will be useful."

"Oh thank you."

"Now this – do you know how to use it?" I had unwrapped the yellow chamois leather. Inside was a small silver .22 revolver, mechanical, easy to clean and hard to break. Lying beside it in the hollow of my hands was an almost full box of bullets.

"Oh no, I couldn't!" Mrs Leibowitz cried, her voice cracking. She clutched the water to her breast and looked from my face to the gun with a mixture of horror and confusion. Between the water and the gun I had both confounded and confirmed her fears about me. She squeaked, turned and ran.

I closed the door, placed the gun on the hallway table, nudged the rat's cage to the wall with my foot and went to the refrigerator. I took a drink to the balcony and watched the mayhem across the city islands. There was a barge on fire floating up Market Street, flames were lighting up the waves in the darkness. I sat in the cold night air and drank, safe in my tower and immune. Presently my doorbell buzzed. It was Mr. Leibowitz, face ashen, asking for the gun.

They must have left early the next day, for when I awoke they were gone, and the rat was hungry. I picked up the cage and tried it in many locations throughout the apartment, before settling on a card table in the corner of the living room by the front door. I sat in my leather armchair, staring across the room at that cage for a long time, the electric light flickering all the while, until finally I pulled the cover off the cage. We stared at each other, the rat and I. It sat frozen, on its hind legs, head in hands, it had been washing itself, and was now paralyzed by fear or immodesty at the rude removal of its privacy. I felt equally invaded by its watchful presence.

I fear the rat won the staring contest – the first of many – and then wandered triumphantly across its cage to its empty food dish before sitting in it and turning round to look at me, as if to say, 'You owe me.'

I looked in my kitchen cupboards, knowing full well I had little to offer a precocious black-eyed fiend, and retrieved a packet of granola I had never opened. I poured the packet through the bars in the room of the cage, tipping clumps of cereal onto the animal as it shook its hide and ran its paws through its fur.

I settled down to read, after shutting the windows firmly in an attempt to keep out the incessant wailing from below and the ever-present smell of smoke, but peace was not to be mine. The rat shuffled. Just occasionally. Just often enough to make its presence felt. When I looked again, the rat was still sitting in its food dish. It had cleaned itself and pushed all of the granola out onto the sawdust floor. Heaven knows where Leibowitz had gotten sawdust, but the rat was soon to find it a luxury his new provider-prisoner could not afford.

Sustenance however, was a necessity, and although my fridge and freezer were at that time well stocked, I was in the habit of making regular forays out onto the streets to see what I could find. I usually waited until 4 a.m. before venturing out. It was both as late as I dared, being an hour and a half before sunrise (when the looters would rise), and late enough that the majority of the night-favouring cutthroats had drunk themselves to sleep on moonshine made from meths – the less crazy ones that is – those that were out for the pickings, and not the action.

Whilst I must admit it is the more crazy ones – the ones that enjoy the business of cutting another – that I find more diverting, I do not care to be outnumbered. At about 3.30 or 3.45 I locked up my little apartment, and made my way slowly down twenty flights of steps, cursing the constant brownouts that meant that riding the elevators was something akin to playing a game of Russian roulette with a machine gun.

That night I had stood in my kitchen and pondered my supplies. I knew exactly what I had, even as I looked through the cupboards. I had food in bags and jars – things that had never been opened. There were boxes of matches and lighters, candles. A medicine kit with bandages and peroxide – how I love that sting. I have an extra small pantry – between the kitchen and dining room, and an extra large freezer, well stocked, as I said.

The bathroom may seem an odd place to keep fuel but it is a sealed, tiled room with nothing to burn. Tin tanks of gasoline sit in the white enamel bath; bottles of propane go on the floor. That door stays firmly locked. I use my small en-suite to wash up – when there is running water that is.

The water I keep in a Victorian mahogany cabinet in the living room. The guns rest in a Japanese wardrobe of about the same period. It is ebony with brass inlay and has a secret keyless locking mechanism that is mostly just for show – any fool with a flick knife or a spoon could prise it open. The wardrobe sits in the corner of the room and looks marvellously inconspicuous – the sort of object that appears to have no use but to stand there and decorate a room – not something you'd actually keep things in – a unique achievement for something the size of a wardrobe.

My generator stands outside on the balcony so that I will not be disturbed by the fumes. There is no escaping the noise however – it's enough to wake the dead. I actually bought it after the first fuel crisis, when things started to get shaky and before the first riots. It has a little plug and socket arrangement for the freezer, and turns itself on whenever the mains cuts out for more than a few seconds – which is about twenty times a day – on the days we have any power on the island.

That night I wandered around my apartment with a scrap of paper, pen in mouth, writing a list of things to look for. It was a short list:

Water
Fuel
Ammunition
Anything useful.

The rat rattled its cage.
Rat food.

2

Much of Russian Hill was residential, which meant there was little left to pick through, but I could go as far east as North Beach before hitting water, and there were shops and warehouses there that had been defended longer and were not yet empty. There was one building in particular that I wanted to take another look at, by Broadway and Montgomery. Although it was on the edge of the water, it didn't appear that anyone had been inside. The doors were welded shut and there were no windows on the first floor. I had had my eye on it for some time. Besides, I had a feeling there had been a pet shop on Broadway and Columbus.

I made my way down the stairs quietly. The stairwell is a cold empty space with a propensity for echoes. Whilst most of the building was empty – those that had the least to lose and the most to preserve had up and left when the waters began to rise – there were several groups of squatters on the lower floors and I liked to avoid them.

The lobby doors had been chained shut and ringed with razor wire some months before – when looters had smashed the windows and broken into the estate office. Whilst the barricade was mostly for show, for there were a dozen ways to get into the building, it was a shame it did nothing for the brass and mirrored deco styling of the lobby. I continued down to the garage, and made my way through to the dumpsters, which, although they had not been filled for months, they had not been emptied either. The putrid smell of the contents was over-sweet and rancid at the same time, and always hit me with the force of a streetcar.

With some trepidation I climbed onto the dumpster nearest the bay doors and lifted myself through the broken window above it, dragging my flesh over glass fragments and sharp wire mesh from the safety glass. Half in, half out, this is the moment you are most vulnerable. Stuck like a pig in its slaughter pen, someone outside could slit your throat as you hung there. For this reason you pull yourself through as fast as possible and run from the building as soon as you hit the ground.

It is amazing how quickly a city decays once people stop caring for it. Making my way down towards the Broadway Tunnel, past the burnt-out shells of million-dollar Victorian townhouses and silver Mercedes flipped onto their roofs, what I notice most is not the human damage, but nature. There are rats and foxes and crawling things everywhere. The concrete of the pavement is splitting into squares as weeds run down the mould lines. The roads are green and crumbling where pipes have burst, algae-laden streams running downhill. A fissure has appeared in the middle of the street where a sewer has collapsed and the tarmac subsided. Flames roar at the top of the hill where the subsidence has sheared a gas main. It has been burning for weeks.

I avoid the Broadway Tunnel itself, for I like my head connected to my shoulders as it is, and join Broadway a couple of blocks down, sticking mostly to the shadows. I pass through Chinatown, where even the prostitutes have gone to bed, and find the pet shop I've been looking for. It is mostly for fish, the windows are shattered, the tanks dry and overturned. Broken glass crunches beneath my feet, the air stinks of decay. I do not linger.

In the hardware store next door I have more luck. The store has been gutted, shelves smashed, strip lighting swinging from the ceiling, but in the back room there is a medicine cabinet. Someone has taken the drugs but left the sterile cotton gauze – fools. On the floor in the corner are a crushed hypodermic and a human turd nestling in shredded newspaper like an exotic bird. I stuff the gauze in my pocket, wanting to flee, but not before I have checked under the sink. Half a bottle of bleach. I take it. It thuds against my back in my small bag as I run from the mounting claustrophobia of that dark back room.

I run downhill, a little too fast to be quiet. I do not want to look in more shops, or any more buildings where I have no business, although no one has business being anywhere these days – but we all want to survive. I am outside the warehouse before I know it, and I look up and down the street. I check my watch. Twenty minutes before dawn – I should go, but I do not want to have to leave without knowing. Most of all, I do not want to come back here. Half a block down hill, the waters of the bay are lapping at the pavement.

I slip my shoes off quickly and stuff them in my bag. I will not leave them on the street. I climb up a dead telegraph pole, the way I have seen islanders climb palms, hanging back on their arms and pushing out with their feet. A thousand rusty staples from fly posting bite into my palms and soles, and then it is creosote and splinters all the way up. I keep climbing until I am level with the warehouse windows, but they are four feet away and twenty-five feet up. At this point I realise there may be a slight flaw in my plan. I strain to see through the window, but I can only see across, not down into the space. I want to fling myself onto the warehouse wall, but there is nothing to hold on to, and I am running out of time. I slide down the pole, risking more splinters, and walk around the building.

On the side of the warehouse that descends into the water there is a fire escape. I could kick myself. I will have to come back. I wonder how secure the fire door is. For a moment I am caught staring out at the bay, and I walk down onto a makeshift jetty – the cremated remnants of a Victorian, a store that used to sell T-shirts and CDs. Now all that's left are the foundations and the shelf of the ground floor, graded flat away from the incline, stretching out into the water to form a pontoon. From here people take small boats out to the shanties on Alcatraz or try and make it across to Berkeley and the interior.

The bay is bigger now, swallowing up the land we'd reclaimed, and I am struck by a sight I'd never imagined. Treasure Island has drowned under many metres of water, betrayed only by a dark slick of fuel oil in the threatening swell above it. Beyond the oily stain and the peak of Yerba Buena Island, the Oakland section of the Bay Bridge was conspicuously absent – collapsed during a continuous series of earthquakes the later, more flexible span was never intended to survive. The new pillars stand naked out of the water, bewildered and alone. Sparse lights glint across the bay from Oakland and Berkeley, few of them electric. The sky must be breaking above the mountains in the East, but I can't tell – the scrub on Grizzly Peak has been burning for two weeks and the horizon is blood red.

I walk further out onto the jetty, the brick and concrete crumbling into the water. I am careful to avoid the rotten floorboards and the failing concrete, burnt stakes of wood that had been doorframes, and sharp spikes of rebar rusting down to a lethal point. I'm looking out towards Yerba Buena Island, which has become a fortress for the looters and pirates and the police that protect them, a fortress, for those that have. I almost don't notice the steps down into the black water; I almost fall into the drowning hole, for the steps are not on the outside, leading to the sea, they are in the middle of the pontoon, leading to the basement.

I am straining to see the lights on the Bay Bridge, peering between the ruined skyscrapers of the Financial District. Those few towers that have survived the earthquakes, the fires, the riots, are slowly toppling one by one as the water rots their foundations, set as they are in sawdust-rich reclaimed land. They lean quite gradually, shifting so slowly that you don't notice the difference day by day, and then reinforced concrete pilings snap one after the other, bang, bang, bang, an explosive sound like battleship artillery, and the tower goes down like a felled tree, or a pile of plates, fracturing in the middle on the way down. Each tower leaves a valley of destruction in the concrete around it, knocking off wings, roofs, burying whole buildings. The water is criss-crossed with fresh sand banks of lethal rubble, each fall sends waves across the bay to Berkeley, but the explosive noise beats them to the shore.

There used to be regimented strings of lights dancing along the piers and cables of the Bay Bridge, lighting it up like a Christmas decoration. Now the decks are dotted with their camp fires and Coleman lamps, their fishing poles, looters and families living in tents, surrounded by the parasites that support them – mechanics, clothiers, food dealers, all hoping for crumbs, for the first pick of the leftovers. Anyone whose usefulness expired lost their place on the bridge – the supply line to the fortress and the big boys. The parasites promptly expired themselves, to be replaced by two others. Light from the fires shimmered on the wavelets below. The water had almost reached the lower deck.

I looked away from the pirates' trophy and notice a body lying face up in the water, hands bound above his head, snagged on a piece of the rebar that lined the edges of the pontoon. It is Mr. Leibowitz. His throat has been cut. The fish have nibbled at his milky eyes and his bloated lips. I have seen this death-grimace before – the Yehudi that taught me English in Prague – matted hair wafting in the dark waters of my memory.

There is something stuffed in Leibowitz' mouth, unfurling, wafting gently in the current. It is packaging, plastic shrink-wrap emblazoned with the brand of mineral water I gave his wife. I feel sticky somehow, something catches in my throat as I trace the line of events from my doorstep to the black death bobbing in the water. My face flushes and the backs of my palms crawl, the world abandons me to the lonely, yearning emptiness gathering in my gut. I hurry back to the tower as the sky brightens. I do not want anyone to see me.

It was a little while after the Leibowitzs had moved out that the squatters really became a problem. I had barricaded the top floors, but people were moving in down below. You may have guessed by now that real estate above the rising sea level was at a premium, and I enjoyed a neighbourhood clientele of crack whores, muggers and desperate refugees.

One evening a meth addict tried to mug me on the stairs. This is precisely what one moves to Russian Hill to avoid. I was coming up and he was above, waiting. It would have been much more effective if he had had an accomplice below me, but then, I suppose being a meth addict does not require you to be the sharpest tool in the box. But there he was, above me on the corner landing, shaking and rocking back and forth as I approached. He waited, head bowed, shuffling back and forth, flashing the knife. I think he hoped not to have to use it. I think he hoped to intimidate me, but he screamed like a child when I told him I carried nothing of value. He was furious. Stanley knives are not very effective as weapons.

I dealt with him, but it shook me up. A messy business on your own doorstep. Now if I have to go out I make sure I carry a knife, or a gun, although perversely guns tend to increase chances of being mugged. They are both a fashion and a necessity on the streets and you attract a certain kind of attention from teenage gangs if you are seen to be stepping out alone with a piece. It's such a waste of bullets. Of course, when the troubles began there was a glut of guns on the streets, but I guess the factories ran out of metal, or energy, and then transporting anything became difficult. Bullets are so expensive on the black market now that you think seriously before plugging someone. This was, of course, the wager the muggers made every time they tried to take one. I don't know what amazed me more – how often they tried it, or how often the prospective victim didn't shoot them.

I began to realise that I had something that people wanted: height. People were moving in, heading further and further up the tower, attracted by the relative security of the apartments, which had not been burnt, had not been looted, which required the use of a narrow set of stairs. You could not get a gang up those wrought iron steps quickly – or quietly. It wouldn't be long before they reached my flimsy barricades and wondered what it was exactly that they were built to protect.

I have no objection to neighbours – good, decent, hard working folks, who went to their jobs and bought their food, but there were no jobs; there were no shops. You either lived under the police, with their dwindling pile of commandeered food stocks, you worked for the looting gangs, or you fended for yourself. It amounts to the same thing really. I was increasingly certain that once the squatters and gangs had scoured the floor below mine, they would turn to me. They would wonder what I had that they could take.

The looters were moving up floor by floor. I noticed what they were doing as I came down the stairs one evening. There was a group of teenagers wearing torn clothes and nose rings, their hair gelled and coloured in improbable shapes (with what? I wondered). They had the stairwell door open on the sixteenth floor and were breaking into the apartments, going from room to room and smashing up the furniture for firewood. One of them passed me on the stairs. A fragile girl of fourteen trying to look nineteen, she wore an oversized leather jacket – phoenix decal catching my eye, and showed a fondness for safety pin jewellery. She pushed past me carrying a bundle of chair legs under her arm. Fools I thought. Smash the kitchen cupboards, you'll be left with nothing to sit on. I caught myself wondering if there was anything left that I couldn't put to use myself.

The stench of people living badly had gotten stronger on the lower floors, and it was beginning to rise. Given the absence of elevators, the squatters packed themselves in on those floors, forming uncomfortable groups until fights broke out, and the loser would be forced upstairs, further from the outside world – and further from fresh water.

By the time I'd reached the fourth floor the stench of shit and stale bodies was thick in the air, and so was the smoke. People were cutting holes in the carpets and laying fires on the concrete floor beneath. There was graffiti on the walls, much of it in charcoal, much of it beautiful. A little one had stood on the steps and scrawled a group of stick figures low on the wall. A family, a house, a big sun above the wonky roof.

Trash littered everything. Food cans, bits of plastic, dead batteries and burnt wood. People hung around the lobby – the main doors had been cleared courtesy of a joyrider – and anyone who was willing to climb over the bonnet of a burnt-out Chevy, was welcome to join the party and shoot up in the estate office. I stopped leaving through the garage for a time. I would get more attention down there than by crawling over the rusty bodywork and broken glass.

11

Occasionally while I was asleep people 'tested' the stairwell doors that I had barricaded. I wasn't worried about the elevators – I had wedged the doors open, which locked them off, and there had been no power now for weeks anyway. But the stairwell doors were another matter. I had begun by taking the handles off the stairwell side of each door, but that meant having to carry wire and pliers with me every time I went down, in order to be able to twist the mechanism and roll back the bolts. It took me thirty seconds to re-enter – not good if you had a mob behind you. And it would only take someone else thirty seconds too, given a wire hanger and the inclination.

The good thing about fire doors is that they are made of steel. The bad thing is that, being designed as emergency exits, they are hard to secure. I went out one evening, ostensibly to scrounge food for the rat, but mostly because I'd avoided the mayhem, sat in for a week reading and was going slowly mad. When I opened the door I discovered it had been badly dented on the other side and the locking mechanism had been ruined, torn up by a crowbar.

Luckily, in smashing the mechanism the vandal had ruined his chances of sliding the bolt back but the push bar on my side still worked, albeit stiffly. I quickly abandoned my plans and checked the door on the other stairwell. There were deep gashes around the doorframe where the vandal had tried to lever the door with the bar, but he hadn't tried the mechanism again. A good thing too – it might have worked. I would have had an unexpected wake-up call.

I stripped the locks from the Leibowitz' front door and fitted them to the doors. It is not easy cutting a perfect one-inch hole in steel plate. In the end I filed it. One of the locks was stronger than the other, but for a while I felt safe, even when I opened the door to find a small axe stuck in the jam, its wooden handle snapped off, leaving a jagged and splintery amputated stub. Even when I opened the door only to step out onto burnt timbers and find the white walls had turned to grimy black from the bonfire lit against the door. They were fire doors, after all.

What upset me was coming to the door one night after leaving my apartment and finding I couldn't open it! I listened carefully for sounds from the other side, something that had become a habit, and then I pushed down the lever. Something went crunch, but the door didn't open. I panicked. I pulled, I pushed. I kicked the door and then went at it with my shoulder.

I cannot stand the idea of being trapped and helpless. I am going to be stuck up here, slowly running out of supplies 'til thirst drives me mad, 'til like an animal I try to climb down the outside of the building, dropping from balcony to balcony, until I slip on a wet railing and roll and plunge and...

I stop and think, and run to the far stairwell, the one with a different lock that requires I turn a key on either side. I slide the key into the lock and it turns and then! Then I am out into the stale cold stairwell air and the dangerous shadows. The stairwells are not connected so I must go down a floor, across the hallway and up again to discover what they have done. This is risky in itself – I do not want to be seen. Every time I go out now I run the risk of being trapped and flushed out by waiting gangs, like a hunted deer in the woods. The fact that I am locking doors, protecting something is attracting attention. It is dangerous for me to leave, in case they are waiting when I return. No one knows who I am, I do not speak to them, I do not let them see me. I am a phantom. I wonder what I will do about this latest problem – I will not be trapped.

I inspect the damage. Someone has inserted a hypodermic into the keyhole and snapped it off. Turning the lock has smashed it to bits and ground it into the mechanism. I don't need to worry about this door any more, but if I leave it jammed and they do something to the other door I am in real trouble. I sneak back.

In the end I remove the lock from the door, but I leave the circular faceplate and the barrel behind, so it looks like the door is still jammed. I cut the back off one of the Liebowitz's chairs, and chain it to the dead push bar so it is braced across the doorframe. Testing the door I know the arrangement works, but it means there is only one working door, and one escape route from my floor.

One night they tried to trap me. It was my fault. I came down the stairs, slowly and quietly, ready to duck out through the fire doors should anyone come up. I had begun to peek through the doors as I went, checking to see which floors were currently unoccupied and safe for hiding.

You may wonder why I took such trouble to avoid my neighbours, hiding up in my ivory tower while the world around me fell apart. Everything was quiet that night, even the rioting had died down. So I moved with a lightness in my step, anxious to take a walk in outside spaces, and fresh air. Somewhere on the way down I had stopped checking floors, and on the lower levels I was dimly aware that there were people around me, talking, crying, sleeping on the other side of a brick wall or a steel wall.

That was to be expected, people lived on these floors, whole tribes secreted within an apartment or a room, trying to stay alive by trading skills, favours, by foraging outside, by mugging others and protecting their own. I had gotten used to their sounds and their presence and my little ways of staying unseen, so I sailed down the stairs on automatic, thinking about the outside and the glorious moonlight. For once I wanted to go down to the water's edge, breathe fresh air, take a walk and look out across the bay. I wanted space.

Therefore, I was rather self-absorbed when I arrived at the ground floor and turned out into the lobby. I had crossed the floor and reached a broken cascade of a rusting Chevy blocking the entrance doors before awareness cracked me out of my daydream. There was a figure sitting in the dark, huddled in the corner of one of the ruined couches. It was the little punk girl with the safety pins, arms wrapped around herself, shivering in the night breeze. She had a black eye, a bloody nose and a torn earlobe. She had been sobbing quietly, but when I burst into the room she froze, like an animal that had been caught out. When I looked at her with shock she quickly looked away, as if she had seen nothing, as if she did not know who I was. She was smart enough to act like she didn't care who any stranger was, ignoring the presence of strangers as an everyday occurrence. To stare would have been to invite the attentions of an unknown marauder in her building.

She looked away stubbornly, as if to say, 'I have seen nothing, I don't know anything, I don't way to know anything, I am a witness to nothing, now do me the same courtesy.' Fiercely she wiped a stray tear from her cheek, and fought back a sniffle. I imagined her as two years ago, just before the collapse. A little girl playing in the light, a yellow dress and pigtails. Somebody's daughter. Now she is sitting in a derelict building, crying over a black eye and a stolen leather jacket.

I looked away quickly and climbed over the wrecked car to get outside as quickly as I could. I was kicking myself for being seen, and although the girl didn't seem to know who I was, it had brought my mood down. I'd just lost a game I'd been playing with myself.

I made my way North, the quickest way to water, for the Marina had been flooded along with most of Fort Mason. It felt good to be walking, stretching my body free in the space and chill night air. There are some old streetcar tunnels in the hillside above that haven't been used for years. I swung by them to see if the fences had been broken down yet. They hadn't. Hidden under hanging ivy the tunnels go unnoticed. They're not a place I'd like to be trapped, but maybe a good hiding spot should I ever need it. One of those places I file away in my mind for emergencies.

When I reached the water's edge the tide line was thick with oil and debris. An armless doll bobbled in the wavelets. Tupperware boxes swamped with engine oil drifted in the shallows. The shoreline was a deadly tangle of soccer netting and electric flex, trapping old clothing and empty bottles of shampoo. The sea smelled of filth and decay, and just fifty feet beyond the water's edge lay a treacherous reef of submerged homes, their timbers turning to mush in the saltwater. Anything buoyant had liberated itself, floating up through broken windows and open doors, making a break for the shore propelled by the lapping waves. Most of the larger items never made it, stolen away by the undercurrent – there was a steady procession of construction timber and disintegrating furniture trickling out to sea.

I had hoped to gaze at open water, but fog concealed everything this side of the hills, and I was left with a claustrophobic sense of white-blindness. The moonlight filtered through the layers of grey, leaving an impenetrable blank expanse of flat dimness before me, disorientating me. Trapped between that closeness and the filthy water, I couldn't see a hundred yards but I could hear the night encroaching all around me – distant rustlings as people picked through burnt-out houses, a fight in the tent camps occupying the parkland above Fort Mason. Things crawled and gnawed at the water's edge – the click of their jaws ran up my spine. Rats scampered through the netting and the seaweed.

I made my way back walking uphill as the fog rolled further in and took on the dawn glow. I was almost glad when I saw my building with its broken windows, and the smoke stains reaching up the walls. There were no lights on, no campfires in the rooms. You couldn't tell if there was anyone in the lobby until you'd committed yourself to climbing over the Chevy, so I went round the side of the building and climbed through the estate office window. The crunch of broken glass underfoot as I stepped in seemed deafening, but the only ones to notice were the rats.

There's an upturned desk in the office, a safe in the corner with its door hanging off. By the door are the discarded remains of a homemade heroin pipe – silver foil, a plastic lemonade bottle and the tube of a ballpoint pen. I sneak into the hallway that links the office, the lobby and the stairwells behind the elevator. As I approach the first stairwell, the one that leads to the only working door on my floor, I can hear a cluster of feet shuffling, people breathing softly. My first instinct is to bolt but there is little time to find a place to hide. I duck beneath the cracked pane of safety glass in the door and sneak past, crossing the length of the elevator back to the other stairwell. If there are people here I may be looking for somewhere else to sleep, maybe those tunnels – if I can get there in time.

Standing against the wall by the doorframe, I hear nothing. Carefully I sneak a look through the glass – empty – but the field of view is very limited. Hastily I stretch out into the emptiness with my mind but sense nothing. If they are waiting below the stairs or above I will have to run. I turn the handle as slowly as I can, but it clicks anyway. Standing back to the wall, I push the door open a crack. The only sound I hear is my heart thumping in my ears. There is no movement when I look through the gap. If they are clever they will wait until I am through the door and I'm committed. I push the door wider. No smell, no sound. I am through the door and jogging swiftly up the stairs in the darkness, swinging myself around the corners by hanging off the banisters. I am trying to be quiet, but the higher I climb the higher my anger rises. I am furious. I am fleeing for my life like a dog, and I know that outside this stairwell, morning is breaking with a brilliant sunrise.

It seems that I've gone unnoticed, but I still have to cross a hallway to the other stairwell and the working door. As I turn the corner on the fifteenth floor with my heart hammering and my blood burning like fire, I see a small battered face peeking through a crack in the fire door. For a moment our eyes meet as I come up the stairs, and her eyelids leap open in fear. It is the punk girl, and I know I've been made. Then the door slams and there are footsteps in the hallway behind and she is running and I am running, up up up I run, I let her go. She will be crossing the hallway to yell down the other stairwell that I am here, that I've fooled them. It doesn't matter, I am too far ahead, they could never run up these stairs the way I do. I keep going.

There is the sound of slamming doors below, but also above, and the horror spreads out in my mind like a forest fire. They were waiting upstairs! Thunderous voices echo from below, shouting and yelling. I am dizzy with the twisting of the staircase, but must keep going. I count seven different voices. Flashlights pierce the darkness above, two beams spiralling round and round as they thunder down. I consider crossing over to the other stairwell, maybe doubling back, but I don't know who will be waiting behind those windowless fire doors, and it will give those below more time to catch up. I keep going. I have more chance if I allow the men above to get as close as possible before crossing stairwells. If I let them get close and they are stupid, they will come down to follow me through the same corridor and end up behind me.

I can hear them coming. They are very close now, their flashlights bright. I cannot breathe, my lungs are burning and I can hear almost nothing for the rush of blood cutting through my ears. I make it to the landing of the eighteenth floor and a beam of brilliant white light hits me in the face, blinding me. I freeze, knowing I am inches from a fire door. There is thunder rising from below, but above is still and silent.

The beam is lowered. Staring back at me is a skinhead – all cut-off denim shorts and a chain bunched up in his hand, and a longhaired greaser in a leather jacket, phoenix wings curling around from the back. They are leaning over the banisters above, waiting on the landing. In a strange moment of recognition we lock eyes and catch our breath. I am furious, a cornered animal, I could kill them both. I wait for them to come down. I need them to come down. They wait to see what I will do.

I reach out a hand towards the fire door, never breaking eye contact with the skinhead. He smiles, an evil gash opening across his face, crooked teeth glinting. The chain slithers down out of his hand, unravelling into one length, and I make a bet with myself. I am stronger than these men. I am faster.

I yank open the door with a force that sounds like an explosion and I run, I do not wait to see if they have followed. Behind I hear their screams as they tell those below that I've crossed, but that is all I hear, no footsteps. It hasn't worked. I am running, praying for the sound of the door opening behind me, but it doesn't come. They did not follow me. They are crossing above. They will be above me when I hit the other stairwell, but I am faster, my only hope is to climb the stairs and get above them before they cut me off at the far stairwell.

I have to slow down before I reach the second fire door so I can turn and open it. There could be men behind it, but I have no time for guessing – if I stay I will be trapped. I could double back, but that means crossing twice more and there are men closing in from below.

I burst through the door into the stairwell, and am running up the stairs before I realise that I can't hear anyone else. I am alone in the stairwell, they have not come through! Just two more floors to go! My hands are shaking as I fumble in my pocket for the key, and my legs are near collapse. My throat is a constricted tangle of barbed wire and I can barely breathe. I round the landing on the nineteenth, and the fire door explodes open in front of me. The skinhead bursts out, and I run straight into him. I roar, I am enraged. The force of the impact slams him into the door and I wrap my arms around him as we roll around it. As we spin I use inertia to propel us towards the wrought iron banister. I push with one arm and wrench with the other, lifting him and throwing him down the stairwell. Not down the stairs but over the stanchion through the rotten safety mesh and down the well – twenty floors down the well. The mesh, a notional gesture to safety, wraps around him like spider's silk around a fly and he screams all the way down.

As I let go of the skinhead my heels catch the bottom step of the next flight, I fall down backwards. I crack my head open and I am half blind with stars, listening to the bitter sounds of success as the blood rolls down my back. I lie there as the skinhead falls, propped up on the steps and staring into the eyes of the greaser. He is a statue frozen in the doorway, gaping. He is terrified. His eyes widen with every sound of his friend knocking off the banisters on his way down, the horror stare of shock bores right into me. Locked into eye contact by tunnel vision, I cannot break that stare even as the world turns grey, I breathe deeply, he is standing over me, I must not pass out.

Like being in a car crash, the moment lasts forever. I am numb, this is a dream and I am watching it from the outside as always. *How strange*, I think, *how strange*, as I notice the man has time to take a breath and scream anew before he hits the ground. The sound is an explosive crack echoing from floor to floor. There is a commotion downstairs. Someone screams, shrieks. The sound of the impact is still ringing in my ears. The greaser begins to shake uncontrollably, his headlamp clutters to the ground, but he cannot break eye contact with me. He cannot even blink.

As I look at him I realise he is just a boy of maybe

seventeen, filthy red hair, a desperately cultivated beard emerging in patches from his chin. His is the phoenix jacket that used to adorn the little punk girl. She may have earned it back this night, but it has cost us all.

I stand up, trying desperately to look as though I can keep my balance, conscious that shock will soon turn to the thirst for vengeance. I must get inside and make sure the bleeding stops. The ever-brighter colour of dawn in the skylight tells me there is little time. The boy is still shaking as I stand up. I consider threatening him, warning him. It will do nothing – I fear this will escalate. In the end I just start towards him, he bolts.

The wailing sound floods up the stairs in waves as I make my way up. I open my clenched hand for the key to discover that in the impact the metal has torn my skin and buried itself deep in the meat of my thumb. I'd felt no pain till now. The blood runs for a short time as I pull the teeth from my flesh. My last thought as the key slides into the lock is the hope that it will not rust the mechanism.

Another door and I am safe in the shuttered darkness, the peace of my own familiar apartment. My appearance in the calm shocks the rat into stillness. I make straight for the bathroom and wrap a bandage around my head, although the wound is already drying. My veins are shredding my flesh like the lines of razor wire, my head is thudding and I am starving. I take a gun out of the cabinet and a bag out of the fridge. Soon they will be pounding the doors at the stairs. Soon I will be besieged. I know my supplies – my freezer is stocked – I could last for a year if I'm careful, but the generator – I have gas to run the generator for three weeks. I have maybe a month, months, and then things get bloody. I place a chair behind the front door and crawl into bed clutching a semi automatic pistol for comfort. The rat shuffles around in his cage, his gnawing rattles like a Gatling gun. I don't notice – I'm already asleep.

I wake up in a blind panic. I am drenched in sweat, my wounds stuck to the sheets. I sit up, and paw the clock on the table by my bed, but it is dead, wound down, and now I know it is late.

Judging by the sounds from below, and the darkness in the cracks between the shutters, it is past midnight, but I don't know whether I have lost a day, or two, or more. Presently I realize that there is no longer any way to know – I have no one to ask and there is no Internet to tell me. The sense of emptiness fills me then, the sense of loss. I am adrift, drowning in the uncertainty of it. I may have slept a day, I may have slept through several. The time passes regardless, but I will never be certain of the reality of it. The truth of it has been lost to me. For once I miss the constructed human world with its assigned values, its electronic diaries and one-way streets; but the truth is that I am more comfortable within the beautiful destruction that is going on around me. It's a process I understand, a world I can relate to – one where the rules of survival and entropy are hard and solid and come down to strength and determination or death. It's a tightrope walk surely, but you know you can at least walk forward.

Entropy is predictable, I've seen its desires before and I know my rivals well. I know the rules. Survival in the human world is something else. It confounds me. The rules are made and broken according to perception and position. It's a treacherous world where meaning is a fluid thing, it doesn't matter how well you can walk the tightrope – someone is always waiting to cut the line.

But just now I miss the newspapers and the Internet and the goddamn running water. I want a radio station. I want a clock. I want to know how long I was asleep. I want to know if this is the day they call Wednesday or the day they call Monday. I may have slept a week, or an hour. I lie there, trapped in a limbo of my own making as the thought strikes me – this could be the same day. Cast adrift in uncertainty I do not know what I have lost, if anything, and so I *am* lost. I am either/or. I am Schrödinger's Cat.

I am lonely.

I sit and listen to the building, it is strangely quiet. I get out of bed and open the shutters and let the city in. So much darker than it used to be, I miss the electric chandelier that used to illuminate the land. Now I count the islands by the blusters of fire dotted about in the water, gazing out at the narrow strips of land and chains of islands that lead down to San Jose and Santa Cruz.

I take a couple of bottles of water and clean my wounds. They are mostly scabbed over, mostly swollen lumps of flesh. I cannot pick all the grains of dried blood out of my matted hair. I stand before the mirror in my small bathroom, trying to see in the darkness. The only light comes from the city, weak fingers reaching across from the bedroom windows. A dim orange glow. It used to streak across the bed in hard white lines. I could run a lead from the generator, or light another stub of candle. Instead I simply wash in the dark. I take a cloth and use the precious water on my skin. I do it slowly, savouring the feeling as the fibres drag over the surface of my being. It is two months since I have done this. After the first week you start to notice your own smell. After the second it is gone again – so ubiquitous it is. After a month the stickiness doesn't bother you. Strangely, you don't notice the way other people smell much either. I don't mind anyway – this is old, well-trodden ground.

I don't allow myself to debate the necessity of wasting two small bottles of water on such a luxury as washing my skin. I just do it. If I thought about it I would stop, but stubbornly I continue. I am stiff, in pain, I want to feel fresh and most of all I want to feel clean again. I will never feel clean.

I've tried to keep my apartment clean, civilized. It helps me to maintain the illusion of order when all around is chaos. It helps me to feel I have some control. The surfaces are clean, the books are on their shelves – I don't like clutter. I have no way to wash the bedclothes however. I strip the bed and air the sheets on the balcony. It is quiet below. There is no one on the intersection or the streets, and the night's fires are dying down. The windows in the building are dark. It would be peaceful, but for the incessant thrum of the generator, the bitter smell of the fumes.

I dress in fresh clothes I have been saving – another luxury, and take a drink. I must look after myself until I am healed. For the last few hours of the night I read. Feeling mellow I sit in my leather chair, a row of candle stubs dripping wax onto an old table, and finish a book. The stock of unread books on my shelves is dwindling – soon I will have to raid the Liebowitz' – something I've been reluctant to do. She might come back.

It is almost dawn when I look up from the book. I am stiff as I crawl into bed. I do not check the doors in the corridor, although the thought chases me into sleep. If they were not sound I would be dead by now.

3

The next few evenings passed peacefully. I would get up, clear away the things from the night before – glasses, candle stubs, before topping up the generator's fuel tank. Once I had to change the gas bottle on the camping stove in the kitchen. I haunted that kitchen, buzzing around the fridge like a fly, holding off the moment I would open the fridge door and boil the double burner on the little camping stove. I would putter about the place pretending I had something to do, pretending that outside of my apartment everything was fine, pretending I wasn't running out of time.

In the early evening I would turn on my radio. It would hiss and crackle, and then burble its way tonelessly through the digital channels, and I would cycle through the bands, listening for signs of life. Sometimes I picked up echoes in the static, breaks in the vague pattern of hum that I could make no sense of. After a few minutes of searching I would snap the radio off decisively, frustrated by the endless white noise or the incomprehensible silences, telling myself I was 'saving the batteries' – afraid that I was listening too hard – conjuring ghosts and shadows in the chaos, all the time denying a pervasive sense of loneliness I had never experienced before. I must have grown soft in the twenty-first century magic.

With the Internet down there was no reason to turn on my modest computer, and it would have meant stepping up the generator, using more gas. I've never owned a TV – they've always left me with a sense of claustrophobia, but few people had one anyway – video was piped through the net to everyone who could afford it.

Often I would sit on the balcony, drink in hand, and gaze out at the archipelago. My balcony looked out on the Financial District and the Transamerica Pyramid, one of the last skyscrapers still standing, still inhabited, a lonely few of its windows lit eerily at night. Apart from a large burn mark that emerged from the windows about halfway up, scarring one side of the tower, it showed no signs of relenting. It wasn't tilting awkwardly the way most of its tumbledown neighbours were –

something to do with its extreme taper I suspect. As a stretched out pyramid it would have to tilt a whole lot further than most buildings before it was actually compromising its centre of gravity and leaning.

I would rest my arms on the balcony railings and look out, or sit in my recliner and sip the cooling liquid slowly from my glass. Either way I had to work hard to ignore the smells drifting upwards. With no running water, the people in the tower were tipping bedpans out of the windows, and a mound of rat infested shit and garbage was collecting around the base of the building, a deadly moat of filth and decay writhing in extreme slow motion. Fresh water was now the currency on any island in the city, and disease swept through the people like waves of wildfire.

The water was controlled by two factions, the Police, who had retreated to The Sunset, ran the racket along the southern island chain down to San Jose, and the looters on Yerba Buena and the Bay Bridge – the Looter's Causeway – headed by a gang known as the Piranhas, dominated everything east of drowned Van Ness. The two factions skirmished regularly over supplies coming in via tanker, and to guarantee a reliable source of water you had to ally yourself with one group or the other. Otherwise you had dehydration, typhoid and cholera to look forward to. Consequently I was aware that I had a small fortune in fresh water stashed safely away in the cabinet in my living room – enough to keep a normal family of four alive for eight weeks if they were careful, and the longer I saved it the more valuable it became.

I would often look out at night and see lights flickering on the radio masts atop Twin Peaks, for if I turned I could just see Upper Market and the parklands from my balcony. Those were the nights when the army would be broadcasting their secrets. Soon after the riots began, the military commandeered the rusting steel Triton's crown at the top of the peaks and threw up a perimeter fence around the parklands, guarded by machine gun posts. Prefabs sprouted along the roadside, running all the way up to the observation point and the radio equipment above. Satellite dishes bloomed across the old car park, appearing almost over night together with armoured tanks and a helipad.

The army fiercely defended the base – anyone approaching the fence would be tracked by searchlights and thermal cameras and shot down. Other than that, the installation seemed to do very little. The soldiers never left the compound. They never got involved in the battles between the Police and the rioters and the looting gangs. They simply watched the bloodshed impassively with the dead, black stare of a video lens, and reported back. The base wasn't big enough to do anything else, and they had no reason to go outside their perimeter and get involved – they were self-contained. Every two weeks at sunset their heavy lifters would take off with two escort 'copters, returning a day later fully laden with fresh supplies and personnel. In these days of famine and disease, the army's budget was well provided for, yes sir.

I spent a lot of time on that small balcony on the evenings when there was little fog, just looking out at the broken city. Since the warming, the fog doesn't roll in so often, and I did not miss it then, particularly the times when I woke up feeling trapped and breathless. I would throw myself out of bed and rush to fling open my shutters. Before me were the peaks of the islands far across the water, I needed to feel the breeze on my face.

My apartment began to seem very small, and those were the times I dreaded the sight of the fog. It would roll in and smother the building, choking my view of the city and the life within me in a wall of nothingness that seemed as black and deep as the ocean. So deep, the sight of it made me dizzy and I would run to the windows and slam the shutters angrily against the invading gloom. Still I felt the force of it encroaching, heard the deafening, pregnant silence in my bursting ears, pressing me, whispering to me, and I would sit restlessly and try to read, unable to concentrate. I would get up and walk around the flat, going from room to room, unable to escape the fact that I knew where everything was, nothing had changed. I have never been the domestic type – I like to keep my home the way I like to keep it, certainly, but I cannot convince myself to scrub a clean surface, or fluff a pillow like a fretful dowager without acknowledging that these are actions born of desperation and despair. I cannot convince myself that this is normal, that I am not looking for something else, something other.

I used to catch myself staring into the fridge, just staring at the contents as if they were relics in a museum and I was a captivated academic – afraid to touch. The contrast of the warm light and the chill invading my body set me still. I would stand in the kitchen with my hand on the edge of the open door, gazing at the yellow light while the cold travelled up my arm and spread through my heart.

In the small hours I would look up from my book and

realise that it was dark, that the little stubs of candle I used to save up and ration had burned out. I would have no idea of the time, or how long I had sat in the darkness staring at the same page in torpor, not reading, not thinking. When I listened I could hear past the tick of my generator to the whispering voice of the city outside – the lapping of wavelets, the general thrum of fire crackling and people shouting. Sometimes there was gunfire, or a speedboat would scream past the shoreline below. And there I was, sat in the darkness as the world turned about me, trying not to think of myself as trapped, glaring at the shutters. I was angry and afraid, afraid to look outside in case the fog was still there in the night, waiting to cut off the world, waiting to swallow me.

Yet in all those days that seemed to be months, the quietness of the building began to cushion me like a pillow over my face. I expected retribution and still slept with a gun in my hand. I expected to be dragged from sleep by vengeful strangers and burned, but it seemed that people no longer knew how to claw and fight, to bear grudges and collect on their debts after a century of convenience food and lifestyle magazines. If I was sure I could feel relieved I wouldn't feel so sickened.

I am used to fighting, surviving. Living in comfort has been new to me, but not to those outside that invented electric light and personal pan pizzas. I am used to being the object of vendetta, but these folks wander around in the darkness below me like KFC portions on legs, picking each other off and then asking where the hand-wipes are whilst I remain the vestigial urge that's almost worth attending to, the itch yet to be scratched.

Or maybe they were simply too busy surviving. Whatever it was, the longer I remained holed up, waiting for them to come in the limbo of deafening silence, the more nervous I became. I began to question my thinking. I was confused. What if they didn't come? How long could I stay here? If they didn't want what was owed to them how could I understand them? How could I survive in a world where I couldn't relate to the priorities of those I might bargain with, a world where I couldn't fathom or predict the actions of my enemies?

The uneasy silence spread through the building like gangrene, threatening to envelop me in the same dizzying emptiness as the fog. Judging from the rising trash mound below there were still people on the floors beneath, cooking, sleeping, living, but there was no laughter in the rising pressure of the tower, and there was no fighting.

One clear night I stepped out onto the balcony and looked down to see a 4x4 truck parked outside the tower. It had oversized tires and searchlights on the front. A machine gun turret had been welded into the bay at the back. The first thing I thought when I saw it was *How did that get there?* – had it always been on the island? I'd never seen it before. Had someone stashed it somewhere? Who could protect and hold such an asset on Russian Hill? Who could fuel it? It was amazing to see such a vehicle untouched, it wasn't a wreck – apart from the obvious modifications it looked clean and flashy – no dents, no broken windows – it was cared for. With metallic blue bodywork and red, flaming decals, it was like a cake sitting alone on a park bench, complete with icing, whipped cream and the proverbial cherry screaming 'Steal me!'

Yet the truck remained untouched as I watched for the next two hours. I stood up out of my chair as a gang of youths approached, whooping and yelling down the hill, swinging their baseball bats. They ran across the burnt-out ruins and crawled through upturned cars, picking up, examining and discarding titbits as they went. It was good to see them larking about, knocking each other over and throwing bricks. They moved through the street like a loud, straggly pack of wolves, but as they neared the truck they fell silent. One by one they each found something uncommonly interesting on the other side of the road that forced them to cross over before coming anywhere near the truck.

My spirits declined with those of the child-monsters below, and I went back inside. I picked up a book from the shelves and dropped into my armchair. I sat, staring down at the volume in my lap for an hour or more, fighting with myself, refusing to open it. I had been reading all week and I couldn't stand to hold another word before my eyes. I was sick – sick of words, sick of walls, sick of myself and sick of this sick feeling of waiting for a losing fight that may, or may not be coming. The whole world was a losing fight.

I threw down the book and stood up, bent with the need to do something to rescue myself and caught with the knowledge that there was nothing I could do. I crossed the room and threw open the front door, stepped into the hallway and slammed it behind me. Outside of the apartment I suddenly felt exposed. I looked down at the carpet, wondering what to do next. I went past the stairwells and the elevator doors – still wedged open, and found myself outside the Leibowitz', staring in. What was left of their front door was propped up against the wall, I had mangled it with a fire-axe to get at the locks.

I stepped across the threshold and passed into their apartment. Apart from a perfunctory search for the keys and anything of immediate survival import I had avoided this act. I am invading the home of someone I know. Burgling someone I have spoken to. Someone who might come back.

This familiarity has been the source of my reluctance, though I know in truth as I search through the bureau and the underwear drawers that he is dead. She is dead. The little one is dead – if he is lucky. We are all dead already and we are never coming back.

I am running through the bedrooms and the study, ripping out drawers and tipping the contents on the floor. I am looking for something that can help me, that can save me. Tools, or something I can trade, or a weapon, but really I am mad with irritation and I'm simply tearing the place apart. I know I will not find anything. The Leibowitzs weren't that imaginative. Or smart.

The living room is next to useless – I found twenty bucks in the sofa cushions – it's worth nothing to me or to anyone. There are hangings on the walls and poster prints of Duchamp and Van Gogh. Although I tell myself I am searching for the safe I know a cautious man like Leibowitz would have, I take pleasure in the destruction as I tear down the hangings, faint thoughts of those artists stir righteously in the dark of my skull.

There is a domestic computer on a desk in a darkened corner. It is nothing without power. It does not exist without electricity spinning its little silicon cogs. I do not look at it. I tip the desk over with a single hand as I pass on my way to the kitchen. The plastic clutters to the ground with a dull empty sound. The apparatus is too light to wreck itself on the carpeted floor.

The kitchen provides more satisfying sounds. I pull the drawers out and let them fall to the floor. They spill their silvery contents over the black tiles like a noisy starburst. I do not even look. I pick through the cutlery with a toe, separating out the steak knives. All around my head is useless expensive crockery, gilt-edged bone china glaring through glass fronted cupboards. I throw the translucent dinner plates like Frisbees, soaring over the breakfast counter and across the living room. They crash into the walls one by one. I aim one at the French windows, I want to see what happens when the plate hits the glass. Nothing. A dull bouncing noise emanates from the double-glazing and the plate explodes, spattering razor shards across the carpet. The glass remains untouched.

I take a carving knife and cut the flex from the microwave and the breadmaker and every other appliance I can find. The cords make great ropes, or garrottes. The saucepans may also come in useful. I start piling these things in the corner, along with the knives and the cooking oil and the alcohol. All of the glass I gather in another pile, it will make sharp toys to play with later.

The fridge is stale and pungent, the food cupboards are almost bare. It seems the Leibowitz' had taken much of what they had – or they were starving. Some of the heavier items remain – a large can of olives, bottles of tomato ketchup. Do rats eat olives? I don't. The olives go in the pile with the knives, but now I am scouring the living room sideboard for rat bedding. It isn't here. This can't be the spot where the rat was kept.

The room that is the pantry in my apartment has been turned into a study. I am hopeful that I find something here worth trading. There was no water in the kitchen. The study is lined with books. In the centre of the room is an imposing leather topped desk, made with walnut and Japanese maple, inlaid with ebony and brass fretwork. It must be at least two hundred years old. European with hints of Japonism. For a moment I stop, and stare at it in the shadows. Slivers of light cut across the pillars of drawers while the maple shines like quicksilver in the dark. Cold sweat breaks out on my back as the past rushes up to greet me and suddenly I feel quite, quite lost. It seems as if I blinked and the world turned away. Again. And everything I thought I knew had gone.

As I stand in that study, staring at an irrelevant piece of furniture in that frozen moment of time, I simply do not know what to do. I do not move. I cannot think. I do not know how long the moment lasts as I stand and stare, I do not know what I am looking at, or even that I am looking. The thoughts do not roll on in my head one after the other, I am frozen between thoughts. I do not experience time.

I blink, or breathe in, or flinch, and suddenly the universe becomes again a fluid place around me, and I make up my mind. I will have that desk. It must weigh two... three hundred pounds but I will move it to my apartment where there is no place for it.

On top of the desk are a silicon writing pad and a terminal

to the household computer. Leibowitz used to run market projections and economic simulations by the looks of the printouts littering his floor. It is worthless now. Glinting in the thin light is an ancient writing set, an original Bakelite fountain pen, and a cracked inkpot. The pot is dry, the pen mounted in a stand, these trophies have not been used this side of a hundred years. As I sit gingerly at the desk to go through the drawers I yearn for a well of Stephen's ink. I'm sure there is one, somewhere, swimming in an old man's study at the bottom of the ocean.

There is a picture of Mrs Leibowitz, smiling in the sunlight at the top of Telegraph Hill, the Golden Gate behind her. A print of the boy slotted loosely into a gold frame for which it is too small. I snap these pictures face down immediately and then I sweep them and everything else off the desk with one arm. It feels final.

I go through the drawers one by one. They slide open like silk off a stockinged knee. Divine. We start at the top with business things, stationary, papers and disks. There is a small letter opener, the handle engraved 'With love, from everyone at Grayson, Wheeler and Fitch." I read the words and drop the object with a shudder. I shut that drawer. The contents degenerate the further down we go, turning to family treasures and holiday souvenirs. A knitted bootie nestles with a plastic Statue of Liberty in the bottom drawer. Beside them lies a bunch of keys. I snatch them up, holding them to my eye. A string dangled from the glinting prize. The tag at the end read 'Marquez, Elevator and Stairwell.'

Silently I place the keys in my pocket and close the drawers up. They shut with a dull, reassuring thud. I stand up and look around the room. I am surrounded by books. I stiffen as I look towards the door. Hanging from a hook on the back of the door is a man's jacket, left just as it was months ago, by a dead man. I have seen him wear this jacket. Sharing the elevator, passing uncomfortably in the windowless corridors. I have spoken to this man. 'Good evenings,' and 'How are yous?' the language of acknowledging presence without acknowledging existence, the language of politely keeping distance. Now I see his face again, swollen from the water and jaundiced as it was. I step slowly towards the coat, horrified to catch the faint smell of Leibowitz. I am watching myself as I go through the pockets. Loose change and old tissues. Nothing to justify searching the pockets of a dead neighbour.

Quickly I step away and turn to the books, starting again with a new zeal, sorting them into three piles. The first pile rapidly becomes a mound in the corner of the room as I pull volumes from the hardwood shelves. I glance at spines, titles and authors as I go by. With the flick of my wrist they sail across the room, fluttering to the ground like wounded game birds. These are the books I will not read but trade as fuel. Occasionally I stop to scan a back cover, or flick through random pages, and so the second pile accumulates. These are the books I will read before trading. I am more careful with these, I stack them on the floor instead of throwing them in the corner. There is a third pile, the smallest. These books go on the desk. These are the ones I will read and keep. Some of them I'll treasure. There are also some truly awful books that I feel duty bound to save, by virtue of their being signed copies, or first editions. I will keep them safe and some day, when things return to normal, someone will thank me for not burning their Library of Babylon. In case things return to normal.

I am pleased with the book horde anyway. This would not be the first harsh winter that I've burned books to stay alive. I ignore the mayhem around me and step over the scattered books on my way to the door. Crossing the tattered living room I make my way to the master bedroom.

The bed is made. Like everywhere else in the apartment the room is pristine. Mrs Leibowitz cleaned on the morning she left. I casually knock over the Bauhaus floor lamp by the doorway, pushing slowly with one finger. I want to hear the glass shatter. It's a reproduction, but I suspect they didn't know. There is no place for fakes in this house.

There are bedside cabinets with lamps on each side of the bed. Very Mr. and Mrs. On one side there is a crystal glass water pitcher, dry, on the other a cheap romance novel. There is a bookmark buried in the leaves, about a third of the way through. I know before I check that there is nothing under the bed. Not even dust.

As I go through the walk-in wardrobe I find they have taken all the warm clothes, which was smart. Maybe I can trade the lighter summer things if the weather settles. On a shelf at the back there seems to be a collection of 'men's stuff,' a toolbox that has never been used, and a cordless drill still in its shrink-wrap. There are magazines about cars, and a deflated basketball. It's hard to tell if these are unwanted Christmas presents or a secret stash of masculinity. I grab the toolbox and the drill and add them to the piles in the other room. I will use them or trade them. I also find the safe buried in the floor of the corner of the wardrobe. The door lies wide open next to a square of loose carpet. Beside it on the floor is an empty jewellery box. There is nothing else in the shallow space beneath the floor, no other indication of what it had contained.

I am raiding the bathroom cabinet in the tiny en-suite. It contains stale contact lens solution, antiseptic and painkillers. I slip the pills into my pocket, along with the bottle of antiseptic. Analgesics can save your life if you're dying of influenza, and Walgreens is permanently out of stock. I also take the soap, and the fancy shampoos. In the main bathroom I swipe bleach and toilet rolls. I don't know what I'll do with these things, but I will save them. I may never see shampoo again after this.

I am reluctant to come to the last room, the boy's room. I hesitate at the threshold. This is a room I keep locked in my own apartment. With a jerk I push the door open, and I'm through to a child's haven. The walls are sky blue, dotted with fluffy clouds and aeroplanes. There are toy rockets on the shelves along with movies and old antique children's books. There are teddy bears on the little bed and toys erupting from a chest in the corner, a dead nightlight in the power point by the door and a clock by the bed. It has stopped at a quarter to twelve. I barely notice any of this. I bend down and place a hand on the bedpost, pulling the bed up by one corner as I straighten. I look up and stop, stock still, the bed hanging in the air. From the corner of my eye I see a teddy bear rolling off the sloping mattress in slow motion. I wait to hear the crash that never comes.

There is a man frozen in the corner, staring through the darkness in shock. I flinch and he flinches, and then I look up at my own face. Against the wall facing the doorway stands a full-length mirror framed in mahogany. I am looking at myself, and I quickly look away. You have no reason to check your appearance when you are alone and trapped. The bed slips from my sweaty grasp, the wooden legs landing with a bump. The man in the mirror world looks around his child's room as I do mine. The toys would probably trade well to some rich looter's spawn, the clothing also. I cannot bring myself to touch any of it. I don't know what I'm doing here any more, I can't look at myself. I flee the room, stumbling over the wreckage on the lounge floor.

I'm scratching at the balcony doors, gulping for air. They are locked and I am starting to panic as the breath leaves me and the stars rise above my eyes. I am not like this. I am not fragile like this. I gasp airlessly like an exiled goldfish, desperately pulling at the sliding door handle, but the trigger won't depress and I put my shoulder to the glass. It's no good, and I realise my fingers are numb and the room is spinning as the floor of this ocean liner rocks gently beneath me. I have to get out of this death place.

I take a step back from the door whilst clinging to the handle, and then I crash my shoulder into the aluminized triple glazed safety glass. The shockwave runs through my shoulder and up my neck into my brainpan before spreading out in waves of colour before my eyes. My throat has clamped shut as if I've swallowed a concrete tennis ball, and as I run my shoulder into the glass again my diaphragm flutters in electric spasms. I choke as my lungs expel the air I am trying to suck in, and I gag, dry-retching for I have nothing to vomit. Buzzing rises in my ears before a sudden and deafening silence falls over me, and my vision shrinks down to a single point as the universe gently fades out.

Somewhere in the slow and dreamy background, a part of me is sliding down a smooth membrane covering the night. A single rolling eyeball glides past the giant metal door handle within which my twisted fingers are trapped. A forehead, possibly mine, lodges against something cool and flat and shiny protruding from the bottom of the handle. My free hand flops about like a dish drowning on deck as I reach up and grasp the object, and then I feel the lock click round as I turn the silvery key. With a muted sigh, the door glides open and I gently slump over the threshold, melting into the chill night air and my first panic attack since after Nagasaki.

I awoke, flat on my back, soaking wet with the fingers of my left hand jammed into the door handle above me and acid rain burning my eyes. Shivering, I stood up and extricated my twisted fingers before going over to the balcony railing and leaning out, arms wide, looking over to the shoreline and the channel to the Marin Islands in the north. The fine drizzle seeped into my clothes and settled uncomfortably on my dank, sweaty skin.

I supported myself with those railings, feeling sick and wretched and dirty. I wanted to vomit, but my stomach was empty. I wanted to cry myself clean, but I had no tears left and no time for them. Instead I let the contaminated spray trickle over me, a clammy baptism in poisonous waters.

City light is still orange. It has always been orange. From fire, to coal gas, to sodium lamps, the night glow remained stubbornly orange, and now, back to fire, the orange glow pervades the mist and low clouds like a clingy relative you are never entirely free of. There were campfires on the peaks of the Marin Chain and Angel Island, adding to the glow of scrubland fires and the city gloom. On the skyline below me were staggered lines of oil drum fires and piles of burning tires. The acrid smell of burnt plastic hung in the air as the greasy ash filtered down out of the breeze dropping out of the air like demonic confetti. Before me, on this, the opposite side of my building, was parked another truck.

The vehicle sat proudly on oil stained scrubland, a few yards from the building, all oversized tires and welded spikes. Although this one had been decorated with more violence it followed the same basic colour scheme of metallic blue with flames, and was in as improbably good condition as the last. Welded to the rear chassis was a collection of bars and spikes forming a cage. The front grille had been replaced with a ram-raiding plough.

I wiped the water from my face and slicked back my hair in the drizzle. The damp was sitting under my clothes, an oil slick spreading uncomfortably over my skin. Shivering, I went inside. I picked out the microwave, the heaviest object I could think of, and brought it out onto the balcony. Feeling the weight in my arms I estimated the distance from the foot of the tower to the truck, and lobbed the oven over the side.

I stood peering over the railings and watching the oven tumble silently through space. It turned out to be a pretty good aim. The microwave sailed into the driver's side windshield, ripping through the door pillar with an explosive crash. The glass disintegrated and metalwork caved in, the oven bounced and rolled away to settle at the foot of the garbage mound circling the building. There was no car alarm, but rather a lot of screaming. The passenger's door swung open and a dark figure poured out, rolling over on the ground, hugging his knees in shock. Another man ran out of the building towards the truck, screaming drunkenly at the one on the ground and running around the truck in circles. I turned away. I stalked across the living room and out of the apartment. I took nothing with me.

4

Over the next few days more trucks and vehicles appeared and circled the building, the uneasy quiet below grew to a heavy, airless silence. It was obvious now that the trucks were being brought in from off-island, sometimes two or three per day. I would wander out to the balcony after waking and count the new arrivals until the tower was completely surrounded. I watched the clouds gather, wondering when the storm would break.

In the meantime I would go across the hall and make regular visits to the Leibowitz place. Bit by bit I filled my apartment with the books and clothes and other things that I hoped would be somehow useful. After comparing Leibowitz' toolbox to my own, the one I had bought when it became obvious that the city was collapsing and hoarding was the order of the day, I saw that his was junk. I threw the toolbox over the railings at a Jeep with massive searchlights, but I missed and it hit the ground ten feet away. It landed close to some punk kid, and he fell over in shock. It was all I could do not to laugh out loud. The impact left a crater in the mud that slowly filled with oily water.

Throwing things from the balcony became something of a pastime. Whenever I was bored I would lob over something useless, a dead pot plant, or a plate. I developed different throws for different occasions. Movie stacks would spin like Frisbees, while books I would throw against the wind, for I liked to hear them flutter, and their trajectory was completely unpredictable anyway. I seldom tried to hit someone below, it was more of a desperate entertainment. This was not about hitting people, I had a ceramic rifle in the cabinet for that. It felt more like throwing things overboard before abandoning ship. With the vehicles gathering below I knew I was running out of time.

It's amazing how much unwanted detritus you can fit into a well-ordered apartment. I stuffed the knives into kitchen drawers, the books into cupboards and gaps on shelves, I bundled the clothes up and hid them in the pantry. I did not want constant reminders of the Leibowitz' haunting my apartment, but I managed to avoid opening the room I kept locked, I refrained from filling it with things that may be useful one day. Still, I found myself at a loss to find a home for an old first edition and I stopped, my hand hanging in the air, poised to place the book on a shelf. I wondered quite what the point was. It was then that I seriously considered taking out my rifle, setting it up on the balcony and evening up the odds a little. Or bringing on the inevitable.

The doorbell rang. I can't fully describe how strange and impossible it was to hear that sound crashing through my silent thoughts. The first time it rang I jumped. My heart thundered in my chest and I caught my breath. The second time the buzzer cut through the air I had to think hard to recognise the sound. Frozen like an animal I listened, hanging on the silence like a spooked deer. On the third ring I put the book down on the shelf slowly, balanced homelessly on the wooden edge, and went to my bedroom to retrieve my pistol.

I approached the door quietly and looked through the peep hole as a long, drawn out buzz hammered through my brain. I could see no one outside in the fish-eyed corridor. As the doorbell chattered again in its annoying, incessant on-off, I began to wonder at an electrical fault, or the batteries, or my sanity. But the rhythm was reminiscent of an attention-seeking child, look at me, look at me, look at me, and my own particular madness has nothing of the child in it.

"Who is it?" I croaked, surprised at the rusty sound of my own voice.

"Smudge," a small voice came from the other side of the door. It was trying to sound older, trying to sound assured. If she hadn't been trying so hard I might have been more worried.

I opened the door and the little punk girl stood before me, about eye level with my hand and the semi automatic. She had a new safety pin above the tear in her earlobe, and her fragile neck was newly adorned with gold chains. Her hair was pink and spiky, but this only made her grey skin seem green and sick. The girl wore a tartan skirt over filthy leggings, and her top was torn, with stains running down the front in long, lazy drips. She tilted her head and looked up at me through her eyebrows with put-upon indifference, chewing gum loud like she'd invented attitude. Unimpressed, she eyed the pistol as she stepped around me and into the living room. I raised my eyes, but closed the door behind her in case there were others outside. She didn't look, she was turning around in the living room, staring at my paintings and Japanese furniture. I made a point of sliding the bolts across slowly, and not so loud, just enough that she could hear. I wanted to see her body stiffen.

"Nice job you pulled next door. Real mess," she said whilst making a show of examining the fretwork on my cabinet.

"Thank you," I said. "I was annoyed."

"Hate to see you angry," she chuffed, and popped a pink bubble loudly. I have no idea how she got hold of the gum. I paused, and she peeled the film from her lips with her tongue, chewing loudly.

"I think you know what happens when I get angry."

She looked at me for the first time, for a moment the bravado act flickered, but she always fought to be the tough girl. With a little scowl her face clouded over again and she went back to chewing her prop. She crossed over to the rat in the corner, brushed her fingers lightly against the cage, a coquettish little monster staring at the prisoner.

"You did a bad thing." She turned to me. "Now you're going to pay."

I stared at her, incredulous. I felt the sweat prick my forehead.

"If only it were as simple," I whispered. "I hurt you, you hurt me, we're all squared and even and the blood runs from our hands with soap?"

She stared at me with raised eyebrows and shrugged. I was shaking, barely aware she was in the room.

"Whatever you say, Chuck." She walked over to the kitchen, poked at the camping stove, opening cupboards, continuing her mental inventory. "Sounds like you have 'issues,' " she said, peering into a cupboard of tins and stale packets.

"Why are you here?"

"Looking," she said as she popped a stale graham cracker in her mouth. Her face wrinkled and she turned to one side to spit. *Not hungry then,* I thought. A great gob of beige paste hit the fridge door, a drooling splat running down like bird shit. It began to roll slowly down the black surface whilst the bubbly liquid streaked to the floor.

"Surveillance – you know. Seeing what you've got. What kind of fight you can put up." She shrugged. "Who gets what when you're through. I want the canned fruit. The sweet things. And the pictures." She pointed across the breakfast bar to the paintings on the living room walls, and my antique prints. "I'll get 'em too, first pick for doing this. Where do you keep your water? Must be running out yeah? You got any proper weapons?" She started pulling drawers out of the kitchen units looking for knives. She turned to look at me as she slid the drawers back in, one after the other, scanning my face for a reaction, her casual, possessive grace a more sophisticated insult than the predictable cheapness of leaving the trespassed kitchen wide open.

"How did you get in here?" I tried to sound calm.

"Wouldn't you like to know. You really don't have shit, do you." She held up a small peeling knife. "They said it couldn't be done, no one could get up here to look about. They'd have to storm it, bring in lots of guys from the Causeway. But I told Lock I knew a way. I bet him I could get in and I have. He can't ignore me no more." She paused, eyes glazed over. "Now they'll have to listen to me," she said slowly. "He'll be begging to take me back." Her voice cracked. "He's scared of you," she looked up at me. "I ain't."

"Lock is the boy with the phoenix jacket?" I asked slowly.

"Lock is my guy!" She yelled. She stamped her foot and I remembered how young she was. "He gave me his jacket and everyone knew I was his. Then after, he took it back! Said I was just a-" her voice turned to white breath as her anger collapsed.

"Poor little girl," I said flatly, suddenly aware of all the delicacy it required not to kill her. "What will you tell them? You have nothing. You know nothing."

"You're the one who's got nothin." Tit for tat. "Where's the fucking water!" She screamed. Like a manic elf she darted across to the bathroom door and flung it open. She smelled the gas fumes immediately and froze, hand on door, confused and infuriated.

"Careful," I warned. "Be careful what you find. I'll kill you before I let you leave knowing anything useful." I lied.

She hesitated, her back to me, and then she snorted, shaking her head. "No you won't." Still she closed the door carefully before facing me. "Where's the water?"

"What's your name really? Princess? Daddy's Little Princess?" I did not want her to get curious about any more doors, particularly locked ones, and I have no taste for killing little girls. I wouldn't touch her, for if I started I wouldn't stop. Besides, she had a secret I needed.

"Britney?" I goaded. "Is it Abigail? Or maybe Alice?" She began to shake as she stared at me from across the room.

"Where's the water?" she shouted in rage.

"That's it, isn't it?" I whispered. "Cut glass Alice. Poor little rich girl, desperate to prove so much to a boy that will never want a girl like you. One that has to try so hard, to prove so much. So brave, trying to be so *tough*, so *dangerous*. Poor little-"

"Shut up!" she stamped her foot again.

"Alice."

"Smudge."

"How did you get in, Alice?"

"Smudge."

"All he wants is a girl with a tough name, a girl who doesn't have to try. Alice, how did you get up here?"

"Smudge." She said quietly, holding my gaze.

"Your parents didn't call you Smudge."

"My parents are dead."

"So are mine." I held my breath and shrugged. "So are everyone's." I took a breath. "So, Smudge, how did you get up here?" I stared at her.

She opened her mouth slowly to answer, and then frowned a little. "Where's the water?"

I almost screamed, squeezing my palms tight, and I suppressed a sigh of frustration. I could feel my face turn red as the desire to throttle her grew. I made a snap decision. "Look in the fridge." I nodded.

Smudge's triumphant grin was an ugly, goading gash in her face, and she trotted back to the fridge. She placed her small, pudgy hand on the handle and I took a deep breath. The seal hissed as she pulled the door open and peered in. She recoiled at first, took a step back, and then she looked again at the three medical units of blood nestling on the shelves, and she looked back at me. She frowned, frozen in confusion. I felt a rush of naked panic as all of my secrets evaporated before my eyes.

"You see, Alice. It's not water I need." A half lie.

At that moment the fridge motor clicked on, awakened by the warmer air flooding through the open door. Out on the balcony the generator thrummed as it cycled from passive to active operation. The noise roused Smudge from her confusion.

"You sick fuck. You sick fucker. You really are a psycho!"

I'm not, I thought, but the serpent of my deepest fear slithered cold and scaly through my gut.

Smudge began shaking, and fumbled in a pocket of her top. She pulled out a small knife that wobbled in her hand as she pointed it towards me. I chuckled, letting my gun hand drop to my side as I took a step towards her.

"How did you get in?" I took another step towards her. "I promise you, you want me to believe you right now."

"Up the elevator shaft!" she blurted, "from the floor below – I climbed!"

I stopped, astonished. "You expect me to believe that? What if you'd fallen?"

"Lock had me on a rope!"

I stood on the spot, not sure what to believe. "Well, I think you had better leave the same way."

She looked at me for some time, pointing the knife and shivering. I waited. Eventually her hand lowered.

"They're gonna kill you." She stammered. "They won't care. You killed a Piranha, they won't give two shits what you're into, they'll come for you and they're gonna pull you apart alive and screaming. And I'll be watching. I seen it before."

I shrugged with disinterest and pointed to the door. Smudge scowled and tried not to cross the room too fast, glad to be leaving in one piece, annoyed to be leaving empty handed. She stopped by the door, looking up at an original print of the Great Wave I kept on the wall by the doorframe. I knew she'd been a rich brat, she had an eye for the expensive even when she didn't know what she was looking at. She turned to me.

"It could go easy for you. I could make it easy for you. I could tell them you were sick and unarmed. They'd only send a few up then. If you made it worth my while. Or.." She waited. "I could tell them you were a sick psycho with a knife collection and to send up ten guys who like to slice and dice."

Good, I thought. *Tell them I'm a monster. Tell them to be afraid.*

Smudge looked up at the print. "What will you give me?"

I sighed. "I give you your life. Use it wisely."

Smudge scowled and flung open the door. Then she stepped back, and threw out her hand quick as anything, tearing the print from the wall. There was a shower of glass as the frame crashed to the ground. She crossed the threshold with her head held high, with all the forced and trembling decorum of a drunken cocktail party hostess leaving a room with deliberate slowness after causing a scene. I went to the door and watched as she disappeared down the hallway, her nerve breaking as she reached the elevators. Sure enough, she stood by a foot wide crack in the doors, tied a thick rope around her waist and lowered herself carefully into the darkness. I was wrong – the kid did have guts.

I went out into the hallway and checked that the stairwell doors were secure. I removed the chocks from between the elevator doors, and, using Leibowitz' drill I wound thick drill bits into their stainless steel surface. By the third door his toy drill had given out and I had to use my own. In the fumes and screeching flying bits of metal dust I found myself wishing that I'd throttled her. I pictured my hands around that young throat. Quickly I wrapped bike chains tightly around the drill bits, clamping the elevator doors shut. As I sealed the doors a sense of aloneness rushed up to greet me. I thought back over the irrelevant lecture I'd given the girl. It was then that I realised I hadn't had a conversation for almost six months, hadn't had an engaging conversation for years, not since the troubles began and my acquaintances had fled. I ached briefly. I went to the fridge and baited my addiction alone and silent amidst the gathering dawn.

I was alone. I was alone in the world and there was nothing to do but sleep. I shuttered the apartment and paced the rooms, drinking too much, gulping, festering my anger so that I went to bed well after sunup, irritated and restless. I lay in bed turning and thinking of scenarios. They would come. Soon. I would be caught and murdered, or worse – kept out in the sun. I doubted that. They wouldn't know, wouldn't believe.

I could bargain with them. What would I trade? The water? The ammunition? No, they would take that and kill me. What could I offer? Knowledge? Skills? Nothing. Nothing they would care for.

I could hide. I could hide in the Leibowitz'. I could lock myself upstairs. They would find me. They would starve me out until I was a raving psychotic animal. I have no taste for being walled in.

Escape? Could I escape? Run down the stairs? And meet a hundred of them coming up. Or just twenty. Could I survive twenty? Or climb down? Not the balconies, they were staggered around the building left to right. Could I climb down twenty floors of the black and echoing elevator shaft? Sneak out of the parking garage, dig myself in somewhere before sunup? Maybe I could do that. Maybe I would die. Maybe I would slip and freefall in the darkness, time to scream and breathe in and scream again before I hit the concrete. Maybe I would run out of time. Maybe I would live. Maybe.

If I just had more time to plan. To pack. To practice with some rope. I just needed some time, if only I had some more time, but what for? What would I do with it? I'd just pissed away the last month of nights, hadn't I? Drinking and pacing and... and reading! Swanning around looting useless objects, pretending the endless cycle of stealing was helping me, was extending, was delaying the inevitable. Pretending that every second I spent was not a second closer to a pointless, useless, inevitable death, my head in the sand like an ostrich. The whole world was an ostrich in a lion's pen, but not me. I knew better. At least I thought I did. Didn't I? Well didn't I?

I had grown fat and complacent in the last two centuries. The two lazy, easy centuries of blind scientific faith, of the mantra 'It doesn't exist until we prove it in a dish,' of medicine and refrigeration units, of plastic bags and fast food. My own fast food, my own invisibility potion. Now I was cowering, helpless and confused like a rat in a maze whose owners had suddenly gotten bored. The game was up. All the exits had been locked, all the floors electrified. I'd ceased to entertain the man upstairs so now it's lights out and time for bed. A rat in a corner in a maze, afraid to place a step. Indeed I found myself scrunched into the corner of the bed, sweating and clutching the filthy sheets. Shaking.

I understood then. I stopped thinking. I stopped looking. I stopped planning. A strange calm came over me. A welcome silence in the burning morning. I stopped. When the sun had fallen I would do something. I would climb down, or I would run or I would hide but I would try and maybe I would die. But if I did nothing I would certainly die. And there'd be no rhyme and reason to it except for "I did nothing." And there *was* no rhyme, or reason, I knew always. Not to any of it. Not to the world or the men downstairs or the acid rain or my age, there was reason to none of it. Just mistakes and accidents falling one after the other like tributaries to the river of time, tributaries I had watched for so many years that I had lost the source of the flow. But it must mean something? As long as I was watching it would mean something? The trees kept falling in the woods; I wanted to know that they made a sound. Suddenly I remembered the point.

I lay down and I smoothed out the bedclothes, and I turned away from the fire in the cracks in the shutters and I slept. I breathed and I slept. I told myself I would do something tomorrow. There would be time tomorrow. I breathed and I slept.

But I was out of time, out of tomorrows. I awoke with a rising sense of panic and the fumes of burning plastic stinging my throat, and although I could feel the sun above the horizon still, hot and roaring in the sky beyond, the cracks in the shutters were dark. A lump rose to my throat and a hollowness grew in my belly as the sick, fearful panic took hold.

No! Not yet! Not today! Never today! Always tomorrow! I haven't had time! It isn't fair! It isn't! Today was to be the day I saved myself! But I loathed myself as I thought these things.

It wasn't fair, it wasn't right. I leapt out of bed and ran into the living room. The building was burning beneath me and I expected the marauders at the door, bearing flaming torches and pitchforks and throwing rocks. I skidded to a halt in the centre of the room wrought with confusion. The rat was a ball of noisy panic in the corner. I was terrified, for there is nothing in the world I fear as I fear fire, and I could feel its presence in the minds of the human vermin below. They were running and crawling through the concrete boxes of rooms like rats, fleeing, escaping. I turned around, breathing heavily, but they were not here. They were not up here. I looked towards the windows and the covered French doors, deep red shafts of light glinting through the gaps. The light the colour of sunlight and smoke, and all the minds below running downwards, not up. This was provident calamity, not attack.

And yet there was a fire below me! Smoke billowing and curling around the side of the building. The overpowering fumes of burning plastic making me retch. I dared not look out into the light to see how big it was. There was nothing to do but wait, wait an interminable wait.

I paced the room, becoming angrier and angrier as the sense of real danger diminished and the sting of smoke contrived to take up permanent residence in my nostrils. I fidgeted incessantly as the last rays of the sun disappeared to the west, the air around the balcony getting clearer by the moment, and I burst through the French doors as soon as I felt the repeal of the light, gasping for air and information, but all I received was an acrid stench and a hazy view in the twilight.

When I looked down, a great black funnel of smoke was rising from a window below, blocking the view directly beneath my bedroom. An ugly black stain ran up the white wall of the building, but there was little fire. For reasons I couldn't know, the fire had been unable to spread, and the smoke had escaped from only one window in the lower, inhabited floors, perhaps fifteen or eighteen floors below.

As the sense of real danger passed and my fear subsided,

my indignation spread out to fill its place. Anger turned to rage as the shock of the fire seeped through me. *They could have killed me! By accident!* And that of course was the great insult. The fire could have run straight up the building and cremated me alive. I would have turned circles in the apartment like a trapped animal, ultimately choosing between the burning death of my own worldly goods on fire, or throwing myself from the balcony into the brilliant, roaring sun.

They threatened me! They could have killed me and they wouldn't even have known it! Secretly this is what riled the most. The thought that I would die alone, unnoticed, unrecorded and most of all by accident infuriated me. I had always expected to die fighting, a dagger in my back, a killer's voice in my ear. But to die by random accident, with no chance of defending myself, and with no intent to it but the fall of the cards when there were so many good, honest reasons for me to die across all the years – well it seemed such a pointless, hopeless waste. A waste in a careless universe, brushed aside by a disinterested God who didn't care for my opportunities or my debts. And there it was again – that growing sense of meaningless, endless, infinite emptiness. But of course, the thing I rejected the most, the thing that I couldn't bear was to die by indifference, the idea that I could go forgotten.

What about me God? Am I not worth justice? Am I not worth the fight? Am I not worth sullying the sword of your people?

I do not mention God often. I do not often think of it.

I stood on the balcony, knuckles white with irritation as I clutched the railings, unable to force a sound through my paralyzed throat as my body shook. I threw plant pots from the heights, dry and dead begonia stems sailing through the air. I picked up my chair and threw it as far as I could with a grunt. I regretted it immediately.

I watched, sullen, as the chair clattered to the ground, splintering as it hit the trash mound below. People screamed as the fragments dispersed – tiny slivers of wooden shrapnel. I looked below, people lay in the mud, black from head to toe with soot, wailing and cradling each other. Whole families huddled in the filth, children in bewildered silence as their mothers screamed. The dead ones lay, dragged into scattered piles, or alone and curled up wherever they fell.

Yet it was maybe only twenty people, four or five families – a small blaze, only one floor, or even less, a room. Even so, the people were stunned and helpless, lying on the ground in the dark, unable to react. One couple that appeared relatively untouched by the smoke were hauling their things away from the building. A small bundle on the woman's back began to wail like a baby as they set off towards the shoreline. The idea welled up within my mind then.

Desperately I ran through the apartment collecting mixing bowls, containers, and every bit of plastic I could find. I scooped up plastic bags, ran through the litter basket optimistically, even salvaged the plastic lids from water bottles. I lit the camping stove and set a large pan of wastewater to warming. Have you ever smelled old washing water as it boils? It is offensive and pervasive of course, the stench almost knocks you to the floor, but I'd saved the water, dammit, every drop in bloated old bottles, and I'd be damned if I'd waste fresh water now.

With a new vigour I ran down the hallway to the Leibowitz'. I gathered the last of the clothing in my arms and swept the place for plastics. I folded the remnants of the computer into shirts and sheets, and I scoured the kitchen for party plates and cups. Oh and cups, disposable plastic cups stacked together in a long clear bag. I could have kissed suspicious Mrs Leibowitz when I saw those. I found two bags of a hundred in the cupboard above the fridge where she kept the tubs and containers. I grabbed those too. Baby dishes and teat bottles glared at me, I closed the door on them. I rushed to the doorway, laden with stolen goods, and hung on the threshold. I looked towards the child's room and a box of plastic toys. I would come back for them if I needed them.

Back in my apartment I could not work fast enough. I set up a row of bowls and dishes containing hot, reeking water, upon which I floated pans, glass bowls anything inert. I fetched gasoline from the bathroom and removed the pans from the heat, filling each one halfway until my tank was empty. Fumes spread through the apartment, combining with the stench of foul water and the dry presence of smoke to make me dizzy and nauseous. I ran out onto the balcony and heaved into the cool night air. Thin streams of stringy fluid burst from my throat and fell away, drifting over in the breeze on the way down. I stood clutching the railings and shaking, but I checked myself and felt the progress of the moonless night. Perhaps a little under halfway through, and the fog rolling in like a prison guard. Below me the smoke was thin and wispy, the fire was no more than embers but the building's occupants ran in chaos. It had to be tonight, when I was free to move amongst the confusion, or I would lose my advantage. I had to be free by dawn, or I would perish. I steeled myself and went inside.

I opened every window and door, careful to take shallow breaths until the breeze and damp fog air had cleared the vapours a little. With the gasoline warm, I began dissolving plastic into the liquid, dumping little items in each pot, stirring, moving on. The thin disposable cups melted gently into the fuel, and the bags disintegrated like sheets of gelatine in hot water.

An old friend from the war confided in me once that dissolving the right kind of plastic into the right kind of fuel produces an explosive. I forget which plastic, or more likely I have never known – in any case it doesn't matter as I had no way to tell one type from another. Use the wrong kind of plastic in your concoction and you arrive at a sticky, incendiary goo, which was good enough for my purposes, except it was highly corrosive – spatters burned my hands, and the intoxicating fumes stung my eyes and lungs. Several times I had to drag myself out to the balcony where, sometime later, I would regain my senses after finding myself crouching in a corner, gazing at cracks in the floor or staring blindly into the haze. I would shudder at the passing time, and then shudder at my task before stepping inside to play the dizzying game once again.

Other types of plastic don't melt at all, nor do electrical boards. I would break up these things with a hammer, and stir them into the evil gloopy mess. I've found that batteries and electronic things don't so much explode as go 'bang,' but in any case I filtered out much of the computer junk and wire. When the mixture had taken as much plastic as it could, and become something of a stiff gel, I decanted it back into two empty gas tanks. I had many that were empty after running the generator for months. I used a glass pitcher to pour the vile substance into the tanks, it would have eaten a plastic jug on contact. Once the caps were safely screwed onto the gas tanks, I hurriedly repeated the process, warming the water, pouring out more gas. I also began to tear hundreds of pages from books, rolling them into little paper balls.

I only stopped my wicked production line when I ran out of viable plastic. My hands were burned and aching, and I had gained an eye for those types of plastic that would melt, and those that would not. I looked to the collection of five-gallon tin tanks gathered by the door, half of which had rested empty in the bathroom before tonight. I realised two things however through the vapour high and the hypnotic repetition – there were more cans than I could hope to carry or use, and – bloody fool, I had solidified more than half of my remaining fuel stock. I shook my head in horror, but the uneasy tightening in my guts reminded me that the planet was turning. I had perhaps an hour until sun up.

With shaking hands I scorched Leibowitz' jacket and pants over the gas ring. Whilst I was doing this the cheerful blue jets sputtered and choked as the canister ran dry, and in my panic I brought the jacket too close, setting it alight, producing a cloud of toxic black smoke. I swore and flapped the jacket out on the balcony.

I grabbed a vicious little thumb-knife, small and so sharp you wouldn't feel it cut, but staring down at it, I rejected a glinting handgun – it could so easily become an expensive liability that I didn't want to worry about. I took shears and cut random patches out of my hair. I wore odd shoes, and rubbed the grease scum from the boiled wastewater over my face and hands. I thought I might retch the smell was so repugnant. On the balcony I stole earth from my one surviving and sickly potted vine, and rubbed it over my clothes and through my hair. Did I look like a wandering looter? A fire victim? I hoped so. If I was recognised I would die.

I wrestled with the gallon tanks. I had one shot, I had to take as many down with me as possible. In the end I threaded belts and old rope through the handles of two cans and wore them front to back over my shoulders. They slapped heavily against my ribcage with every step.

Weighed down with another tank in each hand, I clutched plastic bags of paper balls in my fingertips. There was no time to pack, nothing more I could carry. Intending to reclaim my home later, I turned in the doorway, taking one last glance at my old familiar den – just in case. I resign myself. *If the worst comes, it is just a place.* I closed the door clumsily, twenty gallons of stodgy, inflammable gel sloshing about my body, I headed for the stairwell at the end of the corridor.

Unlocking the door I pushed it open a crack with my toe. I held my breath, listening, stretching my mind out into the ether of empty space. There was no one waiting outside to kill me. Carefully I made my way around and down each flight of steps, feeling the panic urge to run despite this unwieldy weight around my aching body – for the rising hairs on the back of my neck and the shivers down my spine warned me of the impending sun. I sweated and cursed and stepped slowly, conscious that a fall would destroy all my efforts and, one way or another, prove fatal.

I gave myself up to the dizzy, twisting repetition of one step in the shadows after another, losing my mind to the procession of steps, and suddenly I was on the ninth floor. This was the area I was hoping for – too high up for people to carry water every day when there were lower floors to live on, but not too high for looters to be interested in its contents. This was my theory and my hope, but a quick inspection through the corridor proved me wrong. I carried my cargo with me, too afraid to leave it behind it case it was discovered or I was. The looters had not been as efficient as I had expected. Broken furniture lay in piles in the hallways, the apartments were cluttered with flammable detritus. I did not enter, but peeked around the smashed doors to notice sofas and curtains, rugs and wooden tables and shelves. And windows, with deep purple skies, streaks of red piercing the wispy morning haze. Unfashionably, the corridors do not have windows – one reason I chose to live in this building some years ago, but there are skylights high above in the stairwells, and I gasped when I saw those smouldering skies.

I stepped faster now as I hurried down two floors and burst onto the corridor. I looked around. My arms were burning agony, tearing out of their sockets, my hands shaking, my sweaty grip failing. With every movement the tin edges of a five-gallon tank bit into the flesh of my palm, or crashed into the small of my back. But the corridor was clear. The looters had done their work here. The apartments were almost bare – even the doorframes had been pried from the walls and used as firewood.

The floor was bare, and I felt a flush of relief that I could begin my work. I moved down one more level, hoping that the absence of fuel above would prevent the fire from rising and engulfing my apartment. I stood outside the doorway of a bachelor apartment on floor six and unscrewed the first cap with numb fingers. I paused. I caught the glint of dawn in the corner of my eye. Could I do this? Could I survive it? Was it too late? Or just too dangerous? When I stopped and breathed and listened, and pressed outwards with my mind, I could sense human movement below. They were close. They were ignorant of my presence but they were close, and so was the sun.

I took a breath and tipped the can, spilling incendiary goo over the floor. I dragged my cargo through the apartments, splashing the accelerant across floors and walls, opening doors, sprinkling paper balls as I went. I got as close to the windows as I dared. As I emptied the first can my work became lighter and I spread the second can liberally over the final two apartments – family units that had briefly housed a group of crack addicts and, by the looks of the mad scrawlings on the walls, a paranoid schizophrenic or whatever – I'm not a psychiatrist. The walls were adorned with pictures of the rising waters, the storms and earthquakes, each one carefully annotated with a biblical reference scratched out in charcoal, a line or a verse that seemed completely irrelevant.

I ran fuel trails along the corridor and propped each fire door open with an empty can. My stiff shoulders came to life as I removed my rocket-fuel harness and felt the blood flow return to my arms. I dribbled sticky fuel down each stairwell in turn before setting about spreading the corrosive liquid throughout floor five, moving quickly and not daring to breathe. I had to be quiet as I went from room to room, lest I raise suspicions on the floor below. The apartments were bare, but filthy, and showed signs of habitation amongst the newspaper bedding and the toilet corners. My greatest fear was discovering a mumbling loner in a corner, a wastrel who would no doubt scream and raise hell if not dealt with. Every time I looked towards a window my eyes streamed and clamped shut in sharpened agony, a warning of the searing light burning just below the orange horizon. I had just a few minutes before dawn to get below and light the fire, to hide within a darkened corridor – and the most dangerous moment was yet to come. Without good fortune I would end up trapped between two floors of fuming incendiary and a hundred violent thugs baying for my blood. As I dribbled the last of the mixture down the steps to floor four and propped the stairwell doors open, I resolved silently that, if I survived this, I would never again take a risk, any risk, much less an uncalculated one.

Crouching quietly in the stairwell on the fourth floor, I reached out, listening carefully for a presence in the hallway beyond as the volatile fumes filled my nostrils and soured the back of my throat. People lived on this floor certainly, I could not afford to be seen coming through this door if there was no one living above floor four. I guess I assumed that someone would care. That someone would notice and shout, raise the alarm. What alarm? But surely they could hear me? Could detect this overpowering, dizzying, solvent smell? Four flights of steps below there was an ugly stain on the concrete where a boy had fallen. I didn't care to think about it.

I open the doorway a crack – the push bar creaking as I do so. There is no one. There is no one in the ten feet of corridor I can see. It will have to do. I turn and hold my breath as I light a pile of paper balls and start the trail of flames running orange and red up the stairs. I am surprised – the mixture burns slowly with thick black smoke that smells of carbon and gasoline, but it burns hot and steady. The flame disappears through the doorway above and I can only hope that it is finding its wicked way along the corridor as I slip out of the stairwell to look for a corner to hide. I want to run. I desperately want to run, so much so that my body is shaking, but I am waiting for the panic, for the stampede to empty the building.

I go to the corner of the corridor and lie down to wait, covering myself with soggy newspapers. Gently the fear rises. Nothing is happening! And then there is a noise from below. People outside the building have seen more smoke. A window cracks with a loud bang, a child screams. Somebody yells 'Fire!' and then another, and suddenly there is commotion everywhere. People are running and screaming on the floor below, doors burst open in front of me.

A man in a grey coat runs past me towards stairwell where I lit the fire and pushes open the door. He howls in pain – the metal burns. Black smoke bursts through the doorway, rolling along the ceiling, and a wave of heat slams into me. I am amazed at how quickly the fire has become serious, at how quickly the hallway fills with smoke, the light turning brown with haze, and then shrinking away altogether. I wonder a little at the amount of accelerant in that stairwell, at the gallons in the rooms above, and for the first time I begin to realise what I have done. Suddenly the fire I have fathered threatens me more immediately than the mob in the building, as totally as the solar disc outside.

More people are turning out into the corridor, and the man in grey kicks the door reflexively, and smoke pours through the opening like a liquid floating in the air, thick and fast and black. He turns, he wants to run and I can see the liquid streaming from his red eyes. Anxiously he bunches the sleeve of his coat in his hand and grabs for the handle, trying to pull the door closed against the killer smoke. He makes one attempt before the panic and the acidic blackness overtake him and he turns to flee. But the door is warped by the heat and won't shut properly, leaving the thick smoke free to rush enthusiastically through the gap, flowing like ink in water. The man coughs as he runs. Every breath he takes makes him cough further. He runs past me and around to the other stairwell, the hot smoke following, filling up the corridor and devouring the visibility. I can no longer see the fire door. As the man approaches the corner where I lay he flinches, realising there is a person secreted within the bundle of rubbish.

Time slows down in the moments before his eyes travel along the peaks of torn newspaper and up my face, in the moments when I know his eyes will touch mine. His eyes are dark grey in the thick air, *so grey,* I remember thinking with surprise. And they do meet, his portals and mine, but there is no recognition as he rounds the corner, just the terror in his dark irises reflecting the shock in mine. There is no moment of understanding, no moment of sameness. I can see the stubble on his crown, so close he passes, the birthmark under his right ear, small and blotchy and brown, but he doesn't slow as he rounds the corner, he doesn't stop as the noxious smoke hits me in the face. As his body turns his gaze sweeps over me, his pupils do not focus on me, do not move to the corners of his eyes, do not linger. He has seen me, and I am not afraid he has seen me, the man from upstairs, I am not afraid of that, for I look like a terrified wreck of a man. He turns the corner and I see the back of him. He has seen me and seen nothing at all as he pulls desperately at the second fire door, and I am afraid. Afraid that what he has seen is nothing. Or more afraid that he has nothing within himself to compare to the man on the floor. Is there nothing left within them? No spark of recognition? I know they do not know what I am. They see a man before them, only they have lost the man within themselves, they cannot recognise it within another.

A family runs blindly by me, a little girl clutched in her young father's arms, mother coughing and spluttering. There are wailing sounds coming from the apartments. Somewhere in the distance a man is screaming for someone to get up, get up, but the fire above is beginning to roar in my ears. A heavy man with engine grease in his hair runs past me. He is wearing split plastic trousers and a denim jacket laced with metal studs. The back of the jacket is spray painted with a bad decal of a fish, all teeth. Below it is stencilled, U.S. Army style, the word 'Piranha.' The man slips on the newspapers at my feet and slides around the corner before throwing himself into the stairwell.

I cough as I watch him go, curled up in the safety of my corner. My eyes are streaming but my tears sting like broken glass. I can barely see, and the hot air burns my lungs. I cannot stay here! Smoke is pouring down the corridor and as I scramble to my feet I realise the black cloud surrounding the burning stairwell is flickering with light. The fire is spreading into the hallway!

Columns of smoke chase me, rushing along the ceiling in waves as I run after the flock. The stairwell down is pandemonium; I am stuck at the top of a vertical crowd of panic stricken people, terrified for themselves and their small ones. They stare up at the flames and smoke above, for of course there is a lick of accelerant here too, just one floor up. Strangely, many of the children are quiet. They clutch their mother's hands, their father's legs, looking up, wide-eyed and silent in shock. A little girl on the steps below me, maybe three years old, her dress filthy and her golden hair like string, drops her quadriplegic doll to grasp her father's thumb with her free hand. She rubs her cheek against the back of his hand and gazes up at him with quiet, saucer-eyed resignation. I have seen this infantile fatalism before, and I feel the panic close in on me as the bile rises in my gullet. My body shakes and I scream for the people to move out of the way, to keep moving, to get out of the building once they are on the ground floor.

There are a hundred people packed in and heaving on the floors below, each trying to push through, to get down, pushing through doors and blocking the way. The noxious smell is getting stronger and the light fades as the stairwell fills with smoke from above. I am no stranger to the dark, but people react like frightened cattle and rush. They look up past me and the others at the end of the precession towards the smoke ceiling and scream that it is getting darker, lower.

People tear at the safety netting, cut at it with their flick knives, and begin to climb down the centre of the stairwell. At last the crowd is moving, but people are falling to the concrete. The little girl buries her face in her father's neck.

Suddenly there is a giant explosive noise above, and the throng screams in unison, and then they stampede. We are down a level now, and people on this floor are fighting to get into the stairwell, holding us up. It is almost impossible to see through the smoke and people clutch at their blackened mouths as they cough uncontrollably, for breathing is like inhaling volcanic ash. They begin to climb over each other like a sea of rats. And I grasp at what I have done by laying accelerant through the fire escapes.

Panic rises as the crowd draws in, pushing and squeezing in the vicious darkness until I cannot breathe, cannot move my diaphragm to suck in the toxic air, I close my eyes and I am being buried alive. I scream and explode with rage and sheer terror. I lay my hands on the banister, about to haul myself over to climb down the stairwell like a lizard on a hot wall. But there is little space; a crawling, grasping body fills every gap, the blind crowd seizes every handhold along the air core as it heaves forward. I am still three floors above the ground. I shake at the fatal height as I step up to the banister, forcing my way through the grabbing hands of strangers in the darkness. I place my foot at the base of the banister. There is an almighty splintering sound followed by an immediate and divine gust of cool air rushing up from below as the smoke ceiling rolls up like a mushroom cloud.

The skylights above have collapsed! Instinctively I push back from the railings and press myself into the crowd as a ton of smoked glass falls. Beautiful, glinting black daggers, they pass before I can blink, shattering again as they land. The sea of people below erupts into an orchestra of screaming, an instrumental section of witnesses followed by an instrumental section of victims, just one beat of shock later. I cannot imagine the carnage below, and I don't have time to care.

There is a heavy breeze drawing the smoke up and away, and the cacophony of retching lungs fills my ears, accompanied by the first stirrings of sunlight above me. *No! Not after all of this! Not after all these sacrifices I have stolen! All these sacrifices are not to be wasted!*

I force my way back to the railings and push myself over. As I turn in the air a hesitant sliver of glass screams past my ear, down to join the bloody mess below. I cling to the railings and hang sideways, wedging my feet into the gaps. As I move around and down inside the twisted ribbon of concrete, I pass the little girl cradled in her father's arms above. She will not look at me and neither will the others. There is something uncomfortably wrong about my movements as I scuttle sideways on the metal grid of stanchions, and I am fortunate that the crowds are too harried to allow the spectacle through their subconscious barriers.

For a moment as I pass the little one I want to take her, carry her under my arm and set her outside. I cannot. What if I dropped her? What if I needed my arm? She has her face firmly turned away from me.

I crawl and turn, every breath is sharp like breathing

diamond dust, every movement makes my limbs cry out in pain. I am bruised by the throng, deafened by the oceans of screaming, and my arms are leaden, pulling away from the sockets. My hands run freely with blood where I have skinned them against every painted edge of the metal stanchions I cling to. People are climbing over each other on the stairs. I can see through the bars to the steps and the rows of stumbling, pushing feet. I turn the corner, which effectively brings my horizon up above me, and am confronted with the dead stare of an eyeball.

It is an old woman, wrinkled skin pushed up against the bars as people trample past her. Her face is bruised, blue and swollen. Her nostrils are black with soot, her mouth hangs open. Her tongue is a nauseating shade of blue-purple that I know well, I know she is dead before I catch the glassy look in her dilated pupils. Her face is the captured image of surprise, her brow arched, her hair covered with an old floral handkerchief. Blood seeps from her ear on to the concrete below.

A sick feeling rises in my stomach as I near the ground floor. Beneath me lies a tangled mess of warm and cold bodies, covered in blood, infused with razors of glass. I do not want to witness my own handiwork. Coward. I have no choice, but I keep my mind far from the pain. It's not my pain.

At the bottom of the stairs I find steady ground amidst the limbs, amidst the heaving mass of people struggling to pick themselves up as others scramble over them. I cannot look. My world rights itself and I cannot look. Somewhere close to me a woman pleads, "Help me, help me," through torn lips, her bloodied whisper smothered under a dead weight, another person who no longer speaks, and I cannot look. I do not help. I hear the ocean of crying and I fear I will go mad. With a roar of borrowed rage I push into the crowd at the foot of the stairs, driving myself through the doorway until I am out amidst the lucky ones, the ones that were sheltered on the stairs when the skylight shattered.

There is hope running through the competitors on the ground floor, they can smell safety fifty yards away, everyone is pushing and yelling desperately and making their last push. The lobby lies at the end of the corridor, with the glint of sunlight beyond. I turn away in sheer exhausted terror, desperate, hoping to make my way to the garage unnoticed by the sea of escaping piranhas and looters and squatters – I look for all the world like a filthy, terrified, mad old bastard. I turn into the flow of foot traffic behind me, I have to go the other way, I have to go the other way, but a young woman with kind eyes and a four inch gash in her arm shakes her head and grabs me and pulls me along, well meaning in her mistake, and I am drawn into the inescapable flow of people, pushing, trampling, carrying me off towards the terrible light.

I howl. *I don't want to go, I don't want to go!* There isn't time to think as I roll past the door into the lobby. Natural light laces the room like poison, reflecting off the brass and streaming in shafts from a thousand shards of broken mirror. My eyes erupt with searing, burning pain.

My howl rises to a high scream of absolute terror as the sea of arms and legs spreads out into the wider space. Everyone breaks into a run as they see the doorway and the thin morning light. Women are crawling over the ruined sofas and upturned tables to get out. They pass their children out of windows. For a moment I find myself enjoying a gap in the flow as people spread out around me, but just as I think I might be able to force my way back towards the corridor, to squeeze around the doorframe bursting with human bodies, another gush of men floods through and I am carried off and away in the crowd.

There is a group of maybe twenty men, young and old, old meaning forty years once again in these times, all are wearing different salvaged clothes. Somewhere about each of them is sprayed in different neon colours, the emblem of the Piranhas. It is all I can do to keep upright as I am forced backwards, afraid of lying down and being trampled to death under a sea of terrified, desperate squatters.

The skin of my scalp and my neck prickles up as the crowd drives me ever closer to the doorway, and I am paralyzed by fear. I cannot scream, I cannot fight, I cannot speak. The pain rises as I am swept through the entrance, beyond the salvage-stripped skeleton of the Chevy, into the mud and the long shadows and the morning burning. Crossing the threshold is something like diving into boiling mercury.

I scream. Everybody looks as terrified and shocked as I must, I scream in terror of the sun as they scream in terror of the fire. Sunlight licks my skin like flame. The sky rains daggers as the windows blow out. The stampede breaks up into crowds and groups, dodging the fragments, running away from the inferno before turning to watch. Mesmerised, horrified, they look up. I am pushed to the ground, and as I feel my skin bubble and crack, as the agony of burning alive runs through my body, I am struck by the mundane, crass ugliness of daylight, of a light I haven't seen for truly longer than I can remember.

I cannot describe the feeling of being boiled alive as fluids rose to the surface of my crisping skin. I heard popping, cracking noises, bubbling, the ring of tinnitus in my skull. As the pain set in and my burnt eyelids fused into my bleeding eyes, I rolled over and lay on my side. Above me the sky was a plume of black smoke. It seemed through the immense, burning light that the whole tower was ablaze somehow. Rows of windows exploded, popping like balloons, and there was the occasional gorgeous shadow as a figure stepped over me – man or woman I could no longer tell through my scarring corneas. I curled into a foetal ball, shaking as I felt my clothes fill with my sticky, leaking blood. *I am going to die.* It was all I could think. The flesh of my lips stuck to my teeth as it bubbled and charred.

To the side of the main entrance doors, about six feet from where I had fallen, I saw the round, black form of a manhole cover, an absence of light in the muddy grass. I writhed over to it, every second passing slower than the last as my consciousness receded into the safe, quiet world of tunnel vision. I reached out to prise the cover, and somewhere in my calm little mind I noticed the bones of my little finger poking through the shrivelled skin. As I lifted the drain cover, the bones in my hand cracked. I couldn't lift or move it far, so I pushed it across and slid under, head first. Most of its colossal black weight pressed along my body as I dived into the cool blackness. I remember wondering how much scraped flesh I had left attached to that black iron plate as my neck and shoulder landed in the muck, but then sweet black nothingness came to claim me and the agony became a far away thing.

5

I am not awake, but I know pain. I am trapped in a small dark place with it. It is truly dark, a darkness I have never known – the darkness of nothingness, of void. No thoughts, no sounds, no matter. And then there is pain again, and the walls of the void shrink around me. All I know is pain. Even trapped within my subconscious there is no escape from the relentless, high pitched throb running through every nerve. The sensation coats my skin like treacle. It sears my lungs like Sarin gas. Waves of pain deafen me. I am blind with it. I am drowning in it. I do not know this because I am not awake. All I know is pain.

The waves crash upon me before receding in an endless rhythm. There is no time. I do not know one crescendo from another, perhaps it is all one long experience that I approach and run from. I have no idea, but I cannot get away from the pain as it sits in the room in my head and strokes my hand possessively.

The pain chases me, prods me, laughs at me, but I do not know at first. Slowly I begin to realise that I am thinking. Between the nuclear explosions running through my body there came the beginnings of thoughts, echoes and forgotten conclusions. I had it – what was it? No, it's gone. What's gone? Nothing. Then the deafening pain. It demanded all attention, nothing else existed but the pain. A universe of one. There is no room for consciousness.

And yet brief, terrified half formed thoughts burst in, jabbering and screaming for attention, before being obliterated. Some part of me gropes towards them, away from the dark hunter, trying to hear. And then pieces of sensations float through, but I don't know I'm feeling them. Then the pain.

It takes a long time to realise I am awake because I am blind. My first awareness is the differentiation of agony. Every element of my being is burning. There are many forms of pain. My neck is one high pitched, screaming ache. There is a hot poker sizzling through my side. There are needles in my face because I am lying on it. There is slurry in my mouth and nostrils; I am half an inch from drowning. Cracks in my shrivelled skin widen with every tight breath. I breathe in and choke on the sewage, and suddenly I know I am choking and I know I am awake.

I want to scream. I am flooded with helpless panic. I want to burst out and run, but I am an inch away from the illumination of death. This knowledge overcomes me and the desire to run is all I know, but I am lying on my face in a space the size of an oil drum, a cavity where small septic pipes meet before joining the main sewer. I cannot move. Mad as I am, this straight-jacket saves me from the sun above, saves my life.

But it is an oven. I do not know what time it is. I can feel the hot sun outside and with dread I begin to sense that it is not yet midday. I feel the madness coiling within me, running, pushing, screaming for escape as the seconds of bloody agony pass like hours and I realise I will be bound and trapped here for an eternity, cooking in this oven until sun down. I need water and I need life in my mouth.

Shaking uncontrollably, I push my hands down into the slime. I cannot see, and I am glad. I feel things crawl wet and eager across my face. As I push up I place my weight on my forehead, and I fear my neck will crack, my spine will shatter like glass. I move, and the poker in my side travels down my body, or rather, in my upside down world, up my body, and I collapse, screaming for the first time, a thin, high-pitched gurgle bubbling through the sewage. The searing heat is familiar and I know what it is – a white hot crescent of light from the gap in the manhole cover above. I kick out with my feet, and bustle the cover closed. I am trapped in a concrete barrel of sewage and foul air, an oven of filth. Sweat runs – a burning trickle between my charred skin and my clothes, and I pray to pass out. I am begging for relief from a God who hates me. A God whose invention I witnessed. The darkness comes.

I am mad when I awaken next. I know it is midday. My body shakes with the heat and the pain, and I am delirious with thirst. In the shadows between consciousness and unconsciousness I begin swallowing the sewage my face is resting in. No one has flushed a toilet in almost a year, but the filth breaks into my system like poison, and I vomit in horror and disgust. Every convulsion is like taking a cannonball in the chest. I feel my ribs heave through my taut skin, and stars spin before me in the blackness. My head throbs, and I realise how bad the air is as my prison begins to spin. I push up on the circular plate of iron above. I can barely lift it with both of my legs. This is the first time I realise I am going to die here, and strangely, the threatening madness recedes a little with this recognition. Nothing matters any more, it will be over soon. I wedge the rubber toe of my tennis shoe between the iron plate and the concrete, keeping it open a crack. I am hoping for a gush of cool air, somewhere in my memory a light breeze beckons. All I receive is a burning sensation where the light falls across my bare leg.

I drift into unconsciousness. I cannot move when I wake up, and I have no way to measure the passage of time in those paralysed hours. I drift from one thought to the next, dreaming of cool baths and slave girls, but something keeps bringing me back to the chambers of the hypocaust furnace below. Every time I realise where I am the light from above has moved, and my legs are weeping openly from the burns. I cannot move. I will die here. None of it matters any more. As unconsciousness comes to claim me I consider rolling my face over, pushing my mouth and nose further into the mud and slime, drowning myself. In the distance it seems like too much effort.

I awaken to a sharp new pain, and a disgusting, clicking, chewing sound. A rat has crawled into the drain and is chewing my shrivelled lip. With dim perceptions, more a vague sense of outrage than horror, I open my mouth sharply and clamp down as it screams. I've caught its arm between my teeth, and its repetitive, shrill cry reverberates through my skull. I can feel its panic as it tugs. I have no lips to draw the animal inwards, I dare not work my jaw. We enter a race, the rat and I. Whilst it sets about chewing its own arm off at the elbow, I labour to move my hand through the mud. I begin to sweat anew, fresh drops running into my scarred eyes. My body shakes all over with exertion, but I win, and the rat begins another round of screaming as my fingers curl around its fragile body. I force its head into my mouth and clamp down, feeling the grind and pop of glassy bones under slick fur. The body goes into spasms. I am glad of my blindness as I force the animal into my mouth whole. Fetid liquids run over my withered tongue. I want to feel disgusted as I chew. I want to feel ashamed as I swallow the flesh, but I feel nothing, not even relief.

The sun is low in the sky and I am trapped with my hunger; it will not let me pass out again. Every time the world begins to recede and the noises outside start to face, the panic rushes up to greet me and I am awake and dizzy again. I cannot let myself go, for I fear it will be the end of me. Although I am exhausted and quite fully delirious with agony, and although I know that I will not survive till sundown, I do not want to die. It seems to matter again.

I lie there, upside-down in limbo between paranoid alertness and delirium, barely able to move. My head swims as my thoughts run in circles between the confused agony of my flesh and the sinking sun outside. I begin counting. I stumble after five. I start again. Sometimes I make it to seven. Sometimes I pray for another rat. I lick my teeth. Then I am back in the steam baths with the slaves and the muscle labouring at the furnaces below. I want to be in the plunge pool. My thoughts are of the cold delicious water, the screams of laughter, so why do I keep finding myself in the steam baths goddammit? And then I wonder why I am not swearing in my own language, and I realise I am awake in a concrete oven in San Francisco, waiting for the sun to surrender so I can die in peace.

The sun is retreating, I feel it, I know it, but it lingers slowly, tormenting me. My crusted eyelids droop countlessly, but consciousness remains stubbornly barricaded in my skull. The pain has nailed me into my body, and I cannot surrender while being watched by the solar guardian outside. Paranoia keeps me awake.

My delirium fades with the light, and it is like awakening to the agony all over again. Locked in my blindness I come to know the ruin of my body. I reek of filth. Pus trickles from the dead wells of my eyes. In the places where my skin stretches tight over my brittle, blackened bones, it has charred and split. Elsewhere it has bubbled up in weeping boils. I have lost my face, I know it. I am afraid to think on it. My muscles scream and my organs are sunken and withered.

It is a shock when I realise that the sun has been gone for some time, that the limbo between day and night has passed and the darkness is beckoning outside. I do not believe I can move. I long for the slurry to rise and fill my lungs and drown my tired mind. I have a choice – I can lie on my face in the sewage where, if I'm lucky I will die before the sun returns to head my grave. Or I can try to rise from the earth in my agony and crawl blindly for safety, for something. I do not believe in safety any more.

I don't recall making any decision. I begin to push with my legs against the great black iron disc that has been radiating the days heat into my concrete coffin. The only result at first, aside from the pain and spasms in my legs, is that my face sinks deeper into the sewage. I feel through the layer of muck with my fingers, inching towards the concrete floor that my sunken nose and forehead rest upon, and I push. There is a grinding sound above, and I scream out in pain, fearing my lungs will collapse. But the manhole cover has moved a little, and the toe of my tennis shoe is free. It is all I can do to stop my shaking legs from collapsing. I push again, tensing the length of my body. I grind my teeth as I feel skin split and ligaments snap. The filth invades my open wounds. I hear the plate move, and a tinny whine emerges from my throat as I try to push the cover across and onto the ground above. I feel the width of the opening by waving my leg, and I want to weep with relief as I realise that the cover is half open. I poke my legs through the gap and stretch out, and it feels so incredibly good that for a moment the pain seems bearable. My shrivelled legs dangle in the air, macabre saplings swaying in a cool breeze.

I try to rest like this, heart pounding, pain throbbing through my veins, and I realise there is no rest whilst lying on your face in a cylinder two and a half feet wide. I try to get some purchase on the world above with my legs, at the same time I push my body up with my arms. Nausea rises with the exertion and the sensation of my clothing peeling away from my body where it has stuck to my skin. I whimper as I realise that my peeling t-shirt is taking flesh with it. My legs collapse as my waist rises above ground, and I gain an anchor on the world above, which is just as well for I cannot control my shuddering arms any longer. And there I lie, hanging limply, half in the mouth of hell and half out, dizzy and shaking. I have been upside down for hours, my head feels like an overfilled water balloon.

In small, sharp heaves I push myself out of the drain. I am born again, a breach birth, emerging from the dark tunnel into a collapsing world. Suddenly there is more of me on the ground than in the drain, and I almost die with sheer relief. I can relax without collapsing back down and having to start this agonising wriggle again. I have to keep myself awake as I lie there.

Through the buzzing rush of blood in my ears I become aware of the crackle of campfires, distinct voices in low mutters. I look within, and sense the fragile flicker of other minds, groups of them bobbing around like fireflies in little shanty camps around the tower. Terror rises when I realise how close some of the survivors are, and my inner ethereal vision disintegrates into chaos as panic overtakes me. I am helpless like the newborn.

I struggle desperately the last few inches, and then I am lying on the ground in the cool night air. I want to scream with rage and anguish, I want to lie there for eternity, gulping the air, paralysed by the shock of being alive in the world, but I cannot. There are people abroad. I am unrecognisable, tattered and monstrous, and I do not need to be taken to a tent, and cleaned and bandaged and held to wait, blind and patient for the sun. No matter. Most likely they would just steal my shoes and leave me in the dirt.

I crawl, blind and slow like a worm, trying desperately to remember the direction of the tower, trying to orientate myself. Frustration – a spoilt child – stamps its foot in my head for the first time. I try to stay calm and to think, I know the tower, huge as it is, is just feet away, but I am broken and blind, and am just as likely to be crawling away from it as towards it. I follow the close smell of decay, and when I find the ground I begin to rise with a subsiding bed of filth and rubbish that trickles down about me in small avalanche rivulets, I know I have come to the trash mound that has built up around the tower.

I cannot crawl over it. Instead I follow its line, guessing that I am travelling towards the main entrance, which is clear of rubbish, praying that I haven't groped blindly past it. Sure enough, the trash begins to dissipate, and new smells emerge. I swing round, scraping, following the vicious odour of burnt skin and death, and the ground beneath my writhing body turns from the mushy remnants of lawn and weed ridden flower beds to paving slabs and concrete.

I inch my way towards the wretched smell, crawling on my belly, one arm over the other. As I fumble I come across cold metal and broken glass, at least one of the doors has been ripped from its hinges by the stampede. The dry smell of smoke becomes overpowering, clawing at my throat as I enter the building, but faint whispers of the other smell, bloated and rotten and sweet, beckon gently from dark corners.

My spirits rise a little inside the building, and it seems as if my pace quickens. Under cover, I feel a little safer, and relief spreads through me like a warm glow. I know where I am going now. I have lived in this building for many years, I could walk it with my eyes shut.

I crawl along the threadbare carpet, ignoring the smells of piss and shit and fear, and my madness writhes and coils within me as I pass the scent of rotting flesh. It screams within me, demanding satisfaction, I am horrified as the thirst rises. Then there is the noise.

I lie still, frozen in sheer terror as something scratches in a corner. The sound of claws scraping, and chattering teeth. I relax as I realise it is not human, and go on my way as it takes its meal.

I crawl past upturned chairs and fallen lamps, scratching over fragments of glass and mirror tiles, treasures and trinkets dropped in the escape – dented water bottles and plastic necklaces. It is on the threshold between the lobby and the elevator bay that I find a tiny shoe. My fingers fall into the heel as I grasp my way along, and my fingers close around it gently, confused by its size. Then I feel the tight little grooves of the plastic sole, the familiar prickle of Velcro. The pungent smell lacing the child's shoe is one of rubber and sweat. I clasp it to me, tracing its details with my fingers over and over again. The scent of death is very strong just to my left, I do not wish to investigate. I put the shoe down gently, as if settling down the child, and I find my fingers drawn to my lips. My fingernails graze not my lips but my teeth, where they click like the chatter of beetles chewing, and I remember that my lips are burned and shrivelled like a mummy. I crawl on.

Slowly, I drag myself past the elevator doors and the doomed stairwells. I am not going up. I am broken and exhausted. I am crawling down, back into the ground, the garage. The smell of blood and death overtakes me as I pass the stairwell where so many people were caught under the glass. Every inch I crawl takes longer as the stale and foul blood beckons. It taunts. I will not lose myself.

I pass through the hallway and reach the garage steps with the blood still sharp in my nostrils. I listen carefully at the threshold, impatient to lose myself in the cool blanketing darkness. I hear nothing, I sense nothing but the candle glow of rats' minds scratching around me. I descend. The steps down are cold and greasy, and with annoyance I realise that I cannot hope to secure the door behind me. There are no barricades, no tools. I take the steps one at a time, half crawling, half falling head first into the cavern below. After the slick rounded concrete tomb, part of me savours the dryness and the sharp angles of the steps.

I can smell water when I reach the bottom. If I can smell water it means it is rotten and filthy, but I shudder with relief and grope towards the smell like a mole to a worm. The puddle has formed along the wall of the garage. It smells greasy and slightly green, although there can be no algae in the darkness. I am surprised to find the wall where I find it – my fingers recoil. Carefully I trace along its line, making a scratching sound with my flaking nails. Water is condensing on the cold wall and streaming down to the floor – or else it is seeping through the concrete, I have no way to know. I do not care. I slurp along the joint between wall and floor, I lick the gritty concrete gratefully with my black tongue until there is nothing left, and then I push myself up, licking the trickles from the wall as high as I can reach. I grimace as the toxins from engine oil and fungus break into my stomach. I lie down in the cold wetness and the floor spins, drops away and rises up to catch me in free fall. I am sick, but the water is good. I close my useless eyes as the world spins, licking my fingers when they chance upon fresh drops.

Presently the world settles down and the circus ride stops, my body dispatches the poisons and I am left with a dull ache in my guts. It is overshadowed by my rising hunger. I crawl along the wall, towards what I hope to be a dark corner, waiting for the rats to come. And they do come. I lie still, like the dead. It takes hours. I smell of filth and decay, and slowly they approach to nibble at my dried flesh. My revulsion rises as I hear the vicious click of claws against concrete. The vermin follow the line of the wall – rodents do not venture across open ground if they can help it. This means that I feel their arrival either at my feet or my head, and I must wait patiently as their twitching nostrils sniff me.

I watch with my minds eye. At first there is one, sniffing my feet, crawling over my shoe. I am terrified at the thought that it will run up the leg of my pants, I feel the thunder of my heart against my ribs. I want to move. I want to scream. I want to cross my legs! I stay frozen. The rodent nudges my clothing with its head, and crawls over my ankles. It cannot tell whether I am alive or dead, not that it will care to wait. Suddenly, as if drawn by some unseen signal, two more rats appear, but they approach from the other side, coming towards my head. I am almost relieved as I sense them scampering eagerly along. My right arm is pinned along the wall – but my left arm, that is up by my head and free to swat at them.

But the two that approach are smaller and more timid than the first, and with dread I feel it start to sniff at the flesh of my leg just above my sock. The other two hang back whilst it slices through my waxen skin with its teeth. It feels like someone is cutting my foot off, slowly, by the aid of a nail clipper, but the sound is worse. The juicy clicking, chewing sound reverberates across the cavern and through my bones and I want to vomit with boiling disgust and loathing. Sweat pours from my forehead, but I

Samuel Collins

clench my muscles and do not move, do not shake. I screw up my face, clenching my eyes tight shut, clamping my mouth. How I want to kick.

And then suddenly they rush in from above. The first of the pair clambers over my ear and onto my face. It sniffs my decaying eyes. It sits up on its hind legs atop my cheek and its teeth chatter viciously, and I fear I shall scream in terror and madness. All the while my agonies sing in harmony as rat below gently excises my foot from my sun-scorched leg. Then I feel the brush of slick fur against my fingertips as the third rat comes in, and I explode into action.

What this actually means in the shredding pain of my burnt body is that I clench my fist as quickly as my taut and fibrous muscles can, whilst the rest of my body convulses in pain. I scream out loud, and curl up into a foetal position on the unforgiving concrete, but I never relax my fist. The two rats have yelped and bolted, one from my face the other from my leg, but the third, the third screams in panic as it squirms against my wiry grip. The noise reverberates through me like a fire alarm. The creature writhes and flicks about as I draw it inexorably to my mouth, and then I clamp down and feel its skull pop. I hate the taste as the fluid and gristle slides down my throat. I keep chewing. For the first time I am angry.

This goes on into the small hours before dawn. I lie still, relying on my bouquet of rotten flesh, the perfume of presumptuous death. At first they come in groups, I watch them with my mind as they close in like an army of marsh lights. My movements quicken as their numbers decrease and my body relaxes, as my belly fills. Movement becomes a little less painful, I am less afraid when the rats scamper towards my legs and the places I cannot reach. Sometimes I lie still, ready to strike, and I miss. A juvenile wriggles through my fingers and I experience the urge to laugh hysterically. I'm not sure why. The pain shivering through my body prevents it anyway. Part of me wishes the rat luck, but I watch the light of its mind as the animal meanders, sniffling the rich scents along the wall, it returns later only to meet my iron grasp. Its juices run down my chin.

I don't let them nibble at me any longer. I don't need to. I make sharp movements and they retreat, but their tactic is to harrow the defenceless until he is overcome. I am not defenceless. I am content to lie still and to wait, to strike if I can, if they don't begin to chew first. I feel the sun approach the horizon, and the

64

rats retire, low in numbers. I am somewhat sated, my belly burns warm with raw flesh. I begin to think about sleep, for I haven't slept in almost a day, unless you count exhausting delirium. I am afraid. My blind eyes droop and burst open. What if I do not wake up? What if I am discovered – a slumbering monster? A troll underground? My eyes droop. When you are newly blind, you find it hard to tell sleep from waking.

It is some hours later when I awaken to find I am lying perilously close to a beam of sunlight that is falling on the concrete beside me. I can feel the heat. I wake up and sit up in one motion, panic overtaking me. I scream out aloud with the pain of such a movement, and I am shocked and silent as the sound echoes through the garage. I hold still, listening for a movement, a response to my cry. There is nothing, and I can sense no men close by. Stiffly I wiggle back along the wall until I reach the dampness and the running water. It feels good on my tongue as it rolls down my throat. There is less here this time, it hasn't had long enough to gather.

I am exhausted and every part of me is throbbing. I want to lie down, but I will not sleep in the damp. I crawl further along, wriggling on my hips and elbows, and I settle in a dark spot. The shafts of light from the windows above will swing round as the sun crosses the sky, but I have no idea which way they will fall. I know I will awaken before I burn. I settle down and close my eyes. Once again I draw into myself, into my inner vision, looking for the glimmer of other minds. In the emptiness, sleep rises from the depths to claim me.

There aren't so many rats on the second night, they do not come so eagerly. It's the clever ones that stay away, the ones that want to watch someone else do it first. I've taken all the bold and the curious, the next wave of rats will be timid and sly. Somewhere in the back of my mind I ponder – I've tipped the scales of evolution. I hear the rats scratching in the dark, waiting. They don't know that I am getting stronger with the passing hours.

I find I can sit up without so much pain. It feels good. I start to feel I am a man again, even though I reek of filth and pus and bloated flesh. I am coated in grease and sweat, shivering hot and cold with my wounds, and I am exhausted by the endless feeling of being sticky. My guts are distended with the decomposing flesh. I sit in the darkness with my arms folded across my belly like an expectant mother, listening to the gasses rumble out across the floor. Indigestion is a new kind of pain, a welcome distraction from all the rest. It doesn't stop me from catching rats.

Slowly I become aware of a mind hovering on the stairs that lead up from the garage to the lobby. A human mind. I hold still, I make no sound loud enough to be noticed. I feel no light on my wronged skin – I know I'm lying undetected in the dark, yet still I hold my breath. Once I am aware of the glimmer of consciousness, the knot of meaning in the chaotic ether I focus and see that the mind is truly hovering. Undecided. It is a man, but a young one. He will not step down, he will not go back. It is the darkness that prevents him, the fear of being swallowed by the unknown expanse. I do not know what attracts him – perhaps the same thing again. As I listen I find myself in a similar state of ambivalence. I do not want him to enter, I do not want the threat. And yet I wonder if I could take him down. I catch myself.

I wait in the darkness, listening, unable to breathe. I have no way of knowing how long we wait there, alone with each other in the void. I clutch the little thumb-knife in my brittle fingers, wondering if I have the strength to wield it should the intruder come. There are no clocks in the dark. I feel the man's resolve disintegrate in fear, an abrupt and massive collapse, like dumping boiling water over a snowman. He turns to leave. I hear a door grate as I hold my breath, I am disappointed rather than relieved.

Sluggish with pain and stiffness, I daren't leave my dark corner – someone might enter and see me crawling across the expanse, someone who was faster, stronger than me, someone who could pick me off like a sloth in a tree. I put away the idea of searching the floor for tools or weapons or hiding places – I might grope behind blind eyes, never knowing if I was crawling in circles, if I was a foot away from salvation – or doom. Besides, the only things I had come across between the stairs and my smelly puddle had been an empty oilcan and a filthy clump of newspaper. My head turns as if I am looking out over the concrete expanse. That might have been all there was to find.

I had to be careful with the water. I was parched, my blackened tongue and swollen throat throbbed, but the trickles running down the wall didn't provide enough. In that state there is never enough of anything, and I wanted the puddle to be there the next evening. I made do by dampening my fingers against the slick wall and pressing them to my teeth. I didn't like to feel my lips, drawn back and charred as they were.

There were quiet spells down in that garage. The rats would stop scratching and clicking, the water ran silently. In those moments of sensory deprivation time ceased to exist. An hour was a minute was a lifetime, and the dreams I drifted into consisted of one thought, one frame of a movie. I would awaken with a start, unsure if I had been asleep, unsure if any time had passed at all. But I prayed that it had. I prayed for tomorrow, and the next night, and the next, and the day when I would walk out of the garage, or even crawl. I prayed for the passage of time knowing that with every passing moment the spirit stolen from another creature broke into my body like opium, dreaming my cells back to life.

I greeted the returning sun with relief and settled down to sleep through the light hours, contented. I had survived another night, and although the pickings had been slimmer, the business of breathing and living had been easier. I was getting stronger. I had hope.

I awoke in a state of confusion. My forehead was cold where it was pressed against the wall, and I had drawn my knees up under my chin. There was a shaft of light coming up towards my legs, I could almost smell the heat. Yet I knew instinctively not to move. The man! The human man was here, twenty feet away, scratching and dragging something heavy, the light of his mind burning brightly in the ether, so close I could hear him breathe. He huffed as he dragged his prize along the ground, while I lay there, motionless, begging that I would not be seen, just a bundle of rags in the darkness, but the sun was drawing closer. I hitched my knees up tighter, pulling myself in as far as I could, unable to extract the stubby knife from my pocket. I could not survive another burning, I would scream out. I could not, blind and weak, fight a man in the daytime. Terror chilled my soul as I listened to the man. Sweat ran into my scarred eyes. Every blink felt as if vinegar-soaked sandpaper was being drawn across my corneas.

Whatever the man was dragging, it was heavy. The concrete growled under the weight of it. The sharp sound of metal scraping over concrete filled my ears. Every short, gritty sound expanded to become my world. The man cried out, the square of sunlight on the floor beside me edged closer. I could feel the heat prickle my skin. A new, sick feeling caught in my throat as I began to wonder how the man would get the object up the stairs. He was on them now, heaving. I could smell his sweat, sweet and inviting.

My body began to shake as the light grew closer. It was

unbearable! There was a loud, rolling, thudding sound, and the man across the floor gasped. The clink of metal echoed through the garage. He was rolling the object up the steps. A steady rhythm, man and metal. 'Uuurgh'-kerchink-thud. 'Uuurgh'-kerchink-thud. *Oh God, oh Christ get rid of him, make him too busy to hear, oh make him deaf, oh God, oh* eeEARGH!!!

A strangled scream emerged from my bare teeth, gurgling up through my ruined throat as the sunlight singed. I writhed and twisted out into the wide space facing the stairs, and then I shrank away from the light, scuttling along the wall as fast as I could. A gasp rang through the empty space, a heavy metallic thud, and then the clatter of a door slamming. The man had run. I put my head in my hands and shook uncontrollably.

After a time I settled down. I crawled over to the puddle and licked up all the oily water I could find. I didn't care. I kept crawling along the wall, and experienced a flush of relief when I came to a corner. I sat up in the darkness, wedged into that corner with my knees under my chin, and I tried to breathe. I was disgusted with my own helpless fear. Occasionally a great shudder of relief would bubble up and surprise me. It was many hours before dusk, but it took a long time for sleep to claim me. It was that third evening that I realised that I could see a little. Everything was black as I awoke and opened my eyes, but as I shifted my head I noticed forms in the blackness. I wanted to weep in gratitude. My retinas were regenerating. The body supports the nervous system above all else. That's true of all organisms.

My sight was very weak, and the darkness of the artificial cavern was true and unfamiliar to me, but I could sense the solid black of concrete pillars against the deep, vacuous black of empty space before me. Objects littered the floor like woolly shadows. I couldn't see very far in the fuzzy black and white darkness – I found the beginning of the steps but not the end.

In my excitement I attempted to stand up, pushing my hands against opposite walls of the corner to steady myself. Waves of nausea and a thundering, world-spinning disorientation hit me. I couldn't straighten my head. I slid back down, clinging to the floor and praying for the spinning to stop as the ground rolled like a ship in a storm. I was eager despite this. I was optimistic. I wanted to get upstairs to the safety of my locked doors and my freezer. In the fuzzy distance by the foot of the stairs there sat a dark object taunting me.

I crawled. I waited for the floor to stop rocking and I

crawled across the concrete. Every speck of grit cut into my seared palms. My clothing sheered across boils and burned skin. When I got to the foot of the stairs I could see what the man had been dragging. I peered at the metal block, squinting through weak eyes at the veiled mechanical shape, all lumps and spikes. The metal was cold and smooth, moulded. Dark shadows across its surface were deep, circular boreholes. I felt it with bent fingers. It was a sump block. Presumably the man had been in the process of removing it from a wreck when I started the fire. A thin plastic rope was tied carefully around its greasy waist, my hands followed a long line up the stairs. The man would be back for his prize in daylight.

Impatiently I bumped myself up the stairs. Every jolt was agony running through my abused body with the force of a tsunami. It was all I could do not to cry out. I reached the top of the stairs, I hesitated before the doorway. The evil stench of death lingered in the still air. *This is it*, I thought. Was I ready to leave the safety of my dark cavern? Did I have time to reach my apartment? Did I have the strength? Fear and impatience and irrationality drove me on and I crossed the threshold without looking for danger.

It was brighter here. Reflected light from the bush fires and the night sky passed through the broken windows and open doors, cutting through the shadows. The light helped me to navigate in the moments where I could hold my head up. I was beside the elevator bank, the air reeked of bloated bodies, a sweet, rotten smell that stuck in your nostrils and sank into your skin. The stairwell where I had set the fire was nearest. This was the one I should take, I knew. The clear one, with the working door above. But something spurred me forward. The other stairwell, the one I had made my escape through, was calling. The swollen bodies on the floor were calling to me and I followed, like a child coming home.

I sat on the floor outside the doorway, head spinning, whilst my joints screamed and complained. The air hummed, the smell of death was electric. I sat up. I remember the vision of that door, half open, blue and grey and brown in the half-light, the colours decayed and thinned in my ruined eyes. It was open, that door, just a crack. Just enough to be inviting. But I knew what lay beyond; I had seen it before. The vision of it called to me, it sang in the voice of my own guilt, and with the bitterness of the rightfully accused I kicked that door open.

As the door flew open I was confronted with a blast of noxious air. The stench was beyond anything I had smelled in a century. I doubled over and rolled to the floor, heaving in confusion. My stomach produced the last remnants of a rat, a jellied mess of fur and sputum and decomposing flesh scratching its way up my throat, but my mind was somewhere else, lost in the flashes of mass graves and genocide, and things none of us should ever see.

I opened my eyes, and spontaneously heaved again, my body convulsing as I retched. I shook with exhaustion at the effort; I was paralysed by spasmodic pain as my body took over its own movements. There I lay, trapped, lying on the floor before the vision of my own handiwork, unable to avert my gaze. I had expected stillness, a kind of sick dignity in the dead, an angry peace. There was none of that. What I saw beyond my cataracts was a writhing, steaming mound of decomposing flesh, yellow and purple.

The grave was crawling with rats, chattering and knowing. It was the movement I could see most clearly, the random, continuous rippling of vermin over the bloated pile of flesh, glittering with the starry flash of glass fragments embedded in the bloodstained clothing of the victims. The bodies groaned and heaved with rising gas. Though I squinted, I couldn't tell where one body ended and another began amidst the twisted amalgam of stiff arms and buckled legs, of sallow faces. There were pools of glistening dampness where liquids collected, surfaces writhed with the fuzzy yellow thrum of happy maggots. And the flies, the noise of the flies was a spitfire scream.

I had expected stillness.

My mouth opened as if to scream, but no voice emerged, just the dull hiss of passing air. I could not cry, I had no tears left. I sat there in a puddle of vomit and shook with shame and anger.

I did not stay there for long. I did not spend my emotion on them like a fraud or an insult. I was sorry they were dead. I was not sorry that I was alive because of what I had done. I turned and dragged myself away from the evil smell, silent and numb, and I wrenched open the other stairwell door, the one that hinted safely at smoke and ash. I crawled, a stair at a time, around and up, around and up. At every landing I rested, flat on my back on the concrete floor while my head pounded with the rushing of blood and the twisting tower above me spun and whirled. I gasped for air and filled my throat with the sticky, acrid burn of smoke. I was dizzy with the smell. I lay helpless on every landing, praying I was alone, praying there was time.

As I approached the fourth floor the blackened concrete became dusty to the touch, and then it began to flake and crumble under my palms. Every time I put my weight down I began to fear I would slip and fall under an avalanche of broken rubble. With every step up I had the sensation of falling. The metal banisters and stanchions had melted away – twisted spikes and shards that had been ornamental wrought iron drooped like wilted flowers. In my dizziness there was little to stop me rolling over the exposed edge and falling to my death, and the realisation made me dizzier still. I pressed up against the outside wall as I climbed up and around, as the world rocked beneath me. Terror rose up within whenever my shoulder wasn't touching that wall, but I had to keep my head down – looking around disorientated me. I lost my sense of space, and, gazing across the airwell to the steps leading down on the opposite side, I couldn't judge the distance, couldn't tell up from down.

I lay on a blackened landing amidst the clouds of fine black ash and cloying concrete dust, and pressed myself into a corner. I closed my eyes to the spinning world, and let the sensation of movement rock my body. The smell of smoke and accelerant was heavy in my lungs, and the fire door was ajar, a warped and droopy plane of metal that would never swing shut again.

The need for water and sustenance burned through my aching body, and I broke out into a nervous sweat. I shrugged off my overcoat, careful not to tear any fragile skin, and lay huddled in that corner, shivering, cold and sweaty. Somewhere at the back of my mind I knew that the world was turning back towards the sun, and this spurred me on. I rolled over onto my hands and knees and started to climb once more.

I lost myself in the endless rhythm of hand over hand, climbing and turning. Every flight of steps was a mountain, every landing seemed an impossible goal. I stopped resting on the landings, stopped allowing the agony and the exhaustion the moments to set in. Instead I paused, I counted to thirty, at first in my head and then, in desperation, out loud. I couldn't form the words with my stiff and shrivelled lips. The angry, guttural quality of my wrecked voice shocked me when first I heard it and I stopped in surprise. I hadn't realised I was speaking aloud.

I'd climbed above the burnt floors now, and the concrete

steps were hard and cold and covered in greasy soot that infected every part of me. The banister was firm and solid, the edge no longer held any fear for me, or any invitation. As I climbed I began to feel the glimmer of success. I might actually do it, it might actually be worth surviving. It was nothing more than that little hope, it could not drive my stiff limbs out faster, but my hunger for life and experience was returning softly.

And so was the day. A wave of panic rushed through me as I realised it was later than I'd expected. There was a deep blue glimmer falling from the skylight above, and it signalled that the horizon was burning. I dragged myself up the steps to the next landing and sat by the door, trying to grasp the handle whilst the world spun away from me. I opened the door, finally, and crawled through onto stinging nylon carpet in a darkened hallway, glad of the shadows in the windowless space. I felt the relief and an almost congratulatory good humour – at least one trial where the solution hadn't come so *hard*. I secreted myself into the corner at the end of the hallway, and curled up to sleep. I lay there a long time in the silence, waiting for the blood to stop rushing through my head. *That's funny*, I thought. *I didn't notice my hands were bleeding.*

I awoke with a start to the protests of a stiff neck and an aching body, while burnt skin screamed against sticky clothing, and realised I had slept late into the night. It was a rare luxury I would have usually relished but I could ill afford the delay and I was annoyed with myself. My insipid thirst and hunger did nothing for my mood, nor did the fact that I had no idea which floor I was on.

As I crawled back out onto the stairwell I felt how taut my skin was. It was beginning to knit together, and it gave the impression that I had been shrink wrapped overnight. For all that, movement was a little easier, a little less painful, and I felt that I was climbing faster than before. I was eager at the thought of blood and safety waiting for me upstairs. When I paused at the next landing I was able to sit up, and the nauseating dizziness of exertion didn't come. I checked the floor number on the fire door, a little metal plate engraved with the number nine. I almost smiled as I realised my vision had cleared a little.

This was how I continued, up and around, in reasonable cheer, spurred on by the promise of sustenance and the threat of the dawn. Every conquered step brought me closer to safety, closer to the moment when I could lock the door behind me and exhale in relief. My body ached and shuddered with sharp new pains, my hands and knees bled freely from split and grazed skin, I didn't care. I could feel the excitement and relief welling up as I got higher and closer.

It was somewhere on the steps between the fourteenth and fifteenth floors that a noise shattered my premature victory cheer. A door slam burst through the stillness like a gunshot. Running footsteps echoed up from below. I froze in shock, not wishing to make a sound. I didn't know what to think. Who it could be and why I had no way to tell, but I couldn't outrun them and I couldn't fight. *They wouldn't come up here surely? What reason could they have?*

A cold, nauseous dread broke out into my guts and spread through my body. No one had lived much above the fifth floor. There was no reason to come above the fifth floor unless... *Unless they're looking for me!* I didn't wait to find out. I crawled as fast as I could manage. I didn't stop to rest between floors, I just kept going, leaving red, clammy handprints on the concrete steps. Sweat dripped into my eyes and I felt my heart thudding in my chest. The pain and the dizziness returned with a vengeance and I breathed in sharp, agonising gulps. I considered standing up, but at this point I could not afford any mistakes, I could not afford to collapse.

Another door creaked open and banged shut, somewhat closer this time. The sound of footsteps had ceased, but I didn't pause to draw conclusions. At best they had stopped on that landing many floors below, but the paranoid worst was that they had heard my slow shuffle and had crossed over to the other stairwell – to overtake me and cut me off. I did not stop to think. I did not stop to flow through the ether and gauge their intention or location. I just kept going with the sound of my heart thumping through my skull.

Pain collected in the wells of my body like treacle, and my muscles began to seize up. Breathing became the process of inhaling scalpels. The rocking motion of the world became so bad that I had to jam my eyes shut and press myself against the wall as I climbed, following its sharp angles as I twisted upwards.

Was that another door opening? I wondered at a distant sound. I had no idea. I pushed myself up, the pain gathered to a crescendo within my mind as I gasped for breath and pinpricks of colour flashed before my lightly closed eyes. I'd just passed the door for the nineteenth floor when I collapsed. I turned the corner, heaved myself up two or three steps, and my thin limbs simply folded beneath me.

I couldn't move, I couldn't think, I could barely take in air. I lay there listening amidst waves of fear and nausea until I could breathe regularly. I opened my eyes, clinging to consciousness. The only thing I could see was the metal plate on the door below, the number nineteen piercing my fragile consciousness. I couldn't turn away, couldn't move my head.

A door opened below. A definite sound. I shut my eyes and listened to the echo of low voices and shuffling footsteps and was overcome by the urge to shrug. I lay there, limp and helpless hardly two floors away from safety and accepted defeat. I was paralysed with exhaustion. An amazing feeling of calm bloomed within me. *Oh well.* I thought. *Oh well. I've done it all. I've done everything I could do to stay alive. If the universe wants me dead I cannot prevent it. Oh well. Bugger.*

I shrugged mentally and somehow my claim to life lifted. I felt relief, freedom, the relinquishment of responsibility and control. I felt liberty from the shackles of care. Then the blackness I'd been staving off rose up and engulfed me. Swallowed me from below like the cavernous jaws of a whale. When I came to it took me a while to realise where I was. It isn't usual to wake up lying at an incline, halfway up a staircase with your face jammed into the hollow of a step. What I did know was that it was quiet below and I was alive. I also knew that it was close to sun up. Carefully I lifted my body from the steps on all fours, and crawled those last two flights slowly and stiffly. And gratefully. My muscles felt weak and shaky, and I made myself rest on the twentieth landing even as my eagerness overwhelmed me. I strummed my fingers on the concrete, waiting for the shakes to settle, and then my resolve crumbled and I was heaving up that last flight of stairs with a lightness that betrayed my stiff muscles and my dizzying relief.

I could barely believe it as I squinted up to the door with the number twenty-one and fished in my tight, sticky pocket for the keys. The smooth, flat metal surface was a beautiful sight. As I pulled, the door swung open freely, and I listened half-heartedly for intruders I did not expect to find and could do nothing about. I crawled through onto the tough, prickly carpet and closed the door behind me, shutting it as tightly as my shaking hands would allow. My face flushed with relief at the sensation of victory. I was safe. I had control back again.

I crawled over to my front door. Sitting up peering at it, I could feel no pain whatsoever. I clutched at the doorframe, pulling myself to my feet, swooning with vertigo. The corridor spun around me and I held on for dear life as the blood rushed from my head, but I was determined to step through my own front door on two feet. I leant heavily on that doorframe until the dizziness subsided. A big grin broke across my ruined lips and I felt skin split as I gripped the cold flash of metal in my hand. I turned the locks gently and nudged the door open.

6

My apartment reeked of gasoline, it was strewn with empty pots of goo, and the windows were open to a chill breeze. But I was home. I stepped through the doorway and then stumbled, tumbling slowly as my legs folded under me, but I didn't care. I was home, and I was safe. Golden relief spread through me, my hands shook as I slid the bolts across. I crawled through the plastic rubbish and dishes of cold greasy water to the cabinet where I kept the fresh water. I withdrew two bottles and I sat up, propped against the wood as I drank the cool, clean liquid. I guzzled the first bottle and sipped at the second, savouring the feeling of my thirst subsiding as the fluid spread through my withered tissues. I discovered it is not easy to drink when you cannot close your lips.

I crossed the floor to the fridge with mounting glee. I withdrew all three bags, and I drank them in the glow of the fridge light. I bit open a corner of each and sucked them the way one sucks a melting lollipop – with gusto and desperation all mixed up. The blood was dead and foul and smelly, as bagged blood always is, and it was cold and clammy straight from the fridge, but I didn't care. I filled my stomach until I thought I would vomit, and then I waited and burped and took further sips, enjoying the feeling of the sticky fluid running slick and salty over my teeth, dribbling slowly over my chin.

I sat against a cupboard door, clutching my bloated belly, examining the feelings running through my body with a detached fascination. I was safe and relieved and almost drunk, and as the blood spread through me I felt the toxic aches break down and slip away. My body twitched and shuddered uncontrollably, blooming with a welcome heat at the presence of blood. I grinned lazily, head lolling against the cupboard door. There I slept, sitting on the kitchen tiles in the light of the refrigerator, content and clutching my bloated belly, hiding as the sun rose.

Sometime during the day I was woken by the light coming through the open windows and shutters. My eyes burned terribly. I shut the fridge and crawled around the living room walls, keeping below the windows until I reached the darkness of my bedroom. I sat on the floor by the bed and peeled off my clothes, grateful for the cover of darkness. It took forever. With every inch of exposed flesh there was an inch of freshly exposed burn, and I took as much skin off with my clothes as there was left behind. I felt my temperature rise as I agitated the burns. It was agony, like pulling a thousand plasters from unhealed wounds. Every slow tug of cloth on weeping flesh felt like rolling through broken glass, and I did it with a similar reluctance. I didn't want to see the ruin of my flesh through hazy eyes. I sat naked on the carpet, trying to shut eyelids that couldn't meet, surrounded by a pile of stinking, bloodied clothes and trying not to feel the air on my cracked skin, trying not to touch my wounds. I didn't sleep on the bed, I slept sitting up. I was afraid that I'd sink into the mattress and stick to the sheets to wake in a desperate bloody mess.

As it was, I woke up at sundown to the machine gun rattle of the rat gnawing desperately, shivering, and with a desperate need to pee. I headed for my little en-suite, flinging a hand towel over the mirror, and pissed a long stream into the bowl. It felt glorious. *Fool! There's no flush!* I sighed, and stumbled out of the bathroom. As I crossed the threshold I realised I was standing up. I gasped, and a big, painful grin spread across my teeth. How a lipless man grins I barely know. I stood there wondering what to do next. The apartment was a stinking, toxic mess. I didn't want to do anything but sleep and eat and recover. And be clean! I wanted to be clean! I felt sticky and filthy and slick with grime over the burns.

I followed the perimeter of the living room in small, uncertain steps, trailing a hand against the wall, careful of my balance. I ignored the mess and retrieved water from the cabinet along with some clean tea towels. Wavering across the room I stared blankly at the rat, thin and dehydrated and manic, and I stood over its cage, unable to think what to do. I couldn't unhook the water bottle with my stiff fingers, so I poured water into the empty food dish, little flakes of cereal and sawdust bobbing about, and I dumped half a box of stale crackers through the bars. The rat stopped gnawing like a jackhammer and drank happily. I was loath to watch.

I followed the wall back, trailing my fingers along it for balance till I reached my bedroom and the door to the en-suite. I sat in my little bathroom and wiped the grime away, dabbing gently with damp cloths. It stung like hell. I was terrified that I would start to bleed all over, leaking like a stuck pig, but it didn't happen. I kept the light off. I didn't want to see, and I had felt more than I wanted to. I had a fair idea of the damage. On my hands and head, where I had been most exposed, my flesh was shrivelled and leathery. When I picked the water bottles up my fingers clicked dry against their plastic surface. The bones of my fingers lay blackened and exposed where the skin had shrivelled and split.

It was a slow process, wiping the dirt and smoke and pus from my wounds. I started at my feet and worked up, changing cloths before they became dirty, lest I spread an infection. Where the sunlight had gotten through my clothing my skin had blebbed and bubbled up into weeping boils, something like smallpox but a little bigger. You wouldn't know what that was. Most of the boils had burst against my clothes, leaving raw, open wounds that seeped a thin yellow fluid. I used a lot of water on these wounds.

For the most part I was numb to the damage. As I moved further up my body I came across folds of skin that had gone unexposed and were almost normal. Seeing this was more disturbing – a reminder of what had happened to me, what I had lost. I discovered my penis, soft and small and undamaged. Pale. In those moments I began to whimper out loud, feeling helpless and alone and simply exhausted by the fight to survive. I wanted someone else to take over for a little while. There was no one.

As I finished cleaning the wounds on my shoulders and neck I began to shake. I sat on the edge of the toilet seat waiting to catch my breath, waiting for equilibrium. I had to touch my face. There was no avoiding the discoveries I would make there.

I moistened the corner of a clean cloth and wiped under my chin with a bony finger. I kept going, eyes closed, mapping the damage in my mind. My lips were drawn back, I knew, but I found my chin sunken and my cheeks collapsed like an old man. My ears were shrivelled, waxen buds – they felt something like crispy bacon. And they were filthy. Every fold of cartilage was full of soot. As I wiped around them I found that my hair was falling out in clumps. I didn't think on it. The skin was peeling from my forehead – I abandoned the cloth and wiped at my brow with dampened fingertips. I poured water into my leathery palms and held my breath as I buried my face in my hands. My eyes were sunken, becoming deep wells, but it was worse than that – my nose had collapsed. I froze for a moment, feeling the realisation draw through my soul. There was a hole in the centre of my face big enough for three fingers. Black, brittle fingernails probed the fibrous mush of my disintegrating palate and sinuses as those skeletal fingers probed, timid and shaking. Water splattered noisily across the floor as I dropped my hands. I drew my knees up to my chin and wept silently.

It was some time later that I emerged from the bathroom, sniffling and unsteady on my feet as snot rolled down my face. I burst out into a short, machine gun staccato of laughter as I realised I couldn't blow my nose. The noise cut through the silence of the apartment and then stopped dead. It wasn't funny.

I wavered across the living room and closed the windows and shutters. I was freezing. The tangy smell of gasoline quickly saturated every room, but I was too weak to clean up. I shuffled through the mess like an old lady in slippers, and like an old lady I was terrified of falling and breaking a hip. I stepped out with both hands in front of me. I removed two bags of blood from the chest freezer in the pantry. The coldness stung my hands and the frost stuck to my shrivelled skin. I left the bags on the kitchen counter to thaw. If you don't treat them right and thaw them slowly the blood separates, but I didn't care, I was hungry.

Exhausted, I made my way back to the bedroom and took a nap, huddled in a corner and wrapped up in a blanket. It was warm and smelly when I woke up. Although I was dizzy from gasoline fumes, and woke with a thumping headache, I couldn't open the windows – it was light outside. I threw the blanket off and went out to the kitchen, knocking over dishes of greasy water as I went. I didn't care, I was hungry. Pain was shooting through my body, shouting for sustenance. The bags sitting out on the counter were a mixture of ice and thick, gloopy liquid, and I shook them as best I could to break up the chunks. I sucked them dry through the IV tubes, fast and careless like an addict rather than a connoisseur. It was cold and lumpy and disgusting and I didn't give a damn. The liquid warmed my body and lubricated my movements, I almost smiled at the speed with which I gained relief. I was annoyed when the flow stopped.

In good health I could hold myself to one bag a week but in my current state I could drink until I was sick every single night. The presence of the sun outside vexed me and I made my way to the parlour in a foul mood. I took out another three bags and left them on top of the freezer, and then I returned to the bedroom and crawled under the blanket.

When I awoke I felt life and energy coursing through me. My wonder drug had worked its magic again, and I found I was able to walk with a little more confidence. It was newly dark and I threw open the windows to the warm evening air. Familiar sounds from the campsites and waterways washed up from below and I smiled a toothy grin. I stooped carefully, holding my legs like an old man, and picked up the bowls I'd used to make accelerant. I shut them out on the balcony, and began to rinse them with the leftover grey water. I tipped the corrosive residue over the edge, and leant on the railings, looking out. My eyesight was gone, of course. It had improved since I crawled, burned and blind out of the sewer, but it was quite ruined. I had to squint to make out the rounded forms of people below, and there was no longer any detail. The Transamerica Pyramid was just a tapering silhouette in the distance. The sharpness of my eyes was lost; all the fat years of wealth and safety were as nothing. It was the same with my hearing. The sounds of the chaotic city were tinny and dim. I sighed and turned away, hoping that blood and time would restore my shattered senses.

The generator was out of gas, and its silithium storage battery was bleeping an S.O.S. cry – almost empty. I shuffled off to the main bathroom where all the fuel was kept. I couldn't lift the five-gallon cans of course. I had to tip some gas into a bowl and pour that into a pitcher. It went everywhere, I was naked and I didn't want it on my skin. When I refilled the generator it clicked on with a thrum, and the little display blinked with a smiley face, as if everything was A-Okay, technological, normal and safe.

I felt sick with effort, and my body began to shake. I stood by the freezer and gulped blood erratically until the shakes subsided. I stared at the final bag, and reluctantly decided to put it in the fridge. More bags from the freezer joined it on the shelf. At this rate I would run out of blood at the same time as I ran out of gasoline. I went back to my bedroom to lie down. On the way I caught sight of two five-gallon tanks of accelerant sitting unused by the front door, glaring at me.

This was how I recovered – wandering around my apartment naked and dazed, drinking copiously. I did little, I tried to think less. Sometimes I would stand on the balcony, glass in hand, and let my mind drift in the night. I'd come to from the jolt of uncontrollable shivering, and shuffle inside to throw a blanket over my shoulders. Circulating air was good for my skin, and once the burns and boils scabbed over I began to apply paraffin cream that I'd squirreled away years ago. It became my evening ritual, I'd spend an hour gently dabbing the pure white grease over my body with brittle fingers. There was a meditative rhythm to the action that I found calming, which counterbalanced the pain that contact caused my skin. Of course I felt like I had been dipped in oil and set out to dry, a sensation that made me sick and drove me spare with itchiness until the moisturiser sank in. Even by the second day I wanted to wash it all off, but I could not afford to use the water. I would have danced my itching out for rain, but there was none.

The blood heals me more than anything else of course, and although my flesh was thick and stiff with scar tissue, the wounds closed fast and were remarkably infection free. More than half of my body was burned; infection would have eaten any other man alive. The thought made me smile as I applied the cream. Blood also gave me energy, and whilst I had the doddery movements of an eighty-year-old, I was desperate to do things. I cleaned the flat. Every day I aired the living room as I slept. It still smelled of gasoline. I sighed, and left the windows open. Some nights I would read, but often I desired sound. I would sit at the harpsichord and bang out a tune with my stiff fingers, trying to blot out the memories of breaking glass and screaming youngsters, sounds that often ran round and around in my head.

It's a funny thing about the subconscious. When you really need to be together it blocks everything out. The only emotions you know are fear and hope. There are no other concerns. Then, when your stress levels have dropped to something bearable and your body has begun to work on its injuries, it starts to let things slip out, things you didn't know you had to deal with. It happens slowly at first. An echo of a scream makes you put your book down and listen for half an hour. The glint from a knife makes you look up for falling glass. You can't get that damned smell out of your nostrils, and then one afternoon you wake up screaming and it takes a quarter of an hour to convince yourself that you're not drowning under a sea of angry bodies at the foot of some stairs. There were evenings when you'd wake up dizzy and exhausted, twisted into the sheets like a madman, convinced you were trapped in an oven the width of an oil drum and half the length, while someone had lit a fire beneath you. I was waging psychological warfare on myself, and there was nothing I could do but wait, and pay.

So I was desperate to escape once again, only this time it was myself I was running from. Some nights I was fine, sitting out on the balcony, pacing my drinking, clinging desperately to the semblance of a civilised life and a clear mind. Other nights I was manic, pacing the apartment awkwardly like a geriatric crystal addict, trying not to scream and shout and claw at my bald head. Trying not to let the floodgates go completely. It did my recovery no good to be this way, but the amount that I was drinking did nothing to calm my mania.

Neither did my improving health. By the end of the week my scabs were flaking off, leaving a mass of thick scars and tough skin. Although the worst burns remained black and charred and leathery – my exposed hands for instance, my muscles were recovering, fleshing out again, and I was mostly free of pain. Although I was stiff and stooped like an eighty-year-old, I felt well inside. I felt like me. On the days where my mind was peaceful I grabbed at life. I laughed and smiled and danced through the apartment, marvelling at existence, at the miracle of having known so much time in the world, at having survived. One evening I practically skipped into the bathroom clutching my tub of body cream and, taking none of my usual care, I caught sight of myself in the mirror.

I stopped dead in shock and the container cluttered to the floor. I didn't notice – I was staring at my reflection and fighting down a thin, guttural wail. It sounded like I was drowning in my own throat. I knew it, of course. I knew what there was to see. A withered, blackened face, an evil, lipless skull's grin, the cauliflower ears and the bald cap with wisps of white hair. But I wasn't prepared. Not for the ugly black hole in the centre of my face, not for the beady, wicked little eyes. My eyes had been deep and cautious silvery blue orbs, now they were black and bloodshot, and they darted around in my skull like a rat watching a baby. Wicked little eyes set in deep hollows. I couldn't get over the deep hollow space where my nose had been, the little spike of bone hanging down where the cartilage had begun. I sat on the edge of the toilet, dizzy and nauseous, and then I ran from the bathroom.

But there was nowhere to run. There I was, trapped in my little apartment, trapped with the face of a monster I didn't recognise. Or so I told myself. I knew him well. And hated him. And he laughed at me from behind myself every time I felt grateful to be alive. He was the monster that had kept me alive. I woke up one evening from the usual nightmare, the one where I am trapped alive under tons and tons of rotting bodies, inside a stone tower or a corkscrewing stairwell, and I am slowly pressed to death while my lungs fill with pus and rot. I woke up from that nightmare and I saw that I was the monster, and I made those choices and maybe they kept me alive. I was grateful and happy for that. The torture became bearable after that.

I grew calmer in the days that followed. I began to wear clothing and was much relieved at the familiar feeling of being covered. I tried to listen to the building beneath me, but I could pick up little. When I looked down from the balcony I could see great black scorch marks covering the whitewashed concrete, but I saw no lights, no signs of life. The trucks had retreated also – I almost felt alone. I began to wonder what had happened in the days immediately after the fire, the days I had spent in the cavernous garage, in the sewer-oven.

It took me a few more evenings of thinking about it, or rather avoiding thinking about it before I could summon up the courage to venture downstairs and look over my handiwork. I would like to say that I crept out timidly, that I sniffed around and then retreated cautiously, something like a rabbit at the entrance to his burrow. This was not the case. The sheer bloody impracticality of living twenty floors up, protective as it was, was beginning to dawn on me now that I was debilitated. It meant that any excursion to the outside was a major expedition. As such it required careful planning, especially now in my weakened state. I dressed warmly in modern fabrics, heavy denim trousers and stout boots. I wore a hooded sweater, and I drew the hood over my bald and blackened crown. I would have worn gloves over my shrivelled hands but I found any kind of friction or pressure against the deep burns to be unbearable. As it was the light fabric of the hood made my scalp tingle and itch. Standing there in jeans and a sweater, with my black-clawed hands and my skull's face buried in the shadows of my hood, I must have looked like a modern day Death. I completed the look with a stout walking stick replacing the scythe. I didn't check in the mirror.

I stood on the balcony in a warm evening breeze and drank half a pint. It was properly thawed and properly warmed. It was still disgusting, thick and rotten – dead blood that had been removed from the body almost a year before. I frowned and licked it from my teeth. Inside the apartment I collected a bottle of water and a revolver – I was in no mood to engage with people who got too close tonight. I made my way to the front door, savouring the anticipation of leaving the damned flat, then with one final, insulting afterthought I turned back, collecting a small battery flashlight from a drawer in the kitchen.

My step was light as I crossed out of my apartment and into the shadowy hallway, but as I shut the door behind me with a click I noticed the smell of death hanging limp in the air. It was just a hint, just the vague undertone of menace, and it was emanating from under the locked fire door. I swallowed and strode over to it, trying not to think what I would find below.

I opened the locks with the Leibowitz' keys and stepped into the cold, concrete tower beyond. There was a gentle, chilly breeze drawing air up the column and through the shattered skylight above, and the perfume of death was rising on that breeze. I took a breath and started down those steps in the darkness. Climbing down stairs is no easier than climbing up them, particularly if you're less fit than you used to be. By the time I'd reached the fifteenth floor I was ready for a break. As I sat on the stairs at the bottom of the landing it didn't escape my notice that the smell was getting stronger. Death was dragging the salt smell of smoke along behind it. I sat on the cold, hard surface, picking my fingers and catching my breath, ignoring the weight of the gun in my hoodie pocket. After a couple of minutes I took up my walking stick and started down again, and the metal banged against my belly with every step.

I rested again on the tenth floor, the muscles in my legs aching a little. The smell had become a presence on the landing, solid and brooding, the angry child in the corner of the room, the one that nobody mentioned, nobody talked to. I left it there, on that landing, I crossed through the hallway to the stairs on the other side of the elevator bay, but like a tiresome lover the undertone of that smell persevered. There I sat, pretending I was alone, pretending I was innocent, pretending I wasn't being summoned down those steps to witness.

I made my way down again, into the smoke and the scorch marks and the powdered concrete. By the seventh floor I could taste the soot in my mouth. The wrought iron stanchions were melted and bent, trapped forever in their depressed droop. I had to tread carefully on the flaking surface of the steps, and I stayed away from the dizzying edge that threatened to swallow me. I was surprised that the fire had made it to the seventh floor. I stepped into the empty corridor, choking back the hard stench of burnt plastic. The carpet was a layer of black tar on the cracked floor. The walls and ceiling were black as midnight, and every so often I'd come across a lump of charcoal and white ash that had once been half a chair, or a kitchen cupboard looted for firewood.

The front doors to apartments were burnt through. All that remained were the hinges and some sharp sticks of charcoal hanging loosely from the wall. I stepped through a doorway and surprised myself. I heard the crunch of charcoal underfoot and almost lost my balance. I reached out desperately with my stick, and found solid ground through the rubble. Looking down I found I'd stepped on an old-fashioned brass knocker – an ornament in an apartment block. I kicked it aside with my toe and went on. Every step produced a crunch like muffled snow and stirred up wisps of dust that stuck in my lungs and pricked my eyes. I took a sip of water and spat it out onto the floor. My mouth tasted acrid and metallic, my tongue shrivelled in the sour ash pervading the air.

I looked over to the kitchen, a twisted mess of sheet steel and molten cables. Every object was black, a thousand shades of black in the thin starlight. I was amazed at the touch of fire on the objects. There was almost nothing left, and it was truly fearsome. Of the cupboards there was only a layer of ash, some fragments of carbonised wood spread evenly over the area. There was a jet black bubble of metal on the floor, bent and curled over itself like a conch shell. I didn't realise what it was until I saw its distorted corners and the lines of indentation in the steel. It was the sink. The copper pipes had melted clean away.

Examining the kitchen was made all the more surreal because all of the internal walls were gone. The piles of ash and scrap that had been furniture ran along lines that had been drywall. Sharp little mounds of gypsum slag divided the floor up into lazy irregular rectangles. The remnants of the fridge – a pile of sheet steel that had sheared through when the compressor exploded – lay under a mound of slag. The wall and appliance had melted into permanent wedlock.

I shivered. Not simply from horror but from the cold also – all of the windows had blown out. The remnants of glass were brown and stringy and sat in the edges of metal frames that were sunken and twisted. The form was organic, stalactites and stalagmites stretching across a gulf to meet each other in graceful curves and pinnacles. In other places the glass had bowed and stretched, and it ran in viscous little rivers. It looked like plastic. It looked like melted sugar, webbed membranes stretching between the strings. The glass was freeform, uncontrolled and released from useful servitude. It was beautiful.

Wild glass, softened and wilted and untamed, was something one never expected to see. Bewitched, I stepped towards it absently, and immediately I lost my purchase on the floor. For a moment I swung out forward and was faced with an abyss. The floor had collapsed! I saw down into the black depths, a hundred feet down. The floors below had given way and there was nothing but a deep, hungry blackness waiting to swallow me. I screamed aloud, a high, thin wail of terror that cut through the night, and I waved my arms, desperate to catch my balance. But I was going over and I knew it. Frantically I wedged my airborne foot between a brittle lump of concrete at the broken edge and the rebar frame that it clung to. As I put my weight to it the concrete disintegrated, and little powdery clumps fell down into the abyss. They hit the unseen bottom, reverberating like a shower of gravel. The rebar mesh that reinforced the concrete floor squealed and shuddered as layers of rust peeled away, but it held my weight.

I threw myself back in terror and landed on my backside in the dust. I broke out into a sweat and my body shook through with nerves. How had I not seen it? Unacquainted with the new vagueness of my vision, I'd assumed one dark patch of floor was as solid as another. As I tried to breathe and calm myself I scrambled for the flashlight in my pants pocket and I flicked it on. The light spread out into the abyss before me, unimpeded where there should have been concrete flooring. The air twinkled with starlight, tiny flecks of charcoal dust scattered the beam in bright, flashing pinpricks. I scanned the room with the flashlight. It was black. Everything was pitch black and dizzyingly uniform. The floor, where it remained, was flat and soft and silent, and covered in a homogenous layer of black powder. When I saw things, I saw them only through their irregular shapes, their twisted forms standing out in the flat, deep blackness. But where the flat, uniform floor ceased to be black floor and became black void, I could make no distinction, not until the beam shone through, free and uninterrupted where it should have struck a hard barrier.

I sat and scanned the apartment with the beam. I gripped the handle too hard and my ruined fingers ached. I would have seen this with my eyes before. It would not have surprised me. Great swathes of floor had collapsed, broken away into the abyss in dangling strings of rebar and rubble. The edges where the floor gave way were sloping membranes of steel and concrete that declined gently and then fell away sharply, a gaping mouth to swallow you in the night. When I shone the light across the chasm to the building's external walls I could see what had happened. The trusses that held this antique floor up had melted and buckled, and it had broken away under its own weight. I gasped at the destruction. It was beyond anything I had believed myself capable of.

I backed away from the edge, and then turned and walked out of the wrecked apartment, careful to step only where the light fell. I was covered in ash and my face and hands felt dry and itchy. My eyes ran constantly and thin mucous slid down my face from my gaping hole of a nostril, dribbling over my mean lips and on to my teeth. I had to keep spitting.

I went out into the stairwell and jumped up and down on the landing, flapping my arms and generating a cloud of black soot. My aim was to free my clothes and myself from the evil black powder. I did nothing but make myself cough uncontrollably until I couldn't stand or breathe. I fell to my knees and clamped my mouth shut, waiting till the cough reflex passed. It was agony and my lungs felt as though they would explode, but I refused to breathe until I no longer needed to cough. I began to see stars and pinpricks of coloured light before my eyes, and my resolve crumbled as dizziness approached. I took in a huge gulp of dusty air, and I held it for fear of coughing. The reflex passed through my chest, buckling my body over, but I breathed out slowly, in small stages, until I was empty and could breathe again. Silly of me. I avoided stamping up dust after that.

I opened the fire door on the next floor and shone my flashlight out, only to find that even more of the floor had given way here. This was floor six, I had laid accelerant here and on the floor below, and so the heat must have been tremendous. The walls separating apartments had caved in, half of the corridor flooring had collapsed. I began to grin. People would not be coming back here. The wind changed direction and blew a wave of air up from below. I caught the stench of decay and stopped smiling abruptly. I continued down the stairs.

I had cleared the scorch marks by the third floor, but the stench of smoke and death persisted. I didn't look through any of the other floors, I didn't need to. I knew I'd find nothing there but rats and decay. By the time I'd reached the ground floor the smell was almost an audible hum hanging in the air. It was so bad I could barely walk, I leant against the wall as I tripped along. When I pulled open the fire door to enter the elevator bay the stench hit me like a freight train, and I doubled over. My eyes watered with the pungent, overbearing odour of decay, and I covered my face with my hands, trying not to gag. I discovered I couldn't hold my gaping nose.

I stumbled and ran past the elevators, past the door to the other stairwell, and out into the lobby. Whilst a path had been cleared through the corridor and the lobby, some of the bodies had been pushed into corners or dragged outside, no one had done anything about what was effectively a mass grave in the stairwell. And why should they? The door was shut. I couldn't remember if I had shut it when I was half blind and half mad. Other people had been here, certainly. I didn't need to open it, I didn't need to check they were there. As I passed, I crossed over a thick puddle of liquid washing out from under the door. Stinking fermented body fluids and the wastewater of rats. And the noise! The noise was almost as bad as the smell. An army of scratching, chewing, biting things running over the mountain of dead people, a chaotic Roman march in miniature, clicking and squealing in an alien Morse code. I could hear it in the lobby, and above it was the high-pitched drone of flies, circling like jetliners over a runway, and just as loud. Even in the chill night the bluebottles and blowflies did their business with a manic enthusiasm – the pickings were too good to pass up for the sake of sleep.

I plunged through the wrecked lobby. Everything had been pushed aside by escapees or looters. Bodies had been trampled where they fell, and then scraped to the walls and out of the way. Sticky brown trails of blood marked their trajectory towards the piles of wrecked furniture in the corners, the overturned antique post boxes and shredded couches. I stood by the doorway, half in and half out, looking at the bloated, blackened remains of a man pressed up against one corner. Except maybe it was a woman. You couldn't tell.

It's hard to know what to feel amidst the smell of rotten meat and the crawling sound of the maggots at their business. It's easy to feel nothing by that state. When you can't tell the difference between man and woman and it's all just a sack of meat wearing Levis, the temptation is to turn away and put it out of your mind. I stood, looking down, looking within myself and past the numbness for a trace of feeling, a trace of humanity. For a moment I forgot the overpowering smell. All I could find was relief, relief and an aching loneliness. I stood there in the dark, shadowy box of a room, a human construction, feeling alone and exhausted and alien, wondering what I would see when they were done destroying themselves. Was I to be the only one left as witness?

I fell out into the night feeling like an old man, leaning heavily on the stick. I stood there facing the wind in the early hours, and filled my lungs with fresh air. It felt good to be standing outside on the earth. There was no one about. It felt fantastic. All around me were the remnants of camp-fires and flattened patches of mud where people had pitched camp, but the area was deserted. Tire-marks led away to the road where the trucks had made their exit. Halfway down the hill to the intersection was a little row of lumps in the mud. Wooden planks protruding from the earth. It was a little bone orchard. Someone had seen fit to bury their dead.

The area that had once been a driveway and gardens for the tower was now a muddy dumping site, covered with bits of wood, dirty blankets, empty cans and burnt tires that were still smouldering. The acrid smell caught my throat and stung my eyes, but it was preferable to the decay inside. In short, there was everything here that people used these days to make a camp, but there were no people. And when I turned and looked at the building I knew why.

The whitewashed walls of the tower were defaced with huge black scorch marks stretching up to the tenth or eleventh floor of the building. Broken glass from the windows lay sprinkled over the dirt. Great swathes of the outer skin of the building had crumbled and peeled away from the sixth floor, leaving the masonry and steel frame exposed. Sections of antique wall lay across the garbage mound, resting where they fell. There was barely an unbroken window before the eighth floor. The tower looked a wreck. It looked like the walls were collapsing and I began to wonder at its safety. But the steel structure looked complete and it had been built on bedrock in an earthquake zone – it was designed to flex if needed. Still, the ravaged tower was a dramatic sight, and one I was grateful for. I was grinning wildly – people would not be coming back here.

I walked around the building looking for damage, looking for evidence of people. I found nothing. As I came back round to the front entrance and the lobby I stumbled across a small, dark hole in the ground, and my stomach tightened. I felt sick. It was the drain that had tortured me, the drain that had saved my life. The cast iron cover plate was still ajar, and it left a gaping, crescent shaped mouth wide open and laughing at me. I spat through my teeth, and pushed the cover across with my foot. I turned away and walked towards the main doors, ignoring the heaving bodies that had been piled up on the waste mound outside the entrance. They were half covered in falling masonry and camp trash – just another layer of dumping material.

I didn't hang about – I had no reason to. There was nothing I needed to examine further. I darted through the lobby and the elevator bay with the cloying smell, darted as fast as one with a walking stick and the movements of an eighty-year-old can dart anywhere, and I hobbled up the stairs as quickly as I could. As soon as I had passed the worst of the smell I sat and rested. I was on the landing of the fifth, and the heavy smell of ash and accelerant made a good try at covering the decay wafting up from below. The breeze, however, was coming not from below but the door to the corridor, carrying the inescapable odour of death with it. I leant over and pushed absently at the handle to close the door, that's when I noticed something caught in the jam, wedging the door open just a crack.

I stood up and pulled at the door. It wouldn't budge. I put my weight into it and heard a grating, scraping sound in the dust beyond, followed by the familiar perfume of decay.

It was a body pressed up against the back of the door, tiny and burned. Leaning at a drunken angle, arm stretched out, its fingers had gripped around the door's edge propping it open. It wasn't like the others I'd seen, it was blackened, and for want of a better word, crispy. And a child. I was sure it was a child. As I moved the door the body fell into pieces, fibrous strings stretching and fraying – most of the torso remained stuck to the door. The smell was intensely nauseating, scorched hair and charred meat. I stood in the fine ash in the darkness, and I don't know why I kept looking. I was aware that the floor was sloping precariously, groaning and creaking in protest to my presence, but something kept me there, staring at the shrivelled skull, the blackened eye sockets, the barbecued leather jacket.

The leather jacket. I knew before I touched the brittle and crumbling garment. I knew as I tugged at the greasy sleeve and it disintegrated at my touch. Trapped on the fifth floor, the flames had cornered her. Maybe the accelerant on the hallway carpet had burned out by the time she had settled here to die with her back pressed against the fire exit. Maybe it was still burning on the stairs behind her and above. Or maybe she just got lost in the smoke and the hell of it. Whatever, it didn't make sense. None of it made sense.

The heat had been intense, and there was little left except cooked leather, blackened bones and white ash. The flesh was withered and consumed, taut membranes the consistency of jerky had split and separated like overstretched cellophane. The skull lolled uncomfortably at an awkward angle, almost horizontal on one shoulder. A couple of wilted safety pins and a melted earring had settled on the floor around her, embedded in the smear of human grease that had dripped down and spread out into the carpet. There was nothing left to see, but I knew who it was before I peeled the leather jacket away from the metal door where it had stuck. Printed on the exposed paintwork in an array of scorched and sticky browns was a phoenix, rising from ashes.

I left her there. God forgive me I left her there. I stumbled up the steps and away from that place for good, running like a geriatric from an escaped lion. I could not outrun it, but I could divert my anger. As I climbed I became angry, and I began to list all the things I had lost in The Collapse. All the things that men had invented and given to me, and then taken away again. God damn them, I missed my digital music. I missed electric light, and goddammit I missed elevators. I cursed the man who had invented elevators so that tall buildings could be built. Goddamn them all. They deserve their own destruction. I want my elevator!

By the time I had reached my apartment, after several geriatric rest stops and a good deal of sweating, I had built up a great angry head of steam. I stomped around the apartment throwing books and composing in my head snotty, amusing letters to the president and 'the management,' but to no avail. The sun was approaching and I was fighting a losing battle with my spirits. I didn't want to sleep alone with my dreams. I peeled my clothes off in silence, and hung them out on the balcony to air, for they were greasy, saturated with soot and the overbearing smell of death. I was reluctant to go to bed that morning, however I'd gotten myself there, whatever games I'd been playing. All I could see in the darkness was Smudge's skull.

7

The Great Collapse surprised men slowly, as the future is wont to do. There were warnings – for half a century there were changes and warnings as the Earth geared up to shrug off its latest pest. At first global warming was just a theory – a whisper in the rear columns of newspapers, something that the press rolled out on slow news days and that governments responded to with the great holy mantra 'But there is no proof!' – and for thirty years nothing was done whilst insular and objective scientists looked on, taking measurements and writing dry, detached papers as the hole in the ozone layer grew and the glaciers shrank.

The winters grew colder, the summers warmer, and for a time this was simply El Nino, or extremes within normal limits, and the oceans crept up a millimetre by millimetre whilst flash floods wiped out thousands, but were only reported when they happened in wealthy countries, and still there was no evidence for global warming. The party line of the faithful – 'This ship is unsinkable, so help yourself to gas,' began to falter as the weather went from unusual, to erratic, to extreme, as the seas rose and small Polynesian islands began to blink out of existence one by one like floating candles in an overflowing bathtub. Global warming was a joke, remained a joke, indeed, the more bloody absolutely obvious it became, the harder everyone tried to laugh.

The people got wise before their governments. They saw the changes, subtle as they were, and their leaders across the globe shifted their tone. The spin was how to cut back on emissions, because global warming could be prevented, and you could still drive your people-carrier to work, because everyone was moving their car production to coal-rich China, cutting their own emissions and buying their vehicles in cheaper. If that doesn't make sense to you don't worry, it didn't to me either. In the meantime smog-based global dimming was masking the extent of greenhouse warming, but the important thing for the people, and therefore the politicians, was that nothing had to change – at least not in their country – whichever country they happened to be in.

Oh, the politicians signed agreements and they bartered emissions allowances, and a whole new global economy in carbon dioxide sprang up as a means to lash the poor and coddle the rich, assuaging middle-class guilt even as it paid for more carbon-belching factories to be built in developing countries. I watched as intensive biofuel agriculture devoured wheat fields and rice paddies, starving the poorest peoples and devastating the topsoil, and I counted off the days in that narrow sliver of the last years where something could have been done, might have been done, where those countries at the top of the technological pyramid could have saved themselves and those whose shoulders they trampled firmly upon, those they owed everything to.

I watched as the richest countries blindly looted the coffers of the ship they were sinking in. They told people that there was time to prevent a catastrophe that no one liked to imagine – they may even have believed it, and the people bought it just as long as they could run their computers and air conditioners and showers and fifty inch televisions whilst cooking meatloaf, but in truth, it was already far, far too late. You see – it was too late when the glaciers began to recede – which was almost the first thing that had happened. But no one liked to mention it.

The developed West could have used the last fifty years of accessible oil to set up renewable systems on the scale needed to support a global population of twelve and a half billion people, to preserve the technological development that cost us the atmosphere. Instead they shifted the party line from preventing 'global warming' to minimising 'climate change,' and carried on as if they weren't pissing in their own well. And I watched, I saw the signs as the hurricanes circumnavigated the planet, as the oceans swelled, as the monsoons raged and the floodwaters stole the land. I waited for the shock. I saw it coming. I did nothing.

Environmental changes that were a minor inconvenience in the developed West – annual coastal flooding, a shortage in tropical fruits and the 'freak' city-threatening storms every couple of years, translated into a human disaster on a global scale being played out across the low-lying plains of the developing world, which, as home to the majority of the human population of Earth, was therefore the *real* world. The flooding that was an annual nuisance in the States and Europe – a regular source of human-interest segments on slow news days – inundated the farmlands of South America, Africa, Asia. The monsoons drowned the savannahs and the plains; the oceans rolled in and over mud-bank defences, poisoning the breadbaskets of humanity with salt. The watery invasion lasted year round, triggering the greatest

Samuel Collins

human migration in the history of man.

Without the resources, oil, or the infrastructure to defend the land, transport food aid or house the victims of the water, millions drowned, starved, died of disease and exposure. An estimated two billion souls took to their feet across three continents, completely overwhelming any political ideology's ability to cope, to absorb the daily tide of human flotsam washing up on every dry border. Refugee camps grew to the size of major cities overnight – and turned to death camps just as quickly as sanitary diseases – typhoid, cholera, plague, swept through, as national armies opened fire on the starving, rioting, frantic mouths. But the mouths kept coming, and coming, and coming, and the populations of small, developing countries doubled, tripled as governments and nations collapsed under the weight of human desperation.

Chaos broke out early in the rest of the world. Guns ruled supreme, militia thrived like viruses in an immuno-suppressed cash cow where violence was the name of the game, where the human urge to take whatever you wanted was rewarded with food and life and success. Bedlam was there for all to see – there were lessons to be learned, preparations to be made – but in the air-conditioned West we simply watched the bloom of black death on our TVs with compassion fatigue, like it was some far away war, or a movie of the week. Under the grand placating medicine of video-on-demand we tutted, and complained about the price of pineapples and diamonds.

As the treaties and protocols failed and the pollution increased, the Hydroxyl Cycle – Nature's own pollution scrubber – collapsed, and the ozone layer folded its cards and caved. The release of two hundred million year's worth of geologically stored carbon dioxide in two centuries had ensured the largest mass extinction event since the Triassic. Entire niche ecologies disappeared as every type of habitat changed under the heat, the desertification, the flooding and the UV radiation. Giant algal blooms smothered the tepid oceans, and seventy-five percent of life across the planet died in two seasons. Only the generalists survived – and thrived in an untamed explosion of life feasting on the spoils of death, scrambling to claim the newly vacated ecological real estate. Grasses clung on, shrubs and the more adaptable saplings burst through the city concrete in the glowering, wet heat. Weeds ran riot. The inevitable end result of survival of the fittest is a cruel joke. As humanity out-competed

94

itself into extinction, the insects and the rodents emerged triumphant as the death-devourers and clean-up crews of a planet shaking itself free of bigger vermin.

Of the larger organisms only the generalists persisted, the scavengers, the opportunists. Pigs turned feral, along with cats and dogs. Coyotes loped through the night chasing the foxes and the 'coons. Bears reclaimed the mountains while wolves and horses roamed the foothills. Life ran rampant in the melting pot of death and heat – all the rules were upturned and nothing was as it should be. In the pressure-cooker of the refugee camps, viruses jumped between chickens and pigs, ducks and people, all sharing the same food, water, air. New plagues were born to decimate humanity with manic glee, people fell like chessmen.

Sea levels climbed further, and allied nations began to fight over the remaining oil, uranium and fresh water in the weapons-poor, resource-rich countries that the West had spent centuries subjugating with the equal violence of guns and economics. Small, legitimized skirmishes at first, one every few years to keep the voters interested (never start a war with a country that can actually defend itself), and then gradually the pretences dropped as weeklong brownouts and mile-long queues at gas stations became everyday. Disease spread across the globe in waves like wildfire as erratic energy supply lead to erratic water treatment, but for six months of the year when your country was winning the war – and not only holding off the armies of those men that live in the oil lands, but every other Westernised power that's looking to muscle in – everything was fine because the TV worked when you pushed the button and there was gas for the SUV. For the six months when our old allies were hogging the barrels and beating the shit out of our boys it wasn't much fun living on fuel coupons and electricity curfews, and you couldn't afford to run your air conditioning in the sweltering hundred and thirty degree heat, but hey, it's gonna be fine folks, because the boys in Washington said we could minimise climate change.

But it wasn't fine. It was never going to be fine again, because the ice was melting and the sea was coming; it was already too late. It was too late from the moment the first ice began to melt. As the sheets receded the amount of sunlight they reflected out into space decreased, and from then on the warming snowballed. With the oil running out, global dimming tailed off, and the mean American temperature climbed a degree in the week that we lost the occupation of the oil lands and went back to fuel rations. But global dimming was known, it was understood – it was factored into the models – even the ones they didn't tell us about. What no one seemed to know, what no one seemed to have factored in, was the amount of gas imprisoned in glacial ice, in the melting permafrost, in the ice sheets – trillions of tiny carbon dioxide bubbles waiting to wreak havoc – a hundred million tons of sleeping danger. From the moment the glaciers began to recede the process was exponential. Global Warming was a runaway freight train.

Washington stopped saying anything at all after a small atomic rash known as the One Hour War broke out across the Middle East, turning the desert sands into an ocean of radioactive glass and ending all the region's problems in one go. With the Persian fields gone overnight and the world's remaining oil fields rapidly drying up, or inaccessible in the iceberg-strewn arctic, the oil economy collapsed, and suddenly there were no platitudes, there were no sound bites or contingency plans. As the worldwide combustion of oil largely ended over the course of a month, atmospheric soot particles cleared and global dimming ceased to be a variable in the warming equation. Temperatures rose accordingly, and without oil to cushion the blow, the West finally knew the power of an environment it could no longer evade with the delusion of superiority. At last the West knew the suffering of the pyramid of humanity upon whose shoulders it had stood in cheerful denial. A culture so disconnected from the reality of its environment bore no survival skills; the middle-classes starved in their living rooms as they waited by their TVs for help, while the meek, familiar with hunger and the necessities of desperation, inherited the Earth, and all its debts.

Somewhere in the warm, acidic Pacific Ocean where the continental shelf is shallow, and the Australians, desperate for fuel to run their desalination plants, were hoovering up methane hydrate ice like there was no tomorrow, the temperature peaked one sunny day and the hydrate shelves destabilised explosively and catastrophically. Two thousand *gigatonnes* of the most potent greenhouse gas, methane, was released into the atmosphere, and a lethal firestorm the size of Kansas devastated the South Pacific, but no one heard about it for a week because there was no power for the domestic internet, which meant no TV, no video feeds, no blogs, no news sites to disseminate the hell of it. Radio was reduced to underpowered, erratic and government-controlled bulletins for those who could afford to use their battery ration to tune in, or had the foresight to buy those wind-up, solar powered units that were such an amusing anathema in the twenty-first century.

Temperatures rocketed and what remained of the polar ice caps melted – salinity dropped whilst sea levels exploded, and as the shifting weight of ice and water was redistributed along the continental plates, earthquakes and tsunamis rippled across the globe, devastating lands that had been dormant and peaceful for a thousand years. San Francisco trembled for months as buildings collapsed and bridges succumbed to continuous stress fatigue. Fresh water became an occasional miracle as the San Andreas Dam failed, and all along the bay a hundred thousand people died in paralysed terror under a shifting glacier of concrete and dust.

It was sometime after this I heard rumours that the Gulf Stream and Namoc Deep Ocean currents had collapsed in the thin, tepid oceans, and the central heating system of the world had just ground to a halt – it was overdue its ten-thousand year service. Even I wasn't around for the last ice age. All over the world weather patterns stopped. Seasons ceased to exist. Ice descended inexorably from the poles and sea levels stabilized, but while North America and Northern Europe asphyxiated under an abrasive ocean of permafrost, mass desertification took hold over Central and South America, India, Africa, Central Asia and China. As the ice moved down from the poles the desert moved up from the equator, leaving two narrow, isolated strips of life clinging on somewhere outside of the tropics. In one season a billion flood survivors starved to death, trapped between deserts of fire and ice in the biggest dustbowl the world has ever known. I heard their souls cry out, and all I could do was sleep and prepare.

That was almost two years ago, and the mass deaths across the open plains make the ten or twelve bodies in my stairwell seem easy to live with. It's a simple calculation to perform, I pretend I am comfortable doing it as I sit on the gently rocking boat, being ferried to the Bay Bridge – the Looter's Causeway. I'm being rowed by a suspicious old man in a leaking tub of a boat, thinking of the chaos and the drowned SUVs and the heat and the hoarding preparations I made over the years, acquiring things opportunistically like some manic, paranoid squirrel. The boat rocks wildly as the old man fights against the breezy currents. Goddamn you people. Goddamn your SUVs and your toaster ovens, your computers that don't know the meaning of standby, let alone the off switch. God Damn you all. I would have taken the bus rather than all this.

The old black ferryman eyes me suspiciously as I clasp a five-gallon tank to my chest, clinging to it as if it were a newborn. There is another at my feet, but it is empty. The man's eyes tell me he wants to know what I am carrying – is it fuel or water? But I have paid him well in freshwater to keep his mouth shut and his oars moving. Still he stares at my blackened, ruined hands as if I am the very devil himself, and he will not look into the gaping darkness of my raised hood. Just as well.

As we get out into the deep water north-east of the Market Street Channel, the ferryman's eyes drift towards the tank I am clutching once again. The water is choppy out here and I realise how vulnerable I am as the boat rocks in the waves. Casually I reach into the wide mouth of my other sleeve and withdraw the handle of my knife, just enough so that the blade glints in the moonlight. The old man flinches and turns away, pretending to look over his shoulder towards Yerba Buena Island and the old, overrun listening station that has become the Looter's Fortress. The man heaved through the thick black waters and the little boat made its way towards the line of surf and reflected lights that betrayed the Looter's Causeway.

I have never liked travelling over water. The helpless vulnerability of it has always left me feeling uncomfortable, but secretly I am savouring the experience tonight. It has been years since I had a man working for me, labouring under my direction and compensation. It makes me feel powerful and comfortable. I understand this world, I am the centre of it. I sit back and attempt to enjoy the salt breeze, the rocking motion and the sound as the oars cut through the crests and wavelets, feeling thoroughly pleased with the sensation of travelling by oar power. When the wind changed I found myself wishing the oarsman would sigh less and wash more, but no matter.

We were rounding a long, flat bank of rubble that had once been the Embarcadero Centre, and the surf kept pushing us towards the steel and concrete wreckage. It was dangerous to drift, as, like an iceberg, ninety per cent of the rubble lay underwater, waiting to rent a hole in our little hull and throw us against the jagged concrete rocks and rebar daggers. Every so often the sound of the waves percolating through the deadly honeycomb of masonry would escalate and the old ferryman would turn the boat out into the bay and row hard against the current. It satisfied me to watch, I had paid him well for the journey.

The city was spread out before me like a petrified forest rising from the waves. The remnants of the Financial District climbed into the sky, broken shards of steel and masonry barring my view of the hillocks descending into the SoMa floodplains. To the east the Tenderloin sank back down into the sea, Van Ness was flooded and formed another channel for cargo barges coming off Market Street. On bright evenings in times gone, when I'd had my full sight, I could stand on my balcony and see the moonlight reflecting off the gilt dome of city hall.

The Transamerica Pyramid still stood, old as it was. There were burning orange lights flickering in some of the higher windows, and I yearned to know who could hold such a building, and how much it had cost them.

Far beyond lay the Haight and the park hills, Twin Peaks Militarised Zone rose up in the distance. My weak eyes could barely make the radio tower out. SoMa was gone, with its low-rise warehouses and lofts built on the sawdust of reclaimed land, it subsided and drowned in a murky swell of thick, oily water. The shattered freeway coming off the bridge descended down under the waves and into the sucking undertow. Dark pools swirled around the intersections, surge currents pushed through the deep channels between submerged buildings. The old man struggled to keep us away from the swells, and once we were beyond the banks of wreckage and rubble, and had crossed south of Market Street Channel, solid land seemed very far away indeed. There was nowhere to go but the Causeway.

The bridge canopy jutted out of the water like the exposed spine of a ravaged prehistoric carcass, the western span rising up at the stubby first pier and terminating at Yerba Buena Fortress, a highway to nowhere, a refuge camp for the forgotten. Beyond Yerba Buena Island, the newer eastern span had tumbled into the water during the months of earthquakes following the Hydrate Disaster. Designed to withstand the Big One with replaceable, single-use sacrificial shear links, the self-anchored suspension bridge succumbed to the continuous quakes, its free-floating deck shaken apart in its cradle by the endless shearing. Unmaintained and ravaged by the tremors, much of the western span's upper deck had buckled and failed, dropping down on to the lower roadway. When the quakes ceased the desperate and the homeless swarmed in, installing themselves all the way along the canopy to Yerba Buena, clearing the ribbons of the upper deck over the side or simply pitching camp on top of them. As we approached the Looter's Causeway I could hear the sounds of life drifting over the waters. Fires crackled. Tent canvas flapped in the wind. Taut cables hammered out against hollow steel. Babies wailed in the night. I caught the broken flow of life running through the air and my heart solidified in fear. People!

Clouds ran across the moon, sucking the light up greedily. The encroaching darkness took my breath – I was unused to it. The ferryman became a vague, dark shape swaying about in front of me, the Causeway a string of broken fairy lights twinkling in the dark as campfires flared and lamps hanging from bridge beams flickered in the wind. I swallowed as the shape of the old ferryman turned around fast to check our course. I had no way of knowing if his sight was better than mine, or worse.

The old man wouldn't tell me his name. The rasping grate with which I voiced my enquiries did nothing to encourage him. The more he looked at me the less responsive he became – his eyes kept sticking on my ruined hands. At least once I'd shown him the knife he'd stopped trying to peer at my face through the darkness of my hood. I'd taken one of the Leibowitz' thick curtains and sewn it badly into a sort of hooded gown with sleeves. I looked like a phantom. *Let them think me a monster, that's the idea.*

As we approached the bridge the old man battled with the oars. The currents were strong where the water swelled around the pillars, and we could not afford to get sucked under the low canopy of the road deck. It was perhaps a metre above the waves at this point, and the treacherous swell would smash us against the iron girders of the bridge. The ferryman brought us alongside the bridge. He rowed us along to the giant concrete pier where it climbed out of the water and the freeway emerged from beneath the waves. The deck beyond the pier accommodated the gatehouse, no one got onto the Causeway without passing the little fortress there. To tie a boat up further along the bridge was to risk a quick and brutal death, no questions asked.

The freeway formed a makeshift jetty where it descended gently into the water. Tied to stakes hammered into the crumbling tarmac was a collection of boats of various sizes. Some were better-maintained than others. There were small rowing boats like ours, made from bright yellow plastic or fake wood. Nestled between them were larger boats, a single mast rising from each hull with tattered rigging. There was nothing much larger than a fishing dinghy, except for a low-slung speedboat towards the gatehouse and a concrete barge the other side of us. The speedboat glinted with painted metal, a row of mismatched outboard motors hung over the bow, propeller blades whistling in the chill wind. The cab of a truck peeked out above the sides of the hull. Along the roof ran a series of spotlights. I thought back to the trucks that had besieged my tower with alarm, and sat up, straining to see more of the vehicle. There was an emblem painted on the cabin door in coarse, dripping strokes, but I didn't recognise it. It wasn't a Piranha.

The ferryman pulled the boat in between two dinghies, I heard the alarming, grating sound as it ran up along the sodden tarmac. He stood, rope in hand to tie the boat up, and erupted in streaks of cold, white light before he had stepped out. Men were running around, shining headlamps at him and lighting fires in old oil drums further up the ramp. A shaft of light ran along the boat, strafing my chest, and then I was caught in two or three spotlights. I pulled my hood down and held out my empty hands. The spots focussed on the five-gallon tank in my lap. My heart thundered.

"Who the fuck are you then?" A beam of white light swings from me to the paralysed ferryman and another sweeps out into the night.

"It's all right. Just Reg and some old dude."

I shiver in surprise and draw my hands into my sleeves as I realise the old man in question is me.

The ferryman is still standing, frozen, rope in hand. "Let me tie up then," he whines as the boat wobbles.

"Go on, you old bastard."

We are left in darkness as the beams blink off. I realise uneasily that I want to squint. Reg jumps off the boat onto the tarmac and ties up quickly. I wait for him to finish before I move, I swear he's shaking softly in the darkness. I stand up and step out of the little boat, carrying my two tanks, one heavy, one light. The weight in my hands pulls my body down to the left, and I struggle to stand straight. It is important I show no frailty, even as an old man. I do not look at the ferryman as I pass him.

"Wait for me if you want another bottle," I rasp.

Speaking through my wrecked throat takes effort and slow, careful concentration. Still there is something cold and slithering in my voice, and the old man represses a shudder, trying not to flinch as I go by.

It's hard to speak. Hard to hear myself in such a condition.

Every slurred syllable a reminder of what I have done to myself, what I have lost. The voice I use in my mind, the voice I think with, is me. The same old asinine, pensive man, the sound is quiet and gentle and smooth. Then I speak aloud, slow and clumsy through whistling teeth, wisping through a broken palate, and the illusion is shattered, replaced with a reminder of my condition just as bitter as a mirror held to my face. I have lost myself. I have lost myself in the thick guttural hiss erupting from my scalded vocal chords. *That's not my voice! That's not me! Is it? But is it?* There is something of the grave in my voice, heavy and damp and laboured, and every forced sound batters my eardrums, shouting, screaming, *'You. Are. Not. You. You are dead, you must be.'* I died, trapped and alone in that sewer drain, and was resurrected as a filthy grave revenant.

I make my way up the ramp slowly, heading for the guard's camp beyond, up where the tarmac levels out.

"I've come to trade," I call out, wincing at the rust in my vocal chords, hating the stranger's voice I carry. There are low voices ahead, mumbling and laughing briefly. In the flickering light of the drum fires I can make out the peaks of tents across the road, and the eves of lean-to shacks. They form a line along the tarmac, behind which the teaming life of the bridge sprawls. To the left is a low watchtower constructed from scaffolding and wood. A dark figure turns and watches from above as I approach. I lift my head but don't stop moving. I cannot make him out in the darkness, but I know he has some kind of weapon.

As I come closer I realise there is a line of oil drums across the tarmac in front of the tents that make up the camp. They are all filled with mud and rubble. To the right is a more substantial wooden shed, orange light flickering from a wide horizontal window set at shoulder height. A guard post. A lane has been left open across the centre of the freeway between the oil drums, just wide enough to drive a truck through. It is blocked off with rusting barbed wire and wooden boards with protruding, upturned nails – defences that can be removed easily. There is no iron gate, no raising barrier.

There are tents and huts lining the avenue all the way along the bridge to Yerba Buena. The second deck of the freeway is still intact thirty yards ahead, but above me it's just a network of twisted iron covered in loose bundles of concrete that are strung along like dew droplets on a spiders web. There are campfires and Coleman lamps hung up all along the avenue ahead, a mile long necklace dripping with trashcan diamonds, and there are diffuse, moving silhouettes where the light penetrates the thin fabric of the tents. It reminds me of Christmas lights in Union Square. It is beautiful to be sure, but what haunts me is the hope of those who light the lamps. They cling to the light in the darkness, their sheer bloody determined refusal to give up their pretensions of civilisation when faced with a terminal decline sticks in my mind, sticks in my throat. The sounds of laughter and shouting and brawling ride along on the breeze. A violin cuts cheerfully through the night somewhere ahead. I think I hear a child crying, but I cannot be sure, my ears are useless – worse than useless. I hear with a dull, fuzzy undertone that blunts every sound, something like listening to opera whilst being smothered with a pillow. The cries could have been an animal – a goat or a pig. All around was the smell of charred meat and fish guts. Small, deformed fish hung in strings, boned and splayed out like old kippers.

"I've come to trade, do you hear?" I call out, annoyed as I approach the perimeter. Suddenly I am aware that I am surrounded by men, ahead of me, behind me, to the sides, four or five of them. A line of fear shivers through me as I realise I cannot rely on my weakened senses – they do not alert me and I do not know how to listen to them. I stand still and with some effort to remain calm enough, I drop into the ethereal sense, and there they are, four men around me, their minds burning in the empty, fuzzy expanse like beacons in the night. A thousand minds line up along the bridge beyond, humming and flitting like fireflies, a moving, writhing string of fairy lights a mile long stretching way into the vast night.

But it is the mind in front of me that burns brightest, quick and cunning and hungry. Sure enough when I open my eyes he is standing before me, a short, wiry man-child of thirty-five, starting at me with glassy eyes. He is still, examining me intently, but he is relaxed. He holds a knife at his side, a nine-inch straight blade in black iron, rare and unusual, maybe antique. The kind of knife used by Jack the Ripper, but this man would likely not know who that was. He held the blade still, didn't slap his thigh, didn't play with the point. He didn't fidget with the knife – that's how I knew he could use it. My own thoughts went not to the little dagger in my sleeve, but to the pistol hidden under my gown, the pistol I was reluctant to reveal.

Another man stepped in from the left, barring my way. He held his knife out at shoulder height and jiggled it towards me. I stopped at the knifepoint. This one was pure thug, and too much of a bully to be threatening. But it was the gatekeeper in front that was the leader and the menace.

"Let me pass," I croaked. "I've come to trade. I wish to see Papa Bo."

"Bo is dead these six months. If you were welcome here you'd have known it. What could you have that's worth your life?"

I set the heavy tank down, shaking. It had been a year since I had traded with Bo, one of the few men to know my face. I hadn't known. I wondered how he'd died. I wondered what I'd do now.

"Water," I said. "Clean."

The wiry man's eyes narrowed but he stayed still. He made a motion with a flick of his knife, and another man scurried towards the tank, hurrying to unscrew the lid. This one was tall and thin, barely out of his teens, a scraggly beard and holes in his T-shirt. He shivered in the night breeze. As he knelt by the tank he noticed my shrivelled claw and flinched. He didn't look up after that.

The lead Gatekeeper licked his lips and waited as the boy unscrewed the cap and dipped his finger in. He brought it to his nose and sniffed the droplets. Tentatively he placed his finger in his mouth. He blinked. Then he dunked his finger and did it again. His eyes widened.

"It's water!" The boy squeaked nervously. "I mean, it's not rain shit, it's real water!" He licked his fingers again. "It's almost sweet." He choked back excited laughter with the embarrassment of youth.

The thug with the knife gasped and stepped towards me.

"Stop!" the Gatekeeper hissed at him. The thug flinched visibly, and dropped his hand to his side. He twisted his wrist back and forth, slapping the blade against his filthy loose jeans impatiently, angry at being superseded, and embarrassed enough to want to kill me for it.

"Where did you get it?" the Gatekeeper whispered. "Come closer." He beckoned with his hand. He spoke in a soft tone, a smile on his face, but his black eyes were hungry and vicious like mine. He tilted his ear to me, and flapped his fingers towards his breast. He wanted the secret to himself. The one hand beckoned, the other gripped the knife.

I didn't approach. Instead I spoke as loudly and clearly as I could. If my voice hadn't rasped it would simply have been shaking.

"There's more where that came from," I lied. "Clean, safe, sweet water. A lot more. A thousand gallons. In a water tank in a building somewhere out there." I waited. The thug betrayed himself, his face twitched as he tried not to grin. That much water could buy a man a kingdom. The Gatekeeper's face was stony – I wasn't playing ball.

"If you kill me, you will never find out where it is. If you steal this sample you will never find out where it is. If you follow me, or harass me in any way, you will never find out where it is." I saw a wicked idea fire the leader's eyes. His lips curled.

"If you torture me –" I cried out "My heart will give out. I am an old man, after all." I waited for the realisation to cross them. "In short, if you want my water you will have to trade with me."

I stopped and held my breath in anticipation, waiting for my bluff to fail. My throat was sore from the shouting.

"How do we know you're telling the truth?" the Gatekeeper hissed. He was furious, and he knew my answer before I spoke.

"Good question. How do you?" I shrugged under my gown. "But what if I am? Can you risk losing the chance?"

"What do you want?" The Gatekeeper asked flatly, his voice filled with cold contempt for his conqueror.

"An equal volume of gasoline."

It was a fair price, and though they knew it they each of them sighed and complained. Water kept you alive longer than gas.

"We can't measure it out," the boy stammered. The Gatekeeper looked at him sharply but he went on. "I mean – we don't know how to. And we don't have no measuring cups."

I sighed and threw my empty tank at the thug's feet. "Fill this up." I said.

The thug picked up the tank gratefully, and then looked towards the Gatekeeper. The weasely man looked at me, and then sighed and nodded. He ran his fingers through his stubble and huffed. The thug scurried off through the gap in the oil drum blockade, down the avenue, disappearing between a darkened tent and a lean-to shack. The Gatekeeper and I stared at each other silently. Neither of us moved. Forever ticked by slowly.

The thug hurried back through the shadowy avenue, weaving his way around potholes as the tank swung heavily from one hand. He looked at the Gatekeeper as he passed, and set the tank at my feet. Somewhere in the distance of the bridge behind us there was a commotion – rumours were spreading and so was the danger. I was outnumbered by thousands.

"Open it," I said. The thug scowled, but bent and unscrewed the cap with fast, twisting movements of his chubby fingers. I knelt on the hard tarmac and looked into the tank. It was full, certainly, and the vapours struck my defenceless sinuses with the toxic tang of gasoline. I took the cap from the thug. As my brittle fingers scratched against his skin he flinched and pulled his hand away.

I stood up with the sealed tank and turned, wordlessly, hurrying down the slope as the commotion increased behind me. I could see the ferryman waiting at the water's edge.

"Wait!" The Gatekeeper called. "When will you bring more?"

I stopped and sighed, looking up to the stars. "When I need more gas!" I called out. Then I turned – I'd had an idea. "When's the next water tanker sail in?" I rasped.

The Gatekeeper shook his head. "Who knows?"

"And gas?" I asked, although I knew the answer already. The Gatekeeper shrugged. "They stopped sending them. We only get what they smuggle from L.A."

"Ah." I said. "Tell your boss I will trade water for gas. Much as he wants." I lied.

With that I turned and hurried to the little boat. My own water store was dangerously low but it didn't matter. I'd waited three thousand years, watching as man invented science, measuring cups, cars and refrigerators, and now that knowledge was sinking into the mud. I wasn't about to wait for man to reinvent water filtration.

I jumped into the boat and hissed at the ferryman to untie her quickly – I was annoyed that he hadn't done it on my approach. I wanted to be away from there before the gossip brought people to the jetty. The ferryman cast off and jumped into the little boat, and we were off, back into the arms of the black and sucking sea.

People gathered along the bridge and leaned on the pylons as they gazed emptily into the night, eager for a glimpse of the man with water to spare. Word had gotten around. I clutched the square, tin tank to my breast and pulled my hood further down over my face. I didn't want to be seen. As we cut through the black waters one or two eager figures ran out onto the jetty, and fear spiked my guts. I didn't want to be followed, and there were plenty of empty boats tied up. I stared, squinting in the darkness as the boat lurched up and down, waiting for the inevitable, waiting for men to run down to the water and untie a speedboat, but it didn't happen. They'd lost the initiative. Or the Gatekeeper had remembered my words. Either way I was grateful, and somehow disappointed.

The ferryman had brought us out into deep water before I felt able to turn my back on the faces on the bridge, swivelling on my wet seat. As I faced him our eyes met, and he looked away briskly. He'd been watching me. I examined him for a moment, and felt for the weight of the knife in the folds of my gown. But from the way he shrank from my gaze I knew it wouldn't come to that, and I was glad. It was unnecessary. I sat for a time as we made our way towards the Market Street Channel, the Ferry Building's clock tower just breaking the waves. I watched as the foam of the surf glowed eerie blue in the fading moonlight. For those moments I relaxed and enjoyed my success, as I enjoyed the bobbing of the boat in the waves, and the salt air of the bay. I had a few weeks of gas, and a little water yet. I had bought myself a little more time, and although we were all living in the top of an hourglass, I now had more sand than most.

With my thoughts dwelling on time I became aware of the turning of the world. The best of the night was spent. I scowled. The ferry crossings took longer than I had expected, and I had no desire to spend the day sleeping on the floor in a corridor halfway up the building cowering from the light.

"We must go faster,' I rasped. I did not tell the ferryman why. I did not tell him that I wanted to be ashore two hours before sun up. I did not tell him I must be back before the light. He looked at me sourly and opened his mouth to speak, but promptly shut it again. Instead his pace picked up a little as we passed the Ferry Building and crossed the mouth of the Market Street Channel.

As we made our way north along the treacherous reefs that had been the Embarcadero Centre and much of the crumbling Financial District, the moon set behind the islands. A sucking darkness swallowed everything and I surprised myself with my own unease. The rubble banks to my left where the reefs broke the waves became nothing but dancing shadows, flitting in and out of the corner of my eye. I heard the dangerous surf before I saw it. If I could see so little, how could the old man navigate?

He began to waver in the darkness, his stroke faltering,

and the little boat wandered towards the reefs. I could smell his sweat on the breeze as several times he picked up speed to drag us away from the hungry foam. Had I exhausted him? In the darkness of the night I shut my eyes and listened with woolly ears as his rhythm grew ragged and the wash grew louder. My fear grew with it, and I couldn't bear to ride blind in the night. The man gasped as he pulled the oars, my eyes snapped open and I flinched. In the weak light, not forty yards from us, ran a thin line of telltale foam and tiny cresting wavelets – the only sign of a smashing reef beneath the black.

"For God's sake man! Don't you see it?" I shouted in terror. My voice cracked like a teenager's and if I hadn't been so petrified at the impending reef I would have experienced the long ago flush of adolescent embarrassment.

I shot up and pushed the ferryman to one side as he gasped and heaved. He nodded at me in shock that he had seen it. He seemed terrified at what I would do next, so close to him. I snatched up the oar on my side and heaved. He nodded again and pulled as I did. The tide was against us, and running fast. "Heave!" I yelled. But the drowning surf was so close now that I began to shake. I had not come so far to be wrecked by nature, smashed against broken concrete and impaled on rusting rebar before the hellish dawn.

"Heave!" I yelled again, and the boat turned a little. The sound of the rolling waves deafened me as it slapped against our little hull and threw itself against the rubble. "Heave!" And the old man next to me pulled. He was shaking in the darkness, with exertion or fear chasing him. The dinghy cut through the waves, riding high at the prow. I looked out, squinting towards the reef, and we pulled again. We were passing the Transamerica with its glowing windows, passing the drowned piers of Fisherman's Wharf, but not free of the reefs yet. The boat hung dangerously close, running parallel to the deadly breakers just yards away in the darkness. I judged the distance by the crash of the waves and the sound of the boiling foam.

"Heave!" We pulled again and the boat rowed high in the waves, tipping and rocking. The gas can jumped and slid from the bench where I had been sitting, and I yelped, jumped up to save it. I stumbled and fell to the aft, and clasped the tank, setting it down in the guts of the dingy, in the bilge water and the slime, and then I threw myself back into rowing.

I looked up to see that we had turned and were being

driven straight onto the rocks, not fifteen yards from us. I gasped, and screamed as I wrenched the oar through the water, spinning the boat around in two quick strokes, unbalancing the ferryman.

"Pull you old bastard! Pull!"

And we pulled, heaving until the sweat ran into our eyes and our palms burned against the grain of the oars. The tide drove us towards the rubble and we steered a diagonal course out into the bay, and we hung in the balance, just yards from destruction. I gasped again and noted how I sounded like a character from a dodgy book as the dinghy shuddered and scraped and we heard wood splintering against submarine concrete, and we pulled again, turning further out into deeper water. My oar clattered against masonry more than once and I pushed against it until I screamed out with anger, and we kept going, we kept going with our muscles burning and our minds breaking, and nothing to do but heave and hope as the waves rocked and crashed all around us.

And then the old shoreline and the reefs turned away to the west, away from us, and the swell sucked us round and out into the deep channel between the reefs and Russian Hill Island. And quite suddenly we were free in deep, calm water.

I squeaked in relief, but we didn't dare stop moving. We slowed as the adrenaline seeped away and the burning agony set into our backs and our bones. As the boat bobbed in the night waters, the ferryman began to shake all over, I could hear his oar rattle in the rowlock. As I looked at him he turned away, but I fished in my gown for the second bottle I had for him. I held it out and he took it gratefully, avoiding my gaze, but set it down under his seat, and continued to row, and shake.

"Open it," I croaked.

"No Sir," he shook his head violently. "It's for my kid."

I shrugged and continued to row in slow, easy strokes.

We made our way to the makeshift jetty on Broadway where North Beach meets the waves. The place where I'd seen Leibowitz' hollow eyes those months before. I couldn't help but think of him now as the little boat crept up to the shoreline. Cold and slippery blue, a meal for the fish and the crabs. I put those empty, staring eyes out of my mind, but the dead man's gaze hung over my mood like a thundercloud, dark and oppressive, pregnant with retribution. I found my stroke increasing as we drew near the place, I wanted to be gone and done with it as soon as possible. The ferryman struggled to keep up, and after our initial relief he rowed in stolid silence.

Despite my reluctant haste we arrived at the shore later than I would have liked, and I leapt out of the boat without waiting for the ferryman to tie up. I kneeled down to collect the gas tank, and found myself almost level with the old man. I examined him, sized him up. The old, familiar emptiness crept over me – the sensation that I was in the presence not of an equal, but of a child in an old man's body. Someone who would never grow up as I had, would never become emotionally unique and separate and independent. The fact that we had shared something, a danger and a victory, served only to sharpen my dissatisfaction. It was unfair of course. I was his senior a hundred generations over. I had forgotten more lifetimes than he would ever get the chance to learn from, and he was just a man. A normal, human man. I looked at him, and I told myself that what I felt was merely disappointment and not loneliness.

But we had shared something out there on the choppy waters, he and I – the fear and excitement of battle. It made me think of him by name. He was not just the old man, the ferryman, he was a man, a person, he had a life and a family. As I knelt down and looked across at him, my hand entwined in the gas can handle, I very nearly said 'Thank you.' Instead I straightened up, bringing the can with me.

"Be here tomorrow evening, an hour before sundown, if you know when that is." I said it without looking at him. He nodded, and held the boat steady with the oars.

It was an old trick – arrange a meeting before sundown and then be 'unavoidably late.' He would wait, he wanted the water. I didn't need to hide my nature so well. No one would notice, no one would put the clues together and believe them. No one would care. But old habits die hard and I hated to leave any kind of pattern – particularly as I am so good at spotting them.

I kicked the prow of the boat away from the jetty and turned my back, hurrying up the hill. There was little time to get back to the tower and up the cursed stairs. Broadway was deserted in that hour between night and dawn. Too late for anyone to be awake, not early enough for those that rise with the sun. Indeed the streets felt empty, and I had the sense that there were less and less people left in the city with each passing day. Perhaps it was the absence of relief tankers. Perhaps the loot was drying up. Either way I enjoyed having the streets to myself as I hurried along to the intersection and my building, the heavy tank swinging from my arm, sloshing and banging against my thigh. I felt safe and free in the deserted streets.

I reached my ramshackle tower and picked my way through the lobby, past the flies and the bodies and the streaming yellow fluids. There was dog shit in the hallway – strays had been worrying the corpses. I held my breath and ran through the corridor with the elevators and the evil-smelling stairwell, darting up flights of stairs until my legs burned and I had to stop. I stood on the landing, three flights up, with the scent of death and decay heavy in my nostrils, and felt distinctly, irrationally vulnerable. There could be people piling in below at any moment, I could almost picture them on the stairs below me, staring up, angry, accusing, while the sun approached relentlessly. I picked up the gas can and started up those maddening steps, resting every few flights, never comfortable enough to pause for long, always with the feeling that there were people coming up from below. Being chased by ghosts.

The birds were singing and the sky was a deep purple by the time I reached my apartment. My legs were burning and my shoulders and back screamed with sharp pain from carrying the full tank. With every step the liquid sloshed in the can and yanked my arm forward or swung it backward. Taunting me, trying to pull my arm from the socket with a wet, gurgling chatter. I swapped arms regularly, but the relief was temporary. Consequently I could barely lock the door behind me once I had stepped inside and set the tank at my feet – my hands were numb and shaking. Bits of brittle black flesh were flaking off. The skin of my knuckles was cracked and open, revealing angry red flesh glowing beneath.

I forced myself to fill the generator's empty tank on the balcony as the sky burned over the Berkeley hills. I was exhausted and terrified of the orange glow, and my weak arms floundered while I spilt gas everywhere. I hurried inside and screwed the cap on, slamming the doors and winding the shutters down. It was all I could do to flop into bed. I was hungry and thirsty, but I wasn't getting up for anything. I descended uneasily into a fitful sleep.

8

It is some time later that I realise I am awake. My scratchy eyes have been open for a good hour, but I have been dreaming in the shadows of my darkened room. I jump as I realise why I am awake. An invasive, rattling, chattering sound is drilling through my brain relentlessly. I sense it is still early morning, and I am dazed from lack of sleep, from pain and from hunger. I do not quite know what is going on. If I am being invaded I cannot bring myself to care. I cannot get up. No matter – they will come for me in my bed I am sure.

As the noise rumbles on and I lie there stiffly, blinking in the weak slivers of light that find their way through the shutters, my confusion clears and consciousness arises. It is the rattle of steel bars that is jack hammering its way through my skull. The rat is gnawing, hungry. I sigh, and pull myself up, knowing that the noise will not cease until the rat is satisfied, or at least occupied.

I stumble into the lounge and briefly the noise stops. In the far corner the rat sits up and stares at me. It twitches with tension. As I move it follows me, running along the perimeter of its small cage so that it is always as close to me as it can be. I head for the kitchen and retrieve a can of meat. There are no graham crackers left, there is no cereal. The meat will have to do. I pull the quick release tab and the pre-tensed metal bursts open like a razor-edged flower, presenting its pink, jellied prize. I cut a slice off and carry it over to the cage. I am only half awake, and as I walk, eyes half closed and drooping, I stub my toe on the hallway table. I swear and the rat disappears into its dirty bedding. I will have to think about changing it again soon. I break the meat into chunks and force them through the bars in the cage. The water bottle is dirty and a little green, but I refuse to waste good water on a rat. The animal remains hidden under a throbbing mound of shredded paper – it usually does this when I actually give it the attention it begs for. I do not understand. A simple 'Thank you' stare would suffice. A standing up on the hind legs and twitching the nose would be lovely. Instead it torments me from across the room and pointedly ignores me when I get close. I do not understand. I tap the water bottle to check the dropper is still working, and sigh before shuffling back to bed. I have never liked rats. As I doze off I think about the potted meat.

There are snipers on the Transamerica Pyramid. Quite what they hope to achieve I don't know, but there it is. I was sitting out on the balcony in the early evening, drinking slowly and enjoying being alone in the night air whilst mulling over what to do next, when quite suddenly my glass exploded. It was standing happily on the railing an arm's length away, and then there was an eruption of blood and the sliding tinkle of broken glass. Behind me there was a thwack, a puff of acrid, sour-smelling masonry dust, and then I heard the shot. It rang out through the empty city, echoing over the water. I rolled out of my chair in shock before ever I recognised the sound, but there it was, sharp and piercing, a gunshot for certain. I stayed low and scrambled inside on all fours, disappearing behind the wall next to the French doors and killing the modest light bulb that illuminated the balcony. I struck out with one arm, fumbling for blind contact, and pulled the doors shut, wound the handle on the shutters furiously. I scooted across the lounge and into the bedroom, winding shutters down as I went.

I sat with my back against the bed frame and lit a candle stub that I had stuck to the bedside table. My hands were shaking and the lighter refused to catch – it was nearly empty. I cursed my eyes and brought the flame on finally, and then I sat there, panting in the orange flicker. There was a thin stream of dark red running down my shirt and across my right thigh, and for a moment I wondered if I'd been shot, a wave of shock and disorientation hitting me. I was dizzy and disembodied for a moment as I tore my shirt over my head. But there were no holes in my body, I wasn't running with blood. There was no searing, burning agony waiting to overcome me once the soporific, lethal shock set in. I looked up in relief, the stain was from the shattered glass, I laughed out loud.

I sat there in the gloom for half an hour, crouching between the bed and the table, waiting for my heart to stop thudding in my throat, not knowing what to think or do. *Why hadn't he killed me? Had he missed?* He hit a wine glass from a mile away, and my heart was two feet to the left. I was guessing that the shot had originated from the Transamerica Pyramid at this point. It seemed logical – it was the only place high enough. But why had he hit the glass and not me? I didn't understand it, I could only assume he'd missed. But why waste a bullet on a stranger in the first place? I could not know. I guessed he had the bullets to spare, and that was how he kept hold of the building, if indeed he was in the pyramid tower. He was stuck in his building, protecting it, chained to it much like I was chained to mine. He was shooting for fun, and he had the wealth to pay for it. I stayed in for the rest of the night and kept the shutters closed.

I woke early the next evening, and after dressing and packing tools and water in a bag, I paced the flat, waiting impatiently for the late sun to sink beneath the islands. It seemed I had to wait for hours in the clammy heat of my shuttered rooms. Always this time of year I am forced to acknowledge the lengthening of the days and the approach of another Saharan summer. Usually it doesn't bother me, the memory of each year's season blurs into the last, forming one long summer, running parallel in my mind with continuous centuries of deep winter nights. Time means so little to me – or it used to, in much the same way that an old moneyed family doesn't care for money, I never used to think of it. That was before it started running out.

I drank heavily and forced myself to sit down and wait. Reading was impossible, and my frustration only increased with the oncoming dusk, as I knew the ferryman would be waiting for me, wondering when to give up and go home. At last I felt that subtle, tingling sensation bloom through my chest, telling me that the sun had fallen beneath the horizon, and I stood slowly, put on my gown carefully, and locked the door on my way out. All slow, civilized rituals, keeping up the pretence. But I flew down the stairwell until I was dizzy and breathless and had to stop for fear of falling.

I reached the ground floor in record time, eager to be outside and abroad in the world. The smell downstairs coupled with my sweat and exertion made me nauseous. I fled. I did not leave through the front doors for fear they were being watched by my friend with the rifle. I went down into the parking garage, going through the door quietly, looking for the luminescent tumult of other minds. To my relief there was nothing out there in the empty blackness bigger than a cat. The rats had returned too, I noted. When I got to the bottom of the stairs I noticed with unease that the engine block was gone, the young mechanic had been here and claimed his prize. I had no way of knowing when this miniature invasion had taken place.

I crossed the dark expanse and took the easy way out of

the garage – up the vehicle ramp. I still ducked as I came out onto the road. I could sense no one nearby, but would not take my chances with the sniper. I ran through the streets, sticking close to the walls of rotten buildings, never lingering in the open. It was a black and cloudy night and the streets of Russian Hill were empty. Most of the buildings were burnt-out husks, the product of looters and riots ripping through an affluent neighbourhood. It seemed there was nowhere left to live – or maybe simply nothing left to steal.

By the time I hit Broadway I felt a little safer. I crossed over and walked close to the ruin on the south side of the street, nearest to the Transamerica Building so that I would be foreshadowed, even from high up, but I doubted I could be seen in this light anyway, nor anyone else. My heart calmed as I walked briskly down towards the water, and my body pricked with sweat as it released the head of my exertion, but I smiled a little. I could not be afraid forever.

I thought the jetty was deserted when I first drew close enough to see it, I kept on stomping uncomfortably down the hill, and as I got closer I could make out a head and shoulders bobbing up and down apparently unsupported in mid-air. I squinted through the darkness and caught the prow of the little vessel rocking in the waves, the old ferryman, whose name was Reg, had brought the boat up to the far side of the makeshift jetty, most of the dinghy was obscured from view.

Raising my tender flesh I waved stiffly as I approached, more to catch the old man's attention than as a greeting. I had no desire to reach the jetty just in time to see him casting off out into the bay. He caught sight of me in the gloom and raised an arm.

"Thank you for waiting," I croaked as I stepped out on to the jetty. I offered no further explanation. The old man nodded enthusiastically and held out his hands to receive my bag. I was surprised, and passed it down to him before stepping awkwardly into the tilting vessel. I sat down and stared expectantly at Reg. He stared back into the gaping mouth of my hood for a moment and then shifted his gaze, as if startled. I sighed in frustration and waved my scabby hands.

"Lets go!' I whispered. The man raised an eyebrow.

"Where to?"

"Oh! Right!" I said with a little embarrassment. "Could you take me to Ocean Avenue? SF State Campus?' I asked softly as the waves thudded gently against the hull. Reg looked at me with a little surprise.

"What d'you wanna go there for?" He chuffed in disbelief.

Reg cast off without waiting for an answer, and I was glad, for it was a long way to go in a short night. We did not take the route I had expected. I thought we would cross the Market Street Channel and go south, along the shoreline, round The Potrero and west, round the Parks Archipelago to the University. We didn't. When we arrived at the mouth of Market Street, Reg turned the prow of the little boat southwest and we made our way up along the channel. I didn't like it, but I said nothing to the captain of the ship.

Market Street is visibly a channel because the taller buildings running along it break the surface of the ocean. Indeed, that whole patch of the city – Market and north, is filled with stone edifices breaking the waves and marking out the territory of the has-been city. The buildings rise randomly – an arbitrary pattern born out of their height and the ground rising beneath them. They sprout like eager saplings, but the effect is more like a graveyard than a forest. Concrete monoliths – square lines and broken windows resisting the waves that crash against them and mark the final resting place of a frontier town called San Francisco.

It was a clear night, but dark. Fragments of glass in the windows reflected the bitter light as we passed, bouncing it across the channel to us in brief starbursts. I imagined every burst of light to be the muzzle flash of a sniper's rifle, each broken pane the perfect hiding place of some unknown militia, each Art Deco gravestone offering seclusion and shelter to a mindless rifleman. And I was jealous. Jealous of his safety, his position, his power to eliminate any threat at a thousand yards with the squeeze of a finger. How simple life could be. How carefree.

Reg rowed his slow and steady pace down the channel, and gently I lost my mind in the rhythm, watching the darkened office fronts and department stores drift past, on either side, windows becoming gaping black mouths full of sharpened glass teeth, while I felt as though we were caught hopelessly in some watery Death Valley. More than once I jumped in my seat as I caught movement in the corner of my eye, heard the fragile tinkle of falling glass as the wavelets slapped playfully against the buildings.

Then, just as suddenly as we had entered the channel we turned off, passing through an unusually wide gap between stubby concrete buildings with flat roofs and marble walling. The buildings were actually six or eight stories high, but most of their grandeur was drowned beneath the filthy black floodwater, the wide gap did not mark the presence of shorter submerged buildings but was actually the mouth of Seventh Avenue leading south east to the submerged channel of Highway 80 and the 101 Canal. As we rowed down the first few blocks the newer, taller buildings slunk away and SoMa descended beneath the waves. The warehouses and garages of this once-industrial district had always been low rise and rather laid back, but the reclaimed land they'd been built on, sawdust, rotten ship's timbers and landfill trash, had been subsiding for a hundred and fifty years, and rising floodwater was all the invitation the district required to give in and slide slowly into the deep. The intersections and the sidewalks cracked and buckled, forming giant gaping potholes as the land beneath them turned to gaseous marsh loam. Old Victorians folded up peacefully, their foundations sinking through the rotten silt emulsion they found themselves suspended in as the water table rose a metre in a year.

The channels of Market Street and Seventh gave way to mostly open water punctuated by the few buildings that had survived – the last to be built in the thixotropic soil so lethal in this, a major earthquake zone. We turned south to the Canal. Here and there, spread over an area the size of ten football fields, rose the last floor or two of antique loft buildings, preserved and reinforced as they had been, the last vestiges and nationally important examples of the old post-modern style. Some way to the east the penthouse floor of the old Wholefoods building struggled skyward, a couple blocks down from where the slanted roof of the MoMA broke the crested waves. If I squinted I could see the city half-light glancing off the metal eaves of the penthouse, and I could tell that much of the MoMA's superstructure had collapsed into the water.

What was known as the Highway 101 Canal was simply the submerged channel of the road, and not a canal at all. The route stretched between the Bay Bridge where Highway 80 had collapsed into the greedy water (or had been demolished by the Looter King as some had hinted), and Highway 280 where The Ingleside rose up into the long finger of land that formed the backbone of the San Francisco County Archipelago between Golden Gate Park and Daly City. It wasn't the shortest course, it was however a relatively sheltered route through an otherwise treacherous patch of open water – stray from the path and you risk being capsized by the hungry current that swelled through a maze of underwater baffles and reefs composed of the wreckage of old buildings, unmappable and constantly shifting in the strong tidal currents of the engorged bay.

For the most part, the sunken and submerged freeway was just one or two metres beneath the waves, and a long strip of water calmed against its will, resentful and foreboding, stretched out before us, leading the way south to the backbone and Police territory. The waves would crash along with the breeze but go slack quite suddenly at the silent word of some invisible force as they met the line of the tarmac, dispersing and spreading across the lane in taut, angry little ripples.

The surface calm was misleading, however, as strong currents surged along the plane of concrete beneath, sucking us uncomfortably along where the tarmac fell away into the depths, often holding us back where the freeway rose so that Reg had to struggle at the oars, but he would shake his head fiercely when I would motion to help. It was most risky where the freeway was deepest. The boat would rock and bobble as the churning, sucking surface currents gave way to dangerous riptides and a hungry undertow.

Reg paddled on for the best part of two hours regardless and seemingly unaware of the danger, having chosen this route as it left the way round the back of Potrero Island, the narrow gully it formed with Bernal Heights Park concealing our transit between the rival patches of the Looter Kings and the Police Sector from both parties. We spoke little, holding our breath against discovery, and as we moved up the gully Highway 101 truly became a canal where its concrete walls drew up out of the water and enclosed a stiff tidal channel that pushed us fretfully along. We turned west and paddled along the wide channel that marked the line of three concrete and steel canopies where 101 and 280 merged deep underwater, and rowed on, south of Bernal Heights where the streets descended sharply into the waves like layers of melting honeycomb.

The wind whipped up and I clutched my gown around me, chilled to the bone. Clouds descended and covered the night sky, blanketing the land in darkness. I was grateful for the canal then, dangerous as its tidal surges were, for it was hard to see to navigate in the blackness, and we would surely have been sucked out into the open water of the bay had not the steep concrete walls been there to guide and restrict us. Although Reg didn't have to work so hard when the current carried us along, he seemed to sweat no less, nor did he notice the chill night air. It began to spit with rain.

As the spitting turned to a downpour Reg chuckled with delight and then laughed out loud, joyous as a little boy, for it was not only raining money, but life itself, and quite apart from the lagoon of gently poisonous but salt free rainwater forming rapidly in the bottom of the dinghy, he obviously had some water collection contraption pitched out at his camp somewhere. I cursed – I had nothing – no plastic sheeting set out on the balcony, nothing on the unexplored roof. *I could even tap the gutters!* I thought bitterly. I had never thought to collect polluted rainwater before – not when I had had a cupboard full of freshwater and no means of filtration. Soon I would need such a supply of dirty water and a purifier. As the rain fell, steady and unexpected, and both Reg and I became soaked to the skin, the tension between us melted. I splashed him once or twice as I shifted, stiff and cold on the hard wooden seat, and he looked towards me with the relief of water forming a half smile on his face. His gaze lingered a second or more at the darkened mouth of my hood, and he turned away naturally, without shudder or embarrassment, merely to check our course over his shoulder, or to gaze at the raindrops drumming frenetically against the water.

You cannot imagine what an effort it must be to avoid the gaze of the person you are facing for two hours, confined within the cramped space of a two-man boat. Certainly I cannot. Reg managed it. Up until that moment he had looked everywhere but towards my beady black rat's eyes, glinting through the darkness of my oversized hood. It had been a triumph of denial and non-communication between master and servant – one I had welcomed as I always do.

Yet our barriers dissolved in the rain, and there we were, each with a fresh awareness of a fellow mind in our midst, though I doubt Reg's mind would have put it quite like that. I think he began to see the feeling behind the monster's face and the charred hands. And for my part, any creature that can laugh is worth a little value in my book, and even rats can laugh, apparently. Our newfound mutual appreciation did not give birth to a beautiful friendship, it did not give rise to a staggering rapport, it simply made the silence between us comfortable and easy, rather than forced and pregnant.

When we rowed past City College on its hill, and Reg

looked up at it and back to me with a raised eyebrow, question whether it would do, I casually shook my head. I wanted the opportunity to find the best of what was left, I didn't want to be searching for knowledge in a teenager's playground. The canal turned south there, somewhere between City College and Balboa Park, and the freeway rose up with the land, our little boat finally running aground on the backbone with the grating sound of wood dragging over grit. We looked at each other hesitantly, and then I leapt, sodden, out of the boat and onto the cracked and splitting asphalt. As I picked up my dripping bag and turned towards the freeway slip road Reg pointed to the distance.

"Follow Ocean Avenue west a mile or so, then turn left down Nineteenth and you'll see it on the slope. It's not a straight line, but you won't get lost that way"

I paused for a moment. I didn't know what to say. "Thank you!' was all there was. Reg shrugged. "No sweat. Used to drive a cab round here." With that he pushed the boat out into the water and was gone into the wind and the sheeting rain. I cursed and ran down to the water's edge, slipping and yelling "Meet me here tomorrow after sundown." Reg nodded vigorously through the wet gloom before disappearing completely.

I trudged up the slope, wet through, and the weight of my bag and the clothes on my back felt doubled with the sopping water. The acid rain was irritating my burns, making my hands and scalp sting and itch particularly. As I left the canal behind and made my way along Ocean Avenue the rain thinned, and then stopped as suddenly as it had come on, but the sidewalk ran with water and the tarmac clicked and popped where the rain was soaking into the weed filled cracks. I was glad that the rain had stopped, but the sky didn't clear and the clouds hung low, muggy and oppressive in the night sky. I walked faster in the deep darkness, trying to warm up as the wind cut through my wet clothes.

As I shivered and passed a narrow suburban street corner, hidden amongst the wrecked houses and upturned SUVs, I noticed a campfire down the slope. I was conscious of the time, but also the uncontrollable chattering of my jaw and the stealthy danger of hypothermia, so I turned off the ruined main road towards the warmth and the light.

I head down the slope, conscious that the sidewalk was wet and crumbling, and that the weeds sprouting from the concrete would take my feet out from under me. I slung my bag over my shoulder, feeling the water squeeze out of my garments and run down my back. It was an odd street, it felt empty even though most of the houses were strangely intact. I'd pass the occasional burn-out, or an old wartime prefab whose roof had fallen in, but most of the buildings were rows of neat little suburban tract homes. Some of the cottages were locked up, dark and empty, with cracks in the glass panes and weeds sprouting in the gutters. But the curtains weren't drawn. The trash cans were stuffed with uncollected garbage. Garden tools and kid's balls lay out in the tangled mess of marsh vines and thick grass that had invaded from the south, flourishing in the new climate. Everywhere I looked things had been left undone, things hadn't been put away. It was as if the people had left their TVs on and locked their front doors to pop out for a pint of milk, but somehow they had never returned. Some giant force had scooped up their whole neighbourhood and planted it somewhere else while they were out, two hundred miles south, and here was I, lone witness to someone else's empty world.

There was a noise to my left as I passed a mouldy looking wooden bungalow, and I froze. The paint was peeling from the sills and the wooden shingles on the roof were lifting and curling away. I squinted through the tall grass to see the front door, wide open and warped, creaking gently in the night breeze. I tilted my head to peer through the vegetation – there was furniture in that hallway. Some kind of table, wood definitely, and sitting on it a milky white blob that I took in the darkness to be a telephone. Impotent of course, but left intact by some random miracle. I had never known an empty house to go unlooted since the food riots started and people began deserting the city, heading blindly for the empty breadbasket of the interior.

I gazed through the gauze draped behind the bungalow's big front window, and glinting patches of light in the empty darkness told me that that room also was occupied with furniture. Indeed, everywhere I looked there were objects, untouched but rotting, lying in the street or hidden behind net curtains, useful tools or good firewood, or simply the paraphernalia of someone's life, it all lay spread out in this street like a testament to a forgotten civilisation, yet it was only two years ago. Two years since the good people had scooped up their kids and their blankets and left everything else behind, getting into busses or carts or simply walking in their exhaustion, desperate for food and water and most of all the security they had worked all their lives for. It was an illusion, of course, the idea that they were safe in an ordered, human world. They lived coated in a veneer of normality, bestowed upon them by all the others who gladly took their money. But the veneer and the illusion evaporated as quickly as the value of their paper bills, and they were left with nothing, staring at the world and each other, naked in the new dawn, and unprotected from the natural law – eat or be eaten. They saw each other and they saw themselves. They panicked, of course. They panicked in their millions.

I stopped in the middle of the road, deeply uncomfortable. I felt alone, yet crowded by ghosts and trespassing on the accoutrements of their afterlife. Everything was so naturally arranged – casual, from the mail box with its little red arm rusted solidly in the up position, to a child's swing, twisted chain rusted and locked together awkwardly where the tyke had leapt off in mid-air and gone to some other pursuit. I was picking through the carelessly preserved grave goods of a dieing civilization – all that remained was to come across the bodies.

A lump rose in my throat, I felt astonishingly alone amongst those cluttered, untouched houses, those mausoleums to the missing, and yet I felt watched also. I was shivering uncontrollably, teeth chattering from the cold and the deep-seated feeling of unease. I longed to turn back to the major road, but down below at the end of the street, a fire glowed red, and the promise of stolen warmth drew me on. I ran.

I had no idea what force could have preserved these streets and rows of little houses I couldn't imagine the power that could hold back the marauding looters. Whatever it was, I had no desire to learn its name. But my spirits picked up briefly, glowing sharply like embers in a stiff breeze. Perhaps I would find what I was looking for at S.F. State after all.

But when I reached the bottom of the hill my heart chilled. As I approached I became aware that the burning was no camp-fire, no oil drum stuffed with bad timber. Judging from the size it was something else altogether. Drawing closer it became obvious that the flickering glow was actually several small and apathetic fires clustered together. The fuel was an entire house. I stood on the sidewalk in front of it, staring at the low flames and blackened timbers. The house had been built on a brick cellar, the fire hadn't spread. It had burned fiercely though, a day or two ago. The low brick wall was cracked and shattered from the heat, the cement path around the building was buckled and warped. The canopy of a tree that overhung the remains of the garage was almost completely incinerated, the bark of the trunk was black and blistered.

I walked up the short cement driveway to where the garage had been, and held my hands out to a small puddle of fire running along some fallen timbers. There were no walls left anywhere, just charred, stick-like beams and twisted metal studwork. The remnants of power tools lay in a line along the back boundary of the garage where they had fallen from a burning wall. Amongst the rubble and detritus were old, buckled gas cans partly consumed and rusted from the heat, and sticky puddles of burning tar where the felt roofing tiles had melted and pooled together.

I took my gown off and held it out to the flames reluctantly, for the smell of the fire was thick and poisonous, burning tar and burning rubber. My arms were heavy with my knuckles hot, so I hung the hooded gown on a tall spear of wood and watched as it began to steam gently, thinking that I'd never get the smell out now. Still it wasn't bad enough to prevent me from turning around and drying my clammy body in the head of the flames.

I stared through the frame of the house at the wreckage inside. Much of the ash and charcoal had fallen into the cellar, but some of the floor joists had survived and were plainly visible. Slabs of glass lay black and bitter like unpolished obsidian, draped over charred wood and twisted metal window frames. In one corner lay a large concrete tube and some drooping sheets of rusting metal. It took me a moment to realise it was an old-style washing machine.

There was little else. The fire had been too intense. There was no paper, no furniture, no signs of life. A gathering of springs in one area, balanced loosely on thin, charred wooden slats, was a couch or a mattress – I couldn't tell which. Little patches of fire licked casually through the blackened detritus. A deep red glow emanated from within piles of charred dry wall, and slow burning puddles of tar and chemicals dripped fire down into the cellar below. My clothes were still damp and sticky, and I was barely warm. Sick from the sight and the fumes, and with half a mind to snatch up my hood and go, I stripped off the rest of my soggy things reluctantly and hung them on hot beams near loose patches of fire. Naked and scarred, shivering in the night, I crouched next to the flames, trying not to look at the burns running up my arms and across my chest, trying not to think of anything. I was getting used to my scorched and withered finger bones, the deep black wells my eyes had become, but seeing layers of scar tissue stretched over my pale skin in the flickering orange light threatened to overwhelm me.

I sat there, arms wrapped around my knees, watching guiltily for passers-by and singing softly to myself, a tuneless continuous stream of unheeded notes. Half an hour passed or more, until my clothes were almost dry but sour with the smell of burning, and I could no longer think of nothing. I could no longer hold back the thoughts so I chose to think of the time and the lateness of the night and I stood up suddenly, snatching my clothes down and putting them on, damp and stiff over my dry skin. At the garage I folded my hood over my arms and took up my soggy bag, turning to go.

I stopped abruptly and stared at the pale concrete driveway beneath my feet. There, marked out in long strokes of spray paint was the bold emblem of the San Francisco P.D. Beneath that sprawled out was one word. I twisted my head to read it upside down. I was slow to read the awkward blue letters in the darkness, but I took in breath sharply when the word came into view.

S.Q.U.A.T.T.E.R.S.

I started out, stepping uneasily over the warning judgement and walking stiffly back up the street to Ocean Avenue. I was angry and scared and bitter. Frustrated at the treasures that lay untouched in the houses of this street and seemingly many others. Objects like cooking pans and firewood and plastic hose pipe, things that could be useful, things that could save lives. And yet there they sat, untouched and untouchable, waiting for their rich, dead owners to return from the interior and claim them as they never would.

I didn't give a damn about the police mob. I would have gone through every house and sifted its treasures. I didn't have time. I didn't want the bitterness. I was walking fast with anger by the time I reached the main road, hot from exertion and shivering from the wind biting through my damp clothes.

I stopped as I turned onto Ocean Avenue, made myself calm down and walk steadily. I stood still and looked at the dull night sky and the low clouds. The air felt good on my bald scalp, it was good to be out and uncovered. There was no one to hide my scars from. I started out again, walking slowly, and passed an entrance to City College. The buildings hadn't changed in fifty

124

years; in the age of information you didn't need to be at school to study. The campus stood high and distant on a hill crest, square, modernist buildings staring down the valley sternly. At the peak of the hill was a tall, square building, the roofline of which was interrupted by a stubby metal dome. An observatory, the home of a toy telescope by today's standards. I noticed it all seemed mostly intact. A few broken windows here and there, but the fence was good, and a heavy padlock kept the gates drawn shut. I pitched on, puzzled. The fence would not be hard to climb, the padlock could be cracked easily with a looter's tools. But I was not in looting country – that much was clear. This was Police Rule, and they seemed rather good at it.

I continued along Ocean Avenue, past the empty houses the disused MUNI depot and the locked up businesses – nursery school with fading paintings in the windows and little clusters of shops, their signs up and their shutters down. It was almost as if nothing had happened, as if the collapse was some bad drug trip, and I could almost believe that these places were just shut for the night, and they would spring into life with the coming sun. I'd be hiding. I'd miss the resuscitation. It didn't matter, it could go on without me. A flower does not need to be appreciated in order to bloom. But it was not the case. All around me lay the signs of decay and desertion. The sidewalk was sprouting weeds and the drains were cracked. Roofs were missing tiles where last spring's hurricanes had lifted them. There was litter blowing across the street and through the courtesy car parks and crackling noisily as it got snared in the trees and bushes of someone's bedraggled front yard. Their unkempt lawns and sprawling overgrown bushes. Prize winning bushes. And everywhere was rust. Cars rooted where they stood on their perished, deflated tires, watermarks in sticky brown running down the walls of buildings from broken gutters and overwhelmed window sashes. Those sturdy shutters concealing the public face of small businesses and convenience stores were blistered and peeling, brightly painted colours giving way to running streaks of rust red and mud brown whilst vines crawled up the buildings and along the roofs. I walked though that forgotten neighbourhood and I knew it didn't take men to destroy a city.

9

In the end I stopped looking. I have seen enough decay in my lifetimes. I stared down the lumpy street, following its lines as I tackled the erupting sidewalk, watching it undulate in the distance. I'd passed the crest of a gentle hill some time back, and continued on down the slope. At the floor of the shallow concrete valley there were lights and movement off to the left. As I moved nearer I began to pick up the thin sounds of despair drifting on the breeze. Babies crying softly, too hungry to stretch their lungs, the low mutter of a thousand souls too despondent to speak out with pride. I drew closer and the low hum began to fill my ears. Judging from the clusters of Coleman lamps and campfires, and the endless cloud of still and throbbing minds I could see in the ether, I was approaching a large camp of stragglers. But there were no distinct voices, just a wash of vowels and whisperings. It was as if no one dared speak, no one dared complete a word of their own lest they single themselves out as a mind with thoughts and needs, rights and hopes. They were learning how to go unnoticed, all of them, learning how to make do. And in the process they were forgetting how to be human.

Halfway down the slope I stopped and pulled my gown over my head. I drew my hood forward. There were figures milling around in the tents at the edge of the road below. Soon I would be noticed. I clutched my bag under my arm and carried on. At the bottom of the shallow slope, I noticed, on my side of the carriageway, far from the tents and the shanty huts, sat a solitary dark figure. A tiny point of orange light flew about it, sometimes fading sometimes growing my pace I could see it was a young girl, maybe sixteen, dressed in black, savouring a needle thin hand rolled cigarette. She kept holding it to her face and blowing on the cherry to keep it alight. She wore dirty jeans and a baggy black sweater, and her dark straggly hair was tied up in a long ponytail at the back of her head. She sat perched on an old fashioned fire hydrant, her laces undone and scattered across the sidewalk. She wore mangled spectacles, and she kept pushing the bent frames up her nose.

"You shouldn't be out so late," she said, picking a shred of tobacco from her tongue, not looking at me.

"Why not?" I rasped. She didn't blink.

"Curfew," She snorted.

"You're out."

"I know when they're not looking." She tilted her head and looked at me for the first time. "Besides, I'm only over the road. You've been coming from miles off. Where're you from?"

I ignored the question. "What's with the camp? Why don't they all take the houses?"

"Police Rule. They keep us here." She sucked on her cigarette, "In the filth."

"Why?"

"They say it's 'cos we don't own nothing. So they keep us out of other people's houses. Mostly they do it 'cos they can," she said without blinking. "So where're you from then?" She looked at me with a kind of tit-for-tat expectation.

I breathed in. "Outside," I said. "Beyond," I whispered for effect. I raised my eyebrows at her, and then remembered that she wouldn't be able to see them, for they'd been singed off, and anyway they should be swallowed with the rest of my face in the dark vacuum of my hood. I gave up. "An island, other side of Looter's territory."

"I wish I was over with the Looters."

"You don't." I thought of the shantytown of thugs and whores on the Bay Bridge. "You make yourself useful over there. And when you're no longer useful they finish with you."

"At least I'd be free."

I chuffed, "Not with the uses they'd find for a young girl like you, you wouldn't."

"Well," she said. She bent over and stubbed her little fag end out on the broken sidewalk before slipping it carefully into her pocket. She stood up. "I'm off," and with that she was crossing the road. I stood there alone in the breeze, watching her go.

Halfway across the carriageway she looked over her shoulder. "Are you coming then?" and she spun round again and went on, not looking back.

And I wasn't going to, I really wasn't. I was going to carry on the next few blocks to Nineteenth, and make my way to the University before sunup, for it was already well past midnight and I was running out of time. But I stood there, watching that black figure receding into the shadows, remembering the thick smell of a human being – living for once, remembering the timbre of her youthful, ignorant, fearless voice. Standing alone in the dark and the breeze at the bottom of that concrete shallow, I couldn't remember the last time I had walked freely among humans, the last time I had had a casual, meaningless and risk-free conversation. I hurried on after her. She didn't wait.

It was madness of course. I looked a monster, but most of all I was a stranger – I could be lynched. I could be burned, I could be trapped before the sun and... I didn't think. I wanted to hear voices. I ran across the road, the girl was disappearing into the maze of tents and huddled groups of people as I reached the sidewalk. The camp was small and densely populated, a writhing sea of people and debris. It was spread over a patch of muddy waste ground maybe it was once a park, or a schoolyard. The tents and plywood lean-tos had spilled over the boundaries – the premium real estate was next door, the flat tarmac of a supermarket car park. Gritty and lumpy where the weeds were pushing through the asphalt, but blissfully devoid of the ubiquitous mud that characterised the rest of the campsite. The supermarket itself had been burned to the ground.

I passed through the camp like a ghost. Many people were asleep, squashed together in their tents, or huddled around the glowing embers of a dead fire, lying in the mud, wrapped in filthy blankets or a sleeping bag. There was barely any room to tread, but everywhere I stepped there were arms and legs, empty water bottles and puddles of piss in the mud. Disease was rife, there was no effort to help the sufferers, or to separate them from the healthy. It seemed in every cluster of people I came across there was one figure lying in the dirt, shaking or gasping for breath. I began to notice the signs. Sweaty forehead and dark ringed eyes. Crusted lips and sunken cheeks. Piles of bloody shit surrounding the dying. This was diphtheria. This was cholera. This was typhoid. Something I'd seen before and hoped never to see again.

The stench of the camp was enormous and pungent. Old sweat, shit, the familiar perfume of death. Somehow I hadn't expected it. And the noise! The crowded noise of people was hell on earth. The dull, insistent murmur of the hungry, the hidden weeping of mothers that thought they were alone as their children slept, the slow, sucking gasps of children too exhausted with hunger to be angry, to cry, to feel alive. I looked around me at defeated souls everywhere and I wished I hadn't come.

There were no voices for me. No warm welcomes. The camps were pushed up tightly against one another in a honeycomb of despair and misery, and of the two or three people awake around each fire, there were no cheerful smiles, no 'make the most of its', just hollow stares and the slow movements of the starving. These people were broken. They barely looked up as I passed. But all, without exception, fell silent as I did so. It was chilling.

I was completely lost, picking my way through the piles of human terrain, trying to stay upright. Trying not to slip in the filth or drown in the despondency. I had a vague idea that the road was somewhere behind me. Or was it to the right? Where was the condemned supermarket? I didn't know, it didn't matter. Everywhere I turned people paused their lives and their hushed conversations instinctively. As if I were the Angel of Death they waited quietly for me to pass, breath caught still in their throats. I was the moving epicentre of a deadening vacuum, it made me feel, it made me feel monstrous.

My speed picked up and I turned away from the downward looks and the bated breath, knowing that everyone I passed was following my exit with a long suspicious stare. I was running through the tangled mess of lukewarm bodies, feeling them twisted underfoot as I set my step down, hearing them cry out in their dreamless, hopeless slumber. I was terrified. Everywhere I went I felt utterly alone amongst alien beings, and simultaneously accused by every soul. I ran and ran, losing my way, losing my footing, not knowing where I was going or what I was doing. There were bodies everywhere I looked, stretched out in all directions across the plains, and for a moment I was back in Russia, back in 1915. The land was strewn with the dead and the half living, each claimed equally by the mud and the filth, and I said no! I said never again! And so I ran. I ran into the stench, I ran to where the camps were empty and the bodies thin on the ground. I kept running blindly, madly. I was running for my life, I didn't know what I was running for. I stumbled dizzily in the piss and thick clay mud, I stepped out and my foot locked against something. I lurched forward and cried out, a thin, gurgling yelp as I put my hands out. I fell flat on my face. Half crazed I stood and looked and spun. I was somewhere by the far corner of the camp, and the stench was incredible.

I heard the rats before I saw them. The distant, incessant, oil-thick chick and chatter of needle sharp teeth. They were out there, in the shadows, little fuzzy worms of black in the darkness. I saw them in the corner of my eye, I saw them at the distant reaches of my weakened vision, flowing and stopping in clumps, advancing, running, climbing over one another. I squinted, following their direction of travel down into the corner of the muddy field. I heard the buzzing hum in the distance, the yellow drone. Blow flies.

I wiped my hands on my gown, breathing shallow, trying not to suck in the noxious, gut wrenching smell drifting up the field. I scraped my face against my sleeve, feeling the grit and mud and slime drip down my chin. I looked down to see what I had tripped on. It was a body, putrid and yellow. I think it was a young man. Excruciatingly thin from the slow wasting fever that had claimed him. I say young I mean thirty-five. That used to be young. I won't say any more, I am tired of bodies.

"Fun isn't it?"

I jumped and spun around. My bag slipped off my shoulder. It was the girl with slippy spectacles. She wouldn't quite look at me.

"You found it alright then? I was going to show you." She paused. "If you go down to the woods today..." she warbled slowly, off kilter and under her breath, full of menacing, faux cheer. Then she pushed me. "Come on. Lets have a look."

It was not meant to be a playful shove. It was a challenge. The pain that ran through my scorched ribs was explosive. I held my breath so as not to gasp. The girl stepped around me and set off. Then she stopped and waited.

"Let me show you what it means to be here," she said softly. When I didn't follow she turned back and caught my sleeve the way youngsters do. Trying it on. I snatched it back.

"I've seen it. I know. I've seen it more times than you can imagine. I'll not go again."

She stood in front of me and peered up into the depths of my hood. "Then take a good look man," she said in a venomous, iron like whisper. "'Cos unless I make it outta here soon it's gonna be me stiff and dead in that hole."

I shrugged and walked away a little too fast to be calm, picking through the dead and the living alike. I didn't look back. She followed at a distance, but she made no further argument. I made my way uphill, and soon the road was in sight. I went through the camp in a daze, passed flickering Coleman lamps and around tent pegs. I was numb, I no longer saw the people. It was just one rotten, helpless, heaving mass, doomed and endless.

Somewhere towards the middle of the camp field I came

across a little wooden shed. Pasted on it were instructions to digging latrines, a water and food delivery schedule, signs pointing to the mass 'Biodegradable Disposal Area.' Someone had kicked the flimsy door in, but the shed was empty. I pored over the delivery schedule for I had no idea of the day's date, but the printed sheet was soggy and curling at the edges, and quite obviously defunct. It told me nothing useful. From the handwritten scrawls and bitter protests I gathered water hadn't arrived for some time.

Stepping out of the camp and onto the sidewalk was something like breaking the surface after almost drowning. I stood on the pavement, shivering and breathing and wringing my hands. I felt greasy and filthy. I wanted to drink, but I daren't take water out in front of these people, although how they imagined I travelled without it I don't know. Despondent and broken, I don't think they thought anything of me although I was a stranger stumbling in their midst. I think their minds were gone. Certainly they'd given up. They needed to be angry and they weren't.

I set off up the street towards Nineteenth. When I was a few blocks up from the camp I took the water. As I sipped I realised I was hungry. There was little chance of satisfying that need until I returned home. I packed up my bottle and hurried off into the night, berating myself for wasting time at the camp – looking for companionship – a fool's errand for one such as me. I pushed myself along, passing the city blocks and counting as I went, eager for Nineteenth. The street signs would pass and the ache in my body would grow, and soon every intersection and street corner would become an excuse to ask myself *Can I rest yet?*

I pushed on, forcing myself along the crumbling sidewalk, sweating in the night breeze. My bag became lead in my arms, my old man's stoop sunk lower as the night wore on. I set targets in the distance, and stubbornly outdid them. *I'll just reach that tree. I'll just reach that stop sign.* I passed what I imagined to be the halfway point between the camp and Nineteenth. I kept going, unnecessarily fast, stupidly fast. Punishing myself for daring to hope and unused to my old man's constitution. I fell down two blocks from Nineteenth.

I watched myself with a strange buzzing feeling, almost from the outside looking in, as I collapsed in slow motion. I remember the sensation of surprise as first one leg buckled under me and then the other. I rolled and ended up flat on my back on a lumpy, uneven bit of sidewalk, laughing, roaring my head off like a hyena. *Stupid old fool!* I thought. *You've been young too long!*

I lay there uncomfortably, giggling and gasping for breath while my muscles burned and my eyes watered, waiting for my body to recover. The sky was low and black with cloud. One long, homogenous cloud as far as the light could reveal. I sighed and sat up awkwardly, putting my back against the low wall of someone's deserted yard. I heard a low thrum in the distance. At first it was concealed by my own noises, my giddy breathing and my sniffs. It grew louder, though, and I turned towards the noise in time to see a dazzling white light burst out onto the street two blocks ahead. It was a vehicle.

I jumped at the sight, yelped, and grabbed my bag before throwing myself over the wall at my back and lying flat up alongside it. There I waited, pressed into the mud, breathing shallow, listening for voices and praying there were no dogs to sniff me out. The slow rumble of a diesel engine approached, more slowly than I'd have expected, and I hung there in the dirt, unable to move, unable to think.

They hadn't seen me, not from two blocks away – that much was clear from their leisurely approach. Cautiously I drew myself up on all fours, feeling the mud and grit under my fingers, and popped my head up from behind the low wall. They were still a block away. A large, truck-like vehicle approached, with four huge spotlights facing forward, glaring out from atop the cab, and two more directional spots, mounted somewhere behind those and above. I ducked my head as it got closer, listening as the rattle of the industrial engine built and built into a roar.

I looked up again. In the glare of reflected light I could see there were no windows in the cabin, just the glistening ceramic hemispheres of automated gun turrets on each side. No windows meant it was a radar driver – a robot. I heard the clatter of caterpillar tracks behind the cab, and ducked as one of the moving searchlights began to sweep the road and the sidewalk ahead. It was an armoured personnel carrier – a drone in police blue. There would be more of those slick grey gun turrets sprouting from the cargo section, the drone ready to cover the dismounting riot cops with its supersonic machine guns. Or it could be a bluff and the stupid, blind machine could be empty, just doing the rounds to keep the locals down. Either way I didn't want to find out. I kept my head down as the glaring light passed over me in a thick wave. The roar of the engine and the clatter of tracks on hard concrete was deafening and all encompassing. I could scarcely breathe for the thud of my heart in my chest. I was terrified as the ground rumbled beneath me and the huge machine passed, feeling the ground vibrate beneath me, and I lay frozen against that wall listening as the overwhelming roar subsided. I stuck my head up when I thought it safe, but I ducked again quickly. A rear spotlight was sweeping along the concrete maybe fifteen yards from my position, the fly-black lenses of a sensor package protruding from the roof of the cab.

I sat there, picking at the wall like a resentful kid, waiting for the noise to recede. When I stuck my head over the bricks next and saw that the machine was far off below, scanning the camp occupants with its lamps and harassing them, I grabbed my bag and hopped stiffly over the wall. My body was sore and aching, and I hobbled along in the shadows, eager to put some distance between the drone and myself. I began to relax as I made headway, and eased into a gentle walking pace, not wanting to exacerbate my grumbling joints. I plodded on patiently, occasionally catching glimpses of light ahead. I figured the buildings on the slope rising up to the left were the University campus. It was relief that I read the sign for Nineteenth up ahead. It grew larger with every step. I turned onto the avenue gratefully, a half smile on my face, and then I stopped.

Up ahead, hanging from a lamppost and swinging on the breeze was the dark figure of a man. I caught the ripe smell of the corpse as I approached, old and rotten and sweet. Stale. Maggots ran under the putrid skin of the man's face – as I looked up I saw the hollows of his eyes. Nothing in his black sockets but strings of dried pus and paper-thin blowfly cocoons. The rope had cut most of the way through the man's spine and his clothes were rotting through in frayed, blotchy patches. He had obviously been there for some time. Months. His features were quite gone, for that I was grateful. The grey skin was peeling from his blackened flesh in great strips, his hands and fingers swollen beneath the cruel twine used to bind his wrists. His scalp was sloughing off in great sticky patches of writhing insects and red hair, betraying the white of his scalp beneath. In a final indignity his pants had been taken from him before he was strung up. I wondered at that.

I read the word casually sprayed, in fuzzy blue letters, on the sidewalk beneath him.

T.H.I.E.F.

The accusation was accompanied by the emblem of the

S.F.P.D, and at last I understood. Where was the judge that hung this man? Where was the jury? Show me the jury of his peers who would hang a man for thievery in these times? There wasn't one. Not when your children are cold and need food in their bellies. These men were no longer policemen, they were low-rent mobsters and vicious little thugs. Morally bankrupt, they ruled with guns and fists and precious little else – certainly not respect. I thought back to the camp and its inhabitant's apathy, their defeat, and finally I understood it. Their shame. They spoke in low, self-effacing tones because of their shame at being bullied and corralled by cowards. Cowards with guns.

I wanted to cut the man down. I felt for the knife in the folds of my gown but could not bring myself close to the stinking corpse. To reach high enough to fray the rope I would have had to press my face to his putrefying flesh, and I would not. I walked on bitterly. I left the man swinging in the breeze.

I climbed steadily up the hill, I could see the campus in the distance but the sky beyond was turning purple. I was by now deeply concerned over the time. Nothing had gone to plan. I was running behind but my mission would have to wait – I had perhaps an hour to find shelter from the sun. And what if I didn't find a place in the dark? An hour is not so long to one who hates to leave anything to chance. Not so long when it is the rest of his life. With the lights of the campus in the distance and my goal finally in sight I stopped on the road and looked about me. I was on a street of houses, and all looked empty and deserted. I had learned the signs on my travels. The overgrown garden, the peeling paint. The stricken aura of abandonment. I sensed no minds nearby, not even in quiet slumber. I picked the nearest, a vintage 1980's bungalow, and walked up the buckling drive looking for signs of a basement. It was there all right, under the raised ground floor, but no windows to show for it, something to be glad of. I walked around the house to the back garden, and I was surprised to discover that most of the area had been taken up by a ridiculously proportioned swimming pool. The cement had cracked, and much of the water had seeped away into the ground. What was left was green and sour smelling, filthy and thick with dead leaves. The brown lawn had sunken in where the water had run through the ground, and the back porch was sagging. I climbed the wooden steps to the deck, and tried the handle to the back door optimistically. It didn't budge. I took my pistol out and, holding it by the barrel, I tapped the glass by the handle. I hit it gently, and then a little harder, trying to break the pane as quietly as I could. When I did break the glass finally, the noise seemed enormous in the shallow night. I froze, gun handle immersed in razor slivers of glass. My greatest fear now was to see light appear from within the house – I could run but I had little time to lose a pursuer and find another hiding place.

I waited, and the darkness persisted. Satisfied that I had disturbed no one I ran the gun around the little square of wood holding the glass in, pushing out all the sharp fragments. I tapped the gun clean against the wood before gripping the handle with one hand and reaching through the hole with the other. I felt around inside for the latch, and turned it with a click. Twisting the handle I felt the door flex, but it did not open. Something held it fast towards the top, I guessed a bolt.

I smashed the glass at the top of the door with a little less patience, a little more noise. I placed my hand inside and felt around awkwardly, finding a deadbolt. I twisted, feeling it snap open. I retrieved my hand and turned the handle and the door swung open. There came the tinkle of glass from below and I was in. I stood in a deserted kitchen. It was clean, orderly, empty cabinets had been shut, two pans were missing from the row hanging from the wall. A woman had packed supplies carefully, and cleaned the kitchen before she had left, but the dust still gathered.

I searched the kitchen with a little urgency – the skin was prickling up my spine and over my scalp – a sign of the approaching sun. There was no water. I went through the cupboards, some empty, some full, but there were no bottles. I debated opening the fridge, expecting to find a smelly, furry mess of green mould blanketing the white plastic, but when I broke the seal with a hiss I found the insides empty and pristine. I flicked the door shut with disinterest.

There wasn't much actual food left. A three quarters empty packet of cereal, some cans of vegetables. Mostly what had been left were sundries. Cheese sauce packets and dried herbs. Non-essentials. With some relief I grabbed anything I thought the rat might eat, and was rather pleased to discover a small bottle of cooking oil. Not olive oil, not sunflower oil, not even vegetable oil, just 'cooking oil.' That's what it said. I raised an eyebrow but stuffed it in my bag. I was sure I'd find a use for it.

I was getting nervous and irritable, and outside the sky was shifting from black to a kind of luminous purple. I wanted to be underground. A quick survey of the hallway betrayed the stairs down into the basement and I relaxed a little, but I needed to check I was alone truly before I could sleep. Pressing outwards, I saw no minds in the ether, but the sleeping sometimes travel. I ran through the rooms, paying little attention, the place smelt damp and musty and I knew in my being it was empty even as I went through the farce of allaying my paranoia. There was no one in the living room. It was quite strange to walk into that room with its white leather couch and polished hardwood floors and the TV wall. Again I had the feeling that it was all just temporary. That the collapse would rewind over night and people were waiting to return from the interior and take up their old homes. Anyone who'd headed into the vastness of the interior was dead. I was certain of it. Frozen or murdered or starved maybe, but they were dead, and they were never coming back.

I hurried through the other rooms – a study full of books I could not carry home, a parent's bedroom with its neatly made bed. The teenager's room was typical – full of unnecessary silver plastic gadgets, expensive sneakers and e-paper posters that were dead in the night.

Satisfied that I'd checked everything, I poked my head into the bathroom before slipping downstairs to the basement. The subterranean room had been decked out as an entertainment room, with a saggy, threadbare couch and an old TV screen wired into the house network. The room felt damp and sick like a grave, and I could hear the trickle of water running down the walls. The plaster was peeling away from the rear wall in chunks the size of dinner plates. The water had soaked in from the subsiding swimming pool – probably the result of earthquake damage. With no one to maintain the house the foundations were rotting. There was one small, narrow window at ground height along the side of the house. I drew the stubby curtains and wedged it with cushions from the couch, hoping that most of the light would be thwarted and I would be comfortable.

I settled on the musty couch, tucked myself up in a foetal position and closed my eyes. I really was tired, but I found myself unable to relax. Every time I felt myself drifting off my eyes would burst open in panic and I would stare about the room, listening desperately, checking that I was alone. The only thing staring back at me was the dryer in the corner.

There hadn't been time upstairs for me to feel the house. I hadn't absorbed all the personal little things as I rushed around, not the photos in the living room or the saccharine poem framed on the wall above the toilet. Now as I lay there listening to the strange wooden creakings those images welled up and I felt like an intruder. My heart ran with the irrational fear of discovery, sleep evaded my droopy eyelids. Outside, the sun rose slowly and burned the clouds away, and I lay in a half-daze, every crack of the warming timbers rousing me, every shudder seeping into my heart.

Eventually I drifted off, lying on that couch, hugging my damp bag to me. It was a fitful sleep, full of half dreams and bad memories, soaked with the essence of another family's home. These weren't my people. I had no business being here. I woke several times, and settled back down, each time the slumber was a little deeper, until sometime in the afternoon I heard voices above.

I woke with a start, or rather woke slowly and realised with a start that what I was hearing was not a dream. Somewhere on the street above, two young voices shrieked playfully. I could barely make them out.

"Look look look! I'm doing it! I'm doing it mommy look I'm doing it!"

"I can do it too! See. Look, anyone can do it."

"Wow. That's great!" came a warm voice over the petulance. "But guys you need to sit in your seats now."

"Oh come on!" came the protests. For a moment there was the whizzing sound of spokes and pedals cutting through the air, and then a bell rang out, followed by yelping and giggling. I was mesmerised. It was heaven. I thought I was dreaming. I was listening to ghosts. Happy children playing in the afternoon, a mother with only the usual worries. It made me feel light and unworried and hopeful. I wondered at the miracle of it.

"Ok guys time to go back to the compound."

"Oh no! Mommy no! Come on mommy!'

"Pleeaase!"

"I mean it! Don't make me shoot the gun in the air again! It's loud. It hurts my ears!"

"Aaaww! Shoot it! Shoot it!"

My throat dried and a sick feeling swam through my guts, I lay still, trying not to think, trying not to go over the golden sounds of their laughter. It took me a long time to get back to sleep.

10

It was dark when next I woke, and I lay there for some moments, shivering in the damp and trying to remember where I was. I jumped up when my mission came back to me, angry that I had slept into the night. I peeled the cushions away from the high, narrow window, and gauged the time from the colour of the sky. It had not been dark for long. I scooped my bag up and listened to the house for noise, for footsteps, for any signs of intruders or discovery – I was thinking back to the family on the street, how close they had been, how familiar.

There was no sound louder than the aching sigh of the house, no indication that I had company. I broke into the ether for a moment, it was a little difficult to do over the distraction of my whining hunger. There were no minds close by, but I could feel them in the distance, on the fuzzy edges of my shallow trance. Birds slept in the trees above, hanging in the blackness like little rows of candlelight. Their thoughts and dreams glowed dimly through the random fuzz. What do sparrows dream of? I turned away from the window abruptly, and pulled my hood over my head, low down across my face. I made my way up the stairs to the kitchen.

Before I left the house I stood by the kitchen sink, and slowly turned the cold tap. Nothing, as I'd expected. I closed the faucet, and then gently turned the hot tap a quarter turn. A thin trickle of water ran from the head, and a smile cracked wide across my face. There was water left in the hot tank. I fumbled for the bottles in my bag, one empty and one half full, and I placed them under the head as I turned the tap further. I filled them both. I danced through the kitchen looking for bottles, a flask, anything to take more with me. I found an empty lemonade bottle, and I took the water dispenser out of the fridge before filling them both and stuffing them in my bag. The increased weight took its toll on my creaking limbs, but I only wished I could take more.

I emerged from the house feeling like the cat who'd got the cream, unconscious of the time, I practically skipped down the steps from the back deck. I stepped carefully around the crumbling swimming pool and ducked under the trees as I passed through the back gate before heading out onto the street. I shrugged, thinking of the library I hadn't even explored, with regret. It would still be there when I came back. That's what I told myself. How many more rooms like that were there out there, baking in the new deserts or frozen under the icy wastes of New York or Idaho. They would be preserved at least as well as I. Still I stepped onto the street looking up at the stars, and wondering how long those books would last in that room, in that rotting house.

I turned uphill, following the road up to the MUNI stop and the campus. There were people ahead, I knew it. I slowed my pace as I drew up to the University, and kept to the shadows on the far side of the street. There was little moonlight, and the darkness served me well. I clutched my bag tightly to me in an effort to stop it rattling, and when I finally reached the corner entrance of the campus on the other side of the street I ducked into the driveway of a house and examined the grounds in safety from behind a tree.

The campus wasn't gated, and I was disappointed as I took the sight of it in and realised it hadn't fared as well as City College. Every building I could see suffered from broken windows or ugly burn marks. Even the metal 'You are here' map at the entrance was scorched. I exhaled in taut disbelief. The buildings nearest the road were large concrete boxes, remnants from the sixties, and they seemed shattered and empty. The doors were battered in, the windows a mass of melted glass drooping, twisting, dripping down and hanging in mid-air like strings of taffy. Even so I stood behind that tree for some moments, eyes firmly shut, trying in my trance state to focus on signs of the life my instinct told me was there. There were minds – human – but they were further back on the site, away from the road.

I darted across the street in the half-light, staying low and holding my breath. My heart thudded in my ears as I ducked behind the low wall that marked the boundary of the campus. There was no movement beyond as I poked my head up and scanned the area. A wide path led downhill between two square old buildings. Each had doors with steps and ramps, each was a broken husk smelling of smoke and disappointment.

I made my way carefully down the slope, eager to see where it led, eager to find the library. I ran pressed along the walls of buildings wherever I could, I did not want to be seen. As I went by I was puzzled to notice the flowerbeds and patches of grass in the concrete. Every concrete flower box, every strip of ground, every square foot of earth had been raked over. Grass had been torn up, flowers uprooted. In their place stood little rows of seedlings, their green leaves bleached grey in the night.

The path opened up towards the right, and led further down to an open field and something of a courtyard. I heard fragments of voices drifting up, crying or singing or laughing. I stayed pressed to the pebble-dashed concrete of the building on the left, I think it was an old admin block. It was burnt out, windows flapping in the breeze, doors creaking from within. I climbed up and down, along steps and over low patio walls as I followed the line of the buildings, grateful that the ground underfoot was reliable cement, not noisy gravel or treacherous mud. As I drew level with the courtyard and the field across the way I saw that the field was not open at all. Most of it had been built on, shiny new silicon steel boxes, all walls of curving glass and anchor struts of carbon fibre. The contrast between the long wave of a building and the stubby '60's boxes preceding it was sharp, not least because the long wave had not been trashed. The door was ajar, some of the huge sheets of black, metallic glass were cracked and there were signs of burning, but for the most part the modern buildings had endured remarkably well.

I crouched with my back in the doorway of the shell I was currently scurrying along, and I surveyed the scene. The courtyard and most of the field had been dug over, and they appeared to be bearing a crop of potatoes or some low, leafy plant. The path I was following sloped down and across the courtyard, the dip in the middle of which was cluttered with a pile of bicycles. A hundred yards further on, the path was bisected by rows of concrete picnic benches and a large building with an odd, overhanging roof. The building was several stories high, wrapped in glass and concrete, and seemed to be hexagonal in shape. Windows had been smashed out on several floors, and smoke poured out of one such gash, along with the sounds of group singing and the flickering glow of a fire.

I shrank back against the twisted frame of the door behind me as a dark figure emerged from the hexagon. Somewhere in the night a cicada began to chirp, and then stopped abruptly. The distant man's face lit up as he started a cigarette, but I couldn't make out his features, only the dark stick shape he wrestled with in order to free his hands for the lighter. From the way he swung it over his shoulder I knew it was a rifle.

I didn't know what to do – to move forward or to move

back? As the man turned I pressed further into the open doorway, and caught my temple on a metal corner. I turned quickly, and found myself face to face with a metal box. It was bleached and warped, but it featured a large slot of about the shape and size through which you could drop books. Staying low, I backed off from the wall I'd been hugging and looked over at the building. There was the large metal collection box in the doorway, the flaking, painted letters on the doorway that spelled out the word 'Library.' My heart sank. The building had been gutted. Huge greasy soot stains ran up the concrete, the windows had blown out. It was pitch black inside but the salty stench of smoke emanated from within. As I backed away I began to see the word painted on the library wall, a letter at a time set in the spaces between windows. As I read the dripping blue letters my blood began to boil.

J.U.D.A.S.

Of course, I thought. *Of course, of course.*

I crouched on those steps, looking up at the ruined library and half my mission lay spilled out on the floor beside me like my guts. I wanted books on science and engineering, on filters and water management and desalination. I needed something stored – not just the transient virtual information from the internet – no one was going to plug the internet back in for me, I needed memory cards, I needed pages, I needed real, stored information. All I found was piles of ash and plastic residue, fried memory silicon and the wrinkled remnants of burned celluloid microfiche.

I jumped. Kneeling there on the steps leading up to the library, I almost stood in surprise. A loud bang had echoed over the campus. I turned my head to the right to see the doors of the hexagon building swing shut. I squinted. A tiny figure was running up the path away from the building, screaming and giggling in delight. A short ways behind, the man with the rifle was struggling to keep up.

Turn back, I thought. *Please, turn back!* But my hand was already tightening around the pistol laying cold and hard and heavy in the pocket of my gown. The door burst open again and a thin, female voice rang out across the courtyard.

"Jessy! Get back here! It's not safe! Get back here right now!"

The little one squealed with high pitched joy as she took to the air and I realised the man had caught her and whisked her up in mid step. She laughed and clung to him, and I began to breathe again as he turned around. He set her on the ground and talked softly to her, pointing to her mother, and off she went, a little, bumbling shape in the darkness. But my stomach tightened as the man with the rifle turned back towards me and started up the path. A cherry red spot of light whizzed off to the side as he flicked his cigarette end down and reached round for his rifle.

I crept up the steps while he was still many yards away, my belly flat on the ground and my bag balanced on my back. Like a lizard I darted across the patio, crawling up the steps and through the wrecked doors of the library. As I crossed the threshold I felt broken glass under my fingertips. Everything was black with soot. I scrambled to my feet and made my way into the building. I knew the man behind me was still coming.

Inside, the floor was a sea of ash and charred, half burned books. Everywhere I looked there lay warped and upturned metal shelves that littered the floor like an entire forest of felled trees. The remnants of desks and terminal screens lined the walls, and the sour smell of burnt plastic and paper overwhelmed my nostrils.

I could barely see to walk through the sharp debris. There was no source of light, and every surface in the building was matte, carbon black – the room mopped light up like a black hole in space. I knew that the man was still coming up the path behind me, the man with the assault rifle, and the thought drove me deeper into the maze of fallen shelves and twisted furniture.

My only reference point in the swallowing blackness was the row of shattered windows on the far side of the building maybe thirty feet away. The dim night glow drifted in through the tall, thin window slats, and I figured it was my only way out. I started off across the floor, squinting heavily and reaching out, groping with my hands. Almost immediately I tripped and barrelled over the corner of a felled bookshelf, gashing my shin open on rusty metal in the process. Pain ran across my leg like an ugly laugh and then it rushed up my spine. I bit my tongue heavily – it was all I could do to stop myself from crying out.

I lay there in a cloud of dust and ash that burned my eyes and nostrils, and I clutched my leg, feeling the lukewarm trickle of blood run between my fingers. I was ten feet from the entrance and a little over to one side, and in the distance I heard the slow, steady steps of the guard approaching.

I cradled my leg silently as the steps grew louder, and I frozen just another twisted shape in the wreckage, as the dark form of a man blocked the dim, backlit glow in the doorway. He stood there, peering in, checking for endless moments, and then he sighed and turned away, back to his rounds. He knew better than to enter the sharp, invisible maze.

I didn't dare blink.

I lay still, listening to the man's footsteps recede into the night. The sound disappeared quickly beneath the creaking sounds of the carcass I inhabited, and so I waited before moving, lying there flat on my bag with my leg in the air and blood dripping slowly down my sleeves. I was halfway across that minefield of sharp, black objects, I wondered if I should go back or go on. The guard hadn't been looking for me, he had simply been patrolling his rounds, and I had no desire to cross his path again. I flipped over onto my hands and knees in the dust and the ash, trying not to cough as the plumes of soot went up around me, and I began to crawl slowly through the forest of scorched and rusty metal towards the distant light of the windows.

My skin screamed as I scrabbled in the dirt, and more than once I found myself trapped in a dead end, turning back, scorning myself for not risking simply standing up and stepping over two feet of twisted steel. I made it to the windows, and I sat in a puddle of weak light wiping my hands and examining my leg.

The cut was smaller than it felt, of course, an inch long gap under my torn pants, sticky with blood. But it was filthy and that would not do. I stood up stiffly, hand out against the wall, and peered through the cracked window. There was a narrow pathway below, more of a maintenance track than anything, it was eked out from the space between the library wall and a wire boundary fence. From the window it was quite a drop, almost a full storey – the library had been built on a slope. None of the windows would open – they had seized shut in the intense heat of the fire. I hobbled along the wall and around piles of charred furniture until I came to a window where most of the ruined glass was gone, blown and melted out in great dirty brown globules. Carefully I stuck my head out of the narrow slot in the wall, looking left and right along the path, checking for signs of movement. When I was satisfied that I was alone, I lowered my bag out of the window, leaning out as low as I could before dropping it to the ground. It landed with a dull thud and a rattle, and I ducked back inside the building, listening for curious footsteps. They didn't come. I climbed out of the window delicately, hoping to grasp the window frame and lower myself most of the way, but there was nothing to hold onto save molten glass, and I found myself sliding down the pebbledash in a sudden rush, scrabbling for control like an embarrassed cat who's unexpectedly lost its footing.

I landed on the verge with a hollow thump and clenched my jaw in silence as the pain shot up my wounded leg and jarred my spine. I lay there next to the canvas bag in a foetal huddle, not moving, listening to see if I had attracted attention. I began to relax in the outdoors air, and I unzipped the bag, slowly as to cause no noise, and retrieved some water in order to clean the bleeding gash in my leg. I rolled up my pant's leg and sprinkled water over my skin until I could see the flesh where the soot had been. I had no bandage, so I left my black and filthy pants rolled up and let the air get to the wound.

I stood up and slung my bag over my shoulder before turning right and following the path deeper into the campus. I went passed another building, and then one with large windows to the right, and a stage inside. It seemed to be a lecture theatre. It was trashed. The curtains had been torn down and the wooden floor was scattered with seats. I don't know why it hadn't been burned.

Beyond the lecture theatre the path ended abruptly, opening out onto a concourse on the right. It felt very exposed. I crept along the end wall of the lecture hall, and found myself face to face with the Hexagon, not thirty yards ahead. I saw the occupants in the dim orange light of their fire. The flames were pressed against a wall, caged by bricks and rubble, smoke venting through windows above, and a little crowd sat around it, talking and laughing in the half-light. They looked happy.

I could not see them well, I saw them barely at all, but I noticed their long, bushy hair, their brightly coloured clothes. Some of the young ones were bare-chested and carefree, they jumped up and down excitedly as a man picked something out of the fire, black and steaming, and began to pass it around the group. A woman with braided hair put down a guitar and accepted the meal, and everyone talked and ate with their fingers. People milled around the fire, sharing their plates as they chatted and hugged one another. They seemed joyous. They floated about like hippies. Hippies with assault rifles.

I pressed on, backing into the shadows and darting across the concourse, giving the Hexagon as wide a path as possible. The path led down a slope and away past an art block that was all balconies and steps and gangways. All the time I was wandering through a maze of concrete. I passed an accommodation block. Alerted by footsteps I crouched in an alley, hiding from a young blond woman who walked the paths. She sported a tie-dyed shirt and a machine gun holster with equal ease. All in all I felt lucky. There were less patrols than there should have been, and I found myself wondering why.

I kept turning right, and soon I found myself on the far side of the shiny black glass wave building. Its homogenous walls formed one side of a man made gulley – the old concrete pillars of a bronze sign told me it was the science block that formed the other. This was what I had been looking for! Stores of equipment and filters. Engineering labs with tools and manuals. My heart sank as I surveyed the damage. As I looked up I saw that every floor had been ravaged by fire. Piles of desks and chairs lay tangled in the doorway and strewn along the concourse. Computer screens, smashed against the paving slabs, lay where they had been thrown from the fourth floor balconies. A scorched lab coat fluttered in the wind above, snagged on the broken glass of a stairwell window. Blinds clattered in the breeze, and loose papers rustled as the wind whistled through the upper floors. It was a shell, and I didn't want to see it.

A door banged nearby, echoing through the man-made channels of the concrete maze, and I moved off bitterly. The path curved round to the left as it passed the science block, and it let out onto the edge of a sports field before heading back to the front of the campus and Nineteenth Avenue. The field had been turned over, and was covered with an uneven, chaotic patchwork of hand tilled soil and sprouting crops. Standing there, alone in the night, the network of furrows and greenery took my breath away. How many years had it been since I had seen such natural, disorganized labour. Where were the machines? Where were the perfectly square fields and the endless identical rows of machine ploughed soil? Where, in this time of disease and starvation were the hungry masses, ready to pillage and devour this lonely field.

I didn't understand it. People must have known of this encampment – the place wasn't invisible, it was not well defended. I hurried on – my mission was a bust and I was prepared to write it off. The best I could hope for was to get to safety and my bed before the sun rose on another day. Heading in the direction of Nineteenth Avenue I was almost home free, and I pushed on, excited to get off campus, and preoccupied with thoughts of what to do next. I hurried, turning plan B over in my mind as if I was already safe and alone. The path was sloping towards the road and I scuttled along it at a pace, blundering onto a campus roadway and the main car park. I'd followed the concrete as it had wound along the asphalt roadway, and suddenly the buildings opened up, and I was naked and exposed in the wide open space of the car park.

Voices echoed along the road and I looked up. I froze in astonishment. Abandoned cars had been pushed up along the boundary fence between the car park and Nineteenth. They had been turned on their sides and piled up like empty shoeboxes, their axles showing in the night. But this display of power alone was not the cause of the electric shiver tingling down my spine, or the prickly heat spreading across my forehead. Parked in the centre of the barren asphalt, sitting squat and fat like a king tarantula, an armoured personnel drone watched over the campus, its turrets rotating slickly, waiting to strike.

Two guards stood outside the machine, policemen wearing full body armour and helmets, sporting fully automatics and sarcastic grins. They were smoking and joshing with each other, making a grab for helmets, each trying to trip the other up. They were children.

I was astonished that they had not spotted me. A cold sweat trickled down the small of my back as I backed away around the corner, unable to look where I was going, each fumbling step bringing me nearer to a wall that would conceal me, enwrap me, save me. I do not remember the steps. I do not remember feeling my way blind and treading so carefully lest I make a sound or trip backwards. The thing I remember most clearly as the sweat dripped into my eyes and soaked my skin was the thin, drawn shadow of my body lying before me on the pavement. Somehow the weak moon, low in the sky behind me cast its light on my back, and every move I made was magnified twenty times over and played out on the black asphalt of the car park, just yards from the boys and their murder toys.

Maybe my sight was better than theirs. Maybe their helmets narrowed their field of vision. Maybe they were too busy messing with each other, I don't know. All I know is that I backed out of the light slowly and slipped myself behind the corner of a building, leaning heavily and holding my breath. My heart rattled in my chest. I remember listening to their distant sniggers and coming to accept, slowly, gratefully, that those two men hadn't seen me. I squeezed my eyes shut and wiped the sweat from my brow, shaking, and then I set off, pressed against the wall, following back the way I came and trying to stay out of the light.

Whilst before I had been fairly nonchalant, wandering about the campus with only occasional bouts of terror at the thought of being spotted by men with machine guns, I found myself permanently petrified now I knew that discovery would mean pursuit not just by clumsy civilians with sloppy eyes, but also by police, maybe lots of them, and drones that could easily outpace me. Being spotted had never been an option, but previously I had been able to hope that I could escape from such a mess with my life. Now I knew that there was no hope if I were seen.

My hunger writhed within me amid the fear. Different scenarios played out in my brain as I crawled along in the shadows. I would turn a corner and come upon a startled young guard. Forced to silence him – and with lightning speed – I would stab him through the heart, piercing his lung and stealing his scream. Then, as the blood washed down his chest I would lower him to the ground and kneel, sucking on the wound as his eyes turned glassy. I fingered the knife as I ran. I could taste it. What a glorious excuse.

Except that I would always hear footsteps at a distance – ample time to hide, and in my current state of fitness I would be dead before I'd drawn my blade. I hurried along, amazed that I was able to fantasize whilst my life hung by a thread. I slipped by the accommodation block like a ghost, and flew past the Art Block. I didn't come across any young, blood rich guards that needed relieving of their voices.

The most critical task was that of slipping past the Hexagon building. I crouched in the shadows under the steps leading up to the Art Block, watching the figures move in the distant flicker of flames. There was no one guarding the Hexagon.

I crept along the concourse, sticking to walls and shadows, grateful as I came level to the Hexagon that it seemed quieter. The dying fires were on the far side of the building, and only a dim flicker made it across the floors and through the windows to the hollows of my face. Children lay on the floor in piles of blankets, the adults had paired off and sat on stairs, or lay in corners, their backs to the glass. I crept on by.

I was almost past the Hexagon, almost into the concealed corner that led to the maintenance path behind the library, the path I had guessed and prayed led all the way to the road, when I caught movement in the corner of my eye. A little girl. Tiny.

She'd been sleeping, huddled up in a bundle of rags against a window on the ground floor, and she'd rolled over as I spotted her, her eyes popping open in that magical way they do when you know you're being watched, when you know you will meet the eyes of your observer. I sank into the shadows. I knew, even as I froze on my haunches, my deep stare glinting out in two beady pinpricks from beneath my hood, I knew deeply that we'd made eye contact. I knew that she'd felt my mind, my presence. I knew it the way you know in that silent, infinite moment, I knew that she would be certain, she would not be dissuaded. Our souls had touched in the darkness.

She screamed.

I exploded into a run, making the short dash across the concourse into that blind corner by the lecture hall whilst her first, thin little cry pierced the night. I was fleeing down the narrow path behind those buildings before she'd taken a breath. I bolted down that track squeezed between the buildings and the fence, past the lecture hall and the torched library, not looking back, hardly breathing.

The path twisted to the left, opening out, and I realised I was already at the burnt-out admin block – the building closest to the street. I slowed my pace and forced myself to breathe as I approached the end corner of the block, the place where the path petered out. My shin cried out in aching agony. I snuck along the wall, stopping where it turned abruptly, and stealing a look around the corner.

Between Nineteenth Avenue and myself lay bushes, the charred paintwork of the campus map, and open land. And the young rifleman that had propelled me into the library. He was no more than ten yards from me on the other side of the building, standing at the corner where the campus met the sidewalk, clutching his machine gun and staring down the street. I stood still, wondering what to do, trying to breathe, trying not to breathe so loud, trying to think. I had a pistol in my pocket. But could I risk the noise and expect to get far running down Nineteenth Avenue? Not after proving the presence of an intruder. I felt for the handle of the gun, not knowing whether I would take the chance.

A bell rang out in the distance, the guard and I jumped in unison. I flicked myself back around the wall as he turned and looked to the source of the alarm – the Hexagon. They had taken the little girl at her word. I heard heavy footsteps as the rifleman turned and ran, and I watched him in the ether, him and several others as they made their way across the little courtyard to the alarm and the people.

As he receded I crept along the end of the building towards Nineteenth Avenue. I waited. When he'd gotten far enough away I ran.

I fled out into the night, shooting across the road and straight up the drive of the nearest house as my screaming wound trickled blood along the concrete. I kept going, running right through to the back yard before I turned, bolting over fences and scrambling through hedges, passing all the way down Nineteenth Avenue from one back yard to another, acquiring cuts and scratches as I went.

It was twenty minutes later that I allowed myself to slow down, I was halfway over a fence between two yards. I was far enough away that I could feel ridiculous – climbing for my life in some giant steeplechase. I climbed over the fence and stopped for a moment in a neglected back yard. I took a moment to breathe, and I looked around. It was a sad and drooping place, fully of overgrown plants and weeds in the patchy lawn. *The rot is everywhere*, I thought. *The rot is everywhere.*

I sat, and took some water, and it occurred to me that I didn't precisely know where I was. I screwed my bottle cap back on, and carefully made my way out onto the street. I stood in the shadows and looked up and down, and guessed I was about halfway along Nineteenth Avenue. I took a breath, deciding to follow the sidewalk, and set off slowly while keeping out of the light.

The sliver of moon was setting behind houses and hills, and as I walked I welcomed the greedy blackness that swallowed everything. I kept my head up, looking and listening for search parties, people on the road, or vehicles. It was unlikely as far as I could tell. The police owned the road and the night, my only witness was a three your old girl, my only stage a nightmare. No one credible had seen me. I checked my memory thoroughly. All I had left behind were drops of blood and soot in the darkness, no visible evidence. They were not coming for me. This I told myself.

I made my way up Nineteenth unharassed, and I smelled the hanged man before I saw him. The figure draped from the lamppost twisted gently in the breeze, and I wanted to cut it down more than ever, to spite the wretched police and their authority. I could shin up the post. I looked at it. I really could. But they would know someone had been there. There would be evidence. A hanging man one evening, a knife frayed rope the next morning. I may not have respected the power of the local racket, but I did fear it. I moved on bitterly.

Soon after, with the stench still in my nostrils and the buzzing of night creatures still in my ears, I found myself at the intersection with Ocean Avenue. I turned right towards the camp and the canal, hurrying towards the water and the homeward tide.

The walk back seemed endless, the strap of my bag dug into my shoulder and I felt small and lost in the thick darkness. The wind ran up to the avenue and cut into me, and I began to shiver as I walked. Every street sign became a tantalising invitation to sit and rest, I rejected as many offers as I could. The urge was to keep moving, to spend as little time on the sidewalk as possible, to push and push till I was on the boat and heading back safely. *The boat!* It was only then that I realised I must have been hopelessly late for my rendezvous with Reg. I couldn't guess if he would be there at the water's edge, rocking with the lap of the waves and waiting patiently, calm and implacable with his years. I realised I was romanticising. Life was becoming hard again, and old and leathery and grey now was not old enough to be implacable, to be unsurprised. I shrugged. There was nothing to do but continue.

It was later, as I approached the camp, that I heard the noise. Far ahead, at the foot of the camp and the derelict supermarket was another personnel carrier, its engine rumbling as it idled. It seemed to be parked, or at least stopped – its lights weren't on. I was glad for the noise and I stopped walking, ducking to the side of the road to hide and decide what to do. I squinted to see a few dark figures milling about at the edges of the camp, points of light curling about randomly as they carried Coleman lamps and wind-up flashlights.

I stood for a few minutes, getting more and more frustrated. The half-track wasn't going anywhere, that much was obvious. It didn't appear to be searching for anyone, and I didn't think it had come from the campus on Nineteenth – I'd heard no vehicles pass me whilst I was crashing through the back yards and alleyways. The carrier was simply sitting there, gunning its engine, making its presence felt.

I moved in closer, wondering if I could take a back route, cut through the gardens once I'd reached the camp. The diesel rattle filled my ears, and I realised through the gloom that the camp was remarkably quiet. The few tents I could see from the road were zipped up. Most of the lamps were extinguished, there was no one sitting around camp telling stories and jokes – the fires were all dead. It was as if everyone had dived indoors and battened down the hatches, sticking their heads in the sand rather than facing the intruder. But no one was sleeping, I could smell their running fear.

I didn't want to pass by on the road, I knew that much. The armoured carrier was sitting in the middle of the supermarket car park having crushed its way through camps and tents, it was away from the road, but its surveillance stalk was up and telescoping away above the roof of the cab, the spheres and lenses of its budding sensor package of glinting shiny black in the night, clustered together like an evil bunch of grapes. I could go no further without risking being detected. On my left was an old printing shop, and I hurried up to the building, hoping to find a way around the back. It was more difficult here amongst the commercial buildings and the lock ups along the side of the major road. I had to backtrack until I found a gate that I could climb over.

I heaved myself up and over the wood and metal frame, and dropped down awkwardly into the alley behind. My leg was stiff and painful, making it difficult to move, and it would not heal properly until I had fed. Since the burning my hunger had swelled, and I had conceded to it, blurring the boundaries between need and indulgence, stoking my addiction. Where once I would make do with a bag every week or two, now I took that much a night, to keep my strength up and to nourish my crippled tissues. The absence of blood, coupled with all the walking, was making me light headed and weak. For brief moments I would shake, and my limbs would go numb as I felt my grip on my body loosen, it seemed I would start to float up without moving, light and elastic and carefree, and then down I would crash, back into my limbs, back into my head, and all the pain and heaviness and burning aches. I landed in my body, feeling the impact as if I had fallen out of heaven.

These moments were rare, were only just coming on, but they were trouble enough and I had no way to know how long they lasted. They made me vulnerable, and all the while the gnawing knot of hunger grew within my belly, sending tendrils of aching emptiness through my arms and legs, up my spine and deep into my consciousness.

I felt the dizziness rising as I wobbled downwards from the gate, and in a rush I suppressed it. I had landed badly. I found myself in a narrow alleyway between two buildings built of cinder block and painted a shabby magnolia. It looked grey in the darkness. I headed down the black alleyway, treading over the slippery, squelching remnants of decaying cardboard and catching noisy plastic bags on my boots. At the end of the path I turned right into a service road that seemed to run behind the commercial properties. I hoped to follow this single lane down past the camp and as far along Ocean Avenue as possible.

The space was narrow and dark, the buildings on either side were tall, blank devoid of windows. I'd pass the occasional loading bay doors and rusting roller shutters, but it was effectively one long narrow channel. Strangely I felt comforted, not claustrophobic. No one was watching, no one could see me. At last I could move with freedom and breathe without fear. I made my way through the darkness as fast as I dared, pushing my body with the edge of my hunger to goad it, stumbling occasionally as I came across a rusting exhaust pipe or pile of old newspapers.

The service road was littered with detritus. The back of the print shop was stacked with empty cans of paint and plastic containers of glue and chemicals. I passed a pile of worn tires outside a large garage door, and assumed if was the rear of a mechanic's shop. Further along I caught my toe on a soggy cardboard box, and almost twisted my ankle. The cardboard sheared open, splitting all the way across like an over-ripe melon, and a strange, sulphurous smell erupted from within. It was the rotten remnants of a stack of t-shirts. A bad run, or a company uniform or some-such, no one could tell, all the cotton was being attacked by a strange, blotchy fungus. It left behind the threadbare synthetic skeleton of a t-shirt that felt like slime-coated stockings and curled to the heat of your touch.

As I wiped my hand off and looked about me at the empty spray cans and half finished spools of wire up against walls, I was struck by how mundane the garbage was. The lanes were full of stacks of recycling baskets and sour smelling dumpsters that had sat full for years. This refuse was not the product of disaster, it was not the remnants of desperate people nor the final death rattle of a collapsing industrial civilisation. This garbage was normal. It had been put out before the collapse took hold, as the businesses slowed down, a twilight record of production and workaday life that had never been collected by the garbage men. It could have been yesterday. But it wasn't. It was two or three years ago. The rubbish lay there in the street, the off-cuts, the empties, an inverted imprint of a busy, productive society. A well-trained eye could piece together the shape of a society from the waste it had removed, excised coldly and discarded like so much unwanted body tissue. I stood alone in a long channel of garbage and realised there were no more well trained eyes – there was no one left to care.

I set off again, moving carefully through the leftovers. The lane turned abruptly where it came up against a wire fence. The road turned left, away from Ocean Avenue. Straight ahead was grassland rising to a steep hill. Slowly I scaled the fence, slotting my fingers through the gaps and pulling myself up. I dropped my bag over the top and swung over, I forced myself to climb all the way down properly rather than jumping, but I was becoming impatient and nervy with the passing of the night. It was about midnight. I could feel it. The flow of the evening was stationary – hung in the balance like a high tide – it had ceased its insurgence, but was yet to withdraw.

I turned right and followed the fence, hoping it would lead me past the commercial buildings and back to Ocean Avenue. I found it did, but between the street and myself stood a row of tall trees and another fence. Rather than climb over onto the exposed street, I followed the line of it from behind the trees, invisible and carefree. I had a feeling I knew where I was. The ground rose steeply, and soon I came across the first of the old concrete buildings. I was in the City College campus. Each building was locked up and pristine, and I couldn't believe it, couldn't understand why. For some reason the old modernist blocks had been preserved. There were the usual signs of decay – weeds in the paths, paint flaking from the doors, the sports track was an overgrown mass of bramble, but there were no broken windows, no scorch marks.

I reached the point where the ground levelled out and made my way down, coming to a network of pathways between the buildings. I followed a path down to the car park, and found myself on the opposite side of the padlocked gate I had seen the night before. The lock had rusted solid. I climbed the fence at a spot close to a tree, hoping to make use of the cover. I merely made extra noise as I broke branches with my scrabbling, snapping twigs on my way down. All I could think about was getting back to the canal and Reg.

I hurried along the Avenue, turning off on the slip road to the freeway where I could hear the wavelets lapping and smell the water. My feet slapped against the tarmac as I rushed down the slope, but I slowed to a stop long before I reached the water's edge. The concrete channel of the canal was empty. Unoccupied. Reg wasn't there. Of course, of course. The ferryman hadn't waited. Not when he could be out amongst the water lanes earning his living. I dropped my bag on the ground. I wanted to kick something.

I sat on the ground, feeling the little balls of crumbling blacktop beneath my fingers, simultaneously wondering what to do next and trying not to think. I stared into the black water and the long, narrow channel, half expecting to hear the paddle of a row boat, to see the prow of the little craft bobbing up and down in the waves as it emerged from the darkness. It didn't come. And so I sat there.

But not for long. I'd had enough of feeling helpless and sorry for myself. I was stuck here, I needed a boat. I needed a plan. I stood up and brushed the grit from my hands. The sun would come. I would sleep this side of the water through the day. After sundown I would wait for the ferry by the water's edge, and if it didn't come – when it didn't come, I would use the time to find a boat of my own. Sick of the infertile emptiness of the channel, I turned and headed up the slope, back towards the most secure place I had seen so far.

11

Climbing back over the gate of City College proved no easier the second time. I was just grateful that I was alone and undetected. In my clumsy, noisy, wounded state it seemed that the fact that no one expected night prowlers, no one was looking for lone travellers, was my greatest camouflage. I walked up the car park, away from the fence and past the modern 1960's blocks, all concrete pillars and metal framed glass. I had maybe three and a half hours before the sun, I was looking for an older building – one with a basement. I walked along the paths between the buildings and broke out into an open space near the crest of the hill. I looked about me. The area was dotted with concrete sculptures – strange heads and abstract bodies. There was some kind of hall to my left. Maybe an old gymnasium or an assembly hall. Beyond that was a snack store and a library. I wondered if it had the books I needed – without a computer catalogue it could take hours to find them, and I wasn't about to waste my time just yet. I looked at the low rise building and thought it rather small for a library, I began to question hopefully whether it might have a storage basement. But there were no clues – no windows at pavement height, no obvious lower-ground level, unlike houses these buildings were much less likely to be built with cellars unless there was a reason, and I was looking for a safe bet. Exhaust all the likely options first, check the likely buildings in good time before breaking into the others randomly and searching in vain. I turned about in mild desperation, looking for a central building, an admin block, something that might house files in the basement, or a boiler. Staring wildly across the campus I almost missed it right in front of me, but something caught in the corner of my eye and there it was, the basement I was looking for.

It was the science block, standing tall and proud on the crest of the hill right in front of me. Breaking the roofline to the left stood the solitary galvanised dome of a telescope observatory. Yet that wasn't the feature that had caught my eye, I was staring much lower, much closer to the ground. My eye followed along the very path I was standing on, away from the sad patio slabs behind and the forgotten sculptures, all the way along to a short flight of stairs and the main science hall entrance. You had to climb stairs to reach the ground floor of the building, and that meant there was at least one floor below it.

As I crossed the space with the idea that I might kill two birds with one stone, I saw that the science block was about three times deeper than it was wide, and it flowed down the side of the hill beyond. It had been built into the hilltop, and around the corner from the main entrance, where the path led downhill, there was a steep ditch with steps leading both down to the lower ground and bridging up to the ground floor. I darted down into that ditch, for I always favoured breaking and entering out of sight, and I smashed the glass of the door with the butt of my pistol. My heart raced with the noise. It was the loudest sound I had made since I arrived on this island, hammering through that safety glass with its annoying, scratchy wire mesh, and I was sure the racket could not possibly go unnoticed, echoing and rolling down the side of the hill as it was.

I put my arm through the narrow broken slot in the door and stretched, leaning around for bolts and catches. What I found instead was a fire exit bar, which I had to pull towards me whilst stepping backwards to draw the door outwards. It would not have been so awkward had it not been for the vicious spikes of wire and slivers of glass that were straining to slice my arm off. The door opened with a large cracking creak, a stiff complaint in the night, and I stepped inside, feeling the crunch of broken glass underfoot.

The halls were dark and deep, and smelled like school. The stale odour of old wood and floor polish crossed with dust, and paint peeling from hot radiators. Only they were never hot any more. I pulled the door closed behind me, it was the most I could do to secure it. My survival depended on remaining undiscovered, and thinking back to the rusted padlock on the car park gate, and all the buildings above that were locked and dark, I felt more secure here than the house cellar I had emerged from this evening.

I hurried down the hall, past thick heavy radiators and along uneven linoleum, eager to find a room with no windows. Even just a broom cupboard. On the left were two labs at the front of the building, one seemed to be full of old desktop computers sitting in rows along the antique wooden benches. I stopped as I poked my head through the other lab. It smelled old and rusty and the walls were lined with glass cabinets containing fossils and lumps of minerals, and the occasional stuffed bird. The benches carried cases of samples, each cocooned within their little cube of wood and sealed over with glass. There were rows and rows of shells, fossil teeth, pebbles and crystals. Old maps were pinned to the wall by the side of an old blackboard but they were brightly coloured with layers of land that I didn't recognise. Further along the wall were the scratchy line charts of sonar or ground radar, and a topographical printout of the Marianas Trench. In the corner sat a three-screen modelling terminal, inevitably wired with fibre optics into the college's super-array of processors. It was as dead as the stuffed seagull in the case to the left. This was a geology lab, lower ground yes, but lined with windows like the computer lab, all around the external wall looking out on the ditch, and so quite useless to me.

I turned quickly back into the darkness of the high, narrow hallway. There was a central corridor running down the spine of the building, away from the two labs, and I returned to that gaping dark throat now. I stood before it and saw the dim glow of the light filtering through the glass of the doors on either side. But that light was thin. It had come through the subterranean windows of the building on a dark night, and spread across blackened benches and lab floors like a plague before splattering the frosted glass windows of a wooden door. The light beam itself was exhausted. It was a murmur projected onto those square glass panes, it went no further, it did not illuminate. As I watched the shrinking line of faint squares receding into the blackness, I felt as if I were being swallowed – the trail of light was simply the lure of a monstrous angler fish waiting for me at the end of the corridor, its hideous face and needle teeth poised in thick, murky water a thousand fathoms below.

I have never been afraid of the dark, at least, I don't recall it, but it is a sensation I've had to accommodate since I burned my eyes and the night closed in around me. The fear did not ease with time, and I've become acquainted with the spectre of the unknown as I discovered to my surprise that darkness swallows everything. Consequently I moved down that tar black corridor uneasily, and the sensation of being lured down a gaping throat and swallowed alive did not abate. I stared at the posters on the walls, read the letters etched on to the doors as I passed them, simply to remind myself that I was in a place of man and not a shark's belly, simply to hold back the irrational and bubbling panic that threatened to surface. All the while I had the sensation that something watched me from the shadows and waited, waited for me to stumble into its grasp.

I went slowly, reluctant to approach the unseen end of the corridor. Although a brief, stammering look through the ether assured me there was no mind waiting there I somehow desperately feared the place I couldn't see. It was waiting for me, that dark empty space, like the grave I had cheated for so long, it was waiting to slip its cold wet arms around me and smother my screams.

I stopped and scorned myself. Just a corridor. In a school for heaven's sake. And there was nothing here, nothing to be seen, heard or sensed. I was scaring myself, and had no one else to blame. I sighed with embarrassment and fished a flashlight from my bag, flicking it on while I sat against the wall and assessed my situation. I had passed doors labelled 'Lab 1,' 'Chem Prep Room,' 'Lab 2,' and then smaller rooms with computers and a metalworking shop. I seemed to be heading towards engineering. I stood up and continued along the corridor, much relieved for the light in my hand. There was a stack of lockers running along the wall, and then a door labelled 'Welding and Pipe Work,' after which I came to 'Basement Storage and Services. Danger. Strictly No Entry.'

I flushed with relief and grabbed the handle. It was locked of course, and I had to think of a way to get through. I wasn't entirely sure I could break it down, and I didn't want to – I wanted to be able to shut out the light. I scanned the door with the flashlight, wondering what to do, peering at the lock and the handle. I ran the light beam along the doorframe and found that the hinges were protruding outwards, meaning that the door opened out into the hallway. I didn't know why this should be so, I didn't care, it gave me the opportunity I needed. I fished for my knife in my pocket, and dug the blade edge in between the top hinge and the head of the pin that held it together.

I levered the blade up, trying to draw the pin out, but the hinge was old and the grease was stiff and gritty. I held the flashlight over it as I wiggled my blade, watching it scratch away at the metal and slip from its groove. Slowly I began to draw the head of the pin up and away from the hinge plates, and as soon as it was far enough along I reached up and pulled the pin out with my fingers. The lower hinge was easier, not least because I was kneeling on the floor, able to work from above. I worked the pin out and scooted away from the door as I pulled it free, expecting the heavy slab of wood to fall out into the corridor. Nothing happened. I sat there in the silence and wondered what had gone wrong before realising that the door was standing happily with no reason to fall, probably with its bolt wedged firmly in the jam.

I dug my knifepoint into the wood by the hinges and tried to lever the door out gently, afraid that the blade would snap. The top of the door leaned forward a little, and then stiffened, resolutely refusing to move further. I moved the blade up and down the height of the door, levering as I went until I had shuffled it half an inch out on one side, and was able to pull it the rest of the way with my fingers. The door sighed open with a great, wafting blast of air into the corridor, and I was left holding the disembodied plane of wood upright. It was surprisingly light – hollow I guessed, covered in a plywood veneer, and I could have kicked a hole in it had I wanted to. I set it against the wall and shone the light into the darkness beyond.

I discovered why the door opened outwards – it opened directly onto a downward staircase. There seemed to be two doors at the bottom, one ahead and on to the left, importantly there were no windows. I smiled with relief, a taut, gallows grin across my stiff skin. It was a dark space, all I needed. I could sleep on the landing below if necessary. I left the door propped against the wall and went back down the corridor eagerly. There was still time before sun up to explore, to see what useful items could be liberated from the workshops and the labs.

I tried the welding room door first – it was locked. Impatient, I tapped the wood and found it to be hollow like the basement door. I kicked it without conviction, afraid to make noise in the deserted building, and my booted foot bounced off uselessly. The noise racketed down the corridor, sounding like gunfire in contrast with the silence it pierced. Angry, I raised my foot and kicked the door again, closer to the handle this time. I put my foot through the first layer of wood. The cavity was filled with a honeycomb of cardboard and my boot got stuck, leaving me hopping to regain my balance. I extracted my foot and kicked again, aiming a little higher up, a little further around the handle, trying to separate the lock from the door. I put my shoulder to the door and pushed, listening to the wood splinter and groan, until the veneer around the lock cracked and gave way, and I fell into the welding room.

It was an open space. Welding kits sat in each corner behind screens of draped plastic or rubber. The wall was covered with charts showing proper joints in girders and pipe work. Most of the equipment was far too heavy to be carried, but I gathered a blowtorch head and three small butane cans from under a bench in the corner, although I couldn't find the soldering rods. I didn't waste time hunting around, I grabbed a large iron bar from the floor by a welding station and left. I was sure I would collect more prizes than I could carry back anyway.

The computer rooms were useless to me, and I strode along to Lab 2 on the other side of the corridor, smashing the glass in the door briskly with my newfound weapon, and sticking my hand through to release the catch on the Yale lock. I felt awkward smashing and breaking things that I didn't own and that could no longer be repaired. I was ruining a perfectly good building, a rare and precious thing in these times. I had eased my mourning for the world by washing my hands, by blaming them, the humans, the others – anyone but myself as if I didn't use electricity and gas, as if I'd never picked through a shattered home for tidbits. But now I was breaking in, smashing and looting. A pristine building was too good an opportunity to miss, but I had to swallow my pride and my self-respect – and my self-righteous immunity. Now I was the destroyer, I was the seed of chaos spreading shattered glass across an immaculate floor. I could no longer pretend I was innocent.

Inside it was a basic standard lab I guess, if rather old. There were rows of wooden benches, metal stools, power and gas points. All the cupboards were locked. Posters around the room covered the basics of biology and physics, I knifed the flashlight through the shadows to see a diagram of how the planets formed. *Older than me,* I thought. There was a glass cabinet by the door that contained a small, mammalian brain in a jar, the label read 'Domestic Cat,' in scrawling black handwriting. There was a segmented, plastic model of a human brain and other science rubbish, but nothing that could help me.

I peered towards the back of the room, past the digital whiteboard and the fume cupboard and the square porcelain sinks. There was a door. I crossed the aisle and tried the handle, expecting it to be locked. It wasn't. It swung open gently, and I poked my head through. It was the prep room and it led between two labs – this one and chemistry.

I stepped in cautiously, as if I had stumbled across treasure in the tomb of Ra. There was a stack of glass tubing in four-foot lengths propped up behind the door. I grabbed it, and then I set it down to collect a coil of rubber hose, which I discarded in favour of a box of filter papers, my plans for water purifiers spinning eagerly in my head. And then I stopped. I'd found the real treasure. Something I'd thought I was going to have to bodge together miserably out of desperate memory and luck. Glinting in the corner by the window sat a strange object. It looked like an old-style electric kettle – chrome and round with a black handle. Only it had no spout. And where the lid should have been was a foot-long envelope of glass containing a spiralling glass condenser coil, transparent on transparent as the light twisted and glinted, collecting in the curves, the envelope sprouting rubber tubing and a tap. It was a still. A water distiller.

I sank down in joy and sheer bloody relief, leaning against the door in wonder. It was not the most beautiful thing I had ever seen, but it would buy me a lot. It would solve some problems. And it would be efficient, more efficient than the disaster I had hoped to piece together from books and memories, old coffee pots and bits of pipe. Suddenly the blowtorches and the glass and the rubber tubing didn't matter any more. I leant against the door and stared. Then I unzipped my bag and tipped everything out onto the floor.

The still was everything – it was more important than the water I had in the bag. I packed it carefully, wrapping the glass condensation element in paper towels and an old lab coat, trying to protect it. What a fool I'd been, a snob, rejecting Reg's suggestion out of hand. *Who is he to challenge my plan?* That's what I'd been thinking as I'd brushed his look and his advice aside. *Who is he?*

I sighed. I fitted things around the still, wedging water bottles and old tools back in my bag, taking them out again, swapping things around. Was a butane canister worth taking now instead of the half full water bottle? Little decisions that seemed huge, but could only be seen to matter in hindsight.

I went through the prep room, tipping out drawers and searching through cupboards. I picked out filters and pipe fittings, matches and lighters (ah the luxury), I grabbed the first aid kit off the wall and then I groaned. I felt like a fool. Screwed onto the wall between the door and the first aid box was a metal key locker. It was wide open. Inside, keys hung in rows with labels under each hook – Lab 1, Lab 2, Chem, Astro, and one that caught my eye, a little red plastic key fob with two keys, a label underneath – handwritten in faded ballpoint. I squinted to read 'Basement Storage.' I snatched that key down, and took the others, stuffing them into my pocket.

The prep room was full of tools – scalpels and clamps, and electronic meters. I took those things, and placed them carefully in the outside pockets of the bag. It was getting very full. I made some room for the little bottles of poisons I found. Arsenic and cyanide compounds. Why they were there I don't know, but they must have had a legitimate purpose. All the same I found them in a locked container above the sink, next to a brightly coloured flush kit that I wished I had room for. The poison box wasn't secure. I found the little key in the key locker by the door. It was labelled and colour coded, conspicuous and shouting like the dark little bottles it protected. Steal me, steal me, drink me.

I stepped through the mess I'd made as I'd tipped out desk drawers and pulled bottles off shelves, sliding over piles of paper and broken glass and bottles of purple meths. I stood over my bag and lifted it slowly. The last sound I wanted to hear as I raised that bag was the cracking of glass from inside.

It didn't come. I exhaled with relief and made my way out through the Chem lab. A cluster of squeezy bottles sat on the drainer by the sink, the thin, bent tubes emerging from their tops looked like a mass of giant insect legs in the shadows. My search was casual, the mental catalogue I made perfunctory. I could carry nothing else without setting something down, and I was conscious of the time. How I hated the oncoming summer then. It stole my hours when I could least afford it.

Lab 1 was even less fruitful, just rows of benches – a multipurpose teaching room. At least the Chem lab had had shelves of glassware, beakers and strangely blown tubing. This had nothing, just locked cupboards under the benches and a row of dead wireless terminals along the wall. I stepped out into the hallway and back along to the basement door.

It is an odd thing, to turn a key in the lock of a door that has no place, no home, which balances delicately on a wall. The key worked, so I set about fitting the door back into its frame and driving the pins home. It was hard to align the hinges in the dark, and with nothing of the door to grasp save a quarter inch of turned metal and a door handle I could barely reach, but once I'd gotten the bottom pin in it held the alignment for the top.

I checked the lock and the door once more, turning the key and opening and closing. I would be safe as I slept. Then, in a moment of paranoia, I returned to the prep room and the key locker, and peeled the sticky labels from under all the hooks. If my treachery was discovered in the light of day, I didn't want anyone to know I had in my possession a basement key. I didn't want anyone to come looking.

The glow along the corridor was brighter, the shadows shallow as I walked back to the basement steps. I had an hour, I knew, probably less. I took my bag down the steps and left it safely on the landing at the bottom before climbing back up and locking the door behind me. I walked along the corridor, turned right past the geology lab and darted up the staircase, heading for the top floor and the stars.

When I found the Astro lab I was surprised. I had expected the observatory to be a cramped mezzanine space up in the roof, in fact the sheet metal hemisphere protruded out from the ceiling of a corner room, the telescope was mounted on a tall scaffold, with stairs leading up to steering wheels and an observation seat. I paused as I opened the door and saw it all. What I would have given for an instrument like this in my youth, or a thousand years ago when the Earth was the centre of God's Universe – when I knew the stars meant something, they *meant something*, I knew it in my gut as I looked up each night and they spoke to me. I knew they held the secrets of creation, I hoped that one day they might explain my own astonishing existence. I used to care for those secrets.

Yet here it was, an antique telescope, thin and inefficient and forgotten. A thousand years too late, a thousand times smaller than the giant instruments men built in the final starving years of science, as watery exoplanets said hello and the oily fount of technology said goodbye.

I walked over to the mechanism, all iron supports and brass wheels. It was old and obsolete but well cared for. As I looked about and followed the lines of control cables down to their respective wheels I began to decode the workings of the machine. I stepped over to the wall and grasped the handle of a small brass wheel, turning it, and the observatory shutters rolled open above. The wheel moved freely but the thin sheet metal squealed above as the control lines dragged the cavity open. I stopped winding as soon as the shutters were wide enough to expose the scope's head, they were meant to open further but I was nervous of the sound. I looked up through the gap, felt the cool, damp morning air, and wondered how much time I had left.

The telescope was a long, thin metal tube of brass fittings and blue paint. The steps up to the observation seat were not high

– the cradle was about head height and surrounded with wheels and pulleys. Turning those wheels would move the entire frame, swinging the scope across the sky and pulling the observation seat with it. The whole effect as you sat was rather grand. I dared not – dared not risk being seen or heard. I climbed the steps and peered eagerly through the mounted eyepiece, one of a number of stubby black tubes clustered around a rotating head. I saw a hazy field of points. The scope didn't appear to be trained on anything in particular. I focussed, turning the toothed knob beneath a sweeping the sky, looking at distant tremors of light and fuzzy, gaseous clouds that were probably quite, quite magnificent under a better instrument. I didn't care. I didn't know the modern names for the stars or the constellations, I didn't care. They'd all drifted a fraction since my lost youth on a different continent, a different hemisphere. I sat gazing for the precious few minutes I had, not understanding what I was seeing, knowing only beauty of the heavens, and then I climbed reluctantly down those steps, fleeing the fathomless blue of the new sky and the first of the birdsong.

I crossed to the doorway, looking back from the threshold at the star charts on the wall and the models of the planets inhabiting the room's darker corners. The telescope was an antique, a toy, a conversation piece to the modern college, but oh how I wanted to take it with me, to fit it in my bag and sneak it home. What a luxury to have it in my home. Quite impossible of course, but my heart ached as I climbed down the steps to the lower ground floor and made my way along to the basement.

I was quite uncomfortable in the predawn light of that corridor, and I felt for the hard ball of keys in my pocket, suppressing my paranoia and panic as I slotted the basement key in the lock. It turned of course, and I shut the door behind me, inching my way down the steps in total darkness, and grateful for it. At the bottom of the stairs I groped gently for my flashlight, flicking it on as I went over to the door marked 'Storage,' trying the keys one by one until I found the metal sliver that worked.

I stepped into a room of grey metal cupboards and map drawers, of models and of dust. It was a small room, cold and hard, the air was damp, musty, and smelled heavily of decay. It was a strangely sweet perfume – somewhere between stale biscuits and rotten flesh. It made me a little sick. One dank wall seemed to be covered in shelves of brown glass chemical bottles and endless rows of books. A corridor had been formed leading away from the door by rows of storage furniture opposite the shelved wall. I opened the cupboards to find stacks of papers, worksheets and textbooks, all brown and moth-eaten. There were cabinets of physics models – Newton's Cradles and Van De Graaf Generators. On top of the map drawers lay a pile of old, broken C.R.T. Oscilloscopes so thick with dust that the knobs were swallowed up beneath a carpet of fuzz. This subterranean hole was a graveyard of the obsolete, an oubliette to science. I pulled the drawers out, their sliding tracks tired and squealing, finding old oceanographic charts made from paper. I remembered the feeling of real paper maps as I touched them, so different from the glow of a handheld screen, the trademark of a nav. system up until the Collapse. No one knew how to write maps anymore – the satellites used to do it for them.

I came to the end of the corridor and turned right along the abutting wall, only to discover that the room was not so small. It continued behind the cupboards and cabinets lined up to make a walkway, and as I swept the flashlight across the space I froze in horror. A sick feeling collected in my guts like lead shot. This place was a graveyard after all.

The beam had thrown up strange, alien shadows as it pierced the darkness and filtered through the dust that clung to display cabinets and bell jars in greasy smears. I'd stumbled upon a macabre collection. Glass topped cases of pinned insects lay stacked up against the corner, mandibles spread and bearing sharp, shiny fangs that glinted like knives. There was a row of shelves against the wall cluttered with glass jars of murky preservation fluid bearing slimy pink organs, the red-grey of preserved brains and the sad beige of unidentifiable, undeveloped embryos. Rows and rows of embryonic creatures sporting gills and tails and strange, nauseating deformities in their sickly yellow liquid. They were curled up, a few staring with foggy little eyes that were stunted and blind, not one of them bigger than a tennis ball. I choked. I couldn't say that they were not human.

There was a taxidermy collection also, displays of dead animals arranged against fake backgrounds as if nothing had happened to them, as if they hadn't been butchered and turned inside out so that their flesh could be scraped away. A snake was curled around a tree limb, poised to strike at a rat. The rodent's grimace of terror had been frozen and augmented for posterity, highlighted for all the world to see. Birds flew on wires strung between a network of branches pinned to a plaster and paste stand. As I swept the beam along the sharp shadows of creatures and insects crawled up the walls and along the ceiling, a network of sharp claws and black teeth closing around me, waiting to strike.

The hard edged beam of light crossed the path of a stuffed black jaguar that was trapped for all eternity behind its own over-attenuated and ridiculous snarl as it crouched stiffly, and there, with the shadows all around me, I discovered the thing of horror, the source of the sickly sweet smell. It stood on two feet in the corner of the room. I froze. It was a woman, and I caught her gaze first, dark hollows for eyes and a twisted mouth, staring at me, grimacing, accusing. Her jaw was twisted away but her gaping black eyes stared forwards, her body was contorted, her hands were curled into brown, leathery claws. I stepped back in horror, feeling my grip tighten around the tough rubber of my flashlight as the shakes ran over my body in waves. I was terrified. I wanted to vomit.

The woman was a South American mummy, desiccated in the deserts of Peru. Her eyes had shrivelled up and her skin turned to leather maybe seventeen hundred years previous, and now here she was, forgotten in a basement, rudely impaled on an iron stake to keep her upright. The plaque at the base of the frame was engraved bronze, it read 'Madame Zozho, The Witch' – a freak show exhibit, late nineteenth century, but the beads in her braided hair and the woven shreds of clothing on her shrivelled body told me she was much, much older than the freak shows.

She glared at me in the jealous darkness and I hated her. With her claws and her twisted, gaping mouth she made a haunting figure, she was terrifying, evil-smelling and pathetic, and I was terrified as her empty-socketed stare followed me around the room, and yes I hated her – not because of her stare, not because of her smell, but because I was older than her, twice as old, three times – I saw myself in those dead, empty eyes, I saw my scarred and leathery face in her sunken cheekbones and her collapsed nose. She accused me with her stare, she reminded me of myself. I hated her yes – here was a mummy, a homage to death and decay, shrivelled and decrepit, and I was ancient before she was ever born.

Shuddering, I turned my back and headed for the door, walking stiffly, trying not to break into an all out run. I grabbed at the door handle, and then fumbled with the keys outside, struggling to lock the room behind me. I sat at the bottom of the stairs in that cramped little landing, trying to rationalise, trying to understand how that macabre figure had come to be there, how she had remained undiscovered, how she had avoided repatriation. It didn't matter of course, not any of it. It didn't matter and it didn't help.

I settled a little and sipped water, staring at the door in front of me, wanting to check it was locked. Eventually, I knew, I would have to switch the flashlight off, conserve its batteries, and I dreaded that eternity of total blackness now. I would have embraced it just a few months ago. It would have been comforting, like a warm bath – such was the rarity of sensory deprivation to my over stimulated mind and my sharpened senses. Now that my eyes were burned dull and I was easily frightened in my weakened state, I simply found the darkness threatening. It coated me, it swallowed me. It smothered me in a cloying wave of treacle and it made me sick to my stomach.

And yet I had to turn the light off, or it would flicker out for good and I would be trapped in the dark with the endless unknown, waiting for the eternal hours to pass. I was stuck in this little chamber between fire and horror, and I flicked the light out with the conviction of the condemned, trying not to gag with rising panic.

I lay down on the floor with the bottom step as my pillow, but I didn't sleep for the longest time. I clung to the faint, rectangular outline of light filtering through the doorway above my head, it was my only anchor in space, the only thing that kept the shapes of horror from playing across the blackness that paraded in front of my eyes.

I succumbed eventually of course, and that faint, caustic rectangle of sunlight did not prevent the sickness from infecting my dreams. A deep grey overtone washed across the corners of my dream vision. Everywhere I looked there was something going on just on the periphery, just out of reach. Strange, violent struggles between vicious creatures with sharp teeth, people swiping at each other with daggers. These were more feelings than observations, and I would wake in panic and sweat again and again, tormented not only by the dizzy, sick dreams that seemed to go on for hours, but also by the fact that every time I woke I realised I had hardly slept at all – I knew the burning sun had barely moved in the sky.

I slept on, and a strange heaviness infected my dreams. It wrapped around me with the screaming stiffness of an iron curtain, plate steel pinning my arms and legs and creeping over

Samuel Collins

my face with the inexorable glee of a boa constrictor. In my dream the wind rose up and the light faded, swallowing everything in darkness until I was the spotlight in the centre of a vast empty room, a nothing space. But I wasn't alone in the emptiness. The coating, constricting, smothering force that bound my every pore was a conscious presence riling my skin and fingering through my mind. It howled above the wind, striking me, slapping me, driving metal spikes into my brain and accusing me jealously of having everything it wanted. It screamed its outrage in my ear, calling my name wordlessly and cursing my blood.

I was paralysed within that iron sheath, the black monster screeching in my ear, its tendrils writhing through my mind. The last of the light began to fade, leaving me alone in the dark emptiness, alone with the creature that was bleeding my soul dry with relish. I convulsed in horror as the darkness stroked my cheek, bursting into a sweaty consciousness as the shudder ran painfully hard through my true body.

I couldn't move when my eyes burst open, I felt weighed down by a black force, but there was a powerful presence in that little room crypt. It embraced me, coated me, swallowed, smothered me, and as I struggled for consciousness and movement I felt its purchase on me loosen. There was nothing there, no creature, no mind, no jealous will brooding angrily in the corner, but my half-sight showed a flat, lacy mist curled over my body like cigarette smoke in the ether. As I watched it rose away casually, thunder grey tendrils rolling up and away, drifting casually towards the storage room. The twisted membrane of energy turned into smoky white pinpricks of mist, and it dissipated into the ether before it had fully passed through the wall.

I rolled over on the floor, curling into a ball, choking, gagging, gasping for breath. I ran with sweat and shivered in the darkness, pulling folds of my gown tightly around me. As I lay shaking on the hard floor I was too stunned to think – too dizzy and exhausted and weak. The cogs of my mind would not roll on, I could not move from one thought to the next. I could barely move. I lay there, alone and terrified, saturated with the aching, ice cold emptiness of that presence lacing my bones, its tirade of utter hatred and raging jealousy ringing through my mind.

I was trapped of course, and as I regained my senses and my limbs I began to understand that. My first gnawing impulse had been to drag myself up those narrow steps and fling the door wide open to the night air, a chill ran down my spine when I realised what it was I meant to do. Did I hear wicked, rheumy laughter somewhere in the distance? When I was able to gather myself I sat up on the bottom step, hugging my knees and fingering the button of my flashlight in the darkness. I could feel the outrage boiling in my blood.

It was early afternoon when I awoke, but I wouldn't sleep again in that oubliette. I sat in the darkness, rocking, singing softly, flicking my flashlight on or striking the lighter for a few brief moments, staring at my ruined fingers and passing the interminable hours. It seemed forever. I struggled to stay conscious, I struggled not to pass into a hypnotic stupor in the vacuous darkness. I feared losing my awareness – to do so was to invite another approach of the jealous one.

The hours and the seconds passed, and I would knock myself awake, terrified for my mind, unsure whether I had drifted into oblivion – whether an age had passed between my last thought and this or, whether it was simply a moment in the darkness where I had briefly thought of nothing. I was lost and disorientated both in countless time and empty space. Dizzy and over-tired, I had no reference points to cling to, and I battled drowning in my own mind. I spent many hours sitting at the bottom of those stairs, gazing up at the dim rectangle of light around the door above, needing to look and unable to approach.

I would wait in the darkness, holding off and holding off until the spinning terror rose, and then in panic I would break down and shaking, would push the switch on the flashlight or strike a match, grateful for the wave of relief that washed over me as with the touch of false light on my skin. Then I would count the bricks in the wall or the blackened veins twisting through my hands in unabated dread, until again I could smother the light and face the darkness.

I watched the sun, of course. In my instinctive mind I watched the sun track across the sky. That great, twisted ball of gravity and nuclear wrenchings that spun soundlessly through the ether. It is beautiful, magnificent, overwhelming, terrifying. I was grateful when I felt the evening chill draw close and I knew that the worst – best – of the day had passed. I watched with mounting relief as the light from the cracks in the door turned cool and faded, feeling my time abroad return and bring strength to my bones.

The moment of sunset runs through me like a shudder. It

is a knowing every night. I know when I am welcome. I smiled and got to my feet, drawing up my brittle power. I climbed up the steps with my bag, listening and checking for intruders before smoothly unlocking the door, anticipating the springy click as I turned the knob that drew the bolt across. I left the bag on the floor outside and headed for the ransacked prep room. I wanted to go down to the water as fast as possible to check for Reg, but there was something I would do first.

I picked through the ruins of the prep room, looking for something I had seen earlier and passed over. It was a small plastic bottle of bright purple liquid. Methylated Spirits. I grinned as my fingers closed around it, and I hurried back along the corridor, back down the steps to the evil little mortuary and the prize of its collection.

I stood before her in the darkness, meeting her empty gaze as the shadows curled around me. Twisting the safety cap from the bottle I threw its contents in her face, splashed the liquid down her tattered dress, across her feet. The shocking perfume of meths crawled across the room, mingling with the sick odours of damp walls, embalmed flesh and moulding feathers. I struck a match in the darkness, studied that gaping, twisted face for a reaction, an imperceptible shudder of angry fear in her empty eye sockets, some sign of all that cold hate that had slithered through my soul earlier and violated me so casually. I did not wait for a response to a threat, I flicked the match.

The room erupted in light and flame, I almost heard the screams, the chatter of insects and the roar of animals. Clutching my bag I retreated amidst the crackle and smoke, watching the black wisps curl up the ceiling of the staircase above me as I climbed. I fled the building and crossed the athletics pitch opposite that sloped down the hill directly towards the canal. I heard the crash of breaking glass and turned as the windows lit up. The fire had spread through the building on the hill, soon people in the camp would see the burning orange sky. The police would come.

12

There was a wasteland verge beyond the wire fence at the bottom of the sports field, beyond that lay the canal. I could smell the filthy floodwater. I climbed the fence carefully, my bag with its precious contents slung over my shoulder. As I turned over the top of the fence, praying that Reg would somehow be there waiting for me at the water's edge the flames lit up the sky. The low clouds glowed through the pouring smoke, the gutting flames painting long, flickering shadows down the hill.

You would think I had seen enough fire for even my lifetime, but I watched briefly as the old building burned. The ground floor was aglow, rivers of flame running down the side of the hill following the line of the building. Black smoke was silhouetted in front of the flow as it bellowed out of the shattered windows, and in the centre of the building, above the spot where I imagined the mummy lay screaming silently in her overdue crem, the first floor rooms began to flicker. The crest of the hill was lit up as the smoke and sparks billowed into the sky, and I could imagine the commotion and spectacle the fire on the hill would be causing in the camp. I hurried away.

I crossed the verge of oily toxic ground and looked down into the dark gulley of the canal, hearing the lap of the water, feeling the damp. I couldn't see Reg, but still I hoped. Ducking into the shadows I turned right and made my way the hundred yards to Ocean Avenue and the intersection, to the place where the tarmac climbed out of the water and the canal ran dry. Reg was nowhere to be seen.

There was no time to waste with waiting, and I needed a new plan – Reg wasn't coming back. I stood at the water's edge, turning, staring into the empty distance, thinking. It was a boat I needed, but I turned away from the water and crept up the slope to Ocean Avenue.

Walking further along the avenue I could see the camp in the distance. There was a police vehicle of some kind sitting in the road. I stopped as I realised it was much nearer than I had thought – not opposite the camp, but opposite the college. I crossed the road away and dove down an alleyway between the tract houses and the franchise stores that lined the avenue. I made my way up along the avenue and towards the camp by climbing over brick walls and fences and sneaking through neglected yards. There was no convenient parallel route, no service road or alley for me to use. Most often the knife edge moon was shrouded in cloud and my path was black. I went slowly and carefully, terrified of falling from a climb, terrified of tripping lest I crack the glass element in my bag.

I found myself in a bare line of ground between opposing rows of back yards that loosely followed the line of Ocean Avenue. It seemed to curve away a little, but I didn't care. I would push through the rose beds if necessary. I couldn't risk getting lost in the domestic maze. I crept along and began to hear the low murmur of defeated voices – the camp thrum, more tense than excited at the spectre of the fire.

I drew close to the camp and emerged from the patchy garden alleys into a road at the back of a nursery and strip mall. The street was cluttered with upturned dumpsters and broken glass, dead telephone lines splayed across the tarmac. It folded away from the course of the avenue. Beyond was the community space that the camp had occupied and the ruined shell of the supermarket. I paused, looking for a place to stash my bag. I eased open the lid of a dumpster, but dropped it again as the stench of decomposing slurry assaulted me. In the end I hid the bag behind a stack of old pallets leaning against a thrift store's loading bay entrance. I paused and looked about me, taking my bearings. It was imperative that I remember how to find this place.

When I reached the camp boundary I stayed in the shadows and followed the wire fence and grave stench to the rear of the field. I climbed over close to the humming pit and the bodies where no one cared to look. The residents avoided the smell, and I found that they were gazing at the flames on the distant hill. The smart ones were keeping their heads down.

I passed into the sprawling mass of tents and hovels clustered unevenly around dead camp fires and stinking latrine pits, grateful for my hood. I wanted to go unnoticed, but I wondered whether I should find someone who was awake and ask them for what I sought. People littered the ground in piles of filthy blankets and sleeping bags. Many were asleep, others turned away as I whispered to them. No one wanted to know anything. I made my way through the mud and trash like a shadow, edging cautiously towards the front of the camp and the road – the best place from which to see the fire.

There were lamps on by the tents at the front. People sat in clusters or peered up, sneaking glimpses of the flames from above the tent line. They muttered together in hushed tones. I expected groups of people standing, staring across the road as I approached the sidewalk, but there was none of it. I gazed at the huge fire lighting up the sky in the distance, there was a rustle behind me, and someone grabbed my arm fiercely and tugged me down toward the ground.

I half turned and dropped, more out of irritation than anything, and found the girl with greasy hair and spectacles kneeling before me in the dirt, her eyes wide and her finger pressed to her lips. She led me away from the road urgently, crawling through the mud and the filth without raising her head. She stopped and poked her head up once we were further back and quite lost amongst the drooping tents.

"What are you doing here?" She whispered angrily.

"Do you want to earn some water?" I said in a low voice.

"Sshh!" She hissed. Obviously I spoke too loudly for her still. "There's a lockdown since the fire! No movement. Do you want to get us shot?" She paused. "Water?" She pulled me further back again, crawling on hands and knees until we were at the edge of the tents and the grave scent was heavy in the air.

"It was you, wasn't it! The fire?"

I began to grin in the darkness of my hood, but she couldn't see and she went on.

"You stupid.mother.fucking.stupid.cunt. You *cunt*. They'll kill us you bastard. They'll blame us and they'll take ten or a hundred of us out and line us up along the street and shoot us. Are you fucking retarded?"

I stopped grinning.

I grabbed her vicelike around the shoulders. The speed of my hold chilled her. I felt stupid and foolish and morose, but this was not the time to go soft. She struggled as I pulled her towards me, and I summoned anger that wasn't true in order to strengthen my grip. I needed her to be scared. I drew her face to mine until she could feel my breath on her cheek and she writhed in horror as she got some sense of my skulls face.

"Listen to me youngster," I snarled in her ear. "You can deal with me or you can die right now in the dirt. If you think the boys out there are monsters you can't imagine what I'd like to do to you." I licked her cheek, felt a shiver run through her as she whimpered, and I dropped her down into the mud. She scrabbled backwards and kicked out as she retreated, but she didn't run. She sat in the mud, staring into the gaping black mouth of my hood as she shook.

"No," she said, and her eyes hardened.

"No?" I whispered, incredulous.

"Nah." She shook her head. "Not for water. I'm not gonna die here. I won't do it for water. Whatever," she shrugged. "Take me where you're going. Whatever you want, that's the deal."

She folded her arms and looked at me pointedly, trying to suppress her fear. She knew that if I had come looking for her she must have something I needed.

I wanted to scream. I wanted to slap her. *Why is everything so bloody complicated?* I looked her square in the eye. "I need a boat. I need it by midnight and I need it on the water. Do you know where?"

The girl pursed her lips for a moment and blinked. She paused. "Camp 14," She whispered.

"Camp 14?"

"Camp 14." She said with certainty. "Come on."

She stood up low and wiped her hands before turning to cross the field, but I stopped her.

"This way. Things to pick up." I led her across the mud to the back fence, and she looked at me incredulously. "You can do it? A boat – soon? You should be afraid of failing me." My voice grated in the shadows.

She stood away from me, curious but afraid. "Yeah." She nodded, "yeah."

"Then put your arms around my shoulders."

For all my veiled threats and attempts to sound scary, I think she was more afraid to put her arms around me than to fail in her contract. She snorted at the idea and ran at the fence, jumping up and hitting it noisily, halfway up. She clung and climbed with a child's agility, I just shook my head and followed her as quietly as I could.

The girl dropped to her feet on the other side, brushed her hands off and walked carelessly away into the shadows. She didn't look back. She stopped and waited for me to join her, she looked expectantly to me for directions. I nodded, a gesture possibly lost within the voluminous dark of my hood, but I set off back towards the gutters and the thrift store and my hidden treasure and she followed. She waited impatiently as I threw off the wooden pallets and retrieved my bag, and then she looked back and forth along the soggy ground and rows of buildings, unsure which direction to take.

"There are men all along the avenue." I offered.

The girl said nothing, but a look of teenage scorn flashed across her eyes before she swallowed it. She turned away and hiked into the darkness, not waiting for me to follow.

Like a cat, the girl wound her way through gaps in buildings and along boundary walls. She led me around fences I would have had to climb, and down narrow lanes that twisted sharply and whose destination I could not have guessed. I had to hurry to keep up. I followed her over a low wooden fence and found myself at the beginning of a row of domestic back yards, a line of odd decaying Victorians and bungalows leading off to the left. She waited as I climbed down from the fence carefully, trying not to show too much concern for the fragile contents of my bag. I did not want to give away the value of my cargo. The girl eyed me suspiciously, and then turned and let me through a side gate and onto the street. I caught up with her on the sidewalk as she strolled, having proven that she knew where she was going. Our transit through the maze had been a major shortcut. Without her I would have been sweating my way over walls and fences, endeavouring to travel in a straight line, and getting thoroughly lost anyway.

"What's your name?" I asked, trying to get her to slow a little.

"This street runs by one that comes off the avenue. We'll get down to the freeway then. Follow that round and-"

"What's your name?" I touched her shoulder and she twisted away from me.

"Joany, Ok?" She stuttered. "And if you touch me again you, you freaky old peado I will cut-it-off. Got it?"

I nodded and kept quiet.

We walked down the street and downhill in the darkness, heavy clouds hanging low and black above us like the Sword of Damocles. I was getting used to the houses now – untouched and unloved, a row of boxes planted carelessly down the hill, looking fake like plastic doll's houses that someone had forgotten to box up and ship out. The street came to an intersection and opened out, we turned downhill once more, and I could smell the water on the breeze. It wasn't fresh, it was the slick waft of rotten vegetables and diesel fuel.

Samuel Collins

We turned left when we hit the freeway heading toward the college and the water. I saw the distant flicker of the inferno on the hill silhouetting the peak in the night sky. With no fire trucks, no emergency services, the flames could rage for days, I found myself wondering if the other buildings had caught light. I thought briefly of the library opposite, and then the old telescope in its brass glory stuck in my mind.

We walked in silence. Joany (or Joni – I never saw it written) preferred to keep a couple of feet between us, which was fine by me. She didn't quite walk ahead, she didn't want me behind her. We walked along the wasteland by the freeway and she would check over her shoulder, slowing up whenever I got behind. It became a game for me – how slow could I go? How long would she leave it? When would she become uncomfortable? Silly girl. Silly man.

We passed under a road bridge that crossed the freeway, and the college loomed ahead. In the bouncing echo between concrete decks I began to hear things – the rattle of a diesel engine, the shouted orders of men fading in and out on the breeze. My spine stiffened as I counted the voices out there on the road. I didn't have to tell Joany to tread quietly.

The smell of burning was heavy in the air – competing with the stagnant floodwater stench as we came to the Ocean Avenue interchange. The voices of men who've been taught that guns and flak jackets meant power were plain on the air now, and Joany had heard them a while back. Her spiky mood had dropped. She seemed small and fragile, her shoulders rounding instinctively in the darkness. The freeway sloped off down into the water, we continued above, walking along the dirty verge, trapped between the wire fence of the college on one side, and the increasing drop to the water on the other. Voices hollered along the channel from the avenue behind, the crackle of flames and collapsing floors rolled eagerly down the college hillside.

Joany stopped – she turned to point along the curve of the freeway, indicating our destination, and then her hand relaxed in mid-air, and a strange, confused look passed silently across her face. She frowned at something behind me, and then I heard a sound that brought the sweat out on my face and hands. It was a low, guttural growl.

I turned slowly, peeking around the edge of my hood as the fence behind me swung into view. Standing directly opposite us, nose pressed up against the wire fence stood a huge, black

Doberman dog. Its ears were small and sharp and pointed, and it held its mouth half open in a tense mask of violence. Around its neck was fitted a small, blobby tracking collar, black rubber cubes and a single silver antenna shining out in the darkness. Spittle hung down from its vicious bottom canines.

The dog took half a look at me and barked sharply. I jumped. It was tremendously loud, the sound echoing along the artificial canyon behind. I broke into a cold sweat, chills running down my spine as panic spread through me and men called out beyond. I turned back to Joany and the sheer look of paralytic terror pinning her features wide open across her face confirmed to me that we could not be discovered here by these men. She was trembling and spinning, looking for something to do. She turned to run along the verge as the dog barked again, and I darted forward, catching her by the elbow and steering her towards the water.

The calls of men were drawing closer as I lay down on the hard concrete ledge and swung my legs into the icy water. I meant to slip into the filth as quietly as possible, but my feet splashed the surface below, and the shock of the cold weakened my grip. Joany's jaw trembled and opened repeatedly as she hung from the edge and lowered herself in, she squeaked and I could see her chest contracting, her whole body curling up as the cold hit her and she swallowed her cries.

There were footsteps now, a voice addressing the dog that continued to bark and growl with iron determinations as we shivered in the slime and tried desperately to find purchase on the sheer concrete wall rising above. The cold attacked us both. The water only reached my chest, but was almost to Joany's chin, and her teeth began chattering. Her head lolled around uncontrollably. I reached over and pressed her mouth closed more than a little harshly, and she looked at me with something between murderous indignation and gratitude.

The stagnant shallow end of this isolated finger of floodwater was truly filthy. A dead end for all the trash and disease that was funnelled up the canal. The surface was black and calm – thick with a layer of grimy oil and littered with plastic candy wrappers and splintered wood. A dead sea bird hung in the murk between us, its eyes glittering with the rainbow slick of oil. Its smell was explosively foul but its oil coating was too toxic to rot through, and it floated there, a bundle of stumpy, brittle feathers with the neck of a condom emerging from its throat. I gagged and batted the water away between us, trying to suck it out into the channel as quickly as I could. Joany's eyes were wide with horror as they tracked the evil stinking carcass floating by her chin, but to her credit she kept her mouth clamped firmly shut.

The voices drew closer and somewhere that damned dog continued to growl. Its handler could not convince it that there was nothing to see. Other men shouted and ran along the fence, their heavy steps thudding in the dirt. With panic I realised that I had no idea which side of that fence they were on. We huddled by the concrete wall enclosing the freeway and I jumped as a dazzling white streak burst out onto the slick water to the left of us. And then another. The long beams of light stretched out in wide, sweeping arcs along the black, cutting out before they reached us, overshadowed as we were by the wall at our backs.

I swallowed dryly as I heard the voice of the handler calming his animal, whispering, stroking, saying there was no one here, no one here. At the same time I heard slow, heavy footsteps drawing nearer and nearer.

I looked at Joany and pointed behind her and along the canal towards deep water. Her eyes grew wider and she shook her head vehemently, but the blazing beams swept inexorably towards our position and I reached out, drawing my finger clawlike across her throat, slowly evoking the universal death sign of the cutthroat. For a moment I saw the youngster's face crumple in the darkness, watched as her eyes screwed shut and her lips puckered tightly, and I believed she would crack.

Joany swallowed and forced her eyes open, staring into the deep blackness of my sodden hood, holding my gaze. I was caught, and held her pleading stare firm with my black, beady pig's eyes. She wanted to trust me. She needed to believe in that one moment that I knew how to get through this.

I could not break her shuddering gaze and she held her eyes wide with the question. I matched her stare firm and calm, even though the terror and the wicked icy cold were eroding my will and my being. 'We had a deal,' I said with my masklike stare. 'We had a deal, we're not done yet.' And we hung there, locked together by our glassy windows for a second or an hour, until Joany gulped again and blinked, nodding vigorously and turning in the water.

Joany pushed along the wall, heading for deep water. The wavelets lapped noisily around use and she scrabbled desperately against the oil-ridden concrete – there was nothing to cling to. She gasped breathily and I saw her body dip and slide to one side as she finally went out of her depth, and she tilted her head back, struggling to keep her head above water.

The girl was on the verge of panic, shivering uncontrollably as we splashed the oil slick around us, heading further along the canal side I prayed for something to cling to as the water swirled and the footsteps above approached and I desperately wanted to smile at her, to reassure her to comfort her, to keep her together, but my skull's mask was the last thing she needed to see. The lights swept around again, the centre of their arc closer this time, and I pushed on as Joany swam ahead, the filth reaching my chin.

My entire body was numb, I couldn't feel my legs, so when I stepped out and lost my footing on the slime below I didn't realise I was going over until I had already reached out and slapped the water with my free hand. My eyes widened with the resounding noise.

"Hey! Hear that?" Thundered a voice from above. Joany turned to me in horror, and I heard the thud of running from behind. One of the flashlight beams wobbled up and down across the water and I pointed desperately down into the murk in front of Joany's face. For a sliver of a second I thought she would refuse as her eyes crinkled at the corners, but she looked up towards the bank and the approaching footsteps and drew a breath as I put my palm on her head and forced her down. In the same moment, I tore down my hood with my left hand, and lay in the water over the struggling, wriggling, protesting form below. I turned my head to the side, showing my ruined face through the slime, and pushing all of my weight down on the terrified girl below, who was slowly drowning there alone in the darkness.

A brilliant burst of light shot through my oil-slicked eye, I clamped my jaw shut and tensed every single muscle in my body in a desperate bid to stop my uncontrollable shivering. This does not help, it does the opposite, and my free arm jagged back and forth violently in the water. Joany thrashed below, and with my body tense I began to sink in the swirling water, unable to breathe and feeling the slime crawl up my nose, across my face and into my ears.

"Urgh,' came a voice from above, gurgling and fuzzy through the oil in my ears.

"Man come see this, it's totally gross."

"What is it?"

"Come see."

"Well, what is it?"

"Come see for yourself."

I felt Joany thrash as bubbles escaped from her lungs and rushed about me.

"I ain't looking unless you tell me. It could be something really shitty comin' from you."

"What the fuck is that supposed to mean? Just come over here and take a fuckin look alright!"

"Just tell me what it is Michael, Jesus!" The distant man roared.

"Alright! Christ! It's a fish or something, nibbling on some old guy. Looks like he's been in there a while too."

I felt the thrashing beneath me slow and weaken. Joany was having spasms. A second light crossed over my submerging face, dazzling me as I held my breath and tried to be still. It flicked off.

"That's fuckin disgusting Mickey, OK? It's disgusting. Get that sick shit outta your head."

I heard footsteps receding, and another voice follow.

"Oh c'mon, don't be a jerk! Hey should we fish him out? Hey maybe it was a gator! Lets fish him out!"

The light passed away with the distant voices. Joany was barely moving beneath me, I felt the ripples of her little spasmodic kicks. There were no bubbles. I was afraid she would gasp loudly when I brought her up. I relaxed my body – which immediately improved my own shivering and, tipping my head out of the water, I took in a huge breath over my filthy lips and teeth. I pulled Joany up toward me and pushed my scarred lips to hers under the water, pushing air into her lungs, and I think spraying a good deal of filthy water in too. It was only later that I realised how stupid I had been.

Joany convulsed under water. Her whole body flicked outward, and then she was writhing and flopping and kicking for the surface. I held her mouth shut as she broke through the thick, soft slime, holding her around the shoulders and pinning one arm. She stared at me, wide eyed and confused as her free arm waved wildly in the air above her head. She twisted her face, desperate for breath, I held her vicelike, struggling to keep my hand to her face as her ribs contracted and she tried to cough.

"Breathe quiet or we die." I hissed.

She nodded desperately and I released her nose a little as

she exhaled, blowing plugs of oil and grime out of her nostrils, and then I loosened my hand from around her mouth.

The girl breathed in, wheezing, her red eyes wide with confusion and terror. She scratched for breath and her throat gargled, her body convulsed again as her brain processed the deep, hypothermic cold and the sheer black aloneness of drowning. I knew that we very soon had to get out of the water, but the concrete wall rose three feet above our heads. Joany's eyes went wide again as she shuddered another breath in, and then her face screwed up, her eyelids tightly shut. For a horrid moment I saw her confused panic well up and I thought she might scream. I wanted to slap her. I clamped my hand around her mouth so tightly that her eyes bugged out in panic and I drew her ear to my lips.

"No. Don't crack. Don't crack. You're alive. You're alive here and now, do you hear me? Everything will be fine as long as you stay quiet. Or we can die here. Don't crack up."

I listened for voices in the distance as Joany's eyes told me she understood. The two men were halfway to Ocean Avenue – not far enough. I gripped the girl around the shoulders and paddled backwards with wide, slow, underwater strokes of my free arm. Joany alternated between spasmodic shuddering and going completely limp, and I had to hold her above water. I found my footing again and walked backwards, slipping and faltering, until the girl's feet touched the ground, although it didn't seem that she could stand on her own. The water dropped away from us as we made our way up the submarine slope of the tarmac, and I held our position fast once I could see over the concrete walls at ground level. Joany had stopped shaking and I was afraid that she was going into hypothermic shock.

The dog was nowhere to be seen. I felt dizzy and nauseous with relief. Two figures in padded jackets were swinging their flashlights across the blacktop slip road above. The sharp metal forms of automatic rifles hung from their shoulders. Watching them crawl along for the twenty seconds or so it took them to reach Ocean Avenue and turn away was agony. I kept looking back and forth from their disappearing forms to Joany, checking she was still conscious. She blinked back at me, dizzy and serene, head lolling on her shoulder, quite unsure what all the fuss was about.

As soon as the police had broken the line of sight I grabbed Joany under the shoulders and dragged her out of the water. I stumbled as I laid her on the ground, and I sat by her limp body feeling helpless and numb. She looked at me silently and began to shiver again, and I pulled her wet clothes off. The only thing I could offer her was water and the analgesics from a pilfered first aid kit.

A pulse of dread ran through me. It was something akin to vomiting whilst being hit by a freight train. Where was the bag? The water? The still! I ran along the verge above the canal, looking down desperately for the oblong form of the bag in the concealed depths below. The bag had been hung around my shoulder when the dog spotted us. I reached the point where I thought we had slipped into the muck, and tearing my sticky, sodden, icy gown off, fighting to pull off my leaden boots I once again lowered myself into the filth.

The cold hit me for a second time. And I gasped. My arms and legs were numb, and bright starbursts of pain flowed across my skin and into my joints as the pins and needles bit into me. I reached out desperately in the slime before me, trying to feel my way through the water. I felt through the layer where the oil floated on top, by now my skin was thoroughly coated and slick with grease. *No insulation*, I thought bitterly, clenching my jaw to prevent my teeth from chattering loudly.

I pushed through the water as quietly as I could, bending down to reach along the gritty bottom with my hands, and then my fingertips as the water rose around my nostrils, strangling me of breath. Twisted bits of metal crossed my palms, and shards of broken glass, but no bag! Soon I had to hold my breath and duck my head to cover the depth of water in front of me, and then I was out of my depth, duck diving and scrabbling desperately towards the tarmac floor, searching with increasing panic for stolen treasure.

I broke through the surface, heaving for breath and trying to see as the oil seared my eyes. It seemed that this was the spot where we'd played dead, the spot where we'd hung lifeless and terrified in the icy toxic mucous. It all looked the same. One long black spill of bile running down a uniform concrete channel, I had no idea how far along I was, or where the bag was. This looked like the spot. It all looked the same. The only light in this trench of hell bounced sickly from the glossy, smothering slick of filthy shiny oil. It must be it. Had the bag floated? Had it sunk? Was it somewhere under the thick, evil layer of oil that stretched out forever ahead of me?

As the cold seized up my muscles and seeped into my brain I began to get confused. It all looked the same, I didn't know where I was. I didn't know the way out and I could barely move my stony legs. I turned and turned, aware that I was in a channel and that there were two directions I could go. A sick point of light caught my eye and I stopped. The beady glare of the dead seagull was trained on me, accusing me, laughing at me. It was further on, and I struck out along the side wall towards that hollow bird, confused and hopeful, encouraged and repulsed.

I dived again, feeling my chest contract stiffly in the icy water, clenching my eyes against the burning poisonous waste. I stretched out desperately for the bottom I couldn't see, and I felt rough, wet tarmac and then something flat and hard and smooth. Beyond that my hands shivered across broken bottles and crumpled drinks cans, but no bag. My lungs ached to bursting and as I twisted below the surface my head ran against something rough and flexible. I recoiled in shock, and then reached out to feel the canvas texture, the rounded form, the lumpy contents and the free floating strap. The bag! I exhaled in delight, and thrashed out excitedly for the surface, dragging the strap with me.

I gulped air as I burst through the oil slick, desperate to escape the water, reaching out with one numb hand whilst the other clasped tightly around the canvas strap that tugged hope along behind it. The bag hung lopsided in the water – one end buoyant with air pockets, the other heavy with the waterlogged reservoir of the still. I turned in the night, looking for the way out and thrashing my way along the wall. The bridges were ahead of me. I was heading the right way as long as the bridges of the interchange were ahead of me.

I reached out numbly, clawing my way through the water, unable to control my frozen body or the noise I made. I struggled and fought in the heavy slick, desperate to keep my head above water as my body cramped and the muscles in my chest seized up, contracting my arms uselessly, inevitably inward. Over and over I felt the nauseating slip of oil filling my nose and lovingly plugging my ears, smothering me softly until my mind shrieked in sheer uncontrollable panic. Every time I would thrash out with a burst of terror and pain in my frozen muscles, choking as I exploded through the cloying, dragging surface. I fought for my life inching my way through the water and then the paralysing pain would set into my muscles and the process of drowning slowly would begin again and again and again until I was crying silently,

Samuel Collins

wide eyed with madness and terrorised by a hellish loop of death revisiting me again and again.

It was an age before the tarmac returned beneath my feet and then I dragged myself along the wall, choking back fits of delirium, tugging the bag along after me. As the water level dropped, every step became easier, but the icy bite of the breeze against my exposed skin increased in compensation. Soon I was clawing against the tarmac below, scraping my way out of the canal, dragging the sodden and leaking bag behind me. The padding around the still had absorbed a lot of water, and the bag's weight had increased immensely. It felt like it was filled with lead bricks, and I left it just above the water line.

I crawled up the slope to Joany and fell to the ground at her feet. Shuddering with the cold, I struggled to pull my wet pants off. My numb fingers could barely grasp the zipper, I could hardly grip the slimy material to tug. I looked up at the girl – she'd rolled on to her side and lay shivering, convulsing in the foetal position. There was a faint smell of vomit hanging in the air around her. Lying there, curled up in a ball like that she looked peaceful, and I began to feel the pull of rest – how good it would feel to lie down and sleep off the heaviness pressing my limbs down. It would be lovely to rest, lovely as my mind ran from the sucking terror of the canal, and fatal as hypothermia sucked us gently into oblivion. I crawled up to Joany and turned her over. Her eyes were half closed, and she gazed through me with no recognition. I shook her shoulders weakly.

"Wwaake up! Donnt sleeeep. Muss-sssnt," the words shuddered through me hoarsely.

Joany moaned and her eyes swivelled towards me, I realised my oilslicked death mask was naked, not hidden, as confused shock flitted across her features and her body stiffened minutely. I pushed my finger in her mouth to clear the vomit and she gagged a little, convulsing and trying to sit up. She was weak and lethargic, and we both felt the intoxicating pull of sleep. I knew we had to get warm fast. I struggled to stand, and pulled the girl up with me, crying out as my stiff muscles stretched. Joany lolled across my body as I held her under the shoulders, the cold sweat of her throat wavering under my nose. The odour was one of oil and vomit and spittle, but the sensation – the sensation I had to suppress was a fragile stream of delicate warmth running in a line up the side of her neck, inviting me, calling to me, enticing me, and the black serpent Addiction writhed through my guts with

184

the force of a crowbar strike.

I shook my head hard – I needed her still, and I dragged the girl towards the overpass ahead. I left her in the shadows beneath the bridge, leaning against a concrete pillar and mumbling nonsensically to herself. I stumbled down to the water's edge and dragged the bag up, my arms shuddering and my shoulders aching as the last of the water ran off my skin and the goosebumps rose in the chill air. It felt good to move. Every inch of me ached stiffly and burst with icy pain, but movement warmed my joints.

I knelt by Joany, talking to her softly and rummaging through the bag with speedy desperation. I grabbed the blowtorch head and screwed on a gas cylinder, clicking the ignition desperately and swearing as the gas hissed away into the air. The flame rushed forth on the seventh or eighth click, and I squeaked in delight. Joany looked at me and leant towards the silly, searing flame. There was nothing to burn under the bridge, so I pulled everything out of the bag and emptied out all of the plastic containers and wrappers, piling them up against the concrete pillar. I lit the small stack and it sizzled with filth and groundwater – the first aid box, an empty pill bottle, some plastic wrap and a sterile-sealed (and mercifully dry) bandage. I waved the blowtorch over the plastic, drying it until it bubbled and burned with a thin blue flame and a thick, bitter smoke. Joany leant eagerly toward the tiny pyre, hugging her shoulders, saying nothing. When the pathetic fire was done I turned the flame of the blowtorch up and set it against the concrete. Soon the blackened masonry was flaking and radiating heat, and the warmth slowly seeped into my body, loosening my joints and thawing my extremities so that I could feel the steel sharp, icy pain in earnest.

I took a bottle of water and some soggy paper wadding from the remnants of the bag's contents, and flushed the oily slurry from the gash in my shin, wiping the sticky black filth away. Afterwards I rinsed my mouth, spitting repeatedly, but the toxic taste remained under my tongue, stuck to my teeth, the sour odour wafting through my sinuses. Joany clasped the bottle eagerly with both hands when I offered it – she had been watching me in greedy anticipation every time I spat.

"Don't swallow – you'll make yourself sick."

The girl nodded knowingly and tipped her head back, gurgling and spitting repeatedly with disgust and gusto before taking a long draft and draining the bottle. She handed the bottle back to me carelessly as if there was something I could do with it. I set it in the path of the torch jet and watched blankly as it shrivelled and melted to nothing. My mind was empty.

I looked at Joany carefully, the warmth and feeling returning to my body, the painful shivers and spasms subsiding and rolling on again. She looked at me, following my stare upwards to the burned flesh of my face, and then she looked away.

"Which way?" I croaked. Joany blinked and stared blankly into the darkness of the overpass for a moment, before turning out and looking in the direction of the canal. She pointed, hand hanging too loosely from her flaccid arm.

"How far?" I asked, "How long?" for midnight was upon us.

"One –" she said. She swallowed stiffly and shook her head a little, struggling to move from one thought to the next. "Hour. One. Less." She shook her head again and dismissed the conversation with a disinterested flap of her hand.

"Can you go on?"

She turned her head slowly and glared.

13

We sat in silence, barely a foot from each other but alone with our thoughts as the horrors of the water ran through our minds and the darkness ran across our faces, flitting back and forth from me to her to me. She wouldn't look at me, not my ruined face, the shrivelled claws that had held her under, nor my scarred and naked body. So we sat alone, waiting for the warmth to revive our bodies and tending to the shudders in our minds.

I huddled by that warm pillar, wanting to move and shield my stiff muscles from the breeze, but not knowing how. In my mind I was drowning, I was still endlessly, repeatedly drowning. The oil closed over my face and darkness came to swaddle me as my body seized up and the bag promising life dragged me down.

Again and again the blackness washed over me in waves and I found myself staring into the thin blue light of the blowtorch, desperate for any light and hope, desperate to anchor myself in the reality of here and now, alive and free, huddled in the patchy heat under an abandoned road bridge. I knew we had to move on once the cold in our bodies had passed from the sucking, icy kiss of the water to the mundane chill of being naked in the night. I felt the transition come slowly upon me as I worshipped, palms out before the heat of the statuesque pillar, and I watched Joany out of the corner of my eye, she sat cross-legged, hugging her knees across her immature breasts, and when the uncontrollable, thundering spasms that ran through her body subsided into general, all-over shivering across her grease-smeared flesh I knew it was time.

I turned the lamp off and Joany inched closer and closer to the fading warmth as I packed the bag, squeezing water out of soggy wadding and tipping it out of pockets. We wrung out the clothes. Damp and oil-ridden, they slipped uselessly through our hands and jealously retained most of their water. Shivering, we put them on anyway, the slime and grit clinging to our skin, before hurrying out from the hidden safety of the shelter, stiff and aching and silent, praying that there was no one watching from the road above. We crept along the verge between the college fence and the canal, struggling to move against shock as our cramped muscles screamed. Gooseflesh rose against the wind that coursed along the channel and bit through our sodden clothes.

I began to move faster in a bid to beat the cold, but weakness and gathering hunger cut through me like the wind. I pushed on along the fence and the scrub, pressed on away from the bridge and the overpass and the men with guns searching the avenue. I checked over my shoulder with obsessive paranoia. We were bent double and crawling along the shadows, but I was terrified of the prospect of being discovered, of seeing a dark figure with a gun silhouetted on the bridge behind. Equally fatal was the possibility of a dog discovering us, if it was still on the campus, still hunting for my scent. We would die, we would die if we were discovered, either from a bullet or the sucking black water – we were so far from the shallows and I doubted I could face the icy slick again.

My heart lightened as we stumbled further and further along the muddy verge, away from the gunmen, and I began to believe we could make it. My stiff gait loosened and my aching muscles didn't seem to catch the cold so much. There was a noise in the channel and across the campus above us. The irregular burst of machine gun fire. Retaliation. I stopped dead and had to catch myself from standing in astonishment before I crouched to the ground. Fear slithered clammy over my shock. I remember the cold damp firmness of the mud against my toes. I looked back at Joany who was close behind and glaring at me with a look alternating between wide-eyed terror and accusatory bile. I rested, bent double with my arms pushing up from the knees, listening to the random staccato rhythm of murder in the night. The fire raged along the hilltop above, illuminating the low clouds and silhouetting buildings down the slope. I caught Joany's face in the dim orange gloaming. She hated me just then.

We were almost past the campus, and Balboa Park hung in the darkness across the water. As I rested, shivering and sweating in the night breeze, the stiffness returned to my bones and my stomach cramped with a nausea provoked by gnawing hunger. Joany scowled as I held my belly, and she took the lead with bitter and pointed impatience.

The verge widened out into a broad slope beyond the campus and we came to streets and houses rising up the hill in a flowing terrace. I hissed at Joany and nodded to the left, leading her to the corner where two streets met along the boundary of the verge. I walked across the yard of the nearest house and around to the side, and Joany followed me into the back yard, sullen, too exhausted for warnings or arguments or fear.

Fishing for my gun in the filth-ridden bag, I broke the kitchen window clumsily with the butt and lifted the catch, gingerly pushing the splintered glass from the sill with my sleeve before climbing through. Joany hauled herself through the window wordlessly and stood in the shadowy kitchen, looking around and brushing her hands off. She set about opening cupboards and quickly withdrew boxes and packets. She dug her hand into an open cereal box and shovelled clumps of stale cornflakes into her mouth with a desperate, shaking urgency. She barely gave herself time to breathe, and cared nothing for the dangerous filth she was spreading from her hands to her food.

As I watched her fevered grasping I saw how thin and wasted she was beneath the thin, wet top that grabbed at her skin. Her ribs were visible all the way up to her shoulders, and her unformed breasts sagged, sallow and unrealised beneath waterlogged fabric. Her limbs were stick like – concave from the wideness of her bony joints, painfully thin and slack with wasted flesh where muscle should be. She looked up from eating and glared at my staring, her hand hanging in mid-air somewhere between the box and her mouth. I turned away, grabbed my bag and headed into the hall. I checked the hallway doors for a basement and, reassured once I'd found it, I turned and climbed upstairs.

I was too cold to notice the details of the house – the personal touches that I defaced as I smeared my evil black footprints on the deep pile carpet and trailed my fingers unsteadily along the walls. I paid no attention to the ornaments in the bathroom as I went through the medicine cabinet for antibiotics and disinfectant. I had to make do with the bleach under the faucet. I filled the bath with an inch of cold water from the hot tap, and criminally I washed in it. I scoured my skin with soap and a nailbrush and a bleach soaked flannel, eager to remove the grease before the shivering set in. Most of the black came off on the towels, and I left the bathroom filthy, sticky and rancid. Once I was dry I worked on my wound, scraping the flesh with towelling 'til it had turned from black to red and bloody. Pouring bleach over the gash in my shin was akin to cleaning it with acid, but in my weariness I watched the pain through a distant window. I wandered from the room like a zombie. Barely thinking, I returned to get towels for Joany.

189

I didn't look at the family portrait hanging from the wall in the master bedroom, didn't want to see the personality of a real place, of someone's home, I looked only at the contents of the wardrobe. I felt no guilt, no familiar sense of intrusion as I slipped an unknown man's underwear over my shrivelled genitals, only relief. I tugged on thick jeans, big, floppy tennis shoes, and a couple of cardigans with joy and searched the other bedrooms for girl's clothes. There was no girl's room, and I had to make do with boy's things. I took two pairs of pants, two sweaters, two of everything plus a hoodie for myself, and I found an empty sports bag at the bottom of the closet. I passed the sodden contents of my bag into the sports bag. I winced as I unwrapped the fragile glass condenser element of the still, and flushed with relief when I found it intact. I wrapped it in a sweater and placed it in the new bag.

I took everything down to Joany in the kitchen, and found that she had packed several plastic carriers full of food. She was sitting on a counter top, fingers in mouth, can of cat food in hand, and she froze as I entered, wide eyed and naïve as if I'd caught her in the fridge at midnight. I handed her towels and pointed to the sink. She scraped the can thoroughly clean before sliding off her perch and going over to the sink, raising an eyebrow at me in pointed disbelief and turning the empty cold tap. She gave me another teenage glare and I sighed, stepping over to put the plug in the basin and twist the hot tap. I noted how she backed off as I leant across her and over the sink, but I had to smile when the thin trickle flowed from the faucet and she squeaked in delight. She scooped the water into her mouth with black hands until I handed her the dish soap and made her scrub the oil away, and then she drank again in endless gulps. I pointed upwards and Joany made for the hallway.

"We should rest here." My voice cracked.

Joany looked back at me, shrewd eyes gauging. "I can make it."

"Really, we should sleep through the day, should, should hide out."

"I said I can make it."

I shrugged, defeated, no way to confess that it wasn't her I was concerned for.

"Five minutes then," I said as Joany headed from the room.

I slid down to the floor, my back to the kitchen cabinet, and then I rolled onto my side, drawing my knees under my chin to keep warm. My eyelids drooped. The floor was hard and cold, somehow its solidity was comforting. I realised there was no way to measure five minutes. I let my muscles relax but fought dangerous sleep, forcing my eyes open every time soft black unconsciousness closed in. I heard Joany clamber down the stairs and pushed myself upright, grabbing at the edge of the counter above to help me stand. Joany caught me rising.

I was relieved to see the girl washed and dressed and pulling a towel slowly through her hair. Her hair was only slightly cleaner than the towel. Now that we were both clothed and also, I suspect, now that much of my face was concealed by a teenager's hoodie, we were able to resume our normal, awkward glances in safety.

"I lost my glasses. In the water," she said, still bent double with the towel to her head.

"You going back for them?" I grunted. The girl stiffened. We said nothing more. She finished with her hair and dumped the towel on the floor before going over to the bags of food. For a horrid moment she looked at me as if to offer food, but then she frowned and turned her back, stuffing clothes into the tops of the bags. She stamped her feet into wide, spongy sneakers and began to haul herself onto the counter top by the window. I led her into the hallway and searched half-heartedly for overcoats. To my surprise I found some under the stairs. We left respectably – via the front door. It felt so *normal*, shutting that door behind me and dropping down those front steps. Only then did I begin to wonder what had become of the three people that had lived in that little house. They hadn't even packed.

Joany led me back along the canal with renewed vigour. She seemed more alive with fresh clothes on her back and food in her belly, but she hadn't forgiven me. She tripped along at a pace, refusing to look back, refusing to wait for me. The water stretched out into a wide channel with a string of shallow islands between the drowned floodplains of SoMa and us. To the right, streets and houses descended beneath the waves in rows, like layers of cardboard set end-on. To the left, the crescent of hills and gulleys curled round leading from Bernal Heights to Twin Peaks. The streets curved away up the gentle slope, and we were left following the bank of the widening channel as it broke across the sinking concrete boundary of the freeway.

Joany's mood changed as we went on, she stiffened, becoming sullen, and her pace slowed as we neared our destination. There was a faint new foulness drifting on the breeze, but I doubted it was strong enough that she could smell it. It was different from the canal smell – all oil and fish rot – this was the bouquet of the grave. We followed the water, climbing up the verge, and the streets gave way to what used to be a park – really just a rough strip of ground covered in flattened tents, squares of canvas and tarpaulin, and muddy blankets.

As we crossed onto the field the smell rolling down the slope grew stronger, more definite. Joany slowed to a stop and began to shake, her shoulders hanging loose and limp.

"Camp 14," she whispered as I drew up beside her. For once she looked up at me, and her expression was one of helplessness. She pointed across the field to the first of a series of low slung and collapsing wooden sheds in the far corner by the water. "Boat's in there," she said through her sleeve as she sniffed and wiped a tear bitterly from her cheek.

I moved on, leaving her at the edge of the park with her private sorrow. The field was a gentle, uphill slope, complete with uprooted trees and battered amenities – a toilet block towards the lumpy crest above, a children's playground bulldozed and ruined in one corner. This was St Mary's Park. I had known it a century ago, when it had been grass and trees, and wonderful borders of shrubs and sweet, night-flowering Nicotiana. There used to be allotments and the playground, steps up to tennis courts and a baseball field before the hill had been graded and levelled. It seemed very different now, a wasteland of trash and emptiness devoid of the life I had enjoyed.

The grass had been trodden underfoot and churned into mud. Everywhere I looked the ground was embedded with garbage – tent poles and plastic bottles, foil packets and waxed paper cartons of Government Issue rations. The ground was uneven, and several times on my way to the sheds I crossed the churned mud imprints of caterpillar tracks that had driven straight over tents and camps, indenting the thin materials into the ground and crushing metal tent pegs as if they were liquorice laces.

Exhausted and jittery from hunger, and with a growing limp in my leg, I stumbled on the rough ground as I made my way to the shed at the foot of the water. The sick perfume of old death grew a little stronger as I crossed the field, it began to coat the back of my throat. The entire park felt empty, deserted, and somehow violated, haunted by a lingering sense of menace. As I drew closer to the abandoned sheds I saw that they were little more than a series of wooden fence panels wrapped around piles driven into the mud. There were three structures running in a line up the hill, the one furthest up had almost completely collapsed – the piles had snapped or rotted through and the panels had slanted over and tumbled under the sagging felt roof. It looked something like a cardboard box that someone had pushed down underfoot – each side had been rolled over into a rhombus rather than crumpled. The middle structure was still standing, if slightly slanted and droopy, and it showed signs of repair. The same wooden fence stakes which had gone to make the piles were wedged up against the leaning walls in a desperate bid to hold the sides up, but the wind and the rain had clawed through the gaps between warped fence panels, and the rotting wooden structure was slowly being torn apart. The sheds were arranged end on in a line, each had a series of double doors facing the next so you could walk between them. They were large rooms and I guessed they were for storage – warehouses almost. The final building was almost completely upright, and although the lower foot of the wooden panels was black and speckled – soggy with rot, the structure showed less signs of damage. The far end, nearest the middle shed had been repaired and braced, and heavy chains and padlock held the doors closed. I stood in the muddy alley between the sheds and considered checking the doors at the other end – the end by the water's edge. Then I noted the foot wide gap between the solid wooden doors and the adjoining fence panels, and I simply pushed my way past the warped wood.

It was completely dark inside, and I fumbled around in the bag for my flashlight amidst the scent of seaweed and rotten fish. When I rubbed the lens clean and flicked the lamp on I was confronted with rows of shelves made from steel studwork strips, and piles of empty boxes – cartons stamped 'U.S. Govt. Wheat flour' and 'Cal State Soya Mix', empty crates marked 'U.S.DEF PolyVax REFRIGERATE'. I stepped forward over the mud floor, and came to piles of fishing nets and weights and crab pots that smelled salty and rank. The nets had been piled against the walls and a path cleared through the chaos, and I pushed through to a line of empty oil barrels and water tanks that barred my view ahead.

The barrels were lined up in rows all the way across the warehouse, stacked several layers deep as they receded into the shadows. I didn't search for a route, I simply dropped my bag and crawled over the stack awkwardly. I climbed down next to a large, square oil tank that was set on piles of bricks above the mud. It smelled strongly of gas. The flammable liquid dripped softly from a tap set at the bottom of the tank, and there were footprints in the greasy mud around the puddle of gas.

I had come to a chamber at the far end of the shed and could see that the doors beyond were braced from the inside with fencing stakes. I didn't care. What interested me was a small boat between there and here, lying tilted on its belly on the compacted earth. I went over to the little plastic hull and lay my hands on the gunwale in relief. Formed in one piece in bright yellow, the hull was big enough for two people and a little cargo. I was overjoyed to find a small gasoline outboard engine clamped to the stern.

There was little else in the cramped space at the end of the shed – a pile of crash buoys in one shadowy corner, a gas can lying on its side in the mud by the oil drums. Rope hung from the rafters in various lengths, looped and coiled around the rough-hewn wooden frame. I unscrewed the gas cap of the outboard with the wondrous slow precision of an old man savouring a new toy, and rocked the engine on its gimbals a little to see the level of the fuel as it sloshed somewhere about half empty.

It was then, with the little gushing noises of the gas crashing against the plastic walls of its tank and the peaks of its miniature waves glinting in the beam of my flashlight that stiffness spread from my coccyx all the way along my stooped spine. As I peered down into that little circular hole to gaze on a miniature flammable ocean I felt the icy beam of a stranger's stare fall across my exposed neck. I was being watched, I was sure of it. The stiffness slowed my movements as chilly fear spread through my body, culminating in shivers running across my scalp and zinging down my spine. I tried to finish my task calmly and normally, to appear as if I'd not noticed the intruder whilst I slowly screwed the gas cap on, but my heart thundered loudly in my chest and I had to fight back the urge to turn and stab at the darkness with my light. I sniffed the air slowly and silently, hunting for a trace of my opponent. The air tasted of gas and wood rot, fishiness and the thrumming, earthy undertone of the mud floor. Something else lacing the air, rather faint and delicate beyond the chemical tang of gasoline – greasy air and a little body odour, high and sour – a woman.

But I hadn't sensed her presence, hadn't smelt her, hadn't heard her breathe, and so her gender left me feeling no less threatened. I felt suddenly naked and vulnerable and it made no sense. In confusion and annoyance I stretched out my senses into the ether whilst pretending to fumble with the air valve on the gas cap. The darkness fell away as empty space unfurled before me and the shadows of the unseen emerged from the chaotic fuzz of the ether. There. There it was. Behind me in the far corner where the walls had met a line of empty oil drums there perched an unusual mind, cold and expectant, folding its thoughts over itself protectively in the darkness. It barely glimmered, cool blue-violet filaments, and it recoiled in the illumination of my conscious attention. I began to get a sense of self, the face before the mind examining me, and I straightened, opening my eyes. The game was up.

I turned my body and my light in the same movement, and there before me, standing tall in the darkest corner was a woman – another being like myself, gas can hanging from one hand. I was stunned. She stared back at me, unblinking, and met my gaze of shock with anger and fear. She stood tall and regal, looking at me with her dark eyes. Her hair was straggly and greasy around her face, but her skin was pale, and her features fine. Her eyes were large and endlessly deep beneath her light brow, and her long nose led to a delicate, thin-lipped mouth. She held herself still as we looked at each other in surprise, her self-control betrayed her presence of mind but not her age, for she was young, very young. I guessed at somewhere between twenty and a hundred, such a dangerous first century.

She studied me as I studied her, those hungry eyes rolling over my ruined face and stealing every detail in mounting horror. I found myself wanting to reach up and pull the inadequate hood further over my brow, for her eyes were sharp and accurate, better than mine I was quite sure. I didn't move – I daren't break the moment and set her free. How long had it been since I'd laid eyes on another creature like myself? Another with my wants and needs, another mind that understood my fate and my sight. It seemed centuries. Lost in time.

She thought me very old, that much I could tell. Her glance flitted over my stooped body and hung on my claw-like hands in the reflected glare of the flashlight. Very old indeed. Her disgust peaked as I reached out with my mind, trying to establish a rapport of feelings that could only be open and non-threatening. I felt her shudder, her mind writhe in the ether, and saw her eyes widen in squirming astonishment. Her face was stern and uncomfortable, but also angry. She was angry at my presence, my intrusion into her life. She knew I was older than time and twice as sly – she would not put herself within my grasp. She loathed my extreme age and injuries, she loathed my weakness and she hated me. She hated me for presenting her with the horror she took to be her own fate.

Calmly she took a step forward into the light, and then she turned a sharp left and disappeared down a gap between the oil drums – the passage I hadn't bothered to look for. She thundered through the shed and I bolted after her. She flung the heavy gas tank at me and kicked over crab pots, careful to avoid the piles of netting and line that littered the dirt. As I stumbled over the pots and cages rolling across the floor the woman pushed over a metal shelf and crashed through a soggy wood panel by the doors. I ran around the shelves with my shin screaming in pain, and squeezed past the torn strips of wood and out into the night in time to see her back disappearing into the next shed.

I didn't follow her in – not into another maze of upturned shelves and hand-thrown missiles – I ran over to the lowest part of the sagging roof and hauled myself up, clambering over the treacherously spongy surface until I was higher, and could see over all sides of the building. I waited nervously for the woman to emerge, for the roof creaked and thudded and she must have heard my footsteps above. I was sure the felt and ply would give way and I would crash through, breaking my body against a rafter or falling across oil drums or sharp metal shelves, but I stood still, poised and ready to give chase while my chest gave up breathing and my body shouted in painful jabs.

There was a noise at the far end of the shed – creaking – and then the woman burst out and ran around the wreckage of the third shed and up the muddy slope into darkness. I bolted off the roof, landing hard on my wounded leg, and started loping up the hill as the tingling pain set in and the graveyard scent rose in my nostrils. I scanned the beam of my flashlight across the hillside until I caught her black-clothed figure in the spot, and tracked her across the plain fifty feet ahead of me.

I was losing her. My legs were stiff and leaden and my lungs were a wheezing, spluttering bag full of broken glass. Blood oozed freely from my leg and ran down into my shoe as I stumbled on dizzily, sweating under heavy layers of clothing. The ground was soft and spongy underfoot as I made my way up the hill, and it seemed laced with tree roots and fallen branches for me to stumble on in the darkness, although there were no trees to be seen. Often I lurched into shallow depressions in the trash-strewn turf, or tripped where the mud rose up against me. As the woman seemed to get faster I slowed to a stumbling crawl, and the gap between us grew. I was but halfway across the field as she reached the crest of the hill and mounted the fence that separated the park from the streets beyond. I stood still, breathing heavily in the foul-smelling air and pointing my flashlight up the slope to the wire fence. I watched in the dim, distant light as the woman climbed nimbly over the fence. She twisted at the top and backed down facing me. The only part of her figure that wasn't swathed in black was her face, a ghostly white patch hovering in the night. For a moment she hung in the light at the bottom of the fence, facing me, eyes shining brightly like two stars in a dust cloud. She stared at me, sizing me up, and then she turned fiercely and the stars blinked out all at once. Knowing I was beaten she sauntered casually across the street and into the maze of decaying tract homes beyond.

I stood there, panting and struggling for breath as exhaustion broke out in my muscles and burned through me. Prickling sweat erupted across my skin. Hunger pains stabbed through my belly and as I began to shake I sank to my knees. I kneeled on the soft mud with my hands in my lap and let the flashlight roll to the ground. The beam ran across many short protrusions that broke its path and cut deep shadows out of its spreading glow. For the first time, now that the chase was over and my eye was no longer trained solely on my quarry, I was able to look at them and examine what they truly were. I was regaining my breath and with it my sense of smell. The air was florid – thrumming with the cloying smell of old death – the sweet familiar graveyard odour magnified ten times, a hundred. My sweat ran cold with the realisation. The broken chinks in the light, those roots and branches that had grasped and snagged me as I ran, they were bones. I was standing in the centre of a huge, unmarked bone orchard.

I was horrified and exhausted, both physically and emotionally. I was out of tears for the dead. Unable to get up, unable to move, the sight of it made me want to retch my empty stomach. Bones littered the ground everywhere, leg bones sticking up vertically and breaking the light with their bulbous, flowering ends. The crescents of thousands of rib bones lay scattered over the mud and waste as far as I could see. Teeth and tiny bones in strange, irregular shapes from feet and hands were scattered like dice across the earth. There weren't many bigger bones – I saw few skulls, fewer pelvises – the earth doesn't give them up so easily. As I passed the flashlight across the wasteland before me and saw the numerous sinkholes where the mud had collapsed or the bones had risen up and I saw why – for each sodden depression around me was surrounded by big rat holes. The vermin had turned the ground over and dug up what they could whilst picking it clean. And they had had time to do it.

The idea of thousands of rats beneath me, writhing and squirming, gnawing through guts and giving birth to tiny, pink, wet bundles of needlesharp teeth repulsed me. I leapt up unsteadily and stumbled down the hill as fast as my sagging limbs would allow. I was faced with a disturbing choice – flick the light off and risk falling into a pit of horror – or sweeping the light where I was going, and facing countless body parts – rib cages, arm bones, glasses and jewellery and shoes, reminders of mortality, life, the machinery of my own body splintered and scattered and dumped in the earth like so much garbage. Human garbage – always easy to throw away and forget about, regardless of the era.

I continued down the hill, past the skulls with the perfectly circular bullet holes and hair still clinging to their scalps, past the bloodstained and grease smeared jeans that were chewed through and came complete with the original owner's femur. I kept the light on though I refused to look, and rushed forward into the flickering darkness, eyes fixed on the ramshackle structures below, and the small, living figure of Joany loitering by the side of the boat shed. I tumbled on, legs loose, barely feeling anything through numb, disbelieving shock. I was floppy and almost disinterested – I couldn't take it in any more. I couldn't believe the death scattered so casually around me. It was a bad video set, it was an old Ed Wood flick, it wasn't real, it wasn't real, the brown-stained bones were plaster, it wasn't real.

The ground firmed up beneath me, and with relief I noted the gradual disappearance of bones scattered through the mud. I trod unevenly down the park slope and slowed as I came to the first, ruined shed. With my muscles aching sharply I walked more gently and I fought to control my breath. Joany was looking up with concern, watching me approach and following the loose swing of the flashlight with her gaze.

"What was that?" She asked of the stranger and the chase.

"What was that?" I shook my head and pointed awkwardly

behind me in disbelief, "What was that? What was that?" I shouted, I rasped angrily.

Joany went stiff. "I – we – the, the cops," she stammered, shrinking away from my glare. "The supplies stopped coming. Up the river. They stopped handing out rations. So people stormed the warehouse." Her voice was very small and she looked at me, at my shoulder rather than my face, pleading to stop there. I stared and waited although in truth in the girl's reluctance had chilled me and taken the heart out of my angry, impotent curiosity.

"They rounded us up," she whispered hoarsely, her expression distant and flat. "Everyone they could find. Shot us. All." The girl was shaking, and her jaw chattered as silent tears wandered down her cheeks. She choked, she refused to sob. I saw the horror in her eyes. My only defence against the shame of rousing her pain was panic and denial.

"Over a warehouse?" I said bitterly. "I don't believe it." I stalked off and left the girl weeping in the darkness.

I pushed through the large hole in the flimsy wooden slats and made my way through the warren, still angry and bitter and secretly embarrassed. I retrieved my bag from where it lay by the row of oil drums and blue plastic water barrels, relieved to see it, and followed the barrels along in the darkness until I came to the pathway that led to the boat. I scooped the gas can from the floor and found it was heavy and full – perhaps the woman had been filling the outboard. I completed her unfinished task and hunted around for more cans that I filled from the square tank in the corner.

I hurried, aware that there was maybe an hour and a half left, perhaps two hours until absolute sunrise, I could feel the panic surging up from my scorched soul. I kicked the oil tank, hearing gas slosh around in the bottom, guessing that there was a little of the precious liquid left – maybe another five gallons. After stashing the cans and the bag in the boat, I ran back through the shed, looking for jars, bottles, anything that I could carry that would hold liquid. It was all cardboard boxes and empty crates. I gave up, and wondered if I should get Joany in to search, but I didn't want to. I didn't want to see her.

I was getting greedy anyway – losing time so I could bring back more than I could comfortably carry from the boat. I hurried back to the vessel and placed my hands on the gunwale, and stopped. I looked back into the dark corner by the oil drums. Had I really seen her there in the shadows? Another of my kind? How long had it been since I'd stumbled across another hunter? I gazed into the empty space and shook myself. No time to ponder. I went over to the doors and pulled away one of the braces.

I held it like a battering ram and beat it against the loose hinges that held the door to a fence post. Soon I broke through the flimsy wood surrounding the metal, and I bent low to repeat the process on the bottom hinge before attacking the other door feverishly. The two flimsy panels fell outwards and hit the ground simultaneously, their stiff frames still padlocked firmly together. Joany was stood at the water's edge watching curiously for the cause of the noise. I waved her over and motioned for her to grasp the prow of the little boat. She ran around to the side of the shed, re-appearing with crinkly white bags of clothes and food that she swung over the gunwale into the prow of the boat. She pulled while I pushed, but the loaded boat was heavy and moved stiffly over the mud. The plastic runners squeaked and shuddered over the wood of the fallen doors, and rocked over the hard chain at their heart. My arms felt weak and achy, and my body shook by the time the prow reached the lapping waterline. Joany let go and stepped around the boat awkwardly, obviously reluctant to go into the black water again.

"Get round the back and push then," I scowled, and limped around the front, pulling the boat into the water with a gasp. Dragging until the water was knee height and the vessel was free floating, I heaved myself over the side as Joany climbed the gunwale. I squealed as she stretched her leg out above my bag and pointed desperately.

"Watch it!' I yelped in my thin, cracking voice. Joany looked up at me sharply as I rolled into the boat, and moved her foot to one side. Then we were both aboard and suddenly drifting out into the channel. I scrambled across the plastic benches and leant over the squirming girl to start the motor, realising with dread that I hadn't tested it, and hadn't searched the shed for oars. I unlocked the gimbals and the propeller arm fell heavy into the water. Reaching over to push the button I knew that if this didn't work we could end up drifting back on the tide, back towards the campus and the fire and the waiting gun sights of the Ocean Avenue law enforcement gangsters.

I pressed the large orange blob of rubber down desperately with my finger. The little ceramic engine sputtered into life, churning the water behind us. I exhaled in relief and pulled myself across the gas cans to settle at the stern. The prow rose dangerously in the water as I opened the throttle and steered the dinghy out along the channel, and I muttered to Joany to sit at the front, waving my hands until she reluctantly complied.

We sat in silence, facing each other uncomfortably, but Joany's bitter stare reached beyond me and hung, I suspect, on the death camp behind us. I ran the engine at full throttle, scanning the water ahead with the flashlight and steering gently and slowly only when the channel curved sharply or the water became rough. I was conscious of the time and the approaching sun, but also afraid that I might capsize the boat with its heavy, sloshing cargo of fuel. We curled and buzzed our way through the narrow channel that ran from Bernal Heights to Potrero Hill, and the choppy water made Joany cling nervously to the sides of the hull.

We ploughed on in silence amidst the bay breeze as we rounded the hill chain, and the channel opened out into the SoMa flood plain ahead. It was too dark to see the line of the freeway below, I simply did my best to follow the calm channels of water, to avoid any submerged buildings looming below the waves. I enjoyed the open water – it was my first opportunity to think and breathe freely, and the last before we passed the Looter's Causeway and the gatehouse.

Joany had said her goodbyes to the death camp in silence, and she assumed I was doing the same. I was not. I wasn't brooding over the murdered hundreds. I wasn't shrugging off the sickening images of the bone orchard or gulping the sea air to escape the cloying perfume haunting my memories. I was thinking of the woman – the killer. The one like me.

I thought back across the lonely centuries, through all the years of hiding in the darkness, to the brief moments when I had glimpsed others, to the fruitless dalliances we had played out whenever we glided through each other's orbits and interrupted our own little spheres of influence. I thought of the uneasy shock of recognition, the fear, the hope, the wonder. I thought of the desperate, tedious chess moves as the inevitable paranoia took over and we scrambled to protect our power and hide our people. Countless allies and servants over the eras. I remembered the endless quiet years, strung along like pearls on a necklace, years where it seemed I was alone in the universe, that no one knew the immortal ebb and flow of time as I did, the years of disbelief and blindness where my own existence no longer seemed real or even possible and I denied my memories more readily than my deeds.

Samuel Collins

Through all these times I felt the mad loneliness, swollen and pregnant beneath the cool surface of my own psyche, the desperate need to see recognition on another living being's face, to know they shared and understood my conscious experience of existence. The woman's features hung in my mind – I could see her long face before me, her eyes peering through the shadows as her pale skin lit up the darkness. She had recognised me. In her solemn, wide-eyed shock she had recognised me for what I was alright. The only look that had crossed her face had been one of hatred.

I stared forward blankly as my own kind hung in my thoughts. The waves lapped at the prow and pushed the little vessel up and down across the water. My face grew damp with salt spray, and my hand grew icy as it clutched the throttle.

"It was 'cos it was empty," Joany shouted across to me from the prow, fighting the thrum of the engine and the wash of the surf. Her face looked troubled and defiant, and it took me some moments to realise what she was talking about. "It wasn't 'cos we broke down the walls or anything that they said it was. It was 'cos the sheds were empty. They had nothing left to give us, and nothing left to take away. Everyone knew."

I nodded silently in understanding. I had no words to offer her, no cheap sympathies. As a word, 'sorry' is worse than useless. It was enough to show her that I understood. The stubborn look melted slowly from Joany's face, and she gazed past me once again, content to stare across the slick black plain of water behind us.

"My words before. I was a fool. I apologize." I shouted weakly above the surf, my scratchy voice sticking in my throat. Joany looked across sharply, examining me in the darkness. After a moment she settled, one corner of her mouth raised in a half smile which quickly dropped.

"How did you survive?" I didn't need to know. I didn't need to induce the pain of remembering. I was curious, and held the solemn, distant respect of one survivor to another.

"Under my Mom." I could barely hear her small voice over the wash of the surf. "She kept pushing me behind her and then she fell and..." Joany turned away. I was careful not to scan the light beam in her direction for some time.

The silence stiffened between me and the girl, thick and sticky like beaten egg whites, and we were each alone with our thoughts at opposite ends of the little vessel. It didn't matter that we were facing one another, the distance swelled between us. I didn't dwell on her tale, or the mass grave we'd set behind us. I was numb and aching, and overwhelmingly weary, too tired to close my eyes lest my consciousness skipped straight into the dreaming. Most of all I realised, as I looked across at the warm little figure of the girl huddled in the prow of the boat, I was dangerously hungry. I clutched the throttle and the gunwale tightly 'til my knuckles ached and I stared out across the bay, but every few moments my thoughts drifted inexorably back to her, to how much I ached, to how easy it would be to crush her life into me. How rich.

I let the thought wash through me, I gave it no humour and spent no effort on fighting it. I had no intention of acting on my hunger. The girl had helped me and we had made a deal that I would fulfil. I froze myself still, enduring the whispering, beckoning torment of the hunger in my veins and squirming inside, struggling to ignore the fragile girl pulsing before me. I bribed myself with thoughts of the blood in my refrigerator just an hour away, resigned myself to enduring the hollow, endless craving of my addictive hunger.

I turned the light off completely as we passed through SoMA, squinting in the darkness and pointing the boat between the lonely figures of distant behemoths as they rose silently out of the waves. We were approaching the Bay Bridge, and I had no desire to attract the looter's attention with my noisy gas engine or my lights. I kept my distance, watching the twinkling lights of the Causeway go by like a distant constellation in the predawn glow. I was nervous though, and found it hard to run the engine fast, terrified that I would drive the boat onto rough waves and take on water – or run her aground and be trapped in a ten by eight Petri dish waiting to be broiled by the sun. As I looked to the bridge in the east my urgency hardened. Fear congealed in my guts, cold and sick – the sky beyond the Berkeley Hills was turning pale.

I pushed the engine harder, as hard as I dared, and the little boat shuddered through the choppy water. Joany clung to the sides, watching in fascination as we passed the Causeway half a mile starboard. I turned the flashlight back on as soon as we were past, checking the water and sending the beam out into the swallowing distance. I gunned the engine and turned continued north up the bay.

I took a wide course around the ruinous sandbanks of the Financial District, fighting the currents, all the while watching the colour of the sky with mounting terror. While the west looked black and familiar, the east was a deep, glowing purple, swelling to a threatening blue low down by the crest of Grizzly Peak. I took the boat past the makeshift jetty where Broadway dived into the water – it was too long a walk up to my tower. Swinging west I followed the curve of the shoreline and urged the boat onwards until I could see the black outline of my building pinned against the glowing sky. I ran the vessel aground gently amidst the tangled flotsam at the foot of the hill, taking the propeller out of the water as the hull scraped noisily over the tarmac and debris. Joany recoiled, clinging to the gunwales with her knees tucked under her chin. I was splashing through the water and pulling the boat above the tide line before she had even unfolded herself.

I raced the sky as I unpacked the boat and unscrewed the clamps of the outboard. Joany lingered at the water's edge, bags of food hanging from her arms. She looked awkward and shifty, staring up and down the unfamiliar street with discomfort. The unspoken question that hung in the air was what to do with her next. I desperately did not want another living being in the tower with me, and I'd been avoiding the issue in blind hope since making the deal with her. Taking the girl across the water could only be taking her across the water – anything else was beyond my responsibility. Yet as I looked at her standing small and deflated at the water's edge with the bags of food around her feet screaming to the wolves like neon signs flashing in the night, I realised I might as well kill her myself as leave her for the gangs and the looters.

With the bag containing the still slung over one shoulder, and the outboard balanced across the other, I was left with one free hand for a gas can.

"You need somewhere to stay?" I rasped. Joany looked uncomfortable, torn between her distrust of me and her vulnerability, exposed as she was in an unfamiliar world with new rules, and bags of food like millstones of gold around her neck. I turned and headed up the hill – I knew she would bite.

"Just a few days, no more. Grab the gas." I turned my head expectantly and looked behind. The sky to the east was a shimmering bright blue. A glowing sky and a sight I should never see. "Hurry," I said. "The gangs come at dawn."

Joany darted forward, stooping to pick up a can in each hand, twining the thin handles of the plastic carriers around her fingers as she did so. As I strode up the hill, shivers running down my spine with the approach of the nuclear dawn, Joany waddled after me, swinging heavy plastic gallon cans as she went. We were both exhausted, but I could not afford to heed the pain in my muscles as I limped up the hill, striving to be out of the predawn light. It was a five minute climb up the street to the tower and with every passing moment the sky brightened, turning pale until my skin prickled and I had to squint through streaming eyes.

I reached the intersection the tower sat on ahead of the girl and looked back briefly at the wobbling, crinkling figure below me as she wavered left to right, struggling to maintain her balance. My back was screaming under the hard metal weight of the outboard, and the skin of the backs of my hands was prickling with angry sunburn. I waited just a moment until she looked up at me and I was sure the girl had seen and could follow my path, and then I disappeared through the lobby entrance and hurried out of the shafts of light that splayed across the floor, taking shelter in the shadows.

My reluctance to betray the location of my home was assuaged by my need for the gasoline the girl was carrying – it gave me the excuse to shelter her for a day or two and rest my uneasy conscience. I passed through the tatty lobby with its blood stains and shredded couches, flew by the stairwell and the angry horror it concealed, and lingered uncomfortably by the door down to the garage, waiting for Joany to appear silhouetted in the lobby doorway, her shadow breaking the distant beam of light flooding across the moulding carpet.

I shook with relief to be out of the dawn, a horror I could not face again. Setting down the engine I melted gratefully into the corner shadows. I panicked a little, impatient for the girl who was beyond my help or influence, and waved when she arrived, for I was too exhausted to speak. She saw me and picked her way through the lobby as I stepped down into the garage and settled in the darkness with the rats. There were no intruders.

I piled my loot in the corner by the steps and flicked on the flashlight as the girl pushed the door open and brought the gas cans down to me. She set them down on the ground and backed off, suspiciously. She flinched as I went past her and up the steps, reaching round the door to retrieve the outboard. The boat wouldn't stay put, someone would pilfer it, but the engine might prove useful. Joany watched me move around her.

"What is this?"

"Hiding place." I didn't want her getting comfortable. "I'm

going to sleep. Get out."

I sat against the wall by my stash, and flicked the light out. The girl shrugged and started up the stairs. She grabbed the door and a weak shaft of light widened out and burst across the concrete.

"Watch your step upstairs. Floors are collapsing." The door swung shut and I was alone in the comforting darkness.

Humble relief quickly gave way to ungrateful exhaustion, and sharp, angry fatigue sucked me down into restless dreams. As darkness softened into the dreaming, menace became my companion and I stumbled through a maze of empty rooms – concrete cells buried under a war-torn bombsite. It's black dark and the walls are cold and dank – something is following me slowly, matching my stumbling pace and goading me on. It is playing with me.

I awaken feverish and sweating, and for a moment I don't understand where I am. My mouth is dry and my throat cracking, my hot body aches sharply and my leg is throbbing, but as I lie on the cool concrete, peering through the darkness, I realise I am in the parking garage – I could almost weep for the safety of it. The sun was still abroad, and the high windows in the far wall let in dazzling beams of searing light, but I was safe as I was, tucked behind the steps and joyously alone. I scrabbled for the bag and for water, every movement an agony akin to rolling in crushed glass, and I sucked down the last of the liquid like a greedy child before settling down on my unforgiving stone mattress to slip back into an exhausted and dreamless sleep.

When I awoke next it had been dark for some time. I lay on the concrete, unable to see past the darkness, and I listened to the silence. I sat up when I realised where I was and what I needed to do. Hunger shuddered through my belly with the movement. The room spun and my head pounded, my muscles twitched uncontrollably for need of sustenance. I grabbed for the flashlight and sat in its sharp blue-white beam, trying to work out a way of hanging the gas cans off the straps of the bag. In the end I gave up, fearing that one good swing from a sloshing can would crush the fragile glass element of the still. I couldn't carry everything, I would have to make the trip in stages.

I hid the outboard and one of the cans under the steps, covered them with filthy rags and a battered old car door that lay abandoned in the garage. Hanging the bag over my shoulder, I picked up a can in each hand and set out on the steps above. My leg was swollen and I limped, the pain made me gasp and breathe heavily, but every step brought me closer to home and hunger drove me on in anticipation.

The plan had been to leave the bag and the gas around floor three and go back for the outboard before hiding that somewhere on three and continuing on with the bag and the still. When I got to three however, I wanted to push on. Three floors wasn't far enough to be away from prying eyes, and whilst I was going, I was going. On every landing I experienced the urge to press on, dragging my oozing leg up one step at a time until I passed through the smoke and ash and reached eight where few people had ventured even before the fire. I sat on the bottom step exhausted, needing to piss and wishing for blood and water. I looked at the gas cans and realised the profound impracticality that kept me safe on the twentieth floor. If I didn't do something about it it may also kill me. One accident and I could end up lame and trapped and starving.

I left the loot where it was on the landing and headed down the steps to retrieve the outboard. Each aching step down as an almost-fall, and I corkscrewed around in a dizzy haze. All I had to do was get down.

It wasn't until I was crouching under the garage steps and uncovering the engine that I realised the girl, Joany, was nowhere to be found. I was somewhat relieved. A perfunctory look around confirmed my suspicions – she had taken her things and gone. There was no one in the garage or on the ground floor. I carried the outboard up to the eight floor slowly but with a light heart, sensing nothing more unusual than my own presence as I went.

I rested every couple of floors, but arriving on the eight with an engine balanced on one shoulder and a gas can in the other hand I felt as if I had arrived on the summit of Everest. The metal lump had weighed down every step and the sloshing liquid had swayed me from side to side as I turned the spiral. My feet ached and my shoulders screamed in pain. I hid the engine on Eight, under a pile of broken up furniture in one of the apartments. I dribbled the last of the gas out of its tank into my cans, until each was full up to the cap and the tank was all but empty. If someone did find the engine I'd be damned if they would get far with it.

I gathered up my possessions and made a start for home, the third gas can going under one arm and then the other, and then back again as the aches and pains accrued in my failing body. The journey was arduous, and agonising and insanely repetitive, and everything you might expect, but I remember little of it. One floor looks much the same as the next, particularly when all you can think of is pain and hunger. All I could do was tell myself that soon I would be safe and fed.

I was dizzy and parched, and my leg was swollen by the time I reached the twentieth floor. I stood and stared at the numbers, unable to believe what I was seeing. I pulled the fire door open in a daze and shuffled up to my front door in numb disbelief. Dropping the cans in order to grasp the keys, I shoved the sloshing containers across the threshold with my feet after the door swung open. My hands were raw from the handles of the cans, my arms throbbed and grated in their sockets. I set the bag down gently, closed the door behind me and breathed the scent of home.

Everything seemed so normal as I hobbled to the kitchen and took a cold bag of blood from the fridge. I bit the corner out of the plastic and sucked the dead liquid down, the metallic tasting blood rolling over my tongue and coating my throat as I looked across my clean and ordered lounge. *No one would know,* I thought as I gulped greedily and blood dribbled down my chin, *how crazy it is out there.*

I sucked down all three units in the fridge, feeling the life break into me, spreading out warm and true from my stomach. A fuzzy, soporific heat came over me as my veins relaxed and the pain in my body eased. I was content, and wanted nothing more than to crawl into bed, but I didn't let myself sleep just yet. I took more blood out of the freezer, noting that it was now half empty, placed the solid brown bags in the fridge, and then I grabbed some water and the emptied blood bags and proceeded to the bathroom.

When I had launched the boat and beached it, I had waded through the foul water, and my legs stank worse than the rest of me. I stripped off and took soap and a rag and wiped myself down, cleaning my wound carefully. The flesh was smothered under a layer of oil and filth, I had to scrape it away and flush it repeatedly with disinfectant and this set off the bleeding and swelling. The gash was not deep but it ran with pus and I whimpered as I pressed down on the cold grey lips of skin around the wound, forcing the sickness out. I cleaned the angry flesh again, rinsing it with precious water before squeezing the last drops of blood from the medical bags out onto it. This is an old trick but it sometimes works. I applied the anti-biotic cream that I'd hoarded, and bandaged my leg, and then I used the last scraps of water to wash the grime from my body. It wasn't enough.

With my belly full and my body tended to, I had no will for anything but sleep. The relief of safety and sustenance was overwhelming, and I felt the sheer comfort of being able to shut the world out and lock the door. I could survive on my own supplies – if only for a little while. I had an urge to look upon the city from the safety of my ivory tower, and I shuffled across the lounge and out onto the balcony in darkness. No sniper would see light at my windows, nor my silhouette.

I looked out across the islands and the floodplain, watching the streets of my island descend beneath the glittering waves that ran up from Market Street. The air was clammy and fierce – summer air from the central plains clashing with the soul of the Pacific. It was dark below, darker than I'm used to – just a sliver of new moon and a few campfires illuminating the city streets. Men were running out of things to burn. The Transamerica Pyramid stood tall, an awkward black shard set against the endless distance, beyond it the bay, lit by a chain of twinkling fairy lights – signs of life strung along the length of the Looter's Causeway. The city was quiet and dark, the string of hills leading up to Twin Peaks to the west seemed pregnant and ominous. There was no one in the streets of Russian Hill below me, no dark figures scurrying through the wreckage to entertain and intrigue my eye. I felt small and alone. I stepped back inside and shut the doors firmly, hearing the automated click of the generator as it came on to charge its power cell. I stripped off as I shuffled across the lounge and I crawled gratefully into bed.

14

I slept through the night, and the day, and awoke hot, dizzy and confused. I had a burning need for water, and I stumbled through the darkened apartment to the cabinet and its depleted supply of little bottles. I guzzled a bottle down sitting in the darkness at the foot of the cabinet, and I felt the heat break across my body. My leg was numb and throbbing, and as I unwrapped the sticky bandages I knew already that it was infected. I balled the yellowed cotton into the palm of my hand and stumbled around in confusion. I wanted light, I wanted air.

I popped the windows but kept the shutters closed, resenting the infringement of the maybe sniper and my enforced fear and paranoia. Plugging a lamp into my generator grid and flicking it on, a damp light spread across the kitchen and over the polished granite of the counter tops to lace the lounge. I sat hot and naked in a cool leather chair and squinted at the wound in my shin. It was weeping freely, and the flesh around it had taken on a faint green tint. It was toxic.

I was terrified. I ran around the apartment hunting through my medicine stash for antibiotic pills and ointments, collecting bandages and packing and antiseptic. An infected wound is unusual and can be lethal. I piled everything I could find onto the kitchen counter, along with the blowtorch I had looted and a flat, wide metal spatula. The collection didn't amount to much, a couple of blister packs of pills that would make me want to puke, and the small tube of antibiotic cream. I didn't know what to do, I had no idea, I hadn't sustained an infected wound in centuries.

I had distant, haunting memories of something my Mother had done for my Father. Echoes really, just the sound of her beads rattling, the sense that she was whispering, muttering, but no words, no sounds, just the man's mad twisting and shuddering and then the sizzling, like meat in a pan. My father screamed once, one guttural, strangled cry, cursing the Hunt, and I gasped, but my mother forced me to look, forced me to see what had to be done. She had cauterised his wound, and the smell, the smell as I shrank back from the glowing iron was truly awful. It clung to my nostrils and stuck in my throat as his writhing scream filled my ears, and I was a cold little boy who couldn't get away.

It was the smell that I remembered then more than anything. I don't know how we survived nights like those, I don't remember my distant beginnings, but they taught me what they knew and I am sometimes made grateful. I bit my lip, and I thought of the shadow figure that stood in for my father in that small compartment in my mind that he had once occupied. He would not have screamed out as I scraped the rotten flesh with the heated blade of a carving knife – that is what I liked to imagine. He would have been brave. He would have held his tongue and shrugged off the pain as his wounds ran freely with blood and foulness.

I remove as much of the rot as I can before flooding the pooling blood in my wound with cold, dead blood from a bag. In any other organism this could provoke a fatal immune reaction, but not me. Not us. The blood smears over my hands and the floor and everything I touch like a red plague, and I drink the rest cold and hurried, feeling dizzy and nauseous and shell shocked. I set the flat steel of the spatula in the blue flame of the blowtorch, holding its wooden handle until the metal turns rose, and then a glowing cherry red. I squint, screwing up my face as I hold the implement above my leg, the heat prickling my skin, and with a gasp I press the flat blade down into one side of the wound.

I scream and my arms shake as the burning, searing pain mounts, and I force myself to press harder, to see how much I can take as the tears stream down my cheeks and I lose my breath to a faltering diaphragm. The sizzling, bubbling smoke rises up, grey and wispy, and that evil smell comes back to me worse than ever – something between barbecued chicken and the acrid black stench of burnt hair. I slump over in the kitchen and bat the fumes away, and then I tear the metal from my flesh, and in doing so I scream aloud again.

Cauterising the other side of the wound is worse. I sit before the flame, heating the metal amidst the fumes of burning flesh, trying not to wretch or anticipate the pain. I turn the metal in the flame until it is glowing red and then I jam it down into my leg before I have time to think, to hesitate. I cry out again, a dry, strangled, gurgling scream in the back of my throat, and the pain makes the room spin.

I swallow too many tablets, antibiotics that will make me want to vomit, and analgesics to make me numb. I sit exhausted and naked in a chair with a cold bag to my lips, there is another one warming in the pot of water over the gas burner. I fully intend to get inebriated tonight, to drink until I am glutted and slow and stupid. The brief, stolen life runs through me, flowing to my face and hands and collecting in my leg in sharp little flickers of warmth before being sucked down into my cold, ruined tissues. The blood flows to where it's needed and I swallow again, nursing the flopping bag awkwardly in my arms. I am sick of being ugly. I miss my face, I miss my voice. I am sick of the blackened claws I have for hands, I want my thin, pale skin back. I am tired and broken, sick of being exhausted and sick of being sick; I take another swig. I am feeling sorry for myself, running for the bottle like an alcoholic off the wagon. I'm not hungry any more, I'm just greedy and sorry. I don't care, it feels good.

The warmed blood is better, and I pass out after my third or fourth bag, more from the drugs and the searing, throbbing pain that besieges my rationality than from any kind of blood-induced inebriation. Blood is seductive, conducive – it can be stimulating or soporific depending on the circumstances. I sleep a light, luxurious sleep through the dark hours, and I awaken to find my bare skin stuck to the chair, and crusted blood clinging to my lips like rust. The blood left in the bag feels sweaty and smells bad, and I discard it with annoyance. I burp, loudly, and find myself grinning like a little boy as I stagger to my feet. I am still rather vacant and drunk, content and complicit in a shakeable stupor, the only thing I can do is crawl, soggy and bloodstained into bed. I sleep through the dawn with a childish smile on my face, curled up like a baby.

Over the next few days I drink unreservedly and poison myself slowly with human pills. My leg is infected, oozing pale green pus, and I watch it like a hawk for signs of gangrene, for signs that the poison is travelling up my veins to my heart. I don't know what I will do if such a thing happens. Die I suppose. I can hardly amputate my own leg. Can I? I shrug and drink while I have the excuse, and choose not to think on it. I fancy my burns improve a little, my eyelashes begin to come through again, fine and wispy. I peer in the mirror, staring at my drawn lips, imagining them fuller than the night before. It is madness I know, my recovery will be slowing now, so many weeks from the inferno, and I drank as much then as I do now. Still, to worry and drink passes the time.

I also stare at the still. I play with it. I set it up. I fit it together carefully, I take it apart, I clean it. I fit it back together. It bears pride of place in the kitchen, sitting on the black granite top next to the sink. I hook the rubber coolant tube to my empty cold tap, and lead the drain tube down into the sink. There is no getting away from the fact that up here I have no coolant, and no raw material.

Over the nights the edges of my wound turn black and scab over, and I know I will survive. But I am lame again, as burned flesh closes up so slowly, and I am back to walking with a stick. I feel trapped in my apartment and the frustration becomes more acute than my desire for security. I become edgy and irritable, sometimes I hobble around my rooms, or I cross the hallway outside, enjoying the feeling of space that isn't mine, even though really it is. The stairwell doors taunt me, but I do not go down.

15

I was sitting out on the balcony one night, drinking and reading by the light of one candle, enjoying the air and the summer warmth. It was a large candle that I'd made by pouring old wax into a jar and it stood on the balcony railing two feet away. It was the only light I would allow myself out there since the night of the sniper. This night I was slouched low in the chair, a book perched on my belly and my chin resting on my chest when the candle exploded in a flurry of molten wax and splintered glass. The searing liquid splashed across my face and clothes whilst the bullet clanged against the metal of the shutters behind me. The flame died, of course, and I remember sitting frozen in the dark as the thickened skin of my hand bubbled and blebbed up under a tightening membrane of solidifying wax and razor slivers.

I stayed still, conscious that the only thing to see in the city half-light would be my movement. The French doors stood open just feet away, beckoning, and I intended to slide slowly onto the floor and crawl to safety. I was about halfway off the chair and struggling for control when I lost my rag with the book sliding across my belly. I grabbed it and thrust it onto the wide ledge of the balcony railing. A moment after I had removed my hand the stone sill of the railing cracked loudly in a cloud of dust and chips, and the book leapt off the sill, a flutter of leaves running through the air like a spread of feathers.

I sat still once again, barely able to maintain my half-on half-off position with my pelvis in mid-air as the shot echoed across the city expanse. He could see me in the gloom. He could see me between the carved stone pillars surely. Why wasn't he shooting? I fought back numb terror to confront my confusion. What was he doing? What was his pattern? I thought back. Every shot had been trained on inanimate objects, when in fact my head was just as attainable. I'd assumed he'd missed, he'd been aiming for me and he'd missed, but that last shot – it was almost as if he'd waited for something – a target to shoot – something I'd witness.

I scraped around under my chair with my free hand until my fingers came across the object I was hunting for – smooth and round and a little warm in the night air. It was the mug I had been drinking from. Without raising the rest of my body I reached up and placed the mug on the ledge above. I drew my hand down and waited, biting my lip. Seconds later the mug disintegrated, raining me with shards of broken pottery and blood. I wiped my face and shook the gritty fluid, stinging, out of my eyes, but I was smiling. I knew what the sniper wanted. He wanted to play.

I slid down onto the tiled floor of the balcony and pulled myself through the doorway, before scrambling up and tearing through the darkness to my trash pile in the corner cupboard of the kitchen. Most garbage went out over the balcony, but anything clean that I might re-use or burn I liked to save. I tore through the litter in that cupboard, selecting a cereal box, an empty detergent bottle, a plastic bowl, and I went out to the balcony again, bent double and staying low. I set the things along the ledge quickly, one after the other, and then I turned to scoot inside. As I faced the doors the box fell over, and I twisted to the familiar thwack of a bullet hitting the masonry beside the doorframe. As the shot rang out the bowl jumped high into the air, deformed and spinning, and whistled away into the night below. The bottle fell inwards, bouncing and spinning across the terra cotta tiles.

I was consumed for the rest of the night. I scoured the apartment for new, challenging targets for the sniper. He took longest over glass, so I assumed it was hardest to see and often perched objects on top of it. I would lay a row of jars down and then place boxes or old bottles or bits of wood from the Leibowitz' on the top. Eventually he got it – realising the trick he would shoot under the mysteriously levitating objects and smash the jars. Like a gentleman he would also wait for me to leave the balcony after that first time – once he knew I understood what he had been asking me.

As the night wore on the targets became smaller and I started cutting out circles of cardboard no bigger than the spread of my hand. The bullet holes left in those discs of card were tiny little ruptures – I almost didn't believe what I was seeing. And then I had an idea. I wrote a message. In thick pen I wrote "WHERE ARE YOU?" on the inside of a box that I'd opened out. I looked at it and sighed and crossed through it. On the other side I wrote, "YES. ARE YOU UP HIGH? NO." I stood the banner on the railing ledge, propped up against a lump of wood that used to be a chair leg. A shot rang out, and I retrieved the message. A tiny, circular bullet hole tore through the thin, grey card. 'YES,' it said.

It was shot through the E.

I was running out of card by this point and had many questions – questions that could not be answered with a simple yes or no. 'Who are you? How did you spot me? Are you alone? Who are you?' But these would have to wait. I would find a way to ask them – a way that the sniper could answer. I ran through the apartment searching for something to write on. In the end I scrounged a cereal box from under the rat's table. The stale contents would remain in their bag. The stinking animal sat up and looked optimistically as I rustled its food, but it was out of luck and subsiding on emergency rations by this time. I tore the box open and grabbed the thick, dry felt tip pen.

"YES. ARE YOU IN TRANSAMERIC" I wrote before running out of room. It was my main suspicion – it was up high, and the angle would lead most of the bullets, if not all, into the side-wall of my balcony, where they had each thwacked into the masonry with a puff of dust and flying chips of render. I looked at my half finished message. Best I could do. Hurrying outside I propped it up, weighing the flaps of cardboard down under the chair leg for support. Then I went inside and waited.

But there was no answer. No characteristic sharp cracking echo, no thwack into the wall. Either the sniper was waiting for a 'NO' to shoot, or no shot meant a no. Or he was holding the Transamerica Pyramid and didn't want it known. I stepped out half an hour later, feeling alone, and took down the sign. I replaced it with a tinted glass measuring cup from the Leibowitz' place but the sniper didn't bite. He wasn't playing any more.

My restlessness mounted over the nights, and as I watched my stocks of water and blood dwindle, I knew I would have to go out into the world a hobbling old man. I was still weak, but the gluttonous feeding had seen to most of my pain and filled me with energy as my tissues slowly recovered. I needed water badly, and the first order of business must be to test the still. If it worked I would effectively be able to print money.

My first venture outside the apartment was with an empty five-gallon tank swinging from each arm, and I trudged wearily down those dizzying steps feeling numb and trying to pass the time. The height kept my home safe and hidden, but it made living hard, and short of moving down the tower and losing my advantage I wondered what I could do about it.

I grew quiet as I reached the lower levels, listening for signs of life just above and below those dangerous, fire damaged floors. People had poked through the wreckage certainly, but no one had moved in. I was more concerned when I reached the lobby – the floor had been cleared and the broken red couches had been gathered and arranged in a gappy circle out of the draft. The carpet in the centre of the circle was a sticky black mess, scorched and littered with rocks and ash. I searched carefully through the Estates office and the parking garage – there was no one there, but the place was certainly being used and I didn't like it.

I snuck out of the building with a furrowed brow, making my way quickly down the steep slope to the northern shore of the island. The sidewalk was cracked and full of vigorous weeds, and the slope was hard on my wounded leg. It made me wish for my stick, but I'd rejected it in favour of the second water can I was carrying. I hobbled sideways down the street, sweating under my hood as I passed by burnt-out cars and the charred skeletons of high-class townhouses, scanning the scene for movement and listening all the time for the sounds of people.

I felt both lonely and relieved as I reached the shore uninterrupted, and I looked about carefully before bending to fill the cans. The water's edge was greasy and the concrete was coated in black and green slime. The shallows were choked with a tangled mesh of splintered wood, household plastic and bits of nylon rope. Upholstery foam bobbed in the wavelets, picked at by nesting birds and the crabs. I lay the rectangular tin cans on their sides in the water, trying to fill them wholly without getting wet myself. In the end I had to step into the water to get past the slime and push the cans deep enough under. With twenty flights of steps ahead of me there was no point doing half a job.

I screwed the caps back on and hauled myself back up the street to my tower. I was glad to be walking abroad and I was glad of the air, but my mission for the night was almost over, I felt alone, looking desperately for a reason to stay out late when there was none. The island was empty. There was no fun to be had.

For a moment, halfway up that street and hiding from the moonlight, I was aware of my need for people and company and interaction. My hunger stirred, curious and content in the pit of my stomach. I continued on stubbornly, sweating as I reached the intersection and crossed over to the little patch of scrub outside the tower. I entered the lobby cautiously in case the squatters had returned in my twenty-minute absence. There was no sign of them, so I made my way down the hall, past the dead elevators, past the forbidden stairwell of hell with its evil, writhing stench and its damning liquid stares. I trudged up the other staircase in silence, one step at a time, with the grimy water sloshing at my sides and emitting hollow, tinny sounds from the cans.

I trudged, and I rested, and I dreamed as I turned that spiral, trying not to look at the number of the floor, or stretch my neck upwards to the hundreds of steps left to me. The moments where I truly lost myself were the saviour – the times where a minute seemed an hour, or five floors seemed to be one. The worst times were those where I crashed out of the daydream, crashed out of my train of thought and realised I was on the endless bloody staircase and I'd climbed one agonising flight since I'd looked up, or maybe even less. There is a knack to the perception of time, going forwards at least – over the endless years I've learnt it. A year can seem an hour if you don't dwell on it, and if you imagine your future self looking back at your discomfort in the present, telling yourself you'll be when you want to be – well then in no time you find yourself there, looking back and feeling the shortness, the closeness of there to here.

I've learned the tides of time over the centuries, felt the relentless riptides and currents running through the human years, glimpsed the grand scheme in a way no man can. There is flow in the universe, flow and flux, continuous, but not without order, not without design. Sometimes I stand, still and alone, and I feel the changes of the universe flowing around me. I feel the tide of time wash in and out with every nightfall like a physical action, sometimes I hold my breath and squeeze my legs shut, hoping for a sense of the motion all around me. Does anyone understand this? The pattern of constant change? Of course not. Not in the age of science.

These are the things I dreamed on the stairs that night and all the many others. I let my mind wander through the universe whilst my body turned through the aching, crushing monotony of step after step after corkscrewing step. I reached my apartment in a daze and set the water tanks down by the doorway before slumping into a chair. But weariness did not hold back my interest for long. The still – the prize I had risked my life to retain was poised to give up its secret – did it work or not?

I poured scummy bay water into the boiler reservoir and plugged the heating element into the generator grid outlet next to the refrigerator. As the generator outside clicked on, responding to the increased load on the system, I placed a bowl under the output tap and began siphoning bay water through the glass cooling chamber or the condenser element – a tall glass cylinder blown around the outside of a coiled glass-tube condenser run. The device was a laboratory dinosaur. It looked intact – and even well used judging by the mineral crust lacing the boiler lid, but in this age of back-pressure filters and reverse osmosis, old technology was something to be scoffed at by most and observed with suspicion. Over-engineering was everything in the throwaway, built-to-break society where obsolescence was a design feature. Why use a distributor when you can rig a car with not one but twenty microprocessors? Why use ball bearings and good engineering when you can use computer controlled superconducting floats? It was with more than a little apprehension that I sat and watched a pot boil, wondering whether old-tech could really work in the dying days of new magic.

The pot began to bubble and boiled quickly, pretty soon steam was bursting up the coiled glass tube of the condenser element. Trickling specks of water began to crawl down the corkscrew, heading for the output tap at the bottom, and I had to work continuously at swapping high and low cans over and siphoning the dirty bay water through the cooling system. I sucked the infected, oily smelling water through a bright orange rubber tube, trying not to get it in my mouth, running the same few gallons through the machine over and over until the liquid became hot and stinking and the steam no longer condensed. I flicked the power off and listened as the boiling noises died away, pressing my hand to the hot side of the can of coolant water. The machine was designed to be hooked up to a cold tap, with the coolant water running down the drain – a ridiculous, lazy luxury of waste that I could not entertain. It didn't matter, I realised as I looked down into the glass collection bowl. In the fifteen or twenty minutes I'd been able to run the machine it had almost filled the bowl, producing a couple of pints of clean looking water.

I dipped my leathery finger into the lukewarm liquid and touched it to my lips. It was entirely tasteless and odourless, the only flavour being that of the salty grime covering my finger. This new water brought a strange dryness to the back of my throat as I drank more. I giggled and laughed out loud as I sucked the liquid down, realising with glee that the machine worked. I could make safe, pure water on demand. I could trade it!

Of course the realisation brought with it further complications. As I set the cans of warm bay sludge outside on the patio to cool I realised I would need many more tanks of cooling water – more than I had empty containers for, and I would need an inexhaustible supply of raw water to run through the machine. I squinted down at the scrubland far below with its mound of decomposing trash that ringed the tower. I wondered how I would get that water up here, and how I would get it down again.

There was no simple answer. Over the next nights I practiced with the still, setting up a dance-like routine for swapping full and empty cans, topping up the boiler and rotating batches of cooling fluid so that I could run the machinery for as long as I wanted – at least until my meagre supply of coolant soaked up too much heat. By rotating warm cans on to the balcony and cool cans back into the system I would be able to keep the still going for as long as I wanted – I just needed more coolant, and the temptation was always to process whatever raw water I had.

It was hard, manual work that aggravated my limp, but the feeling of achievement was immense. I was doing something to save myself – for once in these crazy, random times there was a process that worked, just like the old days. I put some work in, I got something predictable out, and the fragile illusion that order persisted within my little apartment had a real basis, if only a temporary one. My haven of security, where things were rational. I could work for my future and I knew what to expect was founded on the same lie as all the order in that illusory human world. I looked around the apartment as the clean water piled up in empty canteens and re-used plastic bottles and I noticed something else. The oil was running out. My fuel, the gas, was decreasing in direct proportion to my productivity. My blood supplies weren't looking none too healthy either.

So it was with stiff apprehension that I awoke early one evening and filled two five-gallon army surplus cans with water, donned a hooded robe made from an old curtain, hiding my fuzzy skullcap, and prepared to go out into the night. I was on a mission to trade, but I packed a knife, a fine scalpel (for one must plan to encounter good fortune), and a gun – a small pistol, just in case.

The lower levels are burned and robbed out, the floors dangerously strewn with steel and masonry from the collapsing ceiling above. It was on the second floor that I became concerned for on the landing, nestled between the bottom step and the fire door, I came across signs of life. I almost tripped and broke my neck on an old, worn through car seat that appeared to be someone's pillow. Brushed up against the wall, moth eaten and hole-ridden there was a filthy, stinking bed roll. I froze amid the humming stench and listened. Down below, just on the edge of my perception, cracked the rolling thrum of a campfire; there were low voices muttering and echoing up off the concrete below.

Extending my senses out into the fuzzy ether I saw minds below, shimmering individuals shining in the emptiness. I made my way down the steps silently, dumping my cargo on the first floor landing before descending gently into the clutter of sounds emanating from the ground floor. I hung on the door, desperately listening against the cool metal surface, peering out into the ether and fingering the pistol under my gown in sheer terror.

There were three of them, three slow turning minds shining out against the smouldering plasma of a camp-fire. And another mind, further off, *further down*, small and urgent and sly. I gripped the cool metal of the handgun and eased the door open slowly, flinching as the hinges squealed, and the campsite chatter ceased abruptly. Sick expectation hung in the air, a pregnant, electric threat that ran between us before we could see each other. I shuffled out into the corridor, trying to move as normally as possible, and joined eyes with three astonished and vicious looking hobos.

They were sitting around the fire on the old couches, one man squatted on the floor. Wrapped in rags, they turned their greasy heads to grimace at me from across the flames, yellowing teeth and beady eyes glinting in the flicker. They were ancient. I hobbled forward slowly, a dark figure making his way to the threshold of the lobby and the gloaming light. The men had been eating scraps, there was a pot steaming on the fire and as I approached, the one on the floor, the youngest, scooped up a small, wicked looking knife and got to his feet.

I withdrew the gun from the cloying folds of my gown, raising my arm to point it shakily. As I did so the hood slipped across my brow and obscured my view, and I panicked, sensing the approach of the man with the knife. He was striding across the room halfway between the others and myself, a dirty grin on his face. I pulled the hood down, but as the folds dropped around my shoulders and I took sight of the man his features dropped and he faltered, coming to a dead stop a few feet from me. There was a gasp from a man behind, and the would-be attacker swallowed hard as his eyes widened. I noticed my pistol arm shaking and I looked up into the face of the filthy man with the knife. It was then that I realised his fear.

I must have looked a sight, my bald scalp sprouting fine, wispy hairs and the thickened and scarred skin melted taut over my shattered features. My narrow eyes and sunken nose must have been lost in the deep shadows of the flickering light, and there I was, an eyeless, skull-faced phantom shaking before them and breathing death. I stood still in front of the man with the knife, glaring angrily into his eyes, and then I opened my mouth, bearing my brown and broken tombstone teeth. I hissed. A long, sharp sound, I let the spittle gurgle up my throat and run over my lips. The man squeaked briefly, more a whistling exhalation of shock than a scream, and he turned and fled. He yelped as he tripped through the edges of the fire, knocking charred wood and bright red sparks across the blackened carpet, spreading the contents of the pot in a miniature tsunami over the floor and the couch and the legs of an unfortunate, howling hobo. The other man, grey and wizened and wrinkled under a mac coat flicked a glance at me and stood up, dragging his scolded compatriot out into the night amidst screams and protests.

I was left there, shaking and bewildered, with my finger pressed gently against the trigger of the gun. I'd realised what had happened – they'd been scared by my face. I'd used my visage and saved a bullet. I stood still for a few moments, the fire crackling before me and casting low, long shadows across the disintegrating lobby. It was all very well, using my deathmask to my advantage, using it when it suited me, but I couldn't take it off. It was becoming uncomfortable to remember who I was under the mask, what my face had been for all those years. It would come back, it would come back to me.

I sniffed and turned, making my way back to the stairwell and my expensive water, and as I leant on the doorframe I remembered the shadow of the mind below. It was still there, I could feel it beneath my feet, and so I turned, gripping the gun in my palm and making my way to the steps down into the garage. I wasn't about to leave a squatter unattended.

The door creaked as I pushed it open and descended into the darkness, feeling exposed and vulnerable. I squinted as I reached the cement floor of the parking lot, hoping to pick my way around the trash that littered my path. I was reaching into the ether with my mind, sweeping back and forth for the bright little signs of life that glowed and flowed fiercely in the speckled grey medium before me. There was a human, small and fierce and frightened, pressed into the corner, and I moved away to the side before approaching, deliberately clearing the path between the person and the exit.

I trailed casually along the wall into the corner as if I couldn't see the precise location of my hidden quarry until I came to a pile of flattened cardboard and rags and wooden packing pallets. I kicked it with my toe, knowing full well that I was being watched by a figure within – I could smell the fear and days-old sweat. I stood back and reached out carefully with one hand whilst I held the gun firmly in the other. I meant to pull down a pallet that leant against the concrete, but as my fingers touched the rough hewn wood the whole structure exploded in a tangle of limbs and rotten blankets and flashing metal.

A small, hard bundle of person bowled me and cracked me to the ground, screaming in high-pitched exertion and flashing a knife before my face. My head thudded where I'd hit the concrete, my vision blurred into two images as the dizziness took over, and I grunted in surprise as I struggled to grasp the thin wrist that held the knife poised dangerously above me. A young boy, black-faced and squinting, sat across my chest and was grasping the knife with both hands now, striving to bring it down upon me. I moaned as the room spun, and lifted the gun into the air, heavy and wavering, until the cold, blunt muzzle pressed into the firm flesh under the boy's chin. The hammer clicked as I cocked it. The unmistakeable click rang out through the darkness, cutting through the sounds of our struggles as if they were nothing when held up to its metallic pedigree. The boy squeaked and went stiff, freezing above me, and then he faltered and whispered "No!" in a short, female voice.

"Joany?" I whispered, struggling to fix a look through the spinning and the blurred vision. The small, almond face was smeared and filthy, tears of effort streaming down from the red eyes, and the dark hair had been cut rough and short with shears, but as her fragile body began to shake and she squinted through the black, short-sighted and defenceless, I knew it was the girl.

"Wha?" She said. "You? What are you going to do?"

"Well I'm not about to shoot you." I said, and then we sat for an awkward, tangled moment, and Joany seemed to relax, and tremble with relief.

"Well I won't shoot you if you let me up," I said, nodding to the knife.

"Oh. Yea. Right." She sniffed and wiped her face before climbing off me and pressing her back to the wall. I lowered the gun to the ground and uncocked it gently, and I lay there, breathing softly and hoping the room would stay in one place.

"What happened to your hair? What are you doing here?"

Joany shuddered and wiped her face again, a long vertical movement from the corner of her eye and her nose down across her cheek.

"Nowhere else to go." She said, bobbing her head in the darkness. She didn't seem able to see me as I could her. She screwed her face up in desperation. "You got any water?"

"No." I didn't want to encourage her. I looked at her then, thin and frail and terrified. "Maybe. It's not free."

The girl nodded vigorously in murmured agreement. I sat up slowly and rubbed my head before scooting back to the wall on my backside.

I sat in cold silence until I caught Joany gazing in my direction.

"I suppose you want it now?"

The girl dived into the collapsed pile of junk that had been her nest, and emerged brandishing a flaccid and disappointed looking rubber hot water bottle. Then she sucked in air and whispered "wait, wait wait," as she turned her back and ran her hands through the rags until she found a tatty clear plastic bottle which she presented to me with great pride.

"Don't you want to know what I want from you?" I asked as the girl held her prizes out. What followed was a tactful, and slightly bated pause that preceded a shrug and a 'doesn't matter' expression that contained a degree of wry bitterness I wasn't entirely comfortable with. I sighed, and took the bottles gently from her clutching fingers.

"Nothing like that. Come to the jetty and wait for me, I might have some things I'll need you to carry."

The girl deflated in relief.

I stood up slowly and shuffled across the concrete towards the steps. As I reached the top step and opened the door I found Joany behind me, and the distant orange light of the fire spread across her face. She waited obediently as I went upstairs and retrieved my cans, she watched greedily as I filled her grimy containers after insisting on sucking the last dregs out.

"Here, taste this," I said, and indicated to the liquid at the brim of an open can. Joany bent and slurped at the rim.

"Is it good?" I asked, and Joany nodded enthusiastically. I smiled awkwardly with pride. I poured the payment out and Joany stuck the plastic bottle in her pocket and the hot water bottle under her waistband. She refused all my suggestions to leave them in a safe place, and we set off out of the building and through the streets to the jetty, bumbling along with one five-gallon tank each.

We crept through the streets in silence, hiding in the shadows and checking over our shoulders with paranoia as we went. The water we carried was as expensive as life and easily worth killing for. What's more, it sloshed noisily in the tin cans, and the sound seemed to carry far in the empty streets.

Joany had no idea how to get to the jetty, so I led her down to Broadway and across, pausing every half block to wait for her to catch up. She was clumsy and noisy by my standards, and the gun was never far from my thoughts. Every looted shop front, every burnt-out shell was a perfect hiding place for the hordes, and I expected to be ambushed at any time. I heard the odd noises of the city, the crashing of steps through a distant shattered building, the mad rantings of a lost crazy rolling gently down the hill, but no one came within sight, and we were ignored by fate that night as the world spun on.

We descended down Broadway past the sad old strip joints with their rows of broken light bulbs and dead plasma screens, and I pointed out the jetty as it ran out into the water, a long, rotten, rectangular finger. We approached cautiously, watching for movement in the alleyways, watching for the predators that wait by the waterside for the desperate traveller. I stepped onto the makeshift jetty cautiously – the old floorboards were spongy and rotten. The water level had risen a couple of inches since I had been here last, and the flooded cellar below was collapsing into the waves. I told Joany to wait on dry land, out of sight, and I sat low on my haunches, waving my flashlight out across the bay, hoping a distant ferryman would see my call and come to make a bargain.

I sat under the stars, feeling the breeze and the moment as the waves chopped across the waters of the bay. It struck me, as it often does, that there would never be another moment like this one, not in all of time. I soaked up the deep, deep blue of the night, listening to the sounds, aware of the small, soft breathing presence that watched me from somewhere behind. Presently I straightened up, spying a boat, a little shadowed crescent in the far darkness, and I blinked my light in its direction as it rounded the northern peak of the peninsular.

As I watched the boat approach, I sized up the darkened

figure of the man at the oars. He rowed in short, sharp strokes, cutting his paddles through the water with relish. He drew the stubby fibreglass vessel up alongside the jetty and gazed at me with hungry, glassy little eyes. I detested him immediately. He grinned a toothy grin and made a point of looking over the two tanks that sat by my side.

"An jus what kin ah do for you Misser?" he said in a slow, gluttonous drawl.

"Take me to the bridge and back. East Bay."

"Whell now, that'll cost ya."

"Half a gallon of the purest. Safest water you'll ever taste."

"Ah dunno about that now Sir," he drawled, sly and pleased with himself. "It's late, and it's dark, and your light there looks mighty perdy."

"Not for sale. I'm sure I can find someone who's thirsty enough to take my deal."

The boatman's face twisted bitterly and he dropped the sickening falsetto charm. "Thuh full gallon."

"Three quarters, on return."

The boatman thought for a moment, hand stroking his stubble absently. "Git in then." He growled.

I grabbed the tanks and stepped awkwardly into the rocking glassfibre vessel, and we set off up the bay as I urged the unpleasant little man on faster – midnight was fast approaching.

As we rounded the reefs and the sandbanks, and I wiped the spray from my eyes, my feeling for the ratty little man deteriorated further. He hid his eyes behind a mop of curly grease-ridden hair, and would look from me to my lame leg to the cans balanced between my feet with a greedy expression before looking back up at me and smiling innocently. He was no doubt wondering if my cargo was expected at the Looter's Fortress, wondering if I would be missed.

For my part I ground my eye teeth and watched him sullenly, fingering the wicked edge of my knife under my gown, and hoping I would get an excuse to drive it into that slimy, smug little bastard's heart, so I could drink the juice I liberated. The middle of the bay seemed a perfect place to dump a body, not that anybody would care or take notice in a city of stinking dead bodies. But who would row the boat? The thought of rowing there and back with a lame leg to push on didn't appeal to me, so I would let the man live for as long as he chose – at least this is what I told myself. I placated myself with the knowledge that my hatred was twisted by prejudice, hunger and frustration, but I kept a suspicious eye on the chancer as we passed Market Street and the spire of the Ferry Building.

The bridge loomed up before us, its familiar string of apathetic lights cutting through the darkness weak and brown and disinterested, flicking on and off like a dying fluorescent tube unchanged and uncared for. The breeze was coming from the south and bringing with it all the ripe odours of the colony that lived along the deck above the water. Smoke and fish and shit laced the air, a heady perfume of human perseverance, with an evil little undertone of death drifting downwind over the water. The weasel of a boatman turned the little craft towards that giant concrete first pier of the bridge, the gatehouse that marked the place where the freeway descended beneath the waves. The boatman rowed smooth and swift, an old hand navigating the waterway expertly.

I first noticed the source of the increasing death-stench as a shadow over the water. As we drew closer the form began to take shape in the darkness. In front of the ramshackle guard post, strung out over the water in a rude warning were the swaying bodies of three men, rotting and florid. The boatman passed them by without a care as he took the vessel around to the front of the gatehouse, and the jetty where the asphalt roadway climbed out of the water. He was looking for a space between the boats where he could moor up.

For myself I hardly glanced at the men, ripe and insect ridden and sagging like bags of meat, but I found it easier to look at them than to raise any sort of emotion over their fate. I gazed dispassionately as we floated by, wondering what they had done. I was becoming accustomed to the rot – everyone was. Desensitized and suffering from shock fatigue, it was only when a broad and a skullcap of fine silver fuzz caught my eye that I looked up at one of the swinging figures and realised it was Reg – the boatman who'd taken me up the channel to Ocean Avenue, the one who'd warned me off the University. I was numb for a moment, and then anger swelled within me, hot, silent and dispossessed. With the boat drawing up to the moorings before the guardhouse there was nothing I could do, nothing I dared say.

The boat scraped along the waterlogged asphalt and ground to a halt. I stood up, unsteady in the rocking, beached vessel, and splashed out onto the sodden tarmac before turning back and taking up my cargo. As I bent down I gave the boatman a brief glance from under the brow of my hood "Have you a bottle?" I said in a low voice. The man took a moment to understand my request and then he jumped up, scrambling to retrieve a battered and distressed clear plastic soda bottle from under his seat. He held it out and I poured out what I reckoned to be a pint of water. "Rest later," I said stiffly before turning up the slope, trying not to limp as I went.

I climbed up the long, shallow slope towards the barricade of barrels and wooden splints, and waited for a guardsman to emerge. There were twisting, grinding steps in the watchtower above, someone at least was following my progress. A figure leant over the wooden handrail above, young and sullen, hungry looking. The muzzle of his assault rifle rested lazily on the rail, pointing up at the stars. The low wooden shed on my right was dark and quiet, but as I passed there came a loud, scraping noise from the watchtower. It was the boy above rattling a spanner in a tin bucket. There were confused noises from within the shed, a man grunted, a chair fell over, the man yelped. There was a grating, metallic rattle and a man emerged, bleary eyed from the doorway, pointing a rifle and screwing his face up in the breeze.

"Oi!" he said as I stood before him.

"Yes?"

"Where you going?"

"Some time ago I did business here. Do you know the man I traded with?" I thought back to my last encounter at the guardpost and the wiry, cunning gatekeeper who had run the place. "He was in charge here, thin and bossy." I looked the stringy guard up and down – I'd not seen this one before. He shook his head and yawned.

"Sorry Pops. Could be anyone. Fuck off."

The man pointed his gun at me and tilted his head.

I sighed. "Then find someone who would be interested in buying fresh water." I turned to make my way through a gap in the razorwire blockade. I had no intention of losing myself down the avenue of tents and shanties beyond, surrounded by hundreds of thirsty, desperate folk, but I wanted to trade fast and I wanted to get some attention.

"Wait –" the guard hissed. He was pale and wide-eyed with excitement. "Is that... Water?"

"Of course."

"Can I... Give us a taste?"

"Well, I'm not sure. This is very pure water." I made a point of looking the scruffy man up and down. "It might be a bit rich for your blood." The man smiled painfully and stepped forward, eyeing the cans I held. I stepped back, and set the cans on the floor, slipping one arm into my gown so I could grasp my pistol. The man stopped and gulped.

"I'm sure we can work something out."

"I knelt without taking my eyes from the stringy man, and unscrewed the cap from the can on the left. Every turn seemed to take forever. I could feel the gaze of the gunman on the watchtower above as his eyes bore into the nape of my neck. I motioned to the can, and the guard bent to taste the water. He dipped two fingers in and popped them in his mouth, and then he did it again. I knelt to replace the cap before he could do it a third time. And then we stood to face each other. He could barely contain his excitement. I dropped the façade.

"I want these two cans filled with gas. And I want two more containers about the same size, empty."

I applied the same old bluff. "If you're fast and honest there's more where that came from."

The man swallowed and nodded, and looked up past my shoulder to the boy in the watchtower. Then he disappeared beyond the razorwire and the rubble filled barrels, crawling into an unlit tent a row or two behind the barricade. Muffled sounds emerged and travelled down the central avenue of shacks and shanties, and the guard emerged with a string of dried fish that flashed in the night. An angry looking head popped through the tent flap and hissed up at him through straggly hair.

"You'd better be right mister. Is it the woman?"
The guard waved her back inside. "Someone else so keep your mouth shut. Some old fella. Get inside!"

The guard glanced at me briefly and then turned away, heading further up the road between the tents, splayed fish dangling over his shoulder. He entered one that was bigger and squarer – more sturdy – and a light went on within. After some long moments he emerged carrying one large, broad aluminium pan under one arm and two white plastic cylinders with screw caps. He looked back at me nervously from a distance and hurried over, anxious to make the deal.

He presented me with the plastic containers – they were slightly translucent and had handles moulded into their round bodies. They were smaller than I liked but I nodded in agreement. The guard put the pan on the cracking tarmac and proceeded to unscrew the lids of the tin tanks before emptying them into the pan one after the other. He shook the last drops out of the cans, and took them off to a little shed behind the watchtower. When he emerged both cans were full of gas, and the guard struggled to bring them over to me. He stood before me and tried to hold them up towards my face for inspection, but I waved him away. I could smell the volatile fumes pouring out into the night.

The man bent to screw the caps on as I fidgeted, and then he attempted to pick the cans up to hand them to me. I scowled and batted him down – I had a sense that disparagement was the language this one understood.

"Get me some string. Thread," I said, and waited awkwardly as he scurried off, feeling vulnerable out there alone on the tarmac deck.

The guard emerged from his shed clutching a strand of blue nylon twisted in his fingers. It was buckled and kinked, and had at some point formed part of a much larger rope. I took the thread and bent to tie it through the handles of my empty container and then I placed them over my shoulders and stooped to pick up the gas tanks, wavering and fighting for my balance.

"Will you be back?" The guard asked, a little too eagerly.

"I will," I said no more. I turned to head down the slope to my waiting ferry.

The ratty boatman watched with interest as I waddled slowly downhill. He eyed my sloshing tanks as I struggled to step over the gunwale. Wordlessly he cast off from the artificial shore, and as his eyes shone in the night I had the uncomfortable feeling that I'd spent all my chips. I had a cargo, I wasn't expected anywhere.

"What's in there now?" He said lightly.

"None of your business," I croaked. We rowed on in stiff silence. The wind changed direction as we struck out onto the bay, and the salt spray drifted into my eyes like a fine smoke. I stared over the boatman's shoulder at the spire of the ferry building as it pierced the distant waves. It loomed closer to the sky as we approached. The boatman did his best not to look at me but I caught his hungry glances in the darkness.

The boat went out into the deep water of the bay to take us safely around the Ferry building and the sandbanks of Fisherman's Wharf when the boatman made his move. We were as far as we would get from any land, I could see it coming. There was no warning, no self appreciating speech of triumph although

I'd half expected one from such a greasy man as this, he simply put the oars down carefully and lunged for me as the smile faded from his lips. His face twisted into a maul of hatred and jealousy, and I caught the flash of a blade in the corner of my eye, but I was ready. I had the muzzle of my pistol pointing at his face and the hammer clicked while he was still a foot away. I'd been holding it under my gown, clutching my insurance for dear life like it was a newborn baby while my palm grew sweaty and the handle grew hot in my hand. The boatman froze awkwardly, arms outstretched as the little vessel rocked wildly.

"How do ah know," he said, panting, "that there is anything in there?"

I moved the barrel of the gun until it was pressed against his forehead. "You want to distrust me at this moment?" I said. "Row."

The boatman ran his empty hand through his hair, drawing it back out of his eyes, and he clenched his jaw. Slowly he sat back down, moving backwards and never taking his eyes off me, and he took up the oars with a sulk and a face like thunder, lips screwed up and his brow knitted. He rowed slow and steady, expending as little effort as possible on my behalf. I was conscious of the time but I made no mention of it, I simply leant back and watched him while balancing the pistol on one knee, my finger wedged firmly into the trigger guard.

We went on in murky silence, past the sandbanks and the sucking eddies and the silhouetted, overcast glares of the crippled towers looming over us out of the waves. As we drew close to the jetty the bile rose in the back of my throat and I had the urge to dispatch him anyway. But I would not do it in front of the girl, certainly not in the way that I wanted to, and I would not see his juices go to waste with a bullet. The boat scraped noisily against the submerged building as we drew up against the jetty, and the man sat still, hands resting lightly on the oars with the air of explosion about his face. He stared at me directly.

"Git out."

I suppressed the urge to smile and I took to my feet, putting one gas tank on the jetty before the other, never releasing the grip of my pistol. I slung the empty containers on the shore and then stepped off the boat with a forced slowness, holding back the instinct to bolt as I kept an eye on the murderous thug below me. I stood on the edge of the jetty, gun in hand, watching him cast of and shrink away into the night. I didn't turn my back on him until he was out of sight, I gave him those precious minutes of the dark hours.

When he was gone I turned and picked up my cargo and wobbled uncertainly along the spongy path to the sidewalk before calling for Joany in the darkness. She emerged silently from behind an upturned dumpster at the mouth of an ally up the hill, looking at me cautiously before descending to meet me.

"Do you still have your water?"

"Why?" She shot back suspiciously.

"It doesn't matter any more." I handed her my empty cans. "Go fill these up. Try and avoid the slime."

I started up the hill, gauging the colour of the night nervously. A little later I heard the girl's footsteps behind me, the water sloshing and swaying at her side. We walked in silence, I had no desire to talk, and I wondered at which point I would leave her and continue on my own. I wanted her to know as little as possible, but tonight, as the corners of the sky turned an endless, threatening purple, I had no time for ruses or deceptions.

We made our way slowly up Broadway and then headed north through the shadows, vulnerable in the open streets with our heavy loads. I limped and sweated my way along, racing the dawn, and barbs stuck in my throat every time I turned to look at the eastern sky. The death of the night is such an abrupt event in summer, and I remained terrified of being caught out. Joany stopped with me every time I paused at the paling sky, confused and anxious, but I went on across the broken sidewalks and the rubble, bitter and wordless as we hit the hill upon which my tower is perched.

To my eyes, the sight of my tower coming into view was that of a tombstone silhouetted against an ultraviolet sky. I'm not sure Joany noticed the gloaming as we hurried on, and I no longer wasted time looking to the east. I was familiar with the process, the approach of the sun writhed urgently through my being, rang through my ears, prickled my skin. I scratched across the wastelands outside the building, the dead grass, the low, crumbling ornamental walls and the mounds of trash, and I burst through the sharp and shattered double doors, racing across the ruined lobby as my eyes streamed with hot tears. Joany was somewhere behind me, and I disappeared past the evil stairs and the elevators and waited by the door to the garage steps.

I watched as Joany appeared, a shadow wobbling through the doorway, and impatiently I waved her over, grinding my heels and wiping the sweat out of my eyes. The girl scurried through the hallway, seemingly immune to the decaying smell, now fragrant with fluids and old rot and dog shit, and I pushed the door open as she approached. I crossed the darkness of the parking floor, heading in my haste for Joany's hideout, and I sensed her hesitance at the top of the stairs. I heard her shuffling movements. With no open doorway behind me, with no weak light shining as a beacon she could not see to cross the desert.

I sighed and turned, calling to her, realising with a little spark of pleasure that I could see her in the depths of darkness – if not her identifying features then her form.

"How many steps are there?" I called out impatiently.

"Dunno."

"Well how many were there last time you used them girl?" I barked uselessly.

She shrugged in the darkness and impatience twisted within me like barbed wire.

"There are five steps down. Take them, and then turn to the ri-" I stopped myself, no desire to highlight the strangeness of my vision or schedules. "Just follow the sound of my voice as I talk."

Slowly the girl made her way over. Her steps were small, her manner unsure. I spoke to her in the darkness, struggling to keep my voice soft as the seconds wore on. Although I was safe I was impatient still. Together we made our way over to the wall and trailed our spare little fingers along the concrete towards the pile of cardboard and rags that I could make out in the corner, the pile that was the girl's nest.

Joany set her heavy load down on the ground and stretched out with her hands, grasping for the filthy bedding she slept on. As she was settling in the middle of the pile, presumably rummaging for food like some rogue hamster, I spoke out across the empty black.

"Hide those containers. I'll be back for them tomorrow and I'll bring a little water. Stay out of sight."

I crossed the strewn floor, following the faint glow of the crack in the doorway beyond. I climbed the stairs and shoved the door open, turning, halting on the threshold.

"It would be dangerous for you to talk of this."

I left.

Hauling my cargo up the endless stairs, dizzy in the corkscrew, I peered up anxiously, judging my progress against the colour of the dawn in the shattered skylight far above. The turning, twisting, trudging journey is monotonous, soulless, I am stiff and painfully exhausted, and the secure knowledge that I will make this evil pilgrimage again and again and again drives me to paralysing despair as my soul dries up and my motivation evaporates. Needless to say, I do not make good progress. I barely make it above the fire damage and the dangerous dilapidation of the lower floors before the morning glow sears my eyes and presses unbearably upon my scarred and thickened skin. I make my refuge in a darkened hallway behind a stout metal fire door somewhere around floor nine, setting down the gas cans and nursing the pain in my shoulders, working the numbness out of my abused fingertips. This is my journey. This is the endless journey and it is always like this, always the same – one long, singularly monotonous, indistinguishable moment of exhaustion and reckless despondency stretching through the centuries. In the darkness I lose myself to the delirium that precedes sleep, it isn't restful.

This is the dangerous feeling, the mortal feeling, the one that will one day kill me. I am scared for the few moments a century when it comes on, and terrified when it is able to infect my sleep this way. What is the point of these stairs? What is the point of this struggle, this constant running to keep up, to stay alive? I banish these thoughts as I lie on the brittle floor huddled and alone. I try to remember the glorious times, the brief, golden moments of universal connection and suspicious coincidence that show me there is a purpose to creation, to even my bewildering existence. I summon the feeling of flow, but there, in the false darkness on a floor hundreds of feet up in the sky, it is a weak brown glow constructed within my mind, not the divine, overpowering blaze that I want it to be, the great flooding source outside myself. In the darkness the memory doesn't matter, nothing matters, and under the feeling of despondency I am unable to care. Under the fug of my exhaustion, sheltering in a space that is not mine and that I cannot fortify, I cannot escape the paralysis and I cannot care. But that is fine, because there is nothing here to harm me save myself, and I am not about to lift a finger. I know as I head off into delirium and restless, drowning sleep that I am safe until dark, and when the sun descends and freedom returns, blossoming like a night flower, I will be able to move again. I can do nothing but watch myself in impassive detachment, but then, all I need do is wait.

16

I wake up with a start and the gradual realisation that it is already dark. Sometime during the dead hours the fug abandoned me, and I find I am able to face the stairs again. They are endless but somehow I do not care and I do not need to think about them, somehow I am more endless, and I am content in this knowledge. Sleeping past sundown has revived my psyche a little. I get to my feet, leaving my gas cans in the hallway, and I make for the door, turning down the stairs to collect the raw bay water that Joany has stashed for me. Halfway down that first flight I sigh, remembering the girl and the promise of water, and I sit on the steps to think, rubbing the sleep out of my eyes and running my fingers through the fine, wispy hair of my scorched scalp, trying to comb the frustration out of my lost brain.

It is one of those silent thinking sessions where there is no voice in your mind, no progression step by step. It appears that nothing at all is going on, a vacuous experience of time and space, and yet somewhere in your mind some part of you already knows what must be done, and the silent, dumbfounded remainder of your mind is simply coming to terms with the inevitable.

I don't bother to sigh, or stamp my foot as I rise. There is, after all, no one watching. I simply return to the hallway and collect the gasoline before heading back up to my apartment. I pay no attention to the twisting, trudging journey, even as the pain in my shoulders rises to a high-pitched scream and my legs stiffen with exhaustion. Instead my mind wanders off into daydreams of hunting and plans to make the still more efficient. I need that copper piping after all.

I am surprised when I randomly crash back into reality. Sometimes I have climbed a floor, sometimes many. In my dreaming I have no sense of time, and there seems no rhyme or reason to the amount of distance that has passed. I pay little attention when I arrive at my apartment – there is no relief in the inevitability. I cross the battered lounge to the balcony and step outside into the night air, hot and dry and stale. The unforgiving summer is fast approaching, brief though it may be. High up above the smoke riddled city the wind gusts, and my eyes run as I unscrew the fuel cap of the generator and top up the gas. The machine bleeps gratefully, and a little ethereal light flickers from orange to green, telling me the tank is full. I pause on the balcony when my work is done, leaning on the balustrade and gazing out over the city as the wind claws my back and ruffles my shirt. I look down at the burning buildings and the twinkling campfires, the lights reflecting off the black floodwaters of the Market Street Channel. I have the expensive compulsion to wash, and so I go inside, locking the gas away carefully in the master bathroom before retiring to my little en-suite with a bottle of water, a sliver of soap and a rag.

I strip off slowly in my stiffness, and remove my cares along with my earthly garments. I am all that exists in this long moment. I stand before the mirror above the basin and stare at myself, the stooped, haggard figure I barely recognise, the emaciated limbs and the ravaged features drowned under the scars and the grime. Yet there are hints of my old self returning – my eyes are brighter, there is a flash of silver in the deep, wounded black of my irises, the whites are a lighter, a little less angry red. There is the bud of a nose, shrunken and pink, emerging slowly out of the central cavity in my face. With a little practice I can close my shrivelled lips over my brown teeth and reduce the persistent, sticky dryness that haunts my mouth.

I pour a tiny well of clear water into my cupped hand and lather the soap before spreading the bubbles over my skin. It takes several turns before my body is coated and sticky. I press the bunched up rag to the mouth of the water bottle and flip the container upside down briefly to dampen the cloth before dabbing the soap from my skin. The pressure from the cloth dragging over my face and muscles serve to release some of the pain and tension in my body, and the moment is slow and silent and peaceful. Although I am only a little cleaner when I am finished, I am more relaxed.

After spending the long daytime lying on a hard nylon carpet I long to crawl into bed and sleep a proper sleep, but instead I hunt for an old soda bottle and I fill it with water. It is dented and the plastic has smoky white creases running through it, I tell myself that this will be Joany's advance – her retainer, knowing that whilst she should drink this much in a day, it may be the most clean, safe water she sees in a week, especially with the rains gone and high summer approaching. I falter with realisation as I pour the water, keenly aware that I have already given the girl a place in my brain. She inhabits a box labelled 'ally', or at least 'employee'. Someone under my wing. Damn.

I block the thought from my mind as I make my escape from the apartment. I flee, leaving the revelation buried in my little en-suite bathroom, but I can hear its heartbeat thudding loudly as I make my way down all those stairs, limping noticeably. I should have drunk something, I realise as the hunger grows, a sickening vacuum within my belly. By the time I arrive on the ground floor I am agitated by my own thoughts, but a promise is a promise. I open the door to the garage and sink down into the depths, crossing the parking floor with blind confidence. I am disappointed as I sense with growing certainty that the girl isn't here. I will have no brittle conversations today.

I stare over the florid little nest, seeing through its disguises and analysing its secrets in the darkness. The plastic containers holding the bay sludge are buried under a filthy duvet, and as I retrieve them I leave the precious clear water behind. I consider leaving Joany a note – 'This is a retainer,' or 'Use it wisely,' – something to that effect, but as I realise I have neither pen nor paper and she has no light, I find myself wondering whether the girl can even read.

I stand alone in the darkness feeling suddenly useless and at a loss over what to do next. I turn, getting my bearings, and orientate myself towards the garage ramp and the shattered rolling shutters. Without particularly deciding to, I find myself heading up that concrete slope, following the smells and the breeze out into the night. The ramp curls around and I climb steadily before coming to a pile of twisted metal strips and wire rope that used to be part of the door mechanism. I pick my way through the sharp and treacherous debris, clawing my way over the sheared sheet metal slats that have been torn asunder. I feel like a cat squeezing through a hole in a fence, ears back, eyes half shut and limbs padding repeatedly, feeling for firmer ground. Suddenly I am out in the open, and I sense the air moving freely around me. It hums vaguely, smelling of trash, death and decay.

My view opens up as I climb the last few feet of the ramp, but all I can see is the wasted grounds of the tower, mud and garbage and bodies where there used to be grass and tended roses and raised beds. Beyond the driveway lies the desolation of the intersection, a broad empty space with rusting streetcar lines and crumbling asphalt. I could almost taste the memory of it – the car fumes in the air, the scent of pollen drifting on the breeze. Now it was nothing, empty and shattered, each building I could see a shell, a shadow that no longer blocked my view of the ruins behind. Looking uphill or down, all across the island, the only structures left composed an endless sea of fractured, pointless walls that held no roofs up, enclosed no rooms. Just relics, shards of gypsum and concrete protruding from the earth, tombstones marking the grave of a city.

As I gaze over the ruined space before me I feel the emptiness of it, the sheer uselessness, and I am chilled. The desolation seeps out of the land and into my soul. The value of this land, this city before me is gone forever, and it seems such a senseless, bitter waste. As I stand there I realise I am alone in this part of the non-city, there is nothing for me here, no one to colour my existence. I turn my back and head down the slope bitterly, holding my breath until the bouquet of destruction fades. As I traverse the garage floor I realise that I am passing under twenty floors of concrete and steel, immense and stiff and solid. Standing in the darkness under all that cold, dead masonry I am struck by the knowledge that it too will crumble into dust and useless waste. I hurry on, heading for the stairs, not wanting to spend another day on the floor of an unsecured hallway.

I drag myself up the stairs, a small barrel of bay water in each hand, and I feel the slow, inevitable turn of the earth as the short night comes to a close. By the time I am at my door, stiff legged and aching, fumbling for my keys and dropping them, I can feel the warning tingles forming at the nape of my neck and preparing to flood upwards and over my crown. The key slides in and turns, I practically fall across the threshold, more pleased than ever to see the inside of my darkened little flat. It is ordered in here, constructed, useful. Although the semblance of civilisation is a weak, isolated illusion that struggles in the coming dark ages, it is still better in here with the polished furniture and the clean kitchen and the sharp odour of gasoline haunting the bathroom. Better than out there, where only the bones are polished, the buildings are picked clean, and the only smell in the air is of the death of an epoch.

I lock the door behind me and brush the sweat out of my eyes, I am tired and the sun is approaching but I realise with indignance that I do not want to sleep yet. It must be only four a.m. – I sleep too much, I avoid too much. But there I am again, trapped in a little apartment with nothing to do but play music and read and pretend and avoid. I sit for a while, resting while the music box soothes my agitations with its compressed sounds, and then I set about with the raw water and the still, running back and forth with containers and bowls and anything I can lay my hands on, but I cannot open the balcony, so the equipment quickly overheats as I run out of coolant water and I overheat also. I don't care in the least – I have something to do. It feels good to be working on something relevant, to be saving myself one more time, even if I am only pushing back the inevitable.

When I am done and the machine is off I look with satisfaction over the bowls of crystal water cluttering the kitchen surfaces. The still creeks and tinks and groans with a metallic itch as it cools down. It must be late enough for bed, I tell myself, especially for a convalescent, but before I retire I reward myself with the bag of blood I have been dreaming of since I set out on the stairs earlier. I savour the rapidly cooling liquid, warming my hands against the slick plastic bag while sitting in my leather armchair. I'm huddled over my meal as if I were cold and sitting outside and it were a steaming mug of soup. As if.

I retired late that morning, drunk with the buzz of blood and warmed through to my fingertips. The next two nights were a blur of action, running the still, organising my containers, water cans, bowls, cleaning and juggling so that fresh water never touched a dirty tank. How domestic, how industrious. My activities allowed me to believe I was saving myself rather than delaying the descent. Over that time I was a little more generous with my use of water, as you are with things when you suddenly have plenty, when you think you have an endless source. I actually washed some clothes, and some bedding. I washed myself first, and then took the grey water to my sheets, then to my clothes, adding soap as I went until the water in the sink was filthy black and thick. Reluctantly I threw the water out and rinsed everything in a couple of litres of fresh water that I couldn't find a bottle for.

The effect was miraculous. Feeling clean, being inside clean clothes and sleeping against air-dried sheets felt incredible. I felt civilised and renewed, and for the next few nights I worked with an easy vigour, taking everything in my stride and overcoming all the little trials of survival. Soon however I was sweeping the floor, or wiping the shutters, for I had processed all the raw water and I was finding other things to do, looking for ways to keep the productivity buzz going whilst avoiding the fact that there was nothing more I could usefully do at the top of my ivory tower, and that soon I would be forced to descend into the unpredictable, disorganised vicious real world once again, avoiding the fact that I could likely not do it alone and would have to place my secrets and my safety in the trust of a teenage girl.

The moment of awareness came to me as I was bent under the kitchen sink, looking for bleach that could not be replaced in order to clean a toilet that I rarely used and that no longer flushed. Like any addict I was locked in the binge/purge cycle, manically cleaning and jobsworthing, compulsively consuming the water that I would need to buy my next round of fuel. Compulsively destroying myself.

The observation had been nagging me for a couple of days, but as I grasped the almost-empty bottle of bleach at the back of that cupboard it slapped me in the face, and I threw myself backwards onto the kitchen floor, staring out across my uselessly spotless apartment. *I may be dead in that chair in two weeks time,* I thought, *but no one could say the floor isn't clean and the cushions aren't plumped.* I sat dumbfounded and confused for some minutes, not knowing whether to laugh or cry. I got to my feet, my first instinct was to grab the water cans and the empty gas tanks and to make a trade that night, but I could feel that it was gone midnight and quite hopeless, and the frustration bubbled up inside me. I went and stood on the balcony and watched the city decay. The short summer nights hadn't mattered three years ago – the blink of an eye for one such as me – a time when the Internet still worked, when home delivery worked. So that is the half-life of a city – three years. Less even.

I dropped the compulsions, the illusions of civilised security, forced myself to let them go. Reducing my blood intake was a different matter, and my finite supply was dwindling to emergency levels. I had perhaps another two months before I would have to find another supply, of whatever kind, of whatever risk, or face the mad, shredding hell of hunger.

I slept fitfully that day, unable to escape the terminal nature of my existence even in my dreams. My finite problems chased me through slumber. Everything was running out, and I was clinging to a way of life that was becoming increasingly impossible, and yet I wasn't ready to let it go. I erupted into consciousness several times, and eventually gave up on sleeping, opting instead to sit out the dead hours, gathering empty cans and spare water, waiting for the darkness to roll around the Earth so I could set out on my next essential trade trip.

I sat in my leather chair in anticipation as the tingling built up within me, waiting for that dazzling click to run through my body as the last of the sun crossed the horizon. I held myself back, arms laying over the armrests as the sensation passed over me in waves, and then I stood, flinging on my hooded gown and grabbing the water tanks and gas cans. I'd tied the empty tanks together with rope, and hung them over my shoulders. All in all it was an effective arrangement, and I made my way down the ever-present steps two at a time with the glow of dusk still burning through the hollow skylight above.

As I descended I found myself thinking about Joany, wondering if the young girl was still in the parking garage, wondering if she was still alive. I stretched my ethereal senses out before me, and certainly there was a faint young mind gloaming through the fuzzy ether somewhere below.

When I found her she was scrabbling around in the ash and rubble of the first floor, sorting through the plastic and the trash for anything useful – Wellington boots and food bowls and rags. The partition walls had caved in, and everything the squatters had left behind – battered chairs and crates, old cooking pots – had been sprinkled with broken concrete from the floors above. Every surface was smashed up, and sharp, twisted spikes of steel rebar were scattered in every direction, laced with rounds of concrete like drops of dew hanging along a spider's web. There was a thick coating of masonry dust covering the scene, and I felt as if I had blundered into a strange, indoor winterland as I watched the girl cough and splutter in the acrid clouds she was raising. She was covered and pale, a twisted snowglobe pixie dancing on the fake-frosted surface of a badly decorated joke.

I stood in an empty doorframe, the gypsum plasterboard either side of which had buckled and melted in the damp bay air, finally shearing away and lying in ribbons on the floor. I watched the girl by the thin light of the dying city that crawled in through the shattered windows, but she searched by the light of an electric bulb. It was electro-catalytic, and almost exhausted by the look of its beam. Every few moments the spotlight would shrink and dim to an ugly orange brown, and the girl would straighten up and shake the small baton in her hand before blowing into the mouthpiece. She did this over and over, and every time it interrupted her slow work in the dust. She didn't bother to swear – she was resigned.

"I told you it was dangerous up here."

Joany squeaked and dropped to the floor in shock, hiding the light and crawling behind a large, flat slab of concrete that had dropped out of the floor above. I stood and waited, knowing that I could be more patient than the youngster, and enjoying the game more than I should. It was only a couple of minutes in the night, but we hung in the distance and the darkness, waiting, wondering, anticipating, feeling each other.

"Who's there?"

"Just me. You're quite safe."

The girl stuck her head up from behind the slab and squinted through the mesh of twisted rebar. Once she was certain it was me she stood up.

"I knew it was you." She proclaimed indignantly.

"If you find anything that will hold water you would do well to pass it to me."

"Oh yeah?"

"I assume you found what I left you."

"Yeah." She stiffened slightly, the attitude dropped.

"There's more of that if you'll stay where I can find you and work with me."

"Got any on you?"

The girl bounded eagerly through rusted spikes and strings of brittle concrete, and as she drew close I could see her face and that she had been able to eat. I found myself wondering what she was doing for it. She never would tell me.

"I need to take another trip. Will you wait for me at the jetty?"

She nodded.

So another spray-soaked boat ride and I am once again standing before the gatehouse at the foot of the Bay Bridge. They've cut the bodies down and I'm relieved. They see me coming, someone strikes a thin, high pitched bell, and a short, awkward little man with a limp emerges from behind the blockade and dashes down to greet me. His enthusiasm does nothing to mask his greed. As he approaches he opens his mouth to speak, and then his eyes trip across my cargo and he smiles a shark's grin.

"Well hello there! I'm Darius. You are?"

I look down at his palm from behind my hood and then to the heavy cans in each hand. I make no sound.

"Uh. Right. You must be one of our independent traders. Welcome! Come this way!

I was led through the gap in the blockade and taken a

short way down the central avenue of the encampment, between the tents and the fires and the little shanty shacks that populated the bridge canopy. A hush spread around me as we went on, old men stopped their campfire gossip and women turned into their tents, not wanting to see or be seen. Yet there were eyes everywhere, youngsters peeking through the gaps in draping plastic, spies sitting in the gatherings beyond, or pretending to fish off the edges of the bridge. Hundreds of tents cluttered the causeway, disappearing into the dark distance and the gaping mouth of the tunnel that ran through the heart of Yerba Buena Island at the end of the bridge. The avenue was lined with Coleman lamps and glowsticks, fires in old oil barrels and strings of El-wire and fairy lights. Fish were everywhere, gutted and splayed out on wire frames that stood over the fires, fish stacked in piles by the rusting girders at the edge of the tarmac where they'd been caught, or hanging in nets strung from the perilous canopy above, out of the reach of goats but not gulls.

The goats were everywhere also, bleating and braying and kicking, mostly tied up lest they eat the nylon from the tents. A filthy little girl with thick, knotted hair gazed at me sullenly, clutching a writhing kid goat in her arms like a doll until her young, haggard mother emerged from a hole-ridden shelter to bring her daughter inside. As I looked on she covered her child's eyes, she refused to look in my direction herself.

All around were signs of construction and improvement – people striving for bigger, better, more. Patches had been sewn over fraying tent skins, additions made and reinforced with flimsy wooden frames. People aspired to wood and cardboard walled shacks, some had even cut down old oil drums and beaten them into flat panels for the roofs and walls of their shanties. The constructions vied for space away from the edges of the bridge and out of the wind. The central avenue was a ramshackle and unspoken, it had more evolved than been defined. Everywhere you looked people wanted to be near it, and to be further along. Your status seemed to rise as you got closer to the tunnel and the island, and off in the dark distance the hovels became more substantial – fully wooden huts and primitive, poured concrete cabins with open windows.

I didn't get that far. I was led through the campsites and the piles of goat filth and sewage that had yet to be collected and sold on, and my guide stopped abruptly outside the large tent that I had seen once before. Through the gaps in the hanging fabric I could tell that the interior was well lit, and as Darius pulled the door flap back and ushered me in, I realised the canopy consisted of several layers of musky, draped carpet. This was the tent from which the last merchant had emerged bearing the water containers I had asked for.

As I entered I had to duck, and I noticed the tent went back a long way. Somehow I hadn't noticed its entire length from the outside, and I had the dizzying sensation that it was bigger inside than out. My smug looking host sat on a pillow on the floor, his back to a net curtain that divided the public space of the trading house from the private home.

The tent and the tarmac were layered with rugs and strips of old carpet thick with dust and soot. On the ground between myself and the languid man was a fire nestling on sheet metal over scorched and melted tarmac where a square had been left out of the matted layers of rugs. The acrid smell of burnt pitch escaped with the smoke through a small gash in the roof, and the man examined me through the thin blue plumes that rose steadily up to the sky. He waved me over to a cushion by his side, and as I passed the glow of the flames I saw the silhouette of a woman nursing a baby through the netting behind, and some way further off there was an older woman, sitting quietly, sowing or weaving, doing something repetitive and hypnotic with her hands, and no doubt listening to every word we spoke.

I sat to the side of the slim, bald, lanky man who had been watching me intently and suppressing his trader's glee.

"I understand you have something for me? Tea?" He said, proffering a tiny, cracked cup containing a muddy brown liquid. The man held it out with both hands, and I took it gratefully, enjoying the warmth as I held it to my lips. I sipped the broth, shocked that it actually was tea, strong and earthy and invigorating.

"It's good," I murmured, but I took no more.

"Just don't ask me for coffee," the man raised his eyebrows. "I'm sure there will be some soon. Worth its weight in water it is. I'm Tim." The man extended a long, thin hand. I shook it, feeling the roughness of my clawed fingers grating against his firm flesh. After some moments of expectant silence Tim lost patience. "You are?"

"A trader. Just as your man said." I answered in my rough, scratchy voice as I looked at him from over the rim of my cup. Tim was absently rubbing his hands together, feeling the coolness of my touch. My cracked voice peaked his interest. He inclined his head a little, struggling to see beyond the wool of my gown in the glow of lamplight and the flicker of the fire. I tipped my cup again and slurped against the liquid loudly.

Tim held his stance for a moment, being deliberate about his veiled attempt to see my face, and I held mine, being deliberate in my casual attempt to obscure his view. When it became apparent that he could force nothing from me he relaxed and moved on, immediately registering that there was nothing further to be gained. He flicked back into a casual manner.

"So what is it I can do for you?"

I nodded to the five-gallon army surplus tin cans that I'd set down in the corner next to me. "I brought water. I'd like to trade it for gas."

"Well I see." Tim paused and allowed a flash of concern to pass across his face. "There isn't so much we can do for people who can only provide small quantities here and there..." The trader's voice trailed off into the night air and the constant thrum of human activity outside. He'd left the space between us open, hoping that I would fill it. I sat in the shadows and blinked at him expectantly, staring over my teacup.

Tim looked at me, and then exhaled. "What I mean to say is – we usually like to deal in larger quantities – regular deliveries, that sort of thing. You understand."

I waited a moment in the hanging silence.

"Usually?" I said slowly. Tim clenched his jaw in the firelight. I could see that muscle on the side of his face, the one that bulges when you press your teeth together. He smiled thinly.

"Is my water not wet?"

Tim nodded.

"Is it not good?"

Tim nodded again, with growing distaste. "I assume so, yes."

"Will it not save your wife and child from thirst?"

The trader gave a stiff nod of admission.

Then what. Is. It. You. Need?" I asked very slowly, gazing at him over my teacup.

Tim lowered his voice and spoke in hard, direct tones, letting his annoyance at my refusals seep into his words, thin and icy and determined. "I want to know when you're coming, how much you're bringing, how much you have and where you get it from."

I raised my eyebrows and drew my head back a little. I think I laughed out loud. The woman nursing the infant beyond the veil looked up in my direction briefly, and then caught herself. She quickly jammed her eyes back down to her child before stealing a glance at the ostensibly oblivious matriarch. Tim's pallid cheeks took on a low colour as irritation or embarrassment rose to his face.

"You must understand," he pressed on, afraid of losing control of the situation altogether, "that we need to know our suppliers are not competing with each other, or with us. And our competitors on the mainland –"

"You cannot know those things." I said plainly, batting the questions away with the back of my hand, spilling the tea on the worn carpet between us. "You will not."

I sat and held his gaze with my shrunken black eyes, and for that short time neither of us spoke. Tim again dropped back into his casual, conversational guise. It was a reflex, but it was wearing thin for both of us. He took his time regaining his composure, he took the cup from me, his fingers brushing electrically against my own, and lifted the pot, dribbling the last of the tea into my cup. He spoke slowly in a quiet voice, but kept his eyes on the thin, sharp column of liquid as it dropped from the spout of the small, chipped pot he held in his hand.

"You know, you're new to the Looter's Causeway, so I'm sure you don't know our ways. I made a simple request. I'm sure you'll appreciate the opportunity to reconsider." He inclined his head as he passed the teacup back to me. "In good faith." He wore a smile like steel.

Tim looked to my eyes as he held the cup out to me. I took it gently from his fingers, but I set it down on the carpet between us.

"You want to know where my stash is. What do I have then? I wonder what it is that you think could induce me to give up my nest egg?"

The trader leant back a little, a broad, ugly smile spread wide across his face and he shrugged bashfully.

"Like I said, you don't know our ways." He frowned, as if to himself, enthralled with his own tedious performance. "Life on the causeway is random and chaotic. Friendships shift, accidents happen. Survival here is viciou- aaah."

The pretender's last sounds sighed out of his body like the death throws of punctured bagpipes. Tired of his clumsy threats, I had reached up and drawn the hood back and down from my scalp. The mangled, fluid combination of old and thickened scars together with new pink flesh, the scorched and shrivelled eyes weeping thin fluid down the side of my face, the corpse' lips and demon's teeth, the miniature, baby pink nose emerging from the black gash at the centre of my face must have been something of a shock. I felt the prickles rise along the fine wisps of hair that struggled for survival on my scalp as all the emotions of horror and revulsion flew across the man's face and mind. His gasp was so sudden and choking that even the old woman faltered in her work, hands pausing as she looked up and peered blindly through the mesh. I didn't wait for him to catch himself, I went on breezily.

"Whatever threat it is that you're proposing, I suggest you do it or move on. It makes no odds. There's nothing left to be done to me."

Tim fought to regain his breath, trying not to stare and unable to help himself. He was possessed with the fascination of revulsion, with car crash voyeurism, and I did not enjoy being the object of his curiosity, some freak to be gawped at and then ignored. I drew the hood back down over my forehead and leant further back into the shadows.

I waited patiently for some time as the man gulped his tea and caught his breath, he looked at me, and he looked everywhere but. It seemed he knew no way to regain his calm persona and save face. As he spluttered I gave him an out and he took it.

"I'll give you a discount. This time." I thought again about the appearance of my brazen charity. "I'm in a hurry."

Tim coughed and nodded, trying to breathe and gulp tea at the same time. He clapped his hands with his eyes shut, and Darius appeared through the door flap where he had been listening. He bore a slightly puzzled expression, but his face was tight and he looked only where he was supposed to. He retrieved the water tanks from my side without so much as a glance at the spluttering trader or myself. Ignorance was most definitely bliss on the Looters' Causeway.

We sat in almost silence, waiting for Darius to return with the gas. Tim tried to recover, tried to laugh and joke and mutter to his women, tried to save face. He couldn't look at me, not because of what he had seen, but because I had beaten him on home turf, in front of his women, and he wanted me gone as soon as possible, presumably so that he could beat his wife in private. He could kill me, and risk losing forever what could be an enormous, life-saving, fortune-making stash of water. But there was a chance I was bluffing and the thought of it galled him, dug into his kidneys. Short of killing me there was little he could do but comply, he at least believed, rightly or wrongly, that torturing me would be futile.

Presently Darius returned with the tanks and Tim looked as relieved as I felt. The stubby man set the cans down and popped the lid from one so that I could smell the volatile tang. Tim watched eagerly, waiting for me to declare the gas good, although all of us could smell the vapour rolling along the floor of the enclosed tent. As I replaced the latch on the lid of the can Tim smiled in relief, and as I stood he practically corralled me through the door flap. He went to place his hand on my shoulder, and then didn't. He muttered loudly, pleasantries and meaningless rubbish, filling his unbearable silence with nervous laughter and face-saving murmurs of the success he had actually lost.

This went on as I picked my way along the avenue towards the blockade and the jetty. Darius carried my load and he walked ahead, strangely silent. We passed the gatehouse and he gave a little nod to the boy in the watchtower with the machine gun, and then we crept down the slope to the black, glassy water and the darkness. I nodded to my boatman waiting in a dingy at the lapping shore, and I splashed through the shallows before climbing into the vessel and holding my arms out to receive the goods from Darius. He passed the tanks dutifully, a pained look on his face as if he were thinking of something that troubled him. The boatman was about to cast off when Darius' expression cracked, and he spoke in an urgent, rapid-fire staccato.

"There's another trader – independent like you. A woman. Ana. You know her right? You know her?"

I was surprised, he was almost pleading for my answer. I shook my head as the boatman pushed off with a jerk and the gulf swelled between us.

"I do not. Why?"

Darius shook his head and screwed his face up in the darkness.

17

It wasn't until I was safely in the boat, watching the bridge shrink away into the gloom that I realised the scale of the bluff I had pulled. As the tension and fear ran through me and out into the water I began to shake a little, and my heart pounded as my face flushed hot and prickly. The journey back was uneventful, my boatman too honest or unimaginative to pull anything. The slow little trips across the bay all blur into one damp evening. We drew up to the jetty and I produced the water payment from a bottle I hid in my gown. Joany was waiting for me as I hurried up the hill, I told her to fill tanks with bay water and catch me up. She looked at me for a moment too long, and something clicked in her mind, but she scurried off, saying nothing.

We hurried into the tower and down into the parking garage, and as I left the raw water in the care of the girl I made a show of leaving the building via the garage ramp before sneaking through the lobby and broaching the stairs. In theory, Joany didn't know the tower was where I made my home, and I had a few things to do before I could lend her such information and make more use of her. The dawn caught me earlier than ever, and I spent a restless day cowering in a spot of darkness on the weakened floor of the seventh, praying the structure would hold.

I'm standing on the roof in the middle of the night, nailing old carpet and plasterboard across the broken window frame of the stairwell skylights, and I don't know why I hadn't done this sooner. It took me two nights to strip the carpets and cut down enough drywall from the seventeenth floor, and then to haul it, limping, up here and force the door to the roof. It felt strange harvesting the seventeenth – an area more pristine and unaltered than my own apartment. I walked around the rooms that had become a relic of contemporary living, obsolete and obscene in their ostentation, and then I smashed the walls down with a lump hammer. It was mildly satisfying.

The wind is fast and cutting up here on the rooftop, and all around me the city glows with tiny pinpricks of orange burn. To the south I can see a few lights on in the Transamerica Pyramid, and I am working in darkness to avoid the attention of the local sniper. We've played our game twice more since the night I discovered it, but I've never asked further questions. Knowledge can be a dangerous thing.

I work in the darkness, slipping on the gravel that populates the roof while the wind gusts and whistles through the heating ducts and the rusting satellite dish. My only tools now are a claw hammer and nails, which seem somehow out of place at the summit of a two-hundred meter man made megaliths, but I enjoy it. I like working, I like hammering, I like the fresh night air and I like the heights. As I hammer nails home through layers of plasterboard and rubberised carpet into the rotting wood of the skylight frame, I enjoy most of all the knowledge that I will be able to traverse the stairwell during the daylight, that I will never again be trapped by the light in some stinking, ash-ridden hallway, left to sleep on floors and cower in corners. This knowledge lends some enthusiasm to my hammer strikes, and the nails that I've scrounged and pulled from walls and furniture, collected and counted like coins in a piggybank, drive home with an ease and a certainty that makes me smile in the darkness.

I am hunting. I am hunting. There is blood in the freezer and I have no immediate need, but soon, for the first time in a century I will be completely dependant on skills I have all but forgotten, so I have fasted for two nights to lend myself the mad keenness of hunger and now I sit on my haunches in a darkened doorway and I wait. I am excited and terrified. I am hunting.

I have a knife, and a pistol that generally I will only use for self-defence. Bullet holes are tiny, but a writhing, screaming human person oozing bile or stomach juices with their blood is little use to me, and very definitely a liability. I sit, listening and fingering the blade of my little knife, studying the layout of the street before me. It is somewhat familiar, for it is on the south side of Russian Hill Island by the shoreline near to where Union Square disappeared beneath the waves, about as far as you can get from my tower. Whilst the rule is generally not to shit in your own back yard, the short nights leave little time for boat trips to unfamiliar areas, especially when my chances of failure and even injury are so high. I know there are still people down here, I have seen their fires regularly from atop my tower.

The air is hot and close, and I sweat uncomfortably under a thin black top and pants. Summers here are unbearable now, endless months of sweaty air and high pressure, building and building until the unholy storms. Until then the air is pregnant with moisture but the ground is bone dry, and the bush fires have begun again, sweeping in glorious terrible waves across Grizzly Peak and Angel Island. As the ash rains down on the shattered city, collecting in the broken doorways, swirling in the gulleys, I sense I am trapped in some perverted snowglobe, a scrawny, satanic Santa Claus. My thumb brushes sideways across the blade of my wicked little carving knife once again. Somewhere out there someone will get an early Christmas tonight.

The doorway I am huddled by is part of an almost normal shop front. The glass is cracked but the frames are intact and the sign says *Peet's Coffee.* It's just a shame that there is no shop behind it. The building was gutted by looters, smashing through the door and tearing the walls down to strip out the pipes and the wire. Perversely this is the one building in the street that has a window intact. It's just a small one to the side of the door, slightly warped and cracked in one corner, but defiantly and bizarrely normal in the midst of the destruction. There is no one here, there is nothing left here but solitary walls looking for a shape to be part of, and rubble earthworks of wood and brick and dust, giant molehills that used to be homes and shops and lifesworks.

The city is a maze of waterways and fallen buildings, cards stacked one in front of the other in an endless parade of parallax and eroded perspective. Those dwellings that weren't felled by the earthquakes or the fires of the storms were assaulted by the looters' lump hammers and the ram-raiding trucks. Across the street, amidst the piles of sticks and slanted superstructures swaying and creaking in the breeze, fragments of a broken shop sign nestle in the dust. The characters are gaudy, cartoonish kanji. The sight is disturbing and familiar, something that haunted me once before, but I have forgotten the language. I do not read it and I do not want to.

There is nothing here, my view is obstructed in all directions by the layers of freestanding wreckage, solitary walls like abandoned termite mounds slowly returning to the earth. There is no one, but I'm sat at the corner of an important intersection on the roads to the shore and the safer interior of the island with its endless warren of basements and hidey-holes. If people want to travel, or sift the floating trash or fish the sick waters, they will have to pass me here.

Across the intersection a broken window flaps in the breeze, banging against its warped frame. Somewhere down the slope water laps at the asphalt, channelled as it is up the streets to rush and stab in light little fingers into the human world of the city. I smell the rats and then I hear them, chittering and clawing as their sour, musky odour pervades the draft running up the hill. And then there is something else. Faint muttering in the night. It fades in and out on the pulsing breeze, but it's getting closer every time I hear it.

It's a man, ragged and tired, hurrying along the street that runs parallel to the water line. He bears a sleeping child, floppy and heavy in his arms, and before he passes me on the opposite sidewalk he halts and jigs the child up in the air a little to regain his grip. He is not what I am waiting for. I do not take them. I will not tell you why – it is not a reason I can be proud of.

So I sit in the darkness and I watch the empty streets, waiting for opportunity to step my way. There are perhaps a hundred minds out there in the night, stretching out in a wide semi-circle from the edge of the invading seas up the hill. A hundred little glowing, writhing, ticking bundles of energy eating and fighting and fucking silently next to their slumbering campmates and compatriots. A hundred or so in the mile and a half I can extend myself across the island, and that is enough. That is plenty lest my faculty be overwhelmed by unfamiliar hopes and alien dreams, voiceless thoughts and simple fears I have never had the opportunity to understand.

There is nothing. The breeze rolls on as the night turns, and the shards of the city creak as the timbers bow under the weight of ruin. I smell the empty air, frozen and patient and mesmerised as minds hover on the edge of my perception, dancing their Brownian motion bee dance as they orbit one another. I am suspended in the infinite moment as it passes along, every loose piece of plaster or paper shifting and vibrating in ways I cannot detect or note as the frequencies of the world sing out under the illusion of solid matter. I cannot tell one moment from the next – in the false stillness has the universe been placed on pause, fast forward or rewind?

A gang of youths drawl past. I feel them coming and pull the hood of my black top down over my face before turning into the uselessly transparent glass corner of the shop front. I loosen my body, pretending to be asleep, but I am listening fiercely and clutching the pistol in my sweaty claw. I cock the hammer silently before the rabble arrive, and I listen to their whoops and their jibes as the tripping footsteps approach, so close and gritty a sound that I know they are on the same sidewalk, the same side of the street as me.

My heart thunders as their footsteps get louder, I watch in my mind as they run and jump, a pack of baby wolves clambering over felled walls and fire gutted chassis, and all the glittering, glittering glass – the stars they grind underfoot. They sweat and boast and joke to hide their fear, they swap tall stories and they swap knives. The oldest is twelve.

I hold my breath and my body stiffens involuntarily as the gang shuffle and jostle above me on the sidewalk. This is the spot they pick for an impromptu wrestling and kicking match, two feet from where I cower, a trapped animal with a last resort. I hear the scraping twist of worn-out sneakers on cement, the yelps and the padding kicks that reaffirm the natural pecking order, the bated silence as the elders get serious, and the laughter as the tension breaks and the loser loses, as the scapegoat takes too much. I listen, cold and sick but impassive as the runt is bullied beyond the point of submission. They do not notice me lying in the dirt at their feet, the old, probably dead bag-o-bones hobo that's no good to anyone. No good for nothing. I breathe again as the boys run off down the street. It is some time before I can hear my thoughts and the night over the rumble of my heartbeat.

It is quiet again, and I sit against the doorframe, hugging my knees against the cold. The night is wearing on and I am despondent. It took me twenty minutes to get here from the tower, it will take my thirty to get back up the hill. I am no longer fascinated by the invisible stillness of time on this particular night, I am just tired and hungry and frustrated. Suddenly the sidewalks are alive with foot traffic. People dribble by in twos and threes, and I don't know who to choose, there is always someone watching. There is a lone man coming up from the water, but there is a couple fifty yards behind him. To my left two girls hurry along the pavement in silence, but behind them two teenage boys are helping an older woman up the street. I have no reason to risk being seen, to risk being noticed. The hunger grinds on in my belly, cold tendrils of mad, driving anticipation reach up into my mind and down into my fingers.

The streets cleared as suddenly as they had become busy, except for a small group that approaches from the right. They are talking and laughing quietly to themselves in low, muffled voices. As they approach I see that it is a party of two girls in front accompanied by two boys behind. Every so often one of the girls attempts to slow down, or one of the boys attempts to speed up so that they might join hands, but the sidewalk is narrow and the girls walk arm-in-arm, clinging fiercely to each other and to girlhood, one girl more so than the other.

The group turned off at the intersection before passing me, and made their way up the hill. There was no one else on the street, and so I slipped out of my hiding place and rounded the corner, following them from a distance on the other side of the street. It wasn't ideal – a group of four – it was completely impractical in fact, but by this point I was taking my chances, or else I might sit there all night with no other opportunity arising.

I was hoping that the group would fragment, that one would separate from the others, wandering off into my waiting arms. I waited patiently as they dithered up the hill, keeping my distance and straining to hear their twilight banter. They seemed to have forever as they lingered in one another's company and muttered inanely about the light on the water – the girls romantically, the boys with the childish cynicism of the hyena. I looked away and kept my head down as a man passed me on the sidewalk. He was older and bearded and he carried a pole with line and a stinking bucket of offal. The ripe smell assaulted my nostrils and it continued to drift uphill as the grizzled fisherman stomped his way down to the water and the predawn feeding frenzy. I considered turning and following him, but it was the wrong direction to be heading in so late in the night, and just then the girls said their goodbyes and turned down a treacherous alleyway that cut through the wreckage of a little shopping strip. The boys hung at the threshold, watching them go, and I focussed my mind ahead of them. A glitter of thoughts laced the space beyond the girls' bobbing minds, they were making their way towards a small group, an encampment of some sort. I crashed back out into solid reality, opening my eyes. The boys it is then.

I watched the boys continue up the hill, scrambling over piles of rubble and making their way around a large crater that engulfed the sidewalk where an electricity junction had subsided. They were oblivious as I crossed the street after them. Dawdling along their path, the youngsters were silent and dopey in the small hours, and I hung back, waiting patiently for my moment.

A sick coldness crept down my throat when I realised the boys were making their way towards another camp bigger than the last. They climbed the hill slowly, talking their night over with the enthusiasm of youth, all the while the glimmering nest of minds somewhere ahead drew closer and closer. Dawdling to a stop on a street intersection, they linger over their excitements and tall tales as though they have all night. I waited in the shadows across the street, somewhere between patience and rage, trying not to listen as well as I am able, trying to hear only the bad things since I spotted them. I was trying not to make them into real people. My hearing excelled in spite of me.

"– trust me, trust me man she's well into me. Didn't you see them signs?"

"Yeah yeah, the signs, the signs! What'd she do? Spray 'Fuck Me Hard' across her tits? B'cos you my friend, you sure as hell weren't paying no attention to her face."

"You just jealous, pencil dick. Just 'cos you got some frigid ice queen with a bee up her ass."

"Hey shut your mouth. Shut your mouth man!" Said the weaker of the two. He was short, and skinny streaks of dirty brown hair hung down across his forehead. His t-shirt was stained and torn.

"Alright, alright! Just 'cos you ain't getting any. Jesus!"

"Oh that's it Mick. Like you are."

And then they were scuffing each other, scrapping like children in a tangle of arms and legs, twisted fingers and bruised shins. Neither of them knew how to throw a punch, but it didn't matter, they weren't trying to hurt one another. Then they were down on the ground, curling up to avoid knees and batting away slaps, laughing as I watched. An empty desperation rose in my gullet like bile. My knees were shaking with hunger, an absent mix of need and withdrawal.

The desperate wrestling dissolved into giggles and the two of them regressed to earlier years and earlier games, a world of wedgies and wet willies that existed before girls and hormones and sex. They got to their feet slowly, each calling truce whilst trying to steal in the last attack, to land the last word.

"All right man, enough – enough! You win ok! Quit it!" Said the elder one, the heavier one. "Where you thinking of putting that? Go on, get outta here." He nodded down the intersection.

"Mick – aren't you?"

"I'll catch you up. I gotta piss."

"But Micky – I'll –"

"Eh piss off Lee ok? I'll catch you up."

The younger boy swore under his breath and turned his back, leaving Mick alone. Leaving him alone with me.

Mick watched the other go, and after a minute or so of

Samuel Collins

standing on that deserted corner beside a rusting street lamp that was bent down across the road like a felled tree, he produced a small pouch from his pocket, and looking up and down the street for spies, he opened the pouch and extracted the tools for smoking. Tatters of paper, shreds of leaf, flints and lights.

I watched him roll his cigarette, knowing that this was not as I would have chosen it. I would have taken a girl, or the younger boy. But this one was strong and not slow, the football player type, sixteen or so with broad shoulders and powerful arms that were not unused to labouring for their survival. Still I felt the empty, gnawing hunger drive me on, the small demon rodent chewing away at my insides with its endless incisors. I stepped out of the shadows as he concentrated on rolling the stuffed paper tube in his hands, I guessed that he would not respond to a cry for help, but would not flee from an outright approach. All I had to do was get within arms' reach.

I got halfway across the street, the cold blade of my knife nestling in my palm, before the boy even looked up. He had been struggling with his clacking flints, trying to light the little twist of fuel that would ignite his smoke and bring relief, and as he succeeded and looked up at me sharply I understood the shock of guilt on his face, something akin to the look of a small child caught with his hand in the cookie jar at midnight, the moment the light flicks on. I understood the look as the smoke smell touched my nostrils – it was not marijuana – the cheap, default smoke in a state where the weed grows abundantly, no, the cigarette was tobacco – old and stale, and harsh like chewing baccie, but tobacco none the less. Lord knows where the boy got it – no one had any growing in the city.

"You got a light? I asked as the boy looked up at me. His features softened in naïve relief. He reached into his pocket for the recently deposited flint clacker, "Sure man, I –"

I struck him across the face, drawing on my hunger in place of a hatred I could not muster. Had I been myself this would have floored him. As it was he staggered as his head rolled.

"What the fuck!" The boy said, thrashing out at me. I leapt on him, wrapping my arms around him clumsily and lunging for his throat while he tried to hold me away. I leered, gnashing teeth straining an inch away from that thick, throbbing vein of life pulsing along the side of his throat. My hood slipped down, baring my face and the boy gurgled in phlegmy horror as one rolling eye caught sight of my scarred and rotten death mask. The boy's grip on my shoulders faltered and I lurched towards that greasy, elastic skin of his neck, salivating with the heady warmth radiating from within. I felt the sharp, exploding pain of his knuckles driving deep into my guts and knocking the air out of me with a gargled choke. Foolish. What a fool. I hadn't even torn his flesh. The hunger had overwhelmed my reason, and without the icy strength I was used to enjoying, I could not afford to make such mistakes, to go for a kill without disabling first, not to discard stealth. Teeth gnashing, I was still straining at his throat when the first punch landed on the side of my head. It was awkward and slow, but I saw stars as the impact spread through my skull like vacuum and my ear erupted with a piercing buzz.

I hit back, and then we were on the floor, rolling together like children in a twisted game, thrashing and fumbling and throwing badly aimed punches that slid listlessly across their targets. I could not reach for my knife whilst struggling with both hands, fool, fool fool. He struck me again in the head, and as the pressure whited my vision out I feared my skull would crack. We slid along the grit, the cracking sidewalk and the needle glitter of broken glass and I caught his flailing fist in both hands before he could bring it down upon me once again. I twisted hard and heard the bones snap, the boy screamed electrically in the night. The sound cut clear through my panic as it echoed along the streets, and I realised just how much danger I was in – I could be discovered at any time. Lost in the kill, I hadn't accepted that I was losing the fight.

The boy's terrified stare met mine for a moment and time slowed. I remember his eyes, clear and bright, glinting in the darkness as the wetness of terrified tears streamed down his cheeks. I wanted him. He screwed up his face and backhanded me across the jaw, and we rolled over into the gutter as I grunted with the pain. I was on my back now, clawing with my withered fingers as the boy tried to get up. I twisted my legs around one of his but he kicked and thrashed and punched me in the guts once again, and I let go as the spasm of shock and pain ran through me and rendered my body limp.

The boy was off and running, yelling after his friend for help. I rolled over in a chorus of pain, willing myself not to curl up into a ball, not to shut my eyes and slip into the agony. My instinct was to go after him, to silence him, but he was strong and fast, and he would bring help from his camp while I crawled in the dirt, and I would be hunted like the animal I am. Still gasping for breath I pulled my knees up to my chest and climbed to my feet as sharp, suffocating pain ran down to my fingertips like lightning. My guts felt hollow and vacuous and blood was dripping into my eyes whilst my ear buzzed and pulsed. I could barely walk, I struggled for breath, wheezing as panic flooded my mind and I realised the danger of letting him escape. I didn't let him escape – he beat me. I stumbled and crawled my way up the hill and right towards the tower, lost in unfamiliar streets of rubble and ruin as terror overwhelmed my thinking and disorientated my oxygen-deprived brain.

The sidewalk cracks opened up to swallow me, the broken walls fell in towards me, and as the rubble tumbled down I lost myself, and lost time in the spinning, airless world, and for a moment I was lost and terrified in Japan, the rubble of Nagasaki closing in on me as the hot, radioactive dust filled my nostrils and choked the stale air out of my lungs. *I'm going to die*, I thought again. I spun with the world and fell flat on my face, landing an inch from the jagged, vicious edges of a rebar stake. The ground twisted and tilted and fell away from me as I clung to it, and I stared at the serrated edges of a broken beer bottle, clutching for breath and reading the same three words over and over as the label spun and swayed in the world an inch from my eye.

Red Rock Lite

In English.

Time slowed. The air returned to me slowly, and the rolling motion of the sidewalk came inshore and returned to the stillness of dry land as the ringing in my ears receded and I began to understand where I was. Somewhere behind me were voices and screams, horrors and angry shouting. It seemed a long way away but the emotion was disturbing, and somewhere within my hollow, aching guts was the lick of fear that it might be something to do with me. I pulled myself up against a rotten telegraph pole, catching the skin of my hands on a century of rusting staples and shreds of posters. My head throbbed, but my thinking was clearing and I began to understand where I was and the danger I was in. The shouting was getting louder.

I set off, checking the sky nervously for colour and zig-zagging my way across to the tower, cutting through alleyways and derelict buildings when I could, and praying that I was not pursued, that I would go unseen. I lost track of the voices as I fled, they disintegrated into a single background murmur. By the time I saw the tower rising in the distance the shouting and the angry chants had faded completely away, but the fear remained. I picked my way through the maze of subsiding streets and ruined buildings, stopping only to pick up a plank of wood that I might use as a weapon.

I circled around the tower from a distance, nipping in and out of wrecked homes and criss-crossing empty streets to check I went unwatched, before entering through the garage and heading for the stairs. The small, huddled form of Joany lay warm and asleep, nestled in her bundles in the corner, I sped past her like a distant phantom before leaping the steps two at a time and slipping through the half open door into the hallway beyond. I climbed the corkscrew stairs stiff and slow, clutching the railing and clutching my guts, driven on by hunger and the mental picture of the liquid, ruby jewels nestling in my refrigerator. My progress was slow and my body ached with the shock of every step.

As I climbed the corkscrew my head cleared and the pain clarified in my abdomen. I dragged the plank along behind me, sometimes I balanced it over my shoulder. The sun was coming, bringing with it the static build-up of energy charging through my body. I felt the approach and hurried my step. The electric pressure of warning that filled my bones did nothing to ease the agony swelling in my guts or the stabbing pain that sliced through my diaphragm with every breath. Safe in the darkness, the urgent sensation of the coming day could not drive me any faster up those coiling stairs. The dream of blood drew me on.

I was on the seventeenth floor when the sunlight burst over the horizon. I felt the crackling release of pressure, the flood of energy shimmer through me. I stepped out from my hiding place in the shadows, tucked under the flight of steps above, and leant on the railings, looking up the airwell to the skylight above. I smiled in the darkness of the blackout I had laid across the skylight above. In the stairwell it was still black as oil and just as thick. Later, after I'd reached the floor of my home, when the sun was a little brighter, a little higher in the sky, I found the edges of the blackout glowed somewhat, a faint, dirty brown stain in the darkness. Nothing I couldn't handle.

I fumbled for my keys like an alcoholic as I stood before my door, shaking with hunger and exhaustion. I kicked the door shut behind me and went straight to the fridge, chewing a corner off the plastic bag and spurting cold, sweaty blood over the floor and my clothes. I drank it down, feeling the sick chill spread through my guts, sickness compounding the bruising and internal turmoil. I drank too fast, and then I grabbed the next bag in the fridge and did the same again while bloated nausea rose from my gullet and the shaking spasms of hunger that ran through my body calmed and subsided.

I stared at the third and final bag in the fridge, it lay on a white plastic tray, beckoning to me as it glistened. Two empty bags lay sticky and cumbersome around my feet, dribbling their last gobbets on the black floor tiles. The blood in the fridge called to me. I did not need it, my belly was full and my bruises would heal without it. But it was there, the ruby, bright red in front of my eyes, and the burning impulse to grab it was there also, to own it and destroy it and consume it. To fall in again and be consumed.

I stare. It calls like the last chocolates in the box, the ones you don't like and yet you eat all at once, compounding the disgust and disrespect for your own mind, and you do it because they are *there,* available, and they shouldn't be. That damn box should be empty, conquered, and so should that blood bag. The obsessive rage builds within me at the idea of denying my indulgence, of doing what I ought instead of what I want. I want it goddammit, I want it, and there's nothing stopping me.

I conquer the fridge, or rather, it conquers me, and in a bitter attempt to remain civilised I stand in the kitchen by the portable gas ring and warm the bag in a pot of water, stirring it patiently, which I don't need to do. But I don't decant the bag into a large glass and sit like a gentleman, sipping until it goes cold and unpleasant. I don't sit like I used to do. When the blood is warm, or a little before in truth, I lever the bag out with a wooden spoon and snip the seal off one of the tubes. I perch on the stool and huddle over the warm, poisonous treasure in my hands, sucking and sucking and sucking until I am sick and there is nothing left. As I finish I catch myself reflected in the black glass of the dead microwave, stooped over my prize like a jealous magpie, and for a moment I don't recognise my own face in the darkness.

18

It is a couple of evenings later before I feel myself again, calm and rational in the pale light. I'm reading on the balcony and nursing my bruises when there is a crack echoing through the distance and somewhere a floor or so beneath me the masonry explodes in a little cloud of dust. The familiar sound of the gunshot never fails to disturb me, and the shock brings me out of my chair as always. Usually the fog means I have the balcony to myself, and I don't linger there on clear nights, but tonight whilst I have been reading the fog has rolled back around the tower, and whilst I can't see Twin Peaks at all, the Transamerica Pyramid and the ruins of Downtown are clear in the night.

Tonight, however, I am prepared. I scramble indoors and pull out a large sheet of cardboard that used to be two boxes. I've flattened them out and pasted them together with flour paste. I light more candles all around the balcony – the last of my paraffin ones and some animal tallow that I bartered for, the smell of which takes me back more centuries than I care to think on. I close the shutters to protect my French doors, and then I take a charred piece of wood and draw a grid on the cardboard, three squares by three in scratchy black lines while the sniper waits. Then I draw a cross in the top left hand corner before I disappear inside, humming with anticipation.

Moments later the crack comes, floating across the abyss that separates us. The metal shutters scream and rattle, and I wait with bated breath for the noise to subside before I step out again and examine the cardboard. It takes me some moments to find what I am looking for, peering nose up to the card with a wind-up flashlight in my hand. There is a tiny, tiny bullet hole, not in a square next to mine as I had expected, but in the top right hand corner of the board. We are playing noughts and crosses.

My next move is the centre square. Naturally the Sniper blocks me off at bottom right, and then I must take the middle right square to prevent his victory. The Sniper takes the middle left square for just the same reason, and although I take the bottom middle square, I know by this point that we are evenly matched. It isn't hard. We play two more games on boards I have prepared, and that is all the cardboard I have left. We sit in silence for a moment when it becomes clear that no one will win the third round. I remember the flicker of candlelight in the stiff breeze, and the feeling of emptiness between us. I am poised with the charcoal in my hand, feeling no need to make the next, superfluous move, and then I break into action, flipping the cardboard over and scratching away at my message in the half-light.

"OUT OF BOARDS. WILL TRY TO CLEAN THESE UP."

There is a crack of acknowledgement in the darkness, and I wonder at the huge expense in bullets that my friend spends in our communication. Then in desperation I scrawl on the back of the card "Y. ARE YOU IN DOWNTOWN? N" But there is no answer.

When I take the boards in and clean up the balcony I find remnants of the bullets scattered along the tiles at the boundary where the doors meet the floor. They are tiny windcheaters – mesh-built and hollow, with a weighted tip. Highly specialised and restricted ammunition for military snipers covering long distances. I stared at the fragments, not knowing what they meant, and then I swept them off the edge of the balcony.

19

"You scared me, shithead."

"I apologise."

"What do you want?"

"I have an offer for you. Regular work, regular water."

I was standing over Joany in the corner, in the darkness, and now she sat up, blinking the sleep out of her eyes.

"Sure. I mean. Depends what you need."

"It's not hard, it's just laborious. I need you to bring water up to the fifteenth floor every day. From the bay."

I sighed. It made me uncomfortable to encourage someone up into the tower. She was a smart kid also, I knew that she would figure out what I was doing with the water – I suspected she already had. The distance between the fifteenth and twentieth floors wasn't so great and she would find me one night, curious and energetic she would find my lair. It filled me with no enthusiasm, but to make the most of the still, to trade with the regularity and reliability that would placate the curious, greedy folk on the Looter's Causeway, I had to set up a regular operation, and I had to have help.

Joany stood up too fast, and I could see she was already sold. Yet she played the tough guy, the bargainer.

"Well how much would I have to carry?"

"Not much, just as much as you can reasonably manage." I spoke lightly, as if it mattered not whether she took the deal.

"How much?"

"Like I said, as much as you ca-"

"No. How much do I get? Paid?"

"Oh. I see. Four pints, plus a tenth of what you bring me, in fresh."

The girl had been standing, squinting up at me in the darkness, scraping her hair back from her face, and now she stopped, eyes wide as her hands dropped to her sides.

"How much?"

"Four pints," I repeated coolly, figuring that was as much as an adult human should drink, never mind an adolescent. "But you're not to trade it to anyone," I added, knowing that she would anyway. "You don't want the sort of attention that will bring. More importantly, I don't."

The girl stood speechless, nodding in the darkness as the main concerns of her survival flashed before her eyes and then melted away. It was as if I was answering her prayers.

"Well?" I said.

"Huh?"

"Will you do it?"

"Fuck yeah."

And that was the start of the operation. Every evening I would wake up and make the brief pilgrimage down to the fifteenth floor with two empty cans, and leave them on the landing where I picked up two full ones. Joany had another empty set downstairs, and it would be those that she would fill next before bringing them upstairs and picking up the empties ready for the next day. I busied myself with the routine of the still – running it, bottling the water, cleaning the condenser, scraping the salt and bay filth from the boiler.

It wasn't long before I found Joany nesting like a giant rodent on the fifteenth floor. I was on the landing, reaching out to grasp the handle of a two-gallon water bottle when I caught the tangle of energy with some surprise, an electric shiver clawing up my arm. It drew me through the fire door and into the hallway. By now of course I had sensed the presence in the ether, and I walked with conviction along the darkened hallway, pushing open a battered doorway, certain of what I would find.

The higher levels were almost untouched, and I squinted through the darkness in an attempt not to trip over unfamiliar furniture and make noise. I crossed a living room and opened shutters, realising the apartment was a different layout than mine, which only made me feel even more like a violator. Looking around the room, it was a strange mix of untouched civilisation and conspicuous vacancy. A glass topped dining table stood by one wall, laid out with placemats and cutlery and candelabra, but there were no chairs. There was a faded rectangle on the wall where the television used to hang. These things and more had been hocked to buy food or passage from this city when such things as videoscreens and furniture still held value. I drifted through someone else's life like a ghost, heading for the one door I knew to be relevant. I didn't want to be here any longer than necessary, an uninvited voyeur to the demise of an abandoned life.

I stood on the threshold and pushed the door open. It creaked a little. The bedroom inside was a child's, and had not been harvested nearly so much. The wallpaper was blue in the darkness, fluffy, reddish pink clouds floating above a banner in the orange half-light of the city. The blinds were rolled up and the dim light was bouncing in off the fog and low cloud. There were shelves with cuddly toys gathering dust, a tiny desk, toddler sized and littered with thick, wooden puzzles and cardboard books.

To my surprise there was a child-sized bed with a mattress, quilts and a patchwork blanket. It was covered with filthy sheets of flattened out cardboard boxes, plastic ties, rags and old water bottles. One corner seemed to be devoted to used takeout boxes, cracked polystyrene and crumpled cardboard and bugs. Joany was curled up in the midst of the rodent's hoard, limbs hanging limply off the bed she dwarfed. A grubbied corner of the quilt was caught up between her arms and pressed to her. She was asleep under a stinking brown blanket. I watched for a moment, listening to her steady breathing. I didn't enter.

20

You know it is summer in the city with the onset of bug season. The first month is hell, but now it lasts longer and the itching, biting, gnashing things go on and on and on. Naturally this onslaught coincided with the start of my regular trips to the Looter's Causeway. I carry five-gallon tin tanks, the square kind, and Joany carries whatever she can. As we approach the jetty and the shore, the hum of bugs rises in our ears, and on bright nights I can see the flowing, rippling flesh-made carpet of flies that covers the slime of the shallows. The shoreline flashes rhythmically from a vertiginous matte black to a stark, lightning shine in rippling, flowing patterns as the bugs turn and move en masse. It is not the blowflies that bother me, however, it is the smaller, silent, biting things that coat your face and crawl into your nose and die with the brush of your hand until your skin is slick and sticky with the greasy blood and guts and spindly legs of things that fly in the night. It was never this bad. It was never this bad.

The girl and I sometimes talk on our way down to the living shore. A word here and there, more often than not she presses to accompany me, and I will not let her. But mostly she is quiet, and so I am quiet. She spends her time alone, working or foraging or sleeping, and although she wears the toughness of the habitual survivor, I feel she has great silent sadness within. She cannot touch it and she cannot approach it. Most of the time she doesn't even know it's there.

The bugs line the shore, hanging in the slime and the puddles of stale water. As I will not let her accompany me, the girl dumps her cargo at the end of the jetty and flees the thick air full of teeth, partly in spite but mostly just in good sense. I am left alone to defend my veins while I wave my light and wait for a boat to come. I do not mind, the girl is right to flee the shoreline and I know there are plenty of bugs further uphill, and indeed all over the city. There is no escape for either of us.

Once the boatmen had gotten to know me, and word got round that I paid well, I didn't have to wait long. Usually there would be someone out there in the dark expanse of the bay keeping an eye out for a light on the northeast shore. I was good custom. I was a meal ticket. I often got the sense that whichever one of them turned up at the edge of the jetty had stayed up for me. They got to know my schedule, and certainly there were three or four regulars out of the bunch who took turns, or drew straws or somesuch.

Very occasionally, just once or twice, it was the greasy haired rat of a man that showed up to ferry me across the bay. He was always sullen with wounded pride, and I kept my face stony, not that it could display much of any expression. I made sure I showed my weapons out there in the deep darkness of the rolling bay. The knife would slip from my sleeve to my palm, or the pistol, as if by accident, as if I were unaware as I looked out beyond his face towards the lights of the Causeway. But we both knew, and we sailed on in cloying silence.

It was at these moments, out over the deepest water and four feet from a killer that the pressure came over me. As the cold of the knife slipped into my palm I became aware of how easy it would be to kill him, to slit that salt-skinned throat and gorge myself on the flood, for he was my prisoner, my captive on that tiny floating island rocking in the waves. I was poised, with hunger burning in my belly and spittle dripping down my crumbling teeth, and all the while he watched me, thinking I would let my guard down, thinking I would be the one to make a mistake.

And yet I never touched him or any of them. Even though I suspected no one would miss this one, I left him be as I did the others, for the grapevine is a powerful weapon and I needed their transport more than I dared let on. I didn't speak to them. Not since Reg did I care to learn their names or remember their faces. They've blurred into two or three people in my memory, and that is plenty close enough.

In the first days I would have to wait my turn at the end of the jetty, sometimes ten minutes, sometimes half an hour as I waived my light frantically and swiped at the midges, growing dizzy with the din of the blowflies rising in my ears till it was all I could hear. All the while I had the sensation that Joany was somewhere above, watching me dance and jibe and twist with morbid fascination.

The boat would arrive when it arrived, the deal would be done and we would be out into the deep water as fast as possible, where I found, to my relief, that there were no bugs. It was the only place in the city where you could breathe without fear of choking on crawling living things. And then we were at the bridge all too soon, and the midges were in every little scoop of standing water in the metalwork. It seemed as if the struts and girders were living columns of chittering, crawling insect flesh. The animals hated it. Pigeons left their nests whilst their chicks screamed, seagulls refused to land. Even the goats were tormented, bleating in a night-time chorus that kept their owners awake and brought forth their deaths.

I remember the first night, climbing up the slope from the water whilst the locals hid behind government-issue malaria nets, scratching and shaking their heads. I got to the guardhouse shed and called inside.

"I want to see Darius," I croaked.

There was no one, but a surly young man with a blotchy face appeared on the other side of the barricade and squinted at me.

"Darius? You mean Douglas. He's jus' putting on airs for ya."

The boy disappeared down the central avenue, and sure enough, the squat, limping man I had met before appeared several minutes later.

"Well hello there!" He called out as he hobbled up to the barricade. "Come through, come through!" He waved his arms and kicked some wooden planks out of the way. I stepped through the central gap and put down a tank, taking Douglas' hand somewhat reluctantly.

"We were hoping you'd show up!" He said as he led me down the avenue.

"There are two more containers by the boat." I said.

"Yes, yes! I'll send someone. What can we do for you?" Douglas was his usual, overly chatty self, and he didn't pause for breath as he led me past Tim's darkened tent and kept on going.

"Am I not seeing Tim?" I called out, hoping not to have to break in another player. Douglas stopped and swivelled on his good foot.

"Well, there's a funny story there, but suffice to say that Tim was used to being a big fish in a small pond, and then he found himself in a rather much larger pond, swimming with sharks you might say."

I ignored the mixed metaphors and followed the funny man uphill and further along the bridge. He walked slowly, and all the while the quality of the dwellings improved slowly from fabric tents to flimsy wooden lean-tos to shacks and sheds with tin roofs. The more to-do residents of the Looters' Causeway had chicken runs or several goats. Often there would be a string of gutted pigeons hanging from a doorway, or even a seagull hanging limp from a garrotting snare. The smell of fish and animal dung was everywhere however and the wind rushed through the alleys and the sprawling maze of hovels with a bitter fierceness. Anything not tied down would roll across the deck and drop off the sides, and then it was lost to the waves and the sea. There was more light here, though just as many bulbs were on as off. Most of the light came from stodgy lumps of clarified animal fat pierced with a string and lit, or jars of oily fluid with a wick protruding listlessly from their lids.

Douglas led me to a longhouse made of wooden fence panels and beckoned me inside. There were low benches running the length of the room, and a fireplace at the far end. In the centre was a circle of chairs arranged around a low table. None of the chairs matched, but they were all in good condition. Some were even upholstered. There were lamps sitting on the tabletop, glowing softly, and in the flickering light I saw an elderly Chinese man watching me from the depths of a leather armchair. A stiffness ran through me at first sight, for the stern expression on his face said he knew exactly what I was, although he could not.

On his left sat a bored, sallow, middle-aged white man, and somewhere on his right was a younger, unhappy looking Chinese – possibly the Elder's son. I was led towards them and I sat on a wooden armchair on the other side of the table where we all watched each other as Douglas made his excuses and left.

The Elder sighed softly, as if bored, and stared at me expectantly. It was a prelude to a waltz I didn't want to take. I would not be intimidated by such a one as this.

"I have water to trade, small amounts, fairly regular."

The Elder sighed again, slowly. "They tell me you have a supply. That it's very good water. They tell me you drive hard bargain."

It was all I could do not to laugh under my breath. The Elder waved his hands loosely towards the cans at my feet, and the Youngster leapt up and brought one over to him before popping the lid. Producing a small steel spoon that had been bent and hammered into something of a ladle, the Elder extracted some water from the open can and slurped it noisily between his lips. He stifled a smile and looked at me.

Samuel Collins

"They say it is very pure. It is not as good as they say."

I looked at the man calmly, waiting. It was true, the product wasn't so good. I'd been cutting it a little – just a sprinkle of the salt residue from the still's boiler. The only thing that was keeping me safe on the Looter's Causeway was the myth that I held the location of a huge, undiscovered tank of water, presumably from the utilities or some building. Tap water is impure. Distilled water, dry and tasteless as it is, tastes of nothing so much as distilled water.

We waited in pregnant silence as the expression faded from the Elder's lips. The Caucasian stared off into the shadows, blank and bored, while the Youngster wrung his hands and looked nervous. Eventually the Elder swallowed, sucking up air and sitting up straight.

"Well, no matter. We give you good price for regular business. What you want?"

The Youngster deflated visibly, while the Caucasian turned his head with the slowness of a basking lizard in order to examine the Elder with mild shock.

"Fuel," I said. And then I reconsidered. "Usually Fuel. Tonight I want a block and tackle. As much rope as you have."

The Elder turned to the Caucasian, who whispered briefly. Then he nodded to the Youngster who darted out of the room and into the night, leaving a blast of cool air behind him. The water was passed around, and the ladle. The Elder didn't hesitate to dip into my stock, and neither did the Caucasian. At one point, as they whispered to each other in perfect English, I thought they were going to send for a bigger spoon or some jugs. They offered me the can and the ladle. I passed.

The Youngster returned looking flustered and sweaty, bearing two different sets of pulleys. One had sturdier blocks and thicker rope, but was fairly short. The other, although finer, would take the weight I had in mind and had more rope. This was the set I chose. The Elder clapped his hands and looked satisfied.

"Now we have tea! Good!"

I sighed inwardly. I had spent enough time picking my way through the avenue and I could feel the peak of the night approaching. I had little time for pleasantries. Mostly I was just tired, done with people for the evening. I shook my head.

"Thank you. I must be going however."

The Elder raised his eyebrows in mock surprise. He was eager to delay me for some reason, and I didn't like it.

"You stay! Please. You do honourable tea service."

I took them all in, looking at them one by one as I raised my eyebrows. "I do business with you. You can drop the lousy accent and the cultural pretensions because I'm not a tourist. You were born here. Your father was born here. Your father's father was born here. Forget the tea, I'm sure there's a hamburger and fries waiting for you out back."

The Elder blushed red and then turned distinctly white, shaking a little with anger. It was a calculated insult, appalling really, and rather ignorant, but I wanted to leave. The Youngster turned bright pink and stared at the wall, and the floor, and his hands in quick succession. The Caucasian looked as if he were swallowing a laugh.

"You go now."

"Yes, I think so."

I gathered the rope, coiling it slowly to stretch out the moment of discomfort, and I picked up the pulley blocks by their hooks and left. A few steps out of the longhouse I heard an eruption of giggles. "Oh fuck off Larry," the Elder said sourly.

Here at the crest of the bridge, the canopy was high above the waves and the wind whistled through the struts. I hurried along the avenue, ignoring the stares of strangers and pulling my hood close about my head. Soon the canopy was sloping back towards the waves and Douglas was calling from somewhere behind, struggling to keep up and escort me. I stalked by the camps with their guy ropes and their racks of splayed fish, eager to get off the bridge before anyone could challenge me or try to stop me. *I am bored of this,* I thought. *I am bored of this.*

I passed the barricade and the gatehouse, perched upon the giant concrete pier that rose out of the waves like a fist, and walked down the steep slope where the deck met the boats and sank beneath the black water. My boatman looked stricken as I approached.

"Some guys come and took the rest of your stuff." He was obviously terrified I would think he had done something with it, although where he could have hidden it I do not know. I clambered awkwardly into the little tub and waved him on without a word. As we set off he stared morosely back at the bridge, wondering what was going on, wondering if I was a fugitive. I assured him there would be no trouble as I set down my goods in the bows, and we made our way steadily up the bay to North Beach.

21

Joany was unimpressed with the block and tackle. When I set it up early the next evening, dangling from a plank hung across the aircore of the stairs, I found it only reached down four floors. The girl said it made her arms ache to pull on all that rope, and she preferred to climb the stairs. I shrugged. I still found it useful, as far as it went.

These were the days of summer, where I would wake up, sweating and delirious in the mid-day heat, pinned down by the listless cooing of dying pigeons on the balcony, or the endless machine gun drilling of the rat gnawing at bars in the living room. *Why can't you just die?* I remember thinking one day as the sun glared fierce through the edges of the shutters and the room spun around my bed. Then I realised that the small rodent was the last Leibowitz alive, and I got up to share some water with it.

The heat was insane. I have never known a summer like it in San Francisco. The air was a strange mix of freshness as the salt rolled over the hills to the west, and sticky, humid grease emanating from the ever more stagnant marshes of the bay floodplains. I lay curled up on a leather sofa during those long afternoons, my bare flesh sticking to the shiny, cherry skin, sipping water and counting the endless seconds until sundown and cool freedom.

Joany had moved back down to the garage – to the darkness and the steady temperature of the underground realm, and when I emerged every three or four days, frazzled and half mad, bearing more tanks of freshwater for trade, she would take one look at me, and, brushing her hair out of her eyes, ask if I was ready to move down yet.

But I wasn't. I wasn't ready to abandon my ivory tower, to concede the white elephant semblance of civilisation I maintained up there in the clouds. And most of all I wasn't ready to give in. To accept defeat. To be beaten by such a random, mindless, inane force as the environment.

The operation went on and on, and I kept trading up the ranks, mostly for fuel, sometimes for padlocks, or containers or rope. Often it seemed I was being brought further up the bridge and further up the Looter's hierarchy, but other times Douglas or some other lackey would be waiting by the gatehouse to make the transaction. I had little time to linger on the bridge and ponder all this, I had to dash back down across the waves, and once or twice run up the hill to the tower to beat the everchasing dawn, with Joany protesting and groaning behind me.

The girl knew what I was doing of course – it wasn't hard to figure out. Salt water goes in, fresh water comes out. She knew I was cleaning it somehow, and she knew I was her best chance of survival. In fact she was doing rather well. She seemed to be growing, putting on a little weight. I never knew where she got food, but occasionally she brought some to me. I took whatever she offered gratefully, in order to disguise the nature of my existence, and I gave her extra water, although I got the feeling she would have brought the little offerings anyway. She brought berries, sometimes roots or flowers that she said were good to eat, once even a can of meat – which was so extraordinary that I knew she must have traded water for it somewhere. I chided her for it gently and she denied such a thing, but she never brought me another can after that. Sometimes I ate a little of what she brought, particularly the berries – I have always enjoyed the life in fruit – but mostly the food went to the rat, who grew tubby and lethargic, which I thought was a little obscene.

I didn't try to hunt again, although I found myself lunging at small animals and insects whenever I was abroad at night. There were bats everywhere, nesting in the abandoned office blocks and breeding like rats at the height of bug season. They emerged into the sky in huge, twisting, viscous clouds, I never caught one. I never caught much of anything actually, and although the situation in my half-empty freezer was no less precarious, I was loath to rock the boat. Life seemed good. I had a regular trade operation, could get the fuel I needed for water, and everything was rather regular. There were few surprises, which was just how I liked it, and consequently I preferred not to think of my growing habit and dwindling supplies, rather than risk another inept, half-hearted attack, the broken ribs, the angry mobs.

And that was the other reason of course. My growing habit. It made life feel good, it made me feel safe as I grew fat and complacent, it made me feel that I was clever enough to overcome any problem, including an empty freezer – a problem which was not so far off as it seemed. But this is the nature of addiction, more and more and more, all the while thinking you are in control so long as you don't check yourself in the mirror – and so you don't. Turn a blind eye and keep on down the road to hell. It's not a problem, it's *helping* you do what you need to do, so why look at it? And of course I had the original excuse for not looking at it. It was food I was addicted to.

And so I kidded myself that it could go on, lost in the delusion of a satiated life, all the while needing more and more to keep up that pretence, to keep up the blindness. It couldn't last, of course, and the end was closer than I thought.

The sniper would make his presence known every few days, whenever the skies were clear. Sometimes he would shoot the birds from my balcony, sometimes he would just call me if I left lights on, three short, sharp cracks in the night as the bullets jack-hammered into the masonry or sheered off metal shutters somewhere outside. Else I would be in the kitchen, running bowls and bottles to the still, or picking my way through the queue of containers that led from the living room floor to the door, and there would be a loud, wet bang. I would turn and glance, open the shutters, and outside there would be an explosion of feathers hanging on the night air, drifting slowly down to hell.

The scale of the drought really betrayed itself when the animals began to die. I would be out looting, or making my way to the jetty when I would hear the relentless insect droning of death, and see a small, emaciated bundle of fur lying where it had crawled into the sheltered foundations of some ruined building, or more and more often simply where it had dropped on the sidewalk. First it was the dogs, wild and crazed by the heat and thirst it seemed a desperate pack would turn on its weakest member and worry it to death, eating out the guts and the meat and the soft bits, chewing bones and leaving the stringy rubbish of the corpse for the insects.

Next were the cats, which seemed to just die where they fell, lying prone and shrunken on the hot concrete sidewalk all day and all night. A starved cat is a wretched, tiny thing, not much bigger than a ferret, and to see it reduced to such scrawny proportions, to come upon an angular, bony, half bald, stinking black sack of putrid flesh that used to be graceful and lithe and living, to watch the bugs writhing under the ripe skin filled me with sick foreboding.

But it was the rats that shocked me most. Dead rats everywhere, not that I understood it at first. I would scuff the sole of my shoe along on something, look down to find a slender grey-pink tube, tapering to a point rolling under my boot. On closer inspection I would find the concentric circles of pale, stubby little hairs running along the length, the bloody stump with the sickening ivory white bone in the core, the grim circle of fine, downy grey hairs lying next to it on the sidewalk. Even the rats were dying in the drought. The more I looked, the more I saw random body parts littering the streets, an endless parade of miniature hands, ears, eyelids, inedible body parts and discrete little piles of fur being scooped up in the breeze and collecting in shattered doorways. A silent genocide going on all around me, invisible, unknowable.

In fact, the only creatures that did well over that summer were those that fed on the bugs. The endless lines of bats weaving through the sky, the geckos, I even saw a tarantula kicking its legs high as it walked along the sidewalk, squeezing itself into the air core of a cracked wall. The insects were everywhere. The insects reigned supreme. Not only the midges, the gnats, the bloodsuckers, but the carnivores and the shit-eaters. The cockroaches were unstoppable, their familiar chattering scurry clicking through my ears night and day. There were wild bees, wasps, hornets and horseflies, tiny jumping things and shiny metallic beetles I had never seen before. And the moths, oh the moths at night would storm my balcony candles, would smother any flame with their sacrifices one after the next after the next. Toads called, crickets chirped in the night, bats swooped on the newly established fireflies. I kept my doors firmly shut for fear of being smothered by pale, glittery moths, choking on their dusty wings and wheezing as their furry bodies filled my lungs.

People leave town as the birds flop out of the sky and paste themselves across the road, as the streets become a continuous parade of desiccated death. I rarely see the exodus, which takes place in daylight, but I feel it. Even when I am not in the ether, the presence of conscious minds nearby coats my skin like grease. It's an almost imperceptible pressure that haunts my days and my dreams. Even if I could suffer the daylight I would walk the nights just for the peace of it while men slept and their minds left this earth. I would walk the nights fast to escape the myriad cacophony of voices that I cannot hear so much as feel bubbling beneath the threshold of my conscious mind. So tiresome. A pressure always chasing me, always threatening to squeeze my *self* out of existence.

The people leave in dribs and drabs and as I sleep, I dream it, as I stand drinking on the balcony in the early night, eyes peeled in fascination as I let the blood seep slowly down my throat. I gaze down like a hawk with my recovering sight, my mind sharp with the blood high and my concentration captured by the flapping tents of an abandoned camp or an overloaded boat struggling southeast across the bay.

They leave in boats and carts and on foot, they pack their meagre things and scramble and fight and drag themselves south across the archipelago to the mainland, or across the bay and the mountain bushfires if they think they know the hill pass, if they think they are smart. It seems prudent to me to head north, to follow the line of the Golden Gate and take 101 up to the lushness of Oregon and Washington, a lushness that is founded in my memory of a hundred years ago, a lushness that is fast becoming ice and dust. Still it seems a better bet than the dust bowl of the central valley, but few venture across the sea-mouth of the bay, afraid it seems that they will get sucked out into the open ocean and be lost forever. Some head for the scorched scrubland of Angel Island in their little boats and makeshift rafts. Where they go from there I do not know. I am sad and afraid. The people are leaving and the city is dying, slipping through my fingers like sand. I am lost. I have the vague, empty feeling that I dropped the hourglass, broke the spell. I wish I could place when.

I am on my way to the bridge with a large cargo. The dinghy I am using sits low in the water and rocks in the wavelets while the boatman tries hard not to look as concerned as he is. Joany wanted to come again. I said no, again. She is growing. Flowing from her small, stunted and starved sixteen-year-old self into that uncomfortable chimera between girl and woman, and she feels it. It makes her seek people, seek comfort. Although she is fond of me, and I, at the least am comfortable with her presence, somewhere deep within she knows I am cold. I cannot offer her even many words of kindness. They stick in the throat of the monster that would use them against her.

I am weary tonight, watching the pillars loom up in the distance is like watching the gallows draw closer and closer. Even the Causeway seems to know this, its Technicolor myriad of lights are dim and apathetic, as if they were struggling through the fog, although it is clear. I know, however, that there is life still on the bridge, for as we draw nearer the tinny sounds of survival stretch out across the water like tendrils, and cut into my soul with their cold, clammy suckers. Babies crying, people shouting, animals screaming in the night, these things tear at my innards.

The night seems dark and close. Although my eyes are greatly improved, thanks to my gluttonous habits, there is no moon tonight, and the boatman steers by the light of the Causeway alone. Offer the ferrymen enough and they will work on these darkest nights, I do not know how they navigate but they have a system. Every so often the man squints at the shore, and he is constantly looking about him with an almost manic paranoia for fear of collisions. Every so often he waves a wind-up flashlight into the thick blackness. I do not tell him that I know exactly where we are in the abyss, that I would hear and see a boat coming from almost a mile away. I wait in silence as he makes his slow progress.

The man relaxes visibly as we approach the gatehouse of the Causeway and the dock, with all its boats tied up in rows, although the swell around the huge brick and concrete pillars that mark the gatehouse and the rise of the freeway out of the water is worse than ever. The boat rocks in deep, erratic swings, and I cling to the sides instinctively, feeling the bay lick my knuckles with an icy rasp as the waves reach up perilously close to the top of the gunwales.

I am relieved to hear the dull scraping sound of wood against submarine asphalt as the boat pulls in to a gap and drives up the slope. I take the rope and hop out of the vessel, splashing through the stagnant scum that laps in the shallows, and walking up to a low iron peg of rebar that has been smashed awkwardly into the blacktop. I stop, dismayed to see the sallow Caucasian whose name is Larry, and two nervous looking guards up at the foot of the little wooden guardhouse, instead of Douglas, who is supposed to be waiting for me tonight.

The guards make their way down towards the water behind me. One of them takes the rope from my hand while the other unloads the cargo from the little vessel. Four square tin tanks full of freshwater. Larry points to the boatman sharply.

"You can go," he drawls, but it is not a suggestion, and the man skitters off across the shallows and into the night. Fast. Larry looks at me and spits to his left. He nods uphill to a horse and cart waiting beyond the barricade, and my stomach sinks as he says "Be my guest."

I sit on the back of the cart, my legs dangling over the side as my robe flaps in the breeze. I feel a faint sense of dread as the world recedes from me. People stare at me, the familiar phantom that haunts the causeway every few days but says nothing. The dark man. I stare back from under my hood. *What has he done?* They are thinking. *Why are they taking him away?* I might ask the same thing.

The journey is slow, and I suspect the horse is more of a mule but I say nothing as I rock uncomfortably from side to side. The surface is uneven, potholed and scattered with rubble from the collapsed upper deck. Every so often the boundary of the traffic lane is marked by a twisted girder, or a large strip of concrete-and-blacktop layer cake that has been pushed up against the tents and shanties. Sometimes the girders have been used in the corners of the sturdier sheds. They rise like Greek columns, holding up an uneven roof. Most of the upper deck has gone over the side, occasionally our vehicle interferes with a dwelling, it grazes a wall that cuts into the roadway, or runs across a stray guy rope whose rebar anchor has ventured too far across the asphalt, and there is a thwacking noise as the tent is pulled down and rebounds, or simply a tearing as the guy comes away from the material. Sometimes an angry head appears, open mouthed or in mind to shout, but they fall silent as they see the guards walking at each side of the cart and they disappear, pretending to busy themselves within. More often than not the sight goes unnoticed, for the dwelling is empty. There are fewer people here, fewer beady eyes staring at me. The Causeway is quiet and still, the forest of girders uncomfortably pregnant with fear. The rats are abandoning ship, and the game now is to squeeze every last drop of value and life out of the cargo hold while waiting carefully for the stampede. No one wants to be the first to go, no one wants to be the last. I lay down flat on my back, I do not need to see again the road to hell.

It is an odd sensation, lying backwards, my head lower than my knees on the tilted cart, my jaw rattling in my head while the water sloshes in my ears. Larry coughs up phlegm as he drives the old horse on over big lumps in the road, fragments of the upper deck two or three feet wide that no one has seen reason to drag into the water; once or twice the animal brays in shock and the cart rises, lurches to a stop and then rolls down and back. Larry swears quietly and the guards each take a side of the cart, pushing as the cart rises and then thuds down, and rolls on, on on. The first time it happens one of the guards, the smaller one, looks at me and opens his mouth, but I stare him down and he quickly takes his position against the heavy old wood. I am not above helping in such situations, but I'll be damned if I drive my own hearse to the execution.

I turn my head and Yerba Buena rises ahead of me, I see its peak climbing through the street of roofs, endless sloping planes running up the Causeway, nestled within a parallel strip of girders and pylons. The island is steep and rocky and covered with dying trees, brown and bleached pines with their bark peeling, bare maples that have given up in the heat. The grass and the moss that covers the rocks are dead, the same dull colour as the mud beneath, what little of it has escaped the relentless erosion of wind and salt. At the peak of the island stands a low, flat-roofed building partially obscured by trees and a cleverly built earthwork – the old monitoring station. Where once there stood satellite dishes and radar sweepers, the crest is now littered with windmills reaching up into the sky like twisted sunflowers.

The dwellings are much more substantial past halfway, past the apex of the bridge where it is highest above the water. We descend gently towards the waves. There are tin huts, plaster and concrete structures, wooden panelling is *de rigueur*. Some other time I would be fascinated by the chaotic, medieval market town sprawling across the bridge, growing randomly like fungus to fill the gaps. Every kind of desperate, rickety, hope-held structure that could possibly be here is here. There are guy ropes of blue nylon and twisted netting that hold the walls up against the strong winds. Fighting off the damp and the salt spray is a continuous battle of scraping and plaster, mud and straw and goat dung. I shut my eyes to everything around me, to the sleeping life around me that was slowly, obviously bleeding away, and I felt the rocking of the cart as it jolted my skull.

The bridge ran through a tunnel bored deep into the heart of the island, but now the remaining deck runs straight into a wall of brick and desperately formed concrete complete with embedded oil drums. As I realise we are nearing the Island Fortress I sit up and turn, watching the choked mouth of the tunnel loom larger and larger ahead. The central avenue leads straight up to the walled off tunnel and a wide set of wooden doors, almost like barn doors. They appear to swing inwards. The upper deck of the old freeway has survived here at the tunnel, it bisects the wall and just out over the lower canopy in a wide proscenium. The wall covering this upper level of the tunnel mouth is made from broad wooden planks laid side by side, almost like an old southern whitewashed fence. There are numerous doors cut out of the wood, man sized, and someone has strung a low rope all the way along the curved edge of the upper deck, mounted on pathetic, skinny twists of rebar driven straight into the blacktop.

Within the last two hundred feet before the gaping archway that is clawed out of the island rock, the residents thin out and the dwellings are replaced by strange emplacements along the sides of the bridge, one and two story buildings constructed of oil drums filled with concrete, pierced all over so that the liquid masonry would run together and mesh. Long, narrow gaps are left between barrels, just wide enough for an eyeball and a gun muzzle. Up above, strung between the girders on a network of cables and pulleys are a series of half drums and plastic barrels which gently drip dust and rust as they swing in the breeze, they are filled with rubble and jagged shards of metal. There are smaller containers – tin mop buckets that ooze a sticky blackness and fill the air with the scent of exhaust fumes. Oil, drops of oil strung in a line like dirty pearls, waiting to be boiled. It takes one rope to pull these things along on their evil conveyor belt, another to tip them over. It's ingenious, and intricate, beautiful and hideous. I follow the lines of cables all the way along the Causeway for the last fifty yards. Eventually I see that the lines and the buckets disappear through hatches in the tunnel wall, just below the upper deck.

As we draw up to the doorway in the gaping mouth of the tunnel, and the hungry shadow of the balcony above falls across me, darkness compounding darkness on this evil black night, I feel both numb and nauseous. The wide doors draw back and the darkness becomes only deeper, stretching out in front of me like the mouth of space. The cart rocks along as the blackness envelopes, and then I watch as the doors draw closed, shutting out the strings of fairy lights outside. Instinctively I shut my eyes. I listen.

There is a loud clunk in the distance, and the chamber erupts with the dull, grating buzz of fifty-hertz hum. The blackness behind my eyelids turns red and the horse neighs in distress. Slowly I open my eyes to the melodramatics. The chamber is wide and low, a fact that surprises me, I was expecting a higher, arched ceiling and not the claustrophobic square box I find myself within. Then I realise the height of the ceiling is the height of the upper deck, and the space makes sense suddenly. There are rows of construction lamps lining the walls, halogens burning on battered yellow stands.

There is a heavy smell of gasoline and used sump oil in the air. Battered trucks and hummers stand parked against the walls. They are rusting, and their tires are patched, and some of them are unrecognisable beneath the modifications that have been welded on to their body shells. Quills of sharpened angle iron sprout from the rusting skin of a giant metal porcupine. In another corner a pickup has been covered with spotlights and machine gun mounts. There are vehicles everywhere in varying states of repair – few are complete – in fact I'm not convinced any of them still run. A mini Humvee sits propped up on cinder blocks with its homebrew battering ram lying bitter on the floor ahead of it, one of its doors resting on the hood. It seems that the tires are propped up against the jeep that sits beside it awaiting the life transplant.

All of the vehicles are sprayed in loud colours, covered in graffiti and promises of doom and the tags of the three major looters' outfits – the round fish with the big teeth is the Piranhas, the biggest and an all out white-trash pirate gang. A little further on I see vehicles sprayed with the vicious ancient faces of the Aztec Gods, the emblem of the mostly Latino 'Tecas. Sprinkled between the two camps are mean-looking vans with stakes protruding at all angles, saw blades and chainsaws front and back, occasionally the odd flamethrower muzzle. These are tagged with a neon blue halo surrounded by red flames. The Angels Of Mercy – a self-righteous, self-deluded pseudo Christian gang that uses the Christian bible to justify its theft, its existence – its vicious and vengeful tactics in taking anything its members want. 'God will provide' translated into 'Take what you can'. The smallest group and the most murderous, I hoped never to encounter the Angels.

"God-*Dammit* Larry!" Someone shouted, their voice tinny in the cluttered concrete space. "Shut those things off!"

"Ok boys," Larry's drawl called out, slow and disinterested as a lounge singer. Somewhere ahead of us there was a sharp thunk-click and the lights pitched us back into darkness. A dim row of working lights strung up along the ceiling came on, and Larry came around the back of the cart and smirked, jerking his head for me to get off. I wanted to smash his face in.

Larry stood by a narrow steel service door buried in the concrete wall. I watched as the cart and my cargo disappeared down the tunnel slowly, the horse crying as the blackness wrapped itself around the animal and the guards. The tunnel is half a mile long, skewering the island before it emerges over the bay and looks out beyond the ruins of the eastern span, a few lonely, jagged piers breaking the foamy waves. I stood and tried to catch the whispers echoing up that canal of darkness, but they merged into one oppressive blanket of white noise that chilled me as I listened, struggling above the clop of hooves and the rattle of loose wheels.

The doorway was simply an opening to a narrow, sweaty set of stairs that zigzagged their way up to the top deck. I followed Larry's slow steps in silence, and emerged out into a bustling maze of rooms and hallways lit by oil lamps and luminescent panels. There was a low, rustling din permeating the dimness. The walls were simply fence panels, sheets of cladding or drywall scrounged from old houses, a clashing palette of luxuriant wallpaper and fittings still evident, a wan testimony to better days. The panels were bolted together at right angles so they sat upright on the asphalt deck, but there was no ceiling to be found. The smooth surface of the tunnel arched over above our heads and as the sounds rose and mingled in that vaulted space the hum spread the length of the tunnel, bouncing and echoing until the disjointed mutterings sank into my ears and made my head swim in their seductive softness.

Larry led me through twists and turns while I tried my hardest to memorise my path to escape, and we passed families huddled around open doorways, crouching by heat pads and Coleman lamps. I glanced through one crooked opening to see two young children bent over the Bible, their mother cradling a newborn in one hand and holding a tatty comic book to her eyes with the other. Somewhere further along the narrow passages I came upon two ancient ladies whispering softly to one another in Spanish, shivering and pulling their shawls tight around their shoulders. They fell silent as my gaze passed over them. I looked away.

The place smelled of oil and sweat and shit. Birds chirped in distant cages and goats bleated in the half-light. There were bugs everywhere, skittering up the walls and hiding in dark corners, their eyes glittering – needle points waiting to strike. Larry led me through a makeshift hallway between two dwellings that opened out into a wider central corridor. He led me deeper into the tunnel, past endless wooden sheets and closed doors and lamps smoking away up in the vaulted ceilings above. He never spoke, and although I felt his constant, smirking gloat even as he had his back to me, his body stiffened as we neared our destination, and I began to sense his rising unease. We arrived at a turn in the corridor, beyond which sat a dozing guard with an assault rifle. Larry opened a gilded set of double doors in the corner that had been kidnapped from some theatre, and nodded for me to go in.

I stepped inside, and looked back to see Larry bending to shut the doors, to shut himself out. I caught his eye and the expression he wore was something between guilt and relief. The doors closed and there I was, alone in a large room, an unlit chandelier hanging from the apex of the archway above. Unusually the walls rose up all the way to the curve of the ceiling, gaps had been filled with foam and plaster. Care had been taken to seal this room against prying ears. Beneath the chandelier sat a large oval dining table, the edges of its glass top chipped and grazed. There were seven chairs arranged around the table, none of which matched. At one end there was a large leather armchair, the other end was barren.

On the far side of the room, across from the table there was a raised platform made from wood, upon which stood a large, fluffy armchair. To one side of the platform was a small wooden door, and a lamp hanging from a bracket on the wall. I crossed the floor and went over to that lamp, pressing down on the lever that lifted the glass. With a sharp breath I knocked the flame from the wick, and I stood watching the room settle into darkness as my eyes grew accustomed to the cracks of light that fell under the doors. Squinting as I crossed over to the table, I settled in one of the chairs and waited in the black.

My mind floated in that time, drifting on the distant whispers that ran through the tunnel, the shallow breathing, the tired sighs. It was easy to lose myself amidst the hundreds of minds that burned like fireflies in the space around me. I felt the earth slipping around the sun, time dripping away as people busied themselves below with the effort of life, sleeping, boiling water, grinding flour under a flat stone. It never ends.

It was some time later that another mind approached, fierce with intent as it weaved through the ether. There were others struggling to keep up. Light splayed across the room as the door opened, and the silhouette on the threshold paused, taking in the unexpected darkness. He seemed to re-establish his train of thought, and he fumbled in his pocket as he entered the room, clicking a lighter as two men with guns filed in after him. He saw his way to lighting the lamp by the smaller door, and then he turned and squinted at me as the flame grew and the light spread thinly across the room. He stood for a moment.

"Ok, you can go now," he said to the awkward shadows standing either side of the door. They filed out as the man crossed the raised platform and lit lamps at either side of the chair, and then moved around the room, lighting Coleman lamps and torches and banishing the darkness to the far corners of the room as his footsteps clicked across the asphalt. Finally he picked up a lamp and came to me. We looked at each other as the light hanging from his fingers threw hard shadows across his face. He sat in the chair next to mine and he set the lamp down between us on the table, the yellow light flickering across our features in the gloaming.

"Well," he breathed softly as we studied one another. The man who had come to see me was a heavy-set Caucasian, with a broad neck and close-cut pale blond hair, pale blue eyes and male pattern baldness. He wore a fraying woollen sweater, some multicoloured pattern, deep greens and blues and reds in geometric diamonds, tan corduroys and steel capped boots. He appeared to be around forty years old, but while he sat clutching the cuffs of his sweater in his palms like a shy teenager, he examined me with the stillness of an old man. His steady self-assurance spoke of implacable determination. The man before me knew himself. He knew his own power in a way that would frighten, enthral and enrage the men around him. He was steady, untouchable. He was a stone.

"May I?" He said, reaching out a broad hand to lower my hood. I raised a withered palm to prevent it and he withdrew his arm, but he'd seen what he was looking for.

"Well," he said. "It is true."

Fear lurched through my guts like a wrecking ball, turning to a sharp wave of alarm.

"What is?" I rasped slowly, eager to hold back the panic from my voice. The man merely shook his head and brushed off the question.

"You must be wondering why you're here."

I nodded.

"The faceless one with all the water," he whispered to himself. "Do you know who I am?"

I shook my head.

"I am the bridge. I am the fortress here. I am the Piranhas and the Causeway and the gangs. I am this place and every place up to the Police cordon. I am the King of the Looters." He said it softly, with no pride, looking down at the spread of his fingers on the tabletop. I said nothing. "Do you understand what that means?"

I made no response. The King changed tack.

"I have a theory about you." My discomfort grew larger as his words spread out softly between us, and I held back from shifting in my seat. "Actually I have a couple, both of which you may prove wrong, but if you wish to leave this place alive you must be completely honest with me." He waited as his words sank into me like shards of ice. "Where is the water?"

I sighed inwardly, unable to decide whether I had just been placed on a hook or let off one. "Why should I tell you?"

"Because I will have you executed if you don't." He whispered earnestly, a gentle sadness in his eyes.

"But then you will never know."

The King shrugged. "Neither will my enemies."

We sat in the stale silence as the time between us bled away, his fingers held in a steeple under his top lip, while I myself sat frozen in horror. The slow pace of his breathing filled the room, growing louder in my ears as desperation sucked the oxygen from the air.

"Come with me." He stood abruptly, shaking off his reverie, and the spell was broken. I followed him out of the room and along the central corridor, past counting rooms and stock rooms and dwellings, past darkened doorways and closed doors and softly weeping women. At one point the animal stench of fear and death rose in my nostrils, and we passed a set of double doors that held back a lot of bleating. Chains rattled behind those doors, but as the noise receded the wash of the bay filled my ears. The King opened a door ahead of us and we were out into the open air, the whole of the Bay Bridge spread out before us, stretching out to the sunken city, one long daisy chain of lights and life, and death.

I realised where I was as I took in the salt air, I was on the balcony formed by the remnants of the upper deck. To my left was a galvanized metal gutter leading across to the slope of the island, and down into the water. It was thick with the residue of blood and piss and gore. Something stirred in my gut and raised a sweat on my brow. Across from the gutter there was a makeshift path leading up the hill to the crest of the island, the grass and shrubs were brown and dead from the summer droughts. As I stared up and down the slope of the island the King took my sleeve and led me over to the centre of the balcony. We stood at the edge, beside the rebar and beside the tatty nylon rope, and the King looked out towards the islands with their twinkling campfires and ragged spires.

"It's beautiful out here before dawn," he said. "All the light. Soon the sky will lighten behind us and blot out all those pinpricks."

The skin on the back of my neck prickled as the King turned and looked at me, seeking my gaze. I had the solid feeling that he knew more of me than he possibly could. It made him all the more dangerous. He turned back to the bridge and produced a small hip flask of moonshine, knocking it back before offering it to me. I waved it away.

"What do you see? Out there?"

I shrugged. "Lights. Fires. Ruins."

"Everything before the hills is mine. I took it, I stopped the decay. I harvested the city and made the ruins liveable for those that stay outside, those that choose to remain free – outside of the corrupt law and the stinking pigs with their machineguns and their locked warehouses full of stolen survival gear and medikits." He looked to me. "They choose me, my life, my rule, my law, and I owe them. From the bridge to the highlands I see family, friends, traders, people who put food on my table and trade for my wares. I am King and Nation. I run it, I make it work. I am everything you see before you, and I'm dying. Slowly. Necrotising limb by limb."

I looked at the man who was King, questioning the unexpected eloquence, and I saw the weight on his shoulders, the responsibility etched deep into his face. "Don't you know that it's inevitable?"

As I spoke the words out loud I realised the horror for myself. There it was, hanging in the space between us like a fairground sign, lit up by a thousand light bulbs.

"It isn't." He shook his head bitterly. "It isn't. It can't be, all I have to do is beat it one more day. It's only ever one more day." I heard his slow, tight breath as I gazed out across the waves. "These people depend on me. They are dying, or running – because there is no water left in the city." He caught my eye. "My city is dying and I will do whatever it takes to protect it. It's my responsibility, it's my job." The King took another swig, sucking in air as the moonshine bit his throat.

"It's also the source of your power."

He fell silent for a moment, glanced at me sideways, and then he nodded.

"Why are you talking to me? I've refused before – why aren't you torturing it out of me? You seem to think you can."

The king sighed and inhaled deeply. "Because I don't want to call your bluff unless I have to. Because I have the time." He looked at me. "Because it's still dark."

His last remark sliced through my heart like a knife of obsidian. He knew me. He knew I was bluffing and he knew I couldn't withstand any of it. I was powerless. I stood before the twinkling city and understood that I was as powerless as all the men before me, as powerless as the man beside me, trapped in the circumstance of my fated position as all the rest. Not unique, just another two-legged rat. All my years, all my scheming, all of my haughty self-appreciation – none of it meant a damn. I grasped for the rope as the freight train ran through my soul and my delusions shattered finally under the weight of the terror they had been masking. I clung to the rebar stake and cut my hand, I didn't feel it. The King spoke to me, I didn't hear it. Time slowed and my vision froze and the train rolled on and on, eviscerating me as I deflated. The pain flooding through my chest and guts was that of being struck by a cannon ball. I was struck by the shame and the shock and the dizzying terror, and as it left me I felt flushed and numb, and weak to the point of transparent.

As I stood shaking before the King, hollow and dry, I felt as though I was made of paper and leaves and bits of string. I turned to the King who watched me with a puzzled mask on his face, and I leant into his ear to whisper the horror of it all.

"There is no water."

I felt the man flinch as I smiled wanly. I saw the sickening horror pass across his face as if he had been slapped by his aging mother. I felt the brief flicker of triumph within me as the dreadful news struck home, but it was shrouded in shame and disappointment and self-loathing as I saw the wound in this man before me, and then the cold nausea spread through me as I realised I had just showed my hand, cashed in my chips. There was no lie, no falseness left to protect me, I swallowed and felt sick and ugly.

"I used a still." I muttered into the fickle breeze.

The King nodded, eyes glazed in a distant expression. "That's what I thought," he whispered, and with that he turned and fled.

I stood dumbstruck on that balcony, and watched the King go. He disappeared through the wooden doorway into the tunnel and the maze he had built around himself. For a moment I stood looking out across the bay at the shattered city, listening to the sounds of life and sleep drift in on the breeze while I registered my surprise. I half expected guards to appear with the hanging rope at any moment, and then I glanced at the sky and realised from the deep purple tinge to its blackness that if no one was coming for me I had better get inside before they changed their minds. As I crossed the threshold and melted into the darkness of the corridor beyond I glanced back, one last look at the twinkling, doomed constellation of human lights beyond. Much of it was obscured by struts and wires, the bridge piers and dead skyscrapers, but it was life – dim, desperate, struggling life, and soon it would be gone.

I hurried through the maze of fence panels and bootlegged plasterboard, trying to retrace my steps from wherever I was to wherever I used to be. None of it made sense. Twice I turned off that central corridor hoping for the Throne Room with its sealed walls and nurturing darkness, only to find myself lost in a forest of drying sheets, or a room stacked with shelves upon shelves of empty glass jars, bottles and plastic containers. I felt the sun's claws sharpen as I wandered on, and eventually I came back to the turning in the corridor, and the double doors leading to the court of the Looter King. The lamp hanging by the door had reached the dregs of its animal grease fuel, and was smoking wildly as the wick burnt down. I blew it out sharply and slipped through the doors. The guard was nowhere to be seen.

The room was bright and empty. No one had seen fit to put out the lamps – perhaps wasted fuel no longer mattered. I looked about for a place to hide, for a place where the darkness could envelope me. With the sunrise tingling and clawing up my spine I went round the room, blowing out lamps, and then, in the black I crouched on the floor beside the far corner of the throne platform, away from the door, and I broke off a couple of planks where the structure was pressed up against the wall. The wood cracked like thunder, and I halted in the stifling silence that followed, listening like a rabbit in the long grass, sure that someone would come. After a few moments I reached into the hollow under the platform and dragged myself through the gap in the wood. The space under the throne was not empty, but rather it was filled with supporting pillars, struts that made it hard to curl up for sleeping. It took a silent age to turn my body round so that I could stretch my arm out through the hole I had made and pull in the fugitive fragments of plank. Slowly, quietly I wriggled deep into that dark womb under the throne, and then I settled down to sleep, flat on my back, cocooned and waiting.

I dreamed I don't know what. I remember feeling hollow and shrunken, impotent. I remember mens' whispered voices washing through me. It seemed as if I were in the darkness under that stage, and then I was on the cart wobbling endlessly along the Causeway, old women glaring at me and young ones sucking their thumbs. In my dream I felt the sun scour its vengeance across the surface of the world, and I realised it was daylight on the Causeway, deadly, although it still seemed dark to my eyes, for I no longer remember what day looks like except for the burning white brightness. And the Causeway went on and on and on, and there I was in the darkness of day, not burning but expecting to burn. Drifting in limbo with the Sword of Damocles hanging above my head. I grew tired. I ceased to care.

When I awoke, drifting hazily in and out of consciousness, afraid to move for the struts enclosing me, there were men's voices all around, but they were not whispering. They were enraged and shouting, the voices of desperation, of fear. I shut my eyes and shut my ears, but the waves of anxiety and irritation spreading out from the men rippled through the ether, washing over me so that I saw piece by piece the exchange that was taking place. Lying still, terrified to move or breathe lest I made a sound and betrayed myself, I saw in my mind the white of an eye, the vein throbbing down a man's forehead. I felt the grinding of teeth and the sinking of guts. I tried to sleep but I was held there in the tide of noise, trapped amongst the emotional cacophony.

I lay still. When it was over one man remained in the room – the King. I felt him, deflated and despondent, drunk with misery and blindness. I waited but he did not leave. The glow of his mind sank lower and lower, and as I listened I caught the tinkling of an upturned bottle, the heavy breathing of the maudlin drunk. When I was quite certain he had made himself slow and stupid I emerged, wriggling noisily out of the crawlspace beneath the stage feet first.

As I stood up at the far end of the stage I saw the King's face, shocked and expectant, turned towards me, turned towards the noise. He held a small stoneware cup in one hand and he uncurled one finger from its girth to half point at me. "You!" He whispered in bitter astonishment. I stood still as he turned away and filled his cup with thin, muddy moonshine from a cracked bottle, and he spoke into the bottom of that cup.

"I oughtta have you put down. Staked down outside so I can watch you burn."

"Then why don't you?" I am not much for empty threats.

He snorted. "Haven't the will." He knocked his drink back and pointed an accusatory finger. "I'll get round to you soon enough. If not a fire, or a quake, or the winds, or the drought," he tried to laugh. "If not those, I'll be your fire. You don't know what you've done. To me."

"I've done nothing." I said in earnest.

"Everything and nothing. Everything and nothing." The king burped loudly.

I moved around the stage to the table, running my fingertips along its scored top until the King waved me to sit down. I picked a chair next to his and sat abruptly. I was so close I could see the throb of his pulse in his neck. It's a funny feeling – to catch yourself staring at your desire while someone is talking.

"The council is disintegrating. They'll leave. They'll all die." The King made an attempt at a bitter grin, a have-it-your-way. He merely grimaced with the pain.

"If it's about water – well – get a still." I offered up. The King turned his head to me with a glare so slow and bitter I could almost hear the screeching of gears.

"I have a still. The council have stills. Everybody and his uncle has a fucking still!" He spat venomously. I was taken aback by his words, and he caught my confusion.

"Yes, yes," he waved. "Didn't know that eh? Mr. Big with his own money tree! Thought you were minted." He smiled an oily smile and glared at me from the corner of his eye as he twisted his little knife. The smile faded, he sipped from that cup of his and cradled it in his palms. "Everyone has a still." He spoke softly into the bottom of that cup. "There's been no fuel since spring equinox."

The King knocked the cup back and found it empty. He set it down on the table with bitterness, and I begun to understand. "No tankers since then, and our messengers don't come back from L.A. I tell them to wait – tell the other clans just to wait and L.A. will send someone back with fuel, with a deal, but they are scared and the people are running."

The King sat in bloated silence, staring at his hands in his lap, nodding as if the drink were about to get the better of him, as if he were about to drift off. He rubbed his thumb around his fingertips slowly, just staring in silence as his head drooped lower and lower. I watched him, feeling the edge of my teeth, the strength in my fingertips. Feeling my own power. Suddenly he looked up, stared at me, looked into my eyes.

"They'll die you know. We're only strong together. The city will die and the people will die. Out there – out there on the central plains. Dead in the dust. And the pigs have all the smotic... Osmotic pumps and solar stills they could want locked up in some bunker somewhere. Puttra. Potrero somewheres."

I held the man's gaze, or rather – he held mine, and I opened my mouth to speak. *Why don't you fight them?* I was about to ask indignantly. *Seize all the disaster gear?* But I knew the answer; I knew it even before my tongue had left the roof of my mouth. Human shields. The Police would find reason to execute – to murder every last one of their camp prisoners before giving up their power. They wouldn't have to go so far, and they knew it. Killing a few on the front line would be enough to paralyse the raiders. A few, a few hundred – what does it matter? What do they care? The raiders may want the pumps, the space blankets, the solar panels, but dump a few hundred refugees outside the gates and shower them with bullets and you'll see how long it takes for their appetite and outrage to shrivel.

The King turned away, shut his eyes, oblivious to my slow thoughts. We sat in silence, the man an arm's length from me. I could smell the heat of him, the grease of his scalp, see his heart straining in the wire of his veins. I felt the hunger rise in my craw, marvelled at his lack of fear, frowned at the mystery source of his impossible knowledge. *How could he know? Does he really know what he alludes to?* And yet I knew he was right. I sat there, filling my senses with the warmth of him, struggling to push my hunger down and back out of my awareness, doubting I could murder a king and leave the castle alive, my fear catching on the glint of the knife in his belt. And yet I wanted him, wanted the taste of him, this man of all men I wanted to know the most. I would have given him my time – my longevity, if such a thing were possible – but it is not in my power. It never was.

The King seemed to follow my thoughts as the heat of him filled my nostrils. I believed him to be asleep, but he looked up and glared at my desire in disgust that anyone should want him or that I should, and then his face shattered into drunken tears and he smeared the back of his hand across his eyes as he cried.

"I used to t... teach, y'know? Now it's just..." He buried his face in his hands, and then he seemed to remember what I was. Through the cracks in his fingers he caught me staring, fascinated and ravenous, and he wiped his face. Looking at me in disgust he spoke – he drawled "Get out," and I did. I fled my *self*.

When I emerged from that sealed room I was shaking with hunger, withdrawal, desire, what's the difference? I had not tasted blood in as much as twenty-four hours. The plasterboard walls of the makeshift central corridor seemed to both loom tall above me, stretching to the ceiling, and close in against my sides. I grew dizzy as I panicked, realising the hunger was upon me and my grip on reality was faltering, my self-control along with it. I stumbled through the maze, drawn on by the strange sounds of people's lives, the fetid smells of blood and warmth and flesh. A couple were fucking furtively and listlessly on the other side of a door made of sackcloth. Through a cellophane window I spied a baby twitching in a milk-crate crib. So easy it would be to reach through that synthetic spider's web and grasp the little morsel, and the hell that would follow would make me pray for the old days of the Inquisition. I drove myself on as my surroundings spun and the vacuum in my belly sent sucking tendrils out through my chest and into my limbs, my eyes, my fingertips. I felt the sharpness of the new eye-teeth that were forming under my gums, pushing out the brittle and crumbling set that sat stained and feeble in my old man's mouth. My saliva thinned and ran from the corners of my tight lips, and I fled like a monster passing from hovel to hovel, from corridor to corridor in the darkness.

There was a smell drawing me on, a stale smell of rancid gore and old death, a stench that I had caught here before, and I bounced through the maze almost mindlessly, clinging to its sickening sweetness with the desperate hope that I could commit my crime there unnoticed – after all, all addicts hide the evidence – if not from others then at least from themselves. All I could think of was the warm, sweaty sensation of blood sticky in my throat. *I need it* I thought, *I need it* – the mantra became my justification as my hands shook and my veins burned.

The smell grew stronger as I doubled back, diving out of one dead end and passing another, and up ahead the distressed bleating of goats connected in my mind. A chill draft stung my face and the foul rancour of an abattoir caught my nostrils. The old, familiar perfume embraced me as with the childhood comfort of a warm blanket. I rushed head on, and fully broke my way noisily through the flimsy fence-panel door. It splintered around my clawed hand, I remember the shards sticking in my thickened skin as I brushed them off against the weave of my gown.

The space beyond was dark and wretched, the air ripe with the stench of cud, spilt offal and shit. There was a steady draft filtering through the gaps in the far wall – it was the wall at the mouth of the tunnel – the wall that closed off the balcony. There were runnels along the floor, tin gutter pipes and misappropriated air conditioning ducts that ran together and led down into one corner where the arched wall met the floor. The pipes were sticky with the thick residue of blood – rust brown and foul, and the air was alive with the incessant hum of blowflies, the constant chitter of insect jaws clicking and writhing through the filth.

In the half-light it appeared as though I had stumbled into some nightmare orchard of death and decay, vertical forms ran from floor to ceiling everywhere I looked. They were chains hanging from blocks pinned to the vaulted roof, sharpened meat hooks drifting in the mid-air draft, or lying on the asphalt floor amid coils of chain and filth. I stepped along as quietly as I could in my hunger driven fervour – everywhere I went the chink of chains followed me, betrayed every shaking move.

I followed the sound of the animals, and found them huddled in pens up against the tiled, curved wall that arched over to become the ceiling. I expected the wretched animals to be asleep, but most of them were not. They were too distressed at their surroundings. There were five or six, mostly billy goats, but there were one or two old nannies, worn out and dried up, straining at their chains, bleating listlessly in distress. Their fear was obvious, and several had taken to biting each other, or chewing the fur from their own bodies.

Quietly, with the shakes running through my limbs and pangs of unbearable anticipation clawing up my throat in spasms, I unpinned the gate and grabbed one of the old nannies by the scruff of the neck. She bleated in distress as I dragged her through the narrow gap, and then I shoved the gate closed with the squeal of metal on tarmac as it scraped along the floor. I jammed the animal's chain between the gate and the pillar, so that she could barely move, and then I knelt on the floor and wrapped my arms around her neck.

I bit slowly into the flesh around the thick vein running up the side to the heavy neck, seeking to break the tough, leathery skin like some fur-ridden piecrust. The animal shivered and stiffened, straining on its collar and bobbling its head, trying to wrench its neck away as its guttural bleating rose in pitch to a distressed goat-scream. I held fast, I held tight.

The fur and skin gave way to my rotten teeth and my mouth filled with salty life, slowly at first, and then faster than I could swallow, pulsing in drowning spurts as I tore the vein. The blood cascaded down my throat, hot and thick and somehow hollow. The animal stamped her legs in shock and pain, and my grip grew tighter. I knew that it would quieten soon.

As low, animal life flooded my belly and my veins, so too it filled my mind and infected my soul. I was grasped by dim urges, faltering thoughts welling up unformed out of the darkness. In our dim mind crawled the scarab fear of death, the need to piss, the fermented taste of cud rising in the throat. But also the exaltation, the heady splendour of stolen life flowing on and on and on in waves of heat and energy, the satisfaction of need, the ever further sucking down, exploring deeper and deeper into that animal's body and mind with hungry tendrils of awareness and emptiness.

This is the drug – this is the drug, again and again I see the endless roll, the infinite procession of life on and on as it moves and pulses, constantly changing and transmuting through all those warm, complete living creatures to whom its ever-golden source is not closed. They play their roles in the cycle of birth, death and rebirth, the endless life and love of God is their reward, and I, empty and dysfunctional as I am, closed to the higher ways of the transcendental universe, and cursed to observe it like no other, see the glowing source of God only when I steal it from another creature.

We faltered together as the dimness closed in, I saw flashes of myself, distorted and shadowed in the sideways vision of the goat as her legs buckled and we rolled onto the floor. Too weak to move or bleat, she twitched and her hide shivered whilst my flesh grew warm and my grip grew ever more vicelike, dragging her down, down, down.

The heart does not thunder, it twitters. It does not stop all at once, but enters a relentless and paralysing cycle of fast twitching and desperate, wrenching spasms. The vision at once closes in, numb and black and tinny, and goes bright with stars and light, and then quite before you realise it the two have become one and you are alive and alone, splayed on a cold floor and shrouded in the drifting soul of the thing you have just raped and ended, gazing at that energetic cloud as it fades and slinks away, both connected inextricably to it, desperately trying to drink it in, suck it down, hold it back, and utterly unable to cling to it, to own it wholly or at all. However much you can take from a living thing, however much of the soul you care to imbibe, there is always that golden nugget of sacrosanct energy that escapes your power, that will do what it will, go where it needs to, immutable. It will not be captured. It will not be consumed nor owned. That is the cruellest joke to one as empty as me.

My mind returned to me, warm and slow and satisfied, I became aware of the wetness on my chin and the blood stuck to my teeth. I was inebriated, retarded, as dumb and stunned as the animal life afflicting me, and the world came back to me in phases, a little here and there as the darkness withdrew. I loosened my teeth from the still, cool flesh and spat out strings of coagulating gore and goat hair. The life within me was alien but strong, as sudden and false as if someone had flicked a light switch in my chest, illuminating my central being. It was a lie to feed on such life, it was a lie, but one of substance. I rocked back on my haunches, struggling through my drunken haze to see, struggling to hear. All should have been right, but it was not. It was not. Floating through the dark depths of my consciousness was the presence of an intruder emerging into my awareness slow and gentle, like a dagger slipping unannounced into your heart, gliding through your lung. It was a mind. Another mind, strange and cool and barely present in the ether above me. I flinched and turned to look over my shoulder, to look up. Standing above me amid the chains and the hooks was the silhouette of a woman gripping a baseball bat. Her face was shadowed but I knew, I knew it was the woman from the park. The woman like me. There was a swish of air as she swung the bat hard, and everything turned to black.

I float between the darkness of a tomb and the darkness of unconsciousness. Most of the time I don't know the difference. I fade in and out of existence as the world shakes around me, exacerbating my shocking head. Sometimes the pain wakes me up, sometimes it send my mind running for shelter, puts me to sleep. Gradually I realise that I cannot move. I am curled up on my side in a wooden box so small that every surface touches my body and every limb is pinned in. My head throbs, and I feel the trickle of blood in my eye, and the box jolts violently and continuously, for I am on a cart and I hear the slow, clopping of horses labouring along. But I am in a box, and it's a box I can't open. For one such as myself, who has found hiding in boxes to be a regular necessity for millennia, being trapped within one is a singular nightmare, but this is worse. This is smaller than anything I have ever been in. I can barely breathe. I contract all my muscles, trying feebly to push the sides of the box outwards, but the pain in my head increases with the pressure and the blackness threatens to drown my mind. I cannot unfold my arms to push, the thick, hot air reaches down my throat to strangle me from the inside, and I start to shake as my intellect disintegrates. I try counting, passing the moments as I have done before when the sun has held me prisoner. I breathe slowly. I feel the pressure of wood against every side of my body and I hear my strange, distant voice crack in the darkness, a single, desperate squeak, and then I am falling in the darkness, falling and screaming, falling and screaming.

Waking up in the darkness is not simply a matter of opening your eyes. You can move, blink, stare blindly into the nothing for hours, dreaming all the while until you *realise* you are conscious, until something tips you off. If you are, like me, someone who sleeps in total darkness, often with their eyes open, the certain knowledge that the difference between consciousness and unconsciousness is not biological but a change in the state of mind is somewhat unsettling. Who is to say you are conscious now just because your eyes are open and moving?

I was 'awake' for some time before I next realised I was actually, truly awake. What tipped me off in my blinking mindlessness, as I dreamed of blood and pain, was the coolness of the air sifting through the seams of the wooden box, and the observation that I was no longer jolting but rocking. Shortly after realising that I was conscious to the outside world I realised that I should be able to hear, and then my hearing came on full and fast. I heard ripples of water lapping against a hull. I heard oars dipping through the waves, I heard the wind and I heard the efforts of another living being.

I was careful not to think about the box. Mostly I concentrated on the pain in my head, the stiffness in my neck and my curled up limbs. I was careful not to stretch, not to tense, not to expand myself and feel the impossible limits of my world. I did not think about the confines of my cage, I thought only, *this will end, this will end. One way or another this will end.* I blacked out again.

It was not until after I felt my cage being hauled onto solid ground, after the other had clambered over the box, as the sound of the oars disappeared beyond the lap of the waves that I considered the horror that could have been, could have preyed on my captive mind: The box could have gone into the water. I was thankful that this nightmare prospect was impossible by the time it came to me. The box was being driven along – wheels squeaking, bumping over thresholds, doors whooshing closed, the jangle of keys, and then flying, rocketing, a light-headed sensation. I wretched suddenly, contracting all of my muscles, fighting hard not to vomit. I was afraid I would drown in my own puke. I lost my grip on time and space and an outside world, my hands twitched as my fingertips reached out, and again I was gone.

I was lying on a mattress low down on the floor, and the woman from the park was wiping my naked flesh with a damp cloth. I was unbound. My head throbbed and the room spun around me. The space was large and warm, but the walls seemed to be at odd angles, collapsing in towards the top. There were many windows, but I was too low to see anything but black sky and effervescent clouds. The light was dim and flickering, I had the impression that there was a fire nearby but I couldn't see it. I found I was naked but I didn't care. What is my body but my body? I was grateful to be out of the box.

I lay still, in pain as the woman cleaned and dressed the wound on my head, swollen and throbbing and tender. My mind was lost somewhere between the life of the goat and the dark terror of the box, all I could do was watch her, and watch myself, from somewhere across the room.

She saw my patchwork flesh, blackened and burned in places, the thickened skin receding up my arms and lightening towards my shoulders where clothing had shielded my skin from the sun somewhat. She saw my weaknesses. I saw hers. Her burning eyes roamed my body slowly, with the steady unapologetic force of a steam train, but she was careful not to look at my face, my taut lips, my browned teeth. She didn't look at my fuzzy skullcap, or the cavernous black hole in the centre of my face from which the baby-pink nub of my new nose was slowly emerging, struggling for the light of day like a fragile flower bud. You would think that this would be my most disturbing feature, especially to another such as myself – the evidence of sunburn written over my ruined face, but occasionally her glance flitted over my injuries, guiltily darting to and fro, somewhat like the dance of the hummingbird and as imperceptibly fast. It was not the ugly truth of my wounds that she avoided, it was my eyes, and the harder I sought to meet her gaze the more avidly she denied me.

The woman held my arms as she wiped them down with slow care. She studied me as she worked, tracing the details of my withered skin, following the lines of my clawed fingers one by one. She worked with a nurse's detachment belying the disgusted, irresistible fascination one leper has while observing her fate on the ruined face of another. As she looked down at her work, her dark, shoulder-length hair fell down in curls about her neck. Her face was firm, with a noble, elegant nose and sheer cheekbones, and those piercing grey eyes that gave nothing away. She was slim, but not gaunt like myself, and she seemed a little taller than average, her slender back running down in curves to strong, shapely hips. Her breasts were small and round, and somewhat cloistered within layers of clothing that were both restrained and functional, allowing for ease of movement. In her movements and manner she gave the appearance for all the world of a calm, controlled forty-year-old human woman, but she was not. She was a hundred and fifty, a hundred at least, still a child.

"I am unbound?" I croaked, my throat dry and cracking.

The woman gave me a sideways look, and then proceeded with her work, dipping the cloth in water and wiping my palms.

"Of course. It would be improper." She spoke in a low, steady voice.

"Am I a prisoner?"

"No," she shook her head. "But we would like to speak to you."

My hand went to the bloody wound on the side of my head. "You hit me with a bat."

"It was the only way to get you off the bridge safely."

My jaw dropped. "What? Screaming in a box as it passed by thousands."

The woman raised an eyebrow. "That is the commonplace. There are a thousand unhealthy ways to leave the Causeway. People turn their backs, pretend they don't hear. They ignore and go on as normal. The young ones simply laugh."

I scowled and sat up. And clutched my head as my brain throbbed and the room set to spinning again.

"What is your name?"

"Ana," she whispered. "What's yours?"

I looked about me and ripped the cloth from her hands. I pressed it to my forehead and shrugged.

"What's it matter? I was in danger, you say?"

The woman nodded. "The King. I could no longer protect you. He would have staked you out as soon as he was sober." She shrugged. "I am an abomination, but occasionally useful. You – you are just an abomination. But mostly you are out of his control. Not part of his 'kingdom'. He can't abide that. It might upset his system."

"He knows..." It was a sort of verbal groan, but she took it as a question.

"I told him."

I was shocked. And horrified. And offended. I stared angrily at her, as soon as I turned my gaze towards her she looked away.

"You fool." I spat.

She was still for a moment, I caught her eyes narrowing. "He is my eyes and ears on that bridge and all around. He brought me you. He – "

But I raised my hand, enough. I did not care. No bargain is worth revealing our Achilles Heel. We sat in silence, I made her wait as I dragged cloth over my shoulders and neck, rubbed down my stringy chest, cleaned my genitals with a calculated, unforgiving slowness, and wiped down my legs. She sat somewhere nearby – exhibiting something between boredom and discomfort. When I was done I threw the cloth down.

"We. Earlier you said we."

22

It was only when the three of us were together that I was struck by the feeling of strangeness, of dislocation and loss that had come to me that first time I was in the presence of another like myself. Ana had led me to an elevator and produced a key from a chain around her neck. I was astonished when the doors swooshed open and she ushered me in, and we rushed up, up, up. I leant heavily into the corner of the moving room, clinging to the handrails as my head throbbed and my knees weakened. I thought back to the dark horror of the box and realised that I had not been flying then but climbing.

I thought I would vomit as the elevator came to an abrupt halt, but the doors slid open with a sigh of cool air. Ana stepped through first.

"Come on, he's this way."

It was all she would say, and there was a strange glow to her voice. She led me down a dimly lit corridor, the carpet feeling harsh and bobbly under my bare feet. It was odd to see clean walls and clear floors, I expected to see ash and rubble everywhere. There was a cool draft running along the hallway, and I shivered in the clean clothes I had been given. Fresh clothes were a rare extravagance, but the pants were too wide and the sleeves too short. There was no hood, and I felt naked and ugly without its cover to hide under.

Ana came to an unassuming single door and halted. We had passed several similar doors – the metal frame with the full-length frosted glass panel, a business name embossed in gold or a plaque on the wall by the doorframe. I was beginning to understand that we were in an old-style office building – the kind with hallways and movable internal walls and rental space – something rooted in the twentieth century. Ana went in, and as she held the door for me I noticed the words on the glass, peeling in black lettering, *Parker, Platt and Sons.*

The first thing I noticed was not the room, but the man inside. He stood by an open window but faced the doorway expectantly. His eyes looked for mine immediately, and they were as piercing as Ana's, and I dare say mine. Yet if her presence was subtle and fleeting, his was enormous and magnetic. His confidence, his belief in himself was obvious in every small movement as he crossed the room and held his hand out to take mine, yet his manner was stately rather than flashy.

"Cyrus." He said as he shook my hand, and everything melted away rather uncomfortably. He seemed to size me up in that moment, and found some cause for relief, for his stance loosened a little, and his face softened. I felt my own small measure of relief, for he was young, so much younger than myself, that he could not possibly imagine my mind.

"You are old!" He said softly. "What do they call you?"

"Oh, many things." I said, watching Ana's face out of the corner of my eye as her hidden expression twitched from excitement to anxiety and back again, irritated at my refusal to give a name I did not own. "Do captives have names here?"

Cyrus made a face and sighed. "There is little of the night left. You will have to put that down if we are to talk."

I looked at them both in surprise. "What do ones such as us have to say to one another?"

The words hung in the air like poison gas, heavy and cloying, because of course I'd uttered the awful truth. Predators do not make good bedfellows. We are paranoid control freaks, power mongers, psychotics and murderers, we know all the same tricks, all the same highs. We know all the same sadnesses.

"Well," he said. "Well." The youngster's face hardened and he turned to look out of the window. I took the quiet moments to look at the room. It was similar to the one I had awoken in. Essentially square, with those strange, sloping walls and windows on two sides, and a door in each of the other walls. The floor was carpeted with tacky, immortal nylon carpet squares, and there was a table in the windowed corner covered with papers and illuminated by an electric lamp that appeared to be running from a wall socket. I was too stunned to ask. Ana was standing between me and the other, flushing alternately between acute discomfort and angry impatience. Her radiation was intense, and so I moved over to the window next to Cyrus, half to study my location and half to study the man.

He was tall, a little taller than myself, and he had short black hair that was quiffed neatly at the front. He was thin, with sharp cheeks and a Russian nose, short sideburns and pale, milky skin. I had some hope that I would find him likeable, indeed both of them, but while his presence was strong within the room, I found him less readable than Ana. I could not catch his eyes, he stared out at the ruined city. I watched his reflection in the glass.

Beyond that mirror face lay the pathetic stump of Coit Tower on its hill, and across the bay the bush fires poured their orange smoke up into the night. The clouds were low and glowing but the air was fairly clear. The ruined towers of the Golden Gate were just visible in the distant gloaming beyond the city, beyond the badlands of the park and the cliff trails. Across the floodwaters lay Russian Hill Island and my neighbourhood, my solitary, flame-scarred tower. My scalp tingled with recognition, but it was not until I looked down and perceived the waist of the building spreading out beneath me floor by floor until it hit the waves below that I realised where we were.

"This is the Transamerica." I said out loud.

Cyrus turned and looked at me, his eyes holding mine. "Yes," he smiled. He turned back to the window and spoke half to himself. "The lighthouse between the Police and the Looters."

I would have laughed out loud but he spoke with such quiet conviction that I had to swallow.

Cyrus stood staring out of that window for some moments, alone with his thoughts. I watched him, trying to gauge his years. It was hard – he was older than the woman certainly. He had the poise that comes with the realisation that this may never end. This was the source of his relaxed confidence. He knew I was staring, and he continued to watch the night. Ana walked towards him and squeezed his elbow. He smiled at her and muttered something, and then he turned to me.

"Would you like to see?"

We descended in the elevator, the hum of excitement passing between the other two whilst I felt trapped in the confined space, dizzy and claustrophobic as my head throbbed. The pain was abating however.

"How do you power this thing?" I whispered. Cyrus simply shook his head and grinned.

We stepped out onto a darkened platform, and the air was damp and salty. Ana stood by the bank of elevators and threw a switch, illuminating the emptiness with rows of powerful lights. The space was vast, it was about three floors tall and spanned across the whole building. This was one complete floor in the lowest, widest part of the tower. The only object to break the emptiness was the single, rectangular column of the elevator shaft behind us.

"This is the loading bay," Ana said, "although if the water rises much further it'll be the swimming pool."

There were rolling shutters pulled down over great bay doors on opposite walls of the tower. On one side there was a speedboat, painted black as the night, nestling in its trailer by the bay doors. The shutters rattled in the wind and the sound of the waves crashing against concrete pervaded the vast space. All of the windows in the angled walls had been covered with sheet steel, which was rusting slowly in the salt air. When I looked above, two ragged scars of steel and concrete ran all the way around those concave walls, one at a regular height above the next.

"You cut the floors down?" I said, conscious of the similarities to my own creaking structure.

"We had it done, yes. And the stairs," Ana replied. "It's defensive."

"How do you keep the people out?"

Cyrus crossed the damp floor, the sound of grit underfoot echoing through the empty cavern. "Simple. We keep the doors locked and the elevators upstairs. They've never gotten through the shutters – they're bullet proof. And it's pretty difficult to use a battering ram from a boat."

I thought on it as we made our way back to the elevator. "Doesn't anyone scale the walls?" Ana shook her head, Cyrus smiled a little.

"Sometimes. When it's calm. They don't get very far. And if they get up to a proper window one of us is waiting."

The elevator took us up, up to another floor, almost as big but not as high. I stepped out to be confronted with rows of metal shelves stretching from wall to wall, each one stacked with brown cardboard boxes and cellophane packets labelled 'Survival Blankets, 1000' and 'Powdered Baby Food'. I wandered through the aisles, past fire kits and agricultural tools, shovels and frozen livestock semen, boxes of preserved crop seeds. Every so often I'd come across a gap in the shelves, a scrap of paper laid down, with 'Hillman Safety Lamps' scrawled on it, or 'Biodiesel Fuel Additive'. Towards one corner the shelves became more and more empty, and at some point I stopped reading the bits of paper and turned to meet the others.

Cyrus wore an amused expression as he opened the elevator on more survival supplies four floors up. There was everything from solar stills to prophylactics, and I grew more and more weary at the endless rows of seeds and equipment not rescued but hoarded.

"Do you see it?" He said excitedly as the doors slid open on the fifth floor of shelving. I shook my head and yawned. Some of the supplies were amazing – water sterilizing tablets, chocolate, coffee beans, but most of it, like hydraulic fluid additive, was simply useless to the three of us.

Up we went again as the floors grew smaller and narrower towards the apex of the pyramid. Cyrus took me through floors with hundreds of fuel barrels, tanks of heating oil, biodiesel, gasoline, caged shelves of propane cans. I was astonished. Floors and floors, and more above, thousands of gallons of fuel, there was enough to last the Looter's Causeway a year or myself a hundred. Beyond the fuel stores lay the generator room. Cyrus walked through it with obvious pride, showing off the machinery and the storage batteries.

"This is the generator. We don't need to run it very much – there's a hundred kilometres of copper wire wrapped around the building – the whole tower is one giant electrostatic condenser – but the salt air corrodes the anode – smell the chlorine?" He led me over to a machine humming in the corner, a thick wire trailing to a connection point by the window, and a large copper strip running straight down like a lightning conductor. The metal was green with moist, fluffy crystals blossoming over its surface.

"It's not much but it tops up the batteries enough for two."

We rode up in the elevator in silence, my confusion had given way to unease. We all turned a blind eye to the floors that were ignored – I didn't want to ask, they didn't want to tell.

"How long have you been storing this equipment? It would have taken hundreds of men to –"

"Twenty years. Easily." Cyrus beamed. "In this building... Well, since it closed. Since the company went under. It did take many men to collect and transfer everything, and we didn't find everything we wanted."

Ana spoke up. "Towards the end it was difficult. There were thefts. Quantities of anything were hard to come by. The Feds 'taxed' any large shipment."

"This isn't all for you, is it?" I said evenly as the elevator came to a stop. Ana shook her head and Cyrus laughed lightly. We were back in the region of old offices, rooms with carpet whose walls had not been taken down in the name of storage. Things were more chaotic here, and more arranged for the likes of us. There were odd little stashes of weapons locked in filing cabinets, one long, boring night Ana had made an igloo out of reams of office paper in the centre of some long forgotten typing pool, the desks having been pushed against the walls. There were little electric heaters dotted about, and the fridges in abandoned office kitchens were all partially stocked – with bottles – screwcap bottles of blood, not sealed medical bags. My unease shimmered, an ice-cold slime running down my spine and collecting like a dead weight in my gut. The place had a bored, tight feeling – something between a neglected playground and a prison.

We passed the room where I had woken, above the rooms where the two of them slept, and bathed, and read. Cyrus was taking me to the observation deck as he called it. When we got there I found the room to be small and dark, tucked up in the eaves of the giant pyramid and bisected by the elevator core and stairs.

"This is the top floor," Cyrus said happily. "Used to be a conference room. You can see everything from here."

The man ushered me over and I grew dizzy as I looked down along the criss-crossed plane of the tower wall, my eyes following the external concrete wings that housed the elevator shafts and service piping. Suddenly up and down escaped me, and I was looking at the path of an uneven, glittering bridge leading to a huge, dark cascade of water. The illusion didn't last.

"This is the best place in the city," Cyrus said, almost to himself. "From here I just watch, and watch, and watch."

"Yes," Ana added softly, a little piqued. "All night long."

I looked out across the city, the low cloud glowing orange from the fires across the bay. To one side lay Twin Peaks crowned with its spiky antenna, a dark and hungry silhouette against the sky, to the other lay the black, sucking waters of the bay, a vast expanse interrupted only by the twinkling necklace of the Causeway, its firefly lights winking above the waves. In between lay the ruins of the waterlogged city, buildings breaking the waves like occasional tombstones, fingers of floodwater running up the sinking streets. Campfires billowed in the night as people screamed and fled, fought and died.

I turned away, exhausted by the familiar sight of decay. On a table in the centre of the room stood a small stack of radio equipment and a portable processor array. It was rigged as a scanner and digital decoder.

"Do you pick anything up?" I nodded towards the stack.

"Yes, all the time. Mostly analogue stuff. Desperate signals in the civilian bands, shipping sometimes – though less and less. There's a Christian radio station out on the central valley, calling people in. I think it's on an old CB radio that someone's boosted. God knows where they get the juice – it's probably a pirate scam. Mostly I get the military channels being repeated out of Twin Peaks, but they're encrypted. And the Police signals. I'm working on hacking the drone controls. Cyrus went over and flicked a switch, orange light from the tuner's display panel illuminating the room with a faint glow as fuzzy voices crackled out, liberated from the airwaves. He turned the volume down a little, and I crossed back to the windows, looking down upon the city to the soundtrack of desperation.

I wandered around the room and found myself beside a ten-inch reflector scope with a night sight. The lens was staring out in the direction of the Golden Gate. It was mounted on an automated tripod, and there was a second tripod standing by its side, empty and ready for another device. A thin cable ran across from one gear head to the other, synchronising the control mechanisms so that they would point in parallel. Absently I bent my eye to the viewfinder, and I restrained a gasp as my body ran cold all over.

The scope showed a beautiful image of my bullet ridden balcony. If the shutters had not been drawn I'm quite sure I'd have been able to see the silks on the wall of my living room.

"Oh yes, oh yes," Cyrus said when he noticed what I was doing.

"Tell me," I said coldly, without taking my eye from the scope. "Do you have armour piercing, as well as windcheaters?"

Cyrus paused. "I wouldn't want to hit you, you know." He said softly. I stood in that little room at the top of the world, with more company than I'd had in longer than I could remember. I was silent and alone. Cyrus looked at Ana and nodded decisively, and she inhaled and held her hand out to me.

"Come,' she said. "You haven't seen it all yet."

They led me back to the coffin-like elevator, prickles running up my spine and over my scalp as I tried to assimilate the fact that they had been watching me, knew me, and in all likelihood knew everything about me while I myself knew nothing. The elevator stopped one floor up and I stepped out after Ana, but Cyrus didn't follow. As I looked back he half raised one hand from the rail where he was slouching. All he said was "food," and then the doors slid shut on him.

We were in a chilly corridor, narrow and glaringly bright from obnoxious strip lighting. The walls were whitewashed cinderblock, the floor was bare concrete. There were red painted pipes running along the ceiling, and two doors in the corridor, one marked "Elevator Service", the one I was led through marked "Cleaning" with a small, vinyl plaque riveted onto the wood. Inside was dark and cramped, and I felt the throttling hand of rising claustrophobia. It didn't abate when Ana flicked the light on. It was a broom cupboard, barely two metres by one, barely big enough for both of us.

The room was lined with shelving, there were brooms, bottles of bleach, buckets and brushes, all the chemical potions that were like alchemy these days – beyond the grasp. It was as if I had stepped beyond time and arrived in a school janitor's closet with all its smells of detergent and floor polish, as if the last ten years had not happened within this little piece of space. And then I noticed that all the bottles were empty. Ana took a broom and knocked a ceiling tile out of place. As I watched she pushed the end of the handle against a latch, and a ladder unfolded with pneumatic smoothness out of the black void above the ceiling. Ana began to climb, and looked back at me expectantly.

The room I emerged into was small and square and windowless, with a low ceiling that was riddled with pipes. Ana was sat on an inflatable sofa near the hatch in the floor, and for a moment I thought that the room was otherwise empty, until I noticed a row of narrow closet freezers lining one wall, a little microwave sitting atop the end unit and a basin in the corner below a little mirror. The only light came from floor lamps in each corner, the floor was covered with rugs, and there was a stack of books on a table by the sofa. There was a media library to the other side of the sofa, its screen black and silent, and in the far corner a fuel cell the size of a small washing machine lay dormant. I stood up, head in the ductwork that seemed to disappear into the high centre of the ceiling.

"I thought the observation deck was the top floor?"

"The floor we just came from is elevator service, but this space doesn't exist," Ana said. "For some reason it's not on the plans, but Cyrus figured it must be here. He followed the pipes I think. It's our bolt hole."

"Why show me?"

Ana breathed for a moment. She watched me. "Because there's nothing more precious to show. This is it, this is all of it.

It's our security and we're sharing it with you."

I shook my head. "But why?"

Ana laughed, soft and treacly. "Bonehead! Cy – we want you to stay here, we're giving you our trust."

"Oh." I said. *Dear,* I thought.

I stood in a corner away from Ana, watching my shadow stretch across the floor. Presently Cyrus emerged through the hole in the floor, carrying a flask and some large breakfast mugs. Ana's face lit up.

"You found the throne room then," Cyrus smiled, his shark's teeth flashing in the low light. I nodded. "Sit, sit," he cooed. When I was positioned on the end of the sofa Cyrus pulled the ladder up and lowered the thick, insulated hatch down. He didn't bother with the submarine-style locking wheel. He sat on the floor before us and poured the blood out into the mugs, taking less for himself than for us.

I held the broad mug like a bowl in both hands, sipping loudly, surprised to find the liquid good. It was human.

"It's fresh," I said in surprise. Cyrus just grinned and put the china to his lips. I drank also, confronted by the warm complexity of the unknown human soul I was imbibing, heady, speedy and moreish, tinged faintly with a sick shame that I pushed out of my mind, a disturbing aftertaste I chose to ignore. I finished a little too quickly, drunk on the fear and adrenaline contained within my little cup as the taint of horror swirled around my belly and sank into my veins.

"You can't spend much time here?" I asked, wiping my mouth on the back of my leathery hand. Cyrus shook his head. "I don't. Ana comes here to read when she's not foraging."

"Don't you have everything you need?"

"Need, sure," she said. "But all the treasure that's out there, and so much time to kill – I like to explore."

"She likes the hunt," Cyrus grinned a little.

"How long have you been hoarding?"

"Years. Since it became clear to me that the decline was truly terminal. You?"

"Oh. I didn't. Not enough anyway." I thought back three short years, buying my toolbox, ordering the generator online. Certainly I didn't do enough. "What are the seeds for? The tools? Mountains of it."

"To rebuild of course," Cyrus chuffed. "When things settle down. We will repopulate the region."

"Cyrus has a plan," Ana added, gazing at him.

"Will you join us?"

I studied Cyrus, and then I shook my head. "No. Not now."

We sat in silence; Ana finished her meal and sucked her lips. I slumped into the cushions as the blood and energy coursed through me pleasantly. "How did you find me?" I asked finally.

"You found me, remember." Ana retorted.

Cyrus shook his head. "The city is dark." He swallowed, chin down, hand on chest as if to burp. "There is no light but the fires, and above the flames just the towers, derelict and black. Except for your windows. The only lights above the fourth floor in all the city besides ours, and lit all night 'til dawn." The man shrugged and opened his palms. "A beacon shining out to us. We didn't know at first. It wasn't hard to understand once we knew *you* were out there. So I played games with bullets. I had to get your attention."

"You never replied. All those questions I asked."

Cyrus shrugged, putting his mug down. "I wasn't ready."

His answer hung in my mind for a moment. "And now?" I said slowly.

"Look around. This is the inner sanctum. You're one of us, you belong with us."

I raised my eyebrows. "You'd think so, wouldn't you."

"Stay." He said gently, as if to a lover, but I shook my head.

"It's too late tonight. But tomorrow I will return to the tower."

"Why? There's nothing there."

I shrugged. "It's my home."

I slept the day out in the windowless darkness of that room while the others returned to their respective chambers. The sofa was short and my mind troubled, I turned in the darkness as the seed of the idea burrowed into my brain and I dreamt of the three of us, laughing and watching as the flames overtook everything below, overtook us. *It never works. It never works.*

It was attractive, certainly, to get to know someone, to spend some of the endless years with the same someones. Part of me reached out through those dreams that day, touched the others, walked in theirs. But the disappointment – the disappointment of slowly finding them as cold and monstrous and static as myself, as unchanging, it was more than I would risk bearing. I wasn't ready to play house with strange creatures.

In the early evening Ana took me back to my jetty by

Broadway, the salt spray stinging my face in the solidifying darkness. She didn't say a word, and I found her mind as ephemeral as ever. In the bows before my feet stood two large cans of gasoline sloshing gently on the calm waters. Cyrus had given them to me, an uncomfortable gift, a pained look on his face as we said goodbye.

"Take some time," he'd said. "Think about it. Don't take too long."

Ana had shown me the intercom by the roller doors outside the loading dock. I was but to say the word and the elevator would be waiting. She said to flash a light in my window and they would come for me, send a boat. I said I wouldn't. She was distant after that, every veiled look an indictment. There was so much to ask – where they were from, the things they had seen, and yet none of it mattered enough to interrupt my silence. They were children of the world, children of time, yet to learn that nothing is new and everything comes round again. Whatever they had done, whatever they had seen, it had been done and seen before – I had probably done it and seen it myself. In my funk I could not bear to speak, could not bear to ask.

The wind that came off the bay was cutting. I stood on the jetty watching the hunched figure of Ana disappear amidst the waves and the darkness. I didn't wave, she didn't look back. There was a genuine chill in the air, and the bugs were dying off. I turned to go, trudging slowly up Broadway with a heavy load wavering on each arm, the liquid sloshing inside tin tanks, a harsh, thin sound rebounding with each step. I kept to the shadows, stumbling up the shattered sidewalks, but there were few people abroad. For the early evening the streets were strangely empty of foragers and cutthroats, and, reaching out into the ether it seemed to me as if the island were just a little quieter than usual. The King was right – the city was dying.

I arrived at the intersection beneath my tower and took the long way around, the back way in via the parking garage with its familiar smells of piss and burnt tires. The flies still hummed in the humid darkness, but Joany was nowhere to be found. I climbed the corkscrew of stairs, weary rather than tormented, slow and steady and mindless. I used the pulleys for my cargo where I could, tying the rope firmly around the handles of both cans at once. It was hard. My heart wasn't in it. Somewhere, barely a mile across the water there was a building with working elevators and hot running water.

23

I watched the season change from the windows of my apartment. It was subtle at first, the gentle emptying of the soul of summer – simply, something was missing, some quality of the air – and then the foreboding coolness came on. The weather broke suddenly – its new habits fickle and sharp – a jealous chill settled over everything in the bay. I had no taste for it, no taste to go outside. I watched as the shrinking camps of people huddled together, I watched as the nights grew long and the rats and the few surviving foxes came out to pick at the dead things they found amongst the rubble. I stayed in and I drank voraciously.

But I found no comfort at the bottom of my cup, and no comfort within the walls of my empty castle. I looked about me at the pictures on the walls, the furniture, the trinkets of another passing era of human luxury and folly. The wealth was over again. *They never realise it will end,* I thought. *It's always for granted.*

Even as I drank myself into a quick extinction, I made water sparingly. Its value had changed – it was money still, it was life still, and yet it was not. I gazed over the still, the fragile condenser element glinting in the lamplight. I wanted to smash it. I wanted to hear the tinkling music of its destruction. Everyone had a still, no one had gas. We weren't drinking water, we were drinking gas and we were dry dry dry. For you see, whilst I could trade water for almost anything, I could not trade if for the gas to make more. It was all finite again, and terminal suddenly. And all the while my generator clicked on and off, keeping that chest freezer cold. I should have been out hunting, but I was not. I was hiding in my rooms with the empty relics – a faceless monument to civilisation, and drinking my reason away with the false satisfaction of too much, too much, too much. Denial is the river to hell, after all.

Joany would come up sometimes, scrounging for water but I think also for company. Ironically she felt safe with me. She knew where she stood at least. And she liked the comfort of my sofa. She'd seen my face after the canal, of course, but I found myself donning hoodies in her presence and pulling my sleeves over my hands like a schoolgirl. She never asked me what happened. She used to stare sometimes, half-squinting through weak eyes when she thought I wasn't looking, but she never brought up the subject of my scars. For that I was grateful.

Joany taught me card games I'd seen invented, changing the rules as she went, and I would go along. I tried to get her to read. She wouldn't.

"What's the point?" She'd say. "None of it's real."
The worlds in books of riches and luxury and comfort she could dream about, but would never see.

Often she would fall asleep on the sofa in the small hours after struggling to stay awake with me. I would watch her grow tired, her eyes drooping and the colour draining from her greasy face. It was a game she played. Push it far, see how long she could stay. My place was relatively clean, it was out of the wind, secure from strangers. But I was terrified to have her in the rooms while I slept the day, she might test her theories, play with the blinds. She was a smart kid. Or else I might do something. Was I more afraid of her or for her? Either way I sent her off every time without fail.

So I fumbled on blindly in my own little castle, all the while that other great tower standing over me. Knowing what was out there made the struggle for survival and dignity meaningless. It could all be so easy. I knew I would go. I knew it. And yet I didn't go. Paralysed by inaction I clung to my aloneness more than my independence, and I barely left the apartment. I didn't read, I didn't entertain myself, I didn't clear up – what would be the point? I merely stood peering past my reflection in the window glass, watching the city disintegrate, watching my supplies dwindle.

And yet what kept me? Not the girl I gave water to – for though I was fond of her I would abandon her in an instant. Our different natures had taught me that long ago. It was more my own stubbornness, and my fear of other beings such as myself – my claustrophobia, even if they were children, particularly as they were children, precocious and unpredictable and dangerous. And ultimately it was easier to do nothing. While the blood flowed, while the walls kept the ever-cooling wind from my face and the antics of the girl kept me distracted it was easier simply to do nothing. And so, for those two brief, paralytic, obscene weeks, nothing is what I did.

It was not until I was down to my last can of gas that I was stirred into action. I stared at it, my emergency can, half empty having just filled the tank in my generator. I powered only the freezer – it made the gas last longer. For light I rationed out candle stubs when my eyes failed me or when the girl arrived. For heat, well for heat I put on layers or went cold. The winter would be bitter, but I would find a stove, I would burn other people's books and furniture. Except part of me never believed I would come to it.

I told myself whilst standing on the jetty and signalling my light across the black waters, that I would simply ask for more gas, more time. I packed no clothes, no keepsafes. I told myself I was coming back. But I knew they would give me the sales pitch. I knew I would relax imperceptibly in the company of fellow monsters. In my mind I had already done so.

"It's me," I said into the intercom as the boatman looked nervously around him. Moored up against the loading bay doors of the Pyramid was not a popular place to be, and he obviously did not want to be seen by his fellows.

"Oh, right. Ok." Cyrus voice floated from the intercom grille some moments later. He sounded distracted, stilted, as if he had to search for the intercom. The line went dead and I waited, shivering in the damp air as the boat knocked against the concrete of the Pyramid with a hollow thudding sound. The boatman looked at me briefly, and turned about him as if to cast off, but I held my hand up, waiting as his fearful eyes implored me. There was a whining hum and then a rattle as the steel shutter rolled up, shaking itself free with a shower of salty droplets. The bottom of the doorway and the floor of the loading dock was a couple of feet above sea level, and I hauled myself up on my elbows before the boatman passed my empty cans up and sped gratefully away.

The vast space within was barely lit, and echoed badly, the sense of emptiness crept over me like frost. I stood and watched the boatman flee, his lamp off, invisible to his passing compatriots. I could not comprehend why he was so reluctant to take me to the Pyramid, but I had paid a heavy premium for the privilege. He was under strict instructions to watch that loading bay entrance for my light, my signal waving in the darkness, and he would receive the same amount again. To be honest, in the current climate such a price weighed heavy on my heart, but as I carried two empty gas cans – the largest I could manage – over to the elevator bank in the shadowed centre of the cavernous space, I hoped I would be returning with a heavy load, and the facility to make water again for another few weeks at least.

Or so I fooled myself. Part of me handed the water away with the light-heartedness of the dying man who has said goodbye to his most valued possessions. I crossed the wide, empty floor and made my way over to the elevators, that rectangular pillar rising to the ceiling. I pressed a call button and the fragile red light glowed in the shadows, twinkling as the elevator approached. The doors sighed open, and I stepped inside, looking at the buttons, noticing for the first time that this was the third floor, and the first above the water. I was at a loss to know which floor to press for, but Cyrus' voice called out crisply from the grille on the control panel.

"We're in the nursery, seventeenth." I dutifully pressed the button for the seventeenth, and felt the world drop away.

The door chimed cheerfully as I stepped out on to a quiet and evil-smelling corridor. With the pictures evenly spaced along the walls, the strip lighting, and the sterile blue carpet it could have been any office of the last hundred years. But something in the stillness of the air told me this was a place of quiet misery, and as I turned instinctively towards the nursery, the sound of my every step swallowed by the cloying presence of terror hanging in the air, I knew by smell and intuition what I would find in the room at the end of the hallway.

Inside it was unbearably bright. Indeed most of them had their eyes tight shut. There were six or seven men and women chained to radiator pipework along the floor, barely clothed, one a boy – barely a teenager. They were pallid and emaciated, and covered in sores and razor cuts. As I looked closer I saw that several of them had had their eyes and mouths sewn shut. The room reeked of piss and shit, and old, sweaty blood. Flies hummed around the limp, despondent prisoners, and in one corner where two empty sets of handcuffs were chained to a radiator there was an ugly black puddle of blood and vomit gently rotting down into the immortal nylon carpet. I was nauseated, but not altogether surprised, I had seen such sights before, had taken part long ago. I thought back to the fresh blood that Cyrus had brought me in that high little room scarcely three weeks previous. Not so long ago then. Ana was huddled over a slave, a half-starved and crazed young man who could barely move under her grasp. She had her lips pressed to the flesh low on his shoulder, a razor-blade glinting between her fingers.

"Found us then?" Cyrus said behind me.

I turned to see him carrying a bucket of water and some

straws, a bunch of keys wedged awkwardly between his fingers.

"This is badly done Cyrus." I said. "Badly done." I nodded over to a naked woman who was shivering and mumbling to herself in a low, trembling voice. The other slaves had done their utmost to distance themselves, to get away from her as far as their shackles would allow. "She needs attention or she might die."

Cyrus followed my gaze. "Well, that one is trouble. It's being punished. And there's plenty more fish in the sea, as it were."

Ana's victim began to whimper, catching my eye and drawing out my hunger and fascination, but Cyrus noticed my gaze, and the gloating, crooked smile he wore made me bitter, and the stench turned my stomach. I wanted to tear that smugness from his face. Shaking, I pushed past him, through the awkward doorway and out into that callous, sterile corridor.

"Come now, you know where blood comes from."

"I'll wait for you on the observation deck." I said with my back to him.

"It didn't bother you before." Cyrus called out. "When you *drank* it. Remember? At least, you didn't feel the need to ask." Cyrus laughed.

It was only once I'd arrived at the elevators that I realised I was still carrying the empty gas cans. My knuckles were white with tension, and deep grooves from the tin weld were etched across my scar-thickened palms.

I entered the elevator, but I could not get away from the ugliness of the seventeenth floor. The machine would not function without a key. I sat huddled against the wall, my fingers lost in the harsh beads of the carpet, angry at my impotence, trying not to listen to the muffled sounds beyond. Cyrus approached sometime later, the smell of blood announcing his arrival as surely as his dull footsteps.

"Come now," he said as I blinked up at him. "It's nothing new, is it. You and me, we're the same."

"It's ugly."

"They're animals. They can be trained. Tamed." He shrugged. "Some take to it better than others. Some follow like sheep. Others are wild till you destroy their minds. I love them, I love the taste of that fire, but I spend all my time eradicating that same sense of self that causes all the trouble." He smiled blankly as the bile rose in my throat.

"Spare me."

Cyrus cocked his head and shrugged one shoulder, but he narrowed his eyes as he offered me the uncapped bottle of blood that had been lingering in his hands. I felt my growing rage, white hot and all consuming. I wanted to take that bottle and hurl it against the walls. I wanted to grind his face into the mess, but I didn't. I took the bottle with shaking hands, I drank the stolen lifeblood down, heady and bitter, grateful in spite of myself. The blood tasted of its owner's terror and shame, and I struggled to keep it down as its inherent horror bated my own anger and recalled the images of that dirty room on the seventeenth floor. Was I angry at Cyrus' cowardice or my own?

We rode up, up, up in that shiny metal box, I stood in angry silence, Cyrus with a hungry little grin playing on his lips. I felt trapped as he looked at me, the smugness dripping from him. He enjoyed my discomfort and my hypocrisy. *It's not me you're trapped in here with,* I heard his soul echo. I wanted to smash his face in.

"What can I do you for?" He asked as I stood by the glass of the observation deck windows. I pretended to watch the desperate city below, wishing to be anywhere but in his presence, to be anyone but whom I was.

"I came to ask you for gas." I said tersely. I could barely speak. I certainly couldn't look at him. He laughed softly.

"Why should I give you any?"

I thought for a moment, helpless really. "Because we are the same. Because you can. I suppose because I will owe you."

"But why should I fund your isolation when you should be here with us? Join us. Work with us."

I turned then, anger hot on my face. "What in God's name do you want from me? Why does it matter what I do? I have no interest in your seed banks and your stupid plans, your foolish dreams. What can you hope to achieve?"

"Not foolish," Cyrus' voice turned to steel. "Is it foolish to plan for the future? To spend years thinking and storing, arranging people like dominoes, placing things to fall just as you'd have them? It's all happening as I saw it. This isn't the end it's a new beginning. It's a cleansing. Mankind has scoured the planet like a plague of rats, unchecked for thousands of years, wreaking havoc as a force ungoverned until the Earth can cope no longer. But every force has its alter, every creature has its predator, and that is us my friend. We are here to keep them in check. We are here to rule them and use them and guide them. The seed banks are the beginning. The tools and the plans are just the beginning of the new feudal society that will spread across the globe. This is the new epoch, and we will keep them in check with a world that can no longer support their rampant, bottomless greed."

And your greed? I wanted to ask. I'd heard it all before. I'd thought it up myself in my earliest years.

"How generous of you. How benign. Are you to be the benevolent Godfather of the whole human race or just this little bay? Tell me – how does your altruism sit with your taste for blood?"

Cyrus shook his head. "There are others like us out there, I know it. I'll find them. They'll be rebuilding the world too. They'll be nurturing the humans too, if only to be safe from them and well fed. It is our nature and our destiny to rule those below us. It's what we do."

"Like lions and gazelles, farmer termites and fungus, yes I've heard the arguments." I shook my head. "You're wrong. Wrong and deluded in a desperate attempt at identity. Such a strange, strong creature, there must be a reason right? There must be a reason you exist, a reason you're here. There has to be an intent for you, for one as extraordinary as you to be part of God's plan. He has intentions for you, right? When everything else, when *everyone* else that you've ever known, has slipped through that powerful grip of yours like so much sand, and you've counted them off as they've fallen away, there's *got* to be a reason. It's frustrating isn't it – to be so strong and yet so powerless to change anything, control anything. Everything changes, but you – you stay the same, you and your fellow monsters who reflect just a little too much of your own hopelessness to be comfortable." I shook my head. "You're a child. A child and a clown. You haven't seen enough of the cycles and it will be a thousand years before you even begin to know the depths of your naivety."

Cyrus looked stricken and pale. He was shaking with anger. He attempted to shout, but his words ran thin from his lips.

"Damn you. Damn you, nameless coward. And damn God. There is no God. I don't believe in God!"

I shook my head. "Of course you don't, but you're still here, right? And there's got to be a reason that you of all people are here, walking, seeing, thinking, experiencing. You who can see *so much.* You're special, right? You're here for a reason. This couldn't be an accident." I sighed and I caught his eye. Defeated and tired, I leant against the wall for support. "This whole thing is an aberration – this whole universe, humans are accidents of consciousness and you're an abomination. No one is meant to see as much as we do – as much of the endless, rolling cycles. I'm so old I don't remember my own name. The image I hold of my mother is a fake, a composite, a dream made up from TV shows and oil paintings, Greek vases and frescoes from old Rome all mangled into one false memory in my head. And that is your fate.

I have seen cities birthed and civilisations murdered, your three hundred years are but dust in my eye. You are young enough to think things move on, to think something must build on the past, that there must be some benefit to the rampant procession of time. It *must* add some value to the universe right? It *must* be better now than Rome? Well things get better for the humans and for us, and then they get worse again, and everything returns to nought, for entropy rules the universe. Nothing lasts, and nothing can build on what went before. There is no cumulative value, there is no meaning to time or space. Everything is transient and subjective, so find what you take comfort from and cling to it, for we are corks floating helplessly in the oceans of time just as surely as any little man out there, and we have no more chance against the dancing whims of fate than any one of them. A life may last a century, a book may last five. A song lasts a thousand years and a statue can five. The right to life is a short-lived ideal and the freedom to kill reappears like an old friend every millennia, but human freedom is no greater now than it was in Rome because it is defined by the human animal, and it is the same for us. Our nature is to compete for blood, so a word of advice – when you find them – these others you dream of – or more likely when they find you, because they will notice your shining use of power – when they find you, *run*. Run for your life. I am old and tired and broken-hearted and you are a child, a babe not yet out of diapers, but those that live between our seven ages will consume you because they have the will and the strength to do it. They won't be rebuilding, they won't be guiding mankind, they will be hunting their greedy little hearts out till they can swallow no more. They will trap you and they will devour your innocent young blood for centuries because that is their nature. When you see those glittering eyes take your woman-fiend and run. Don't make the mistake of thinking their existence shows meaning in the universe – because everything here is just an accident, including us, a mutation – each mouth more successful than the last until we devour the planet beneath our feet. This is a meaningless, closed, self-terminating system, there is *no* value and there is *no* escape, and no one is *meant* to live long enough to see that *as we alone* come to see it."

The words and the rant dried up, turned to bitter ash in my mouth. I found I was shaking in that little room at the top of the world, and I wondered if I had gotten my point across, if I had a point. I felt quite destroyed, a welter of horror rising to the surface of my consciousness as the full meaninglessness of my own struggle for life struck me and laughed in my face. I looked at Cyrus across the room from me as if he were across the gulf of the Grand Canyon. He was white with anger, fists clenched.

"I don't believe it," he said, the struggle of denial betrayed by the taint of his voice, and he looked at me, weighed me up. Cyrus' eyes narrowed.

"I convinced her of you. She warned me. Imagine it!" Slowly he shook his head. "I don't believe any of it. Neither do you. You struggle so hard to stay alive, I've watched you. I've *seen* you. Why live if it's so hard and pointless?"

I shrugged. "Because there's nothing else to do. Is there." I clutched the wall beside me. "Will you give me the gas?"

"No." His voice cracked as he shook his head. "Join us."

"What? And rule the world? I won't be the proof of your self-righteousness. We have no divine right, just the accident of birth, just like anyone." I crossed the room and entered the elevator that was still locked open.

"Come here," Cyrus barked, and then he shouted it. "Come here I said!"

I waved the back of my hand in disinterest as his voice rolled across the room, and I reached out to turn the key in the control panel.

"Wait! Wait!" His voice turned to a high squeal, somewhere between desperation and terror. "Weren't meant to! You said 'meant to'! Meant by who?"

I stopped, quite astonished at myself, and turned my head. Cyrus was clutching the edges of the table, eyes wide with anger.

"Meant to by who?" He shuddered as the words left him.

"Well well," I said, the realisation washing over me. "There really is a God. I guess." And as the doors sighed shut in Cyrus' face I knew then and forever that we are truly cursed.

I watched the shadows cross his features as the doors met – Cyrus clinging to that table for dear life as if the Pyramid were disintegrating along with his convictions.

"You'll be back!" He called out bitterly, voice tinny and desperate through the doors. "You'll be back! You're either with us or against us, you'll be back!"

I shook my head in disbelief as the elevator dropped away. I should have paid more attention.

Standing at the open roller-door I waved my light out across the bay in great, wide arcs as the wind and the salt spray bit into my face. Ana and Cyrus made no attempt to stop me – when I stepped out of the elevator the doors swished closed and it sailed off up to the top floor. Shadows coalesced in the glittering watery darkness, I was relieved to see the little boat cutting across the choppy black water, and I was as glad as its pilot to be gone from the water. I sat in leaden silence as we crossed the bay, rather stunned by the evening's events. Huddled against the cold I listened to the rhythmic sound of the boatman dipping his oars in the water. I produced my payment with a heavy heart as the man brought the little vessel up against the jetty, conscious that my journey had been unsuccessful, that I had blood enough for three weeks or so, but it meant nothing. I had gas for only one.

Still I planned and schemed my way up Broadway, up the hill to my home. I could trade for a solar still, or steal one. I could look for solar panels, or a wind turbine, I could mount one on the roof. Perhaps the Looter King could be induced to trade one from the peak of the Island Fortress. I turned this thought over as I hurried up the stairs, eager to be indoors before the return of the sun. I wanted to rest, to read and relax, to sleep on my problems and forget. I would tackle them tomorrow. Always tomorrow. I had a week, after all, I had at least a week.

I threw my overcoat off as I stepped inside, glad to be alone and safe. It was good to be home in the familiar sounds and smells, the freezer humming gently, even the rat rustling in the corner, gnawing the bars of his cage. I rolled my shutters down and lit candles to read, enjoying the little golden flame, the little ball of heat. The nights were growing longer finally, but there was still precious little time before sun up. I was sweaty from climbing the endless stairs, but I still gathered a blanket around me as I sat down to read, my spine tingling with the distant approach of the sun. I was opening the book when the enormous bang occurred, the first of three sharp cracks that rang out from my balcony. The leather bound volume dropped from my hands as I leapt up in shock, and in the pregnant moments that followed the calamity I stood still and listened, and found the silence.

There had been an explosion on my balcony, three short, disruptive bursts, but even before I rolled my blinds up I knew what had been at the epicentre of the destruction, because, you see, in the silence I discovered silence. The rat, terrified by the noise, no longer gnawed at its bars, it trembled in a corner of its cage, and the freezer – the freezer no longer hummed. In the last hour before dawn I rolled those blinds back up and looked out onto my balcony, but I knew already – the generator was destroyed, and I was out of time.

It was Cyrus of course. He'd waited until I'd returned, or simply left it so late in the night that I could do nothing to save my frozen stores, and then he'd placed three armour piercing rounds into my generator. One had torn through the little catalytic engine, another had detonated within the silithium storage battery, the third had struck and ignited the fuel tank. The whole mess was burning profusely, flooding my rooms with deadly black smoke and giving off prodigious heat. A small mushroom cloud of gasoline had scorched the blinds and masonry, the plaster cracking and flaking before my eyes, spitting blackened grit in my face as it fell about my feet. It was all I could do to take a broom handle and push the toxic pile of flaming plastic to the far corner of the balcony before rolling down the blinds and shutting the doors. I stood inside and screamed.

There was nothing to do but drink the blood. I stood, peering into the depths of that chest freezer, counting the bags, aware that in a day or two, or three at the most, the white sheen of frost that coated the plastic would be gone and the solid, brown-red gemstones resting one atop the next would be quivering, sweating time bombs of odorous decay. I counted the bags, a hundred or so, which was twenty days at my current rate, thirty if I cut down a little. A month. I'd been fooling myself that I had time to live, time to adjust to the new world outside, time to heal and hunt again, and really I had a bare month. A whole month. I might have made it. But the blood was melting, and it would go off faster than I could drink, faster than I dare drink.

I took the top layer of bags out of the freezer and placed them in coolers, stacking them head to toe like giant tessellating building blocks. I would consume these bags first, knowing that the bulk of the blood would remain frozen for longer if I could avoid opening the freezer. It still left me with fifty bags to swallow in the next day. I laughed out loud. It seemed absurd and impossible. It was obscene. After working so hard to conserve my precious stockpile, after experiencing guilt for draining three bags in a night when the world outside grew more and more barren, it seemed obscene that I should be convincing myself to drink such an amount in so little time. I went from scrimping, saving, testing the limits of my strength and my hunger, seeing how very little sustenance I could take and stay alive, I went from such self-imposed poverty to self-imposed gluttony, seeing just how much slick, sticky lifeblood I could force myself to swallow in one continuous sitting.

But then – wasn't a human person eight bags of blood? Maybe it wasn't so very much. I drank and I drank and I drank and I found in those three days that the fifteen or twenty people I consumed weren't so very much. It was a task, certainly, a trial to swallow and swallow and swallow until you were bloated and sick with the blood, stuffed and soporific like a tick on a dog's neck, barely able to move with the swelling, and then to find another bag was melting and to begin again with the urge to vomit rising in your craw, but I would not waste those bags I had collected, I had scrimped over and starved myself to save, I couldn't afford to waste the strength – the health they offered me.

There was no power to run the microwave of course, and so I defrosted and warmed the bags over the camping stove, water bubbling away gently in a double burner so as not to scorch or cook the blood, which could easily turn grey and gelatinous, coagulating into a stringy protein scum that would make me retch.

I drank as I watched the stove, a tube in my mouth, a half-empty bag dangling at my lips, I sipped slowly and continuously. It wasn't bad at first – poor me, having to drink my own body weight in my favourite foodstuff, right? Poor murderous little me. But my anger swelled alongside my nausea with every bag I consumed. My fury at the loss of my stash, at the rising bloodlust I bated with every salty mouthful, the knowledge that the more I had the more I would want, and the less control I would be able to exert on my appetite. I had never done such a thing before, never consumed so many people, even in the rich days, the powerful days, and as I stood, shaking over the toilet that didn't flush, pissing continuously and wondering if my elusive organs would hold out, I felt the beginnings of the addiction's rise, I felt my will go dark and my mind withdraw.

With the endless slick, salty mouthfuls of liquid passing

over my teeth they began to jolt with pain as they grew sensitive, for they were never clean, never neutral and unused. The salt attacked my lips, along with the enzymes and electrolytes, the mysterious things that make up blood. My lips peeled, and then the inside surface of my mouth slew off and I gagged, almost vomited as the pieces of flesh caressed my tongue, before spitting up all over the kitchen. I had lost the powers of taste and smell, I grew fat and swollen as I persuaded myself to swallow just one more rumbling mouthful of fluid, then I would rest, then I would piss again, even shit. I clutched the counter tops for dear life as the room swayed, holding myself upright in the darkened room, but I felt crazed and powerful, I felt strong as I drank and my mind receded. I wanted to swallow. Even through the blinding, relentless nausea and the increasingly sharp ache growing within my guts and organs I wanted to swallow, I wanted to see how much I could take. I wanted more, more, more.

I hadn't slept, didn't sleep, but after the first few bags that was fine. I felt stronger in my body than ever before since the floods had risen and the people had run. I felt incredible, I felt I could achieve anything even as my awareness of my self and my surroundings grew dim and fragile like candlelight. If my previous attempts at gluttony had soothed my injuries, my current excesses were reconstructing my body with a speed I could not have anticipated. I felt the tingling pain of new teeth forming in my gums, my face erupted with a searing, itching sensation as new cartilage, flesh and skin burst forth from the gaping hole that engulfed my baby nose. My vision sharpened in those dark hours, and fine new hairs grew up over my scalp and face, shattering the thickened scar tissue that shrouded my skull. My limbs swelled and my body grew succulent with the blood, and much of my taut, scarred skin sloughed off to reveal soft, pink tissue beneath. The blackened, shrivelled flesh of my clawed hands swelled and split, revealing long, slender fingers beneath, and the strong, fine hands of a pianist. My body grew strong and healthy with the influx of blood, but much of the regeneration took place over the next week as my body raced to make use of the abundant flow of food it was struggling to absorb and store. I wasn't there to witness the metamorphosis as my skin ruptured and I emerged from a cocoon of scar tissue however, for with every mouthful of stolen life I swallowed, my psychosis grew, my connection to a reality outside of myself cracked and disintegrated a little more, and my mind withdrew into a dark, quiet space where there was nothing, no room to move, no time to think, no need for anything at all.

It comes on slowly at first, it is the desire not to stop, to drink more than you should, more than you need. Then it is the desire to swallow even as your guts are screaming with pain and you are so dizzy you have to cling to the floor. You begin to watch yourself with detachment as you go uncontrollably from one bag to the next, faster than you need, faster than you ought, defrosting them impatiently even though they will keep, because you want more, and more and more, because it's doing you good, right – I mean – you feel good, right?

But somewhere in that blood, floating in each bag is the echo of a human mind, a consciousness not so much smaller than your own, not so fundamentally different, and there's just an imprint, just a memory in that fragile little bag of blood. Sometimes it's a sensation, the taste of bubblegum, the sound of kids in the playground across the street, or it's an image – waving your child to school, it's the sadness you felt when you were bullied, it's a human orgasm and it's the utter shame of being raped, it's saying goodbye to your son, it's watching your mom die or it's the first time you drove your new car. It's a thousand fragments of a thousand lives you've never lived, have no right to and will never understand, but for that one, infinite moment when the blood flows and the echo explodes through your mind like a shotgun blast, rupturing your soul with the memories of loved ones you have lost but never known, some part of you is shaken and shattered by the golden dream of a way of life you can never grasp and have no right to experience but you do, oh God you do experience it and you don't deserve to be subjected to something so beautiful and brief and completely alien to one such as yourself, so mysterious and unattainable, that you feel your own hollowness so keenly, such pain at the pointless, empty waste that is your own endless tawdry existence that you struggle so hard to perpetuate, motivated only by the sheer, black fear of death, even when the light of their memories blinds you and reminds you that you are empty, empty, and will never, never ever be fulfilled. You are broken somehow, cold and sterile, unmoving like rock and untouched by time, broken and untouchable as the world moves around you, as everything moves but you, but oh the sunlight, the golden, terrifying sunlight of their memories, it burns you from the inside out but you want it again, you want that beautiful light, that scorching warmth, you want it again and more and more and more.

No wonder your mind withdraws from the world. Sometimes you come to, curled up on the floor, blinded by the tears in your eyes falling down your face, blood in your mouth and over your clothes, shaking like an earthquake. But those are the times when you reach for more, you scrabble for it fast and desperate, praying for the scorching pain, the burning memories stolen from others, screaming because the blood is frozen and will not warm fast enough, until you burn yourself, you swallow it in painful icy chunks, you gulp down your own destruction, because anything, the pain, the terror, the madness, the agony of lost loves that seem in the moment to be yours and never will be, anything is better than being alone with yourself and your own broken emptiness, shaking and grovelling on a polished kitchen floor.

But mostly by this time you are not conscious, you are a thing, a monster, a zombie, driven to madness by greed and gluttony and addiction, you float through the darkness and the nightmares – running on automatic while your mind and your soul and your own god damn sense of self are quite somewhere else until a problem arises in the real world like you've run out of slaves or the gas burner is empty or the inquisition is on to you or you simply can't break the seal on the blood bag your hands are shaking so, and then the light comes, the scorching, searing light of self-awareness falls across your face as your mind stirs desperately and opens the door to the real world outside of your self pity and your misery just a touch, just a crack, just enough so that you can deal with that problem that's keeping you awake, keeping you up, deal with it with just as little thought as possible, as little awareness, so that you can go back to the drunken, delirious oblivion before you are forced to think, before you realise that some small part of you is awake and you have to think, think and scream and agonise over the mess, the useless, pointless destruction, the guilt, the shame, the loss – the total utter bloody inefficiency and loss, the waste of life that is your own life. You struggle desperately for the delirious oblivion of your comfortable, predictable nightmare dreamworld rather than be forced to look at yourself in shame, to count every single, minor, irrelevant mistake you have ever made over and over again as if any of it ever really mattered, even really made a shred of difference to the outcome of a life that was never really in your hands anyway – your life, you reach for the object of your addiction and run and hide before you look at yourself once again and face the terror and the shame that you are sitting at the bottom of a familiar and infinitely deep well that you have dug yourself, that you can never escape, and you are disappointed, disappointed with the sorry, worthless, helpless creature that you are and the irrevocable, valueless non-event that is your life, knowing that the road to hell is paved with good intentions and that you have done this to yourself.

So you drink again, you drink more, you drink again, rather than break down, rather than admit that you are a small, flawed creature, rather than admit that you fucked up in your own eyes and before God, and rather than asking for there to be a force in this world bigger than you so that you can ask it for help, "Please God, please God help me," because that's stupid, right – only a fool asks anything of a God, right? But you're terrified because you have this niggling doubt that you can't make it on your own, you can't help yourself and there's no one to help you – of course there's no one to help you – right? How could there be? Right? But you're too scared to help yourself, and you're not worth it, right? Too scared to take responsibility of every fuck up you have to correct, every nettle you have to grasp, too scared or too unwilling, because that's what addiction is, really, that's what reaching for the bottle, the blood bag, the beautiful, horrific, enchanting sad blackness is – it's an excuse, a fucking excuse, it's a refusal to grow the fuck up and take some fucking responsibility.

Yes, I've been here before. I know this place well. I know this black dog that rides my back. I know this place well.

Fortunately, although I get utterly lost, unconscious in the graveyard of dead dreams, a blood-smeared monster writhing on the floor amidst hundreds of empty plastic bags, I have an in-built escape route. It's called 'The last unit of blood in the building,' and it burns like hell.

I do not know. In my delirium I do not know at first that I have consumed the entire supply, that I have sucked dry the last bag of blood, that there is no more relief from the torment I have created, the torment of being inside me, with only me for company, and a healthy dose of self-loathing. My body knows. My body learns this fact first. It scrabbles continuously at the bottom of the freezer until my hands are grazed and my nails are torn and bleeding. I have dim flashes of consciousness while my body searches desperately – dim, aching moments of horror and awareness, but they are strange, stilted, detached experiences, it's as if I am watching myself from across the room, I am watching as the monster me tips over the freezer, I am watching as the monster me wades through plastic empties looking for dregs, I am watching as he licks the drips from the sticky floor and destroys the kitchen in mad bloody desperation. I watch each or these moments as if they are projected onto a cinema screen, but they seem so far away, so far apart, they seem not to matter.

Each time I watched, these moments got a little closer, each time they felt a little more real. I had watched myself tearing through the apartment, a drunken tornado, as the sounds grew louder, less tinny, and the vision became more relevant, less grey, less disembodied. I had watched myself collapse, an awkward pile on the floor between the kitchen and the lounge, drooling on the carpet. Sometime later I awoke, blinking and stupid in the semi-light and I lay in that mess of crossed limbs for a pure age. I could barely move, I could not co-ordinate my thoughts or actions. I lay in that exhausted pile and blinked. Eventually I pushed myself up on my arms and looked about me. There was not a stick of furniture in the place left intact.

I sat and stared for hours, peering with fresh eyes at the shredded silks on the wall, at my fleshy hands, pink and full under the peeling skin. I had no idea what time it was, it was dark certainly – I had that much sense. I had been lost for days and my body shook with the torment of withdrawal.

If my previous, mild gluttony had done much to slowly repair my body, the great binge and the lost days that followed had restored me so fully to my old self that I barely knew the difference. My hands, as I said, were full once again, and strong, with fresh skin under the dead and peeling surface, and clear fingernails coming through under the brittle and brown claws that the sun had left me with. Indeed my whole body was firm with flesh where once there had only been a mass of emaciation and scar tissue. There was muscle again on my arms and legs, and the leathery old burned skin was sloughing away to reveal a fresh layer underneath, pale and supple and clean.

I glowed with health. I rubbed at the loose skin, grinning like a baby at the magical regeneration beneath, the proof once again that I was untouchable to time or the universe. Immortal. Carelessly I ran my hand over my scalp, crying out as I discovered an ocean of short bristles covering my previously scorched and barren skullcap. Of course this led to a tender exploration of my face with soft and timid fingertips, anxious of what they might find. But there was no disappointment as my fingers wandered over fresh lips, full and flexible, perfectly equipped to cover my teeth completely. The great, vacant gash in my face between the bridge of my nose and my palate was filled, with new bone and thin new skin and yes, I cried out, a new nose. It seemed a little small, a little fragile, but there it was in the middle of my face, and all the tissues around it joined up perfectly. My fingertips explored my new eyelids, delicate and flexible and complete, not the stiff, ragged half-moons I had been left with before, and above them, above them two fine new eyebrows, two delicate rows of bristle sown on my face like young sprouting rice. From there up to my new head of hair the skin was delicate and unfurrowed. And ears! I had ears again! My fingers traced their curves and folds over and over until the thin new skin became hot and angry, but I was amazed again and again at the lightness, the softness of squidgy neonate earlobes, the intensity and firmness as the cartilage curled over and around the rim of the ear. I was complete again.

Every sound, of course, was amplified and crystal clear. Every rustle of the plastic blood bags about me as I moved, every scratch, every fold in my clothes as I stretched, they all sounded fresh and sharp and new to me. But every sense had been renewed, rebuilt, every hair that ran across my fingertips was as sharp as a pinprick, every glimmer of light that fell through the joins in the shutters was a piercing luminance that spread across the floor illuminating the wreckage before me. The gentle wind outside was a raging gale to my new ears, the faint perfume of rotten blood, every coagulating string of foulness on my clothing was a nauseating wave of evil decay permeating my nostrils and lungs with its sour stench. These things seemed new to me, new and unfamiliar and shocking. The smells were somehow different than before, the textures more real, more present, and the sight of my war-torn apartment, well, everything was different from my memories, it was unrecognisable. Even the sensation of breathing the air seemed altogether crisper, fresher, more alive than I could remember. I was new and the world was new in every sense and overwhelming. It was marvellous and bright and fresh and deliriously, terrifyingly overwhelming.

It was shocking to me then, every sound, every breath of air. Every sensation hammered through my fragile, blood-addicted mind. I shied from the crumple of the carpet pile underfoot as I staggered semi-conscious to the bathroom. I shuddered at the garish, feeble light as I checked my new face in the mirror. It was scored and cut by bands of colour and brightness as it swam to the fore of my consciousness, swam out of the shadows. My face was full, and smooth, fresh and pale and unscarred, it was familiar to me despite the thinner lips, the immature button nose, it betrayed that old deception – cherubic youth belying ageless eyes. It was me alright, a little thin, a little crooked, but my face at last, the piercing stare concealing hollowness. I could barely conceive of it, so I could barely recognise myself.

It was my mind you see, quite broken then and for the next few days. I spent the nights staring, staring, staring in the darkness until the mass of lines and shadow before me took form and I knew what it was that I was looking at. A shattered glass, the corner of the broken bed, my face, it didn't matter which. Every sound made me jump. Every miniscule creak of the building, every crack as the tindersticks of my splintered furniture settled about me. I lost myself for hours in the fine new hairs on the back of my arm, swirling them around with a fingertip, tracing a figure of eight – the infinity sign, again and again and again.

But my mind was quite somewhere else. I did these things with the vaguest of awarenesses as my mind wandered its own dark spaces, floating up occasionally out of the darkness only to find my body lost in the perfect roundness of a drop of condensation on a water bottle, or rubbing the dead skin from the cracks between my fingers. There was pain, always there was pain, a searing, shredding pull running through my veins and limbs, it drew my fingertips inward, it tightened my chest till I could hardly bear to breathe. It was the agony of withdrawal, the mindless mad agony of need burning in my guts, an animal clawing through my ribcage from the inside while my head thumped and sickness rose in my craw. More often than not I rose from unconsciousness shaking and fitting, unable to control my motions and helpless to do anything but watch and endure the pain, the nausea and the dizziness.

I would find myself lying on the floor, awoken by the huge sound of my foot rattling against a kitchen cupboard, or bleeding from my sides where I'd fallen in broken glass, but all I remember is the pain. My mind would run from the mad, unbearable pain and holy need of cold turkey. For I needed something greatly, I needed blood – more and more and more. I needed blood to keep me warm and stupefied, safe in my welcoming unconscious where the world didn't matter and I needed nothing, I was nothing and I needed nothing. I longed for those blissful moments where my mind hung frozen in the air unable or unwilling to move from one thought to the next, suspended in the oblivion of nothing, of not thinking.

But without blood, without the drug that glorious oblivion never came, could never come, and the best I could do was descend, descend beneath the waves of torment and conscious sensation, to lose myself in the darkness of half formed dreams and zombie semi-awareness.

The pain dimmed but not the paralysing hunger. My conscious periods grew longer and more bearable, my mind holding together longer each time before fleeing back to the abyss. As the days wore on these conscious periods drew closer together until they began to join up. I would feel my mind slipping as the horrid, debilitating shakes approached, and I would secure myself in a ball on the floor before fixing my eye on some glittering trinket and resolving to stay present, to cling on to the twinkling light. Sometimes it worked. One night – it was two or three nights after my first fleeting moments of awareness in front of that mirror, I awoke with blood in my mouth and a sharp pain in my hand only to find I had half chewed off my own index finger to get at the blood. There were three brittle, mottled teeth on the ground beside my shoulder, my new teeth were coming through and it seemed my unconscious body was making good use of them in my absence. I resolved to stop, to stay awake, and this was probably my first fully formed thought since the long descent had begun.

I bound my finger in slow, jerky movements as I leant against the wall in the filthy, squalid bathroom. Every hour brought growth and repair to my body, my tissues could not keep up with the great influx of nutrients from the feast of days ago. I was strong, stronger than I remembered and flexible. I could move faster than my shattered mind could track, my body felt unfamiliar and I didn't know the measure of my own strength. I staggered through the wreckage in surprise looking for a chair, but there was none, so I sat in the corner on a cushion and rested my head against the wall. I did nothing for hours, I simply stared across the battered lounge and clutched myself for strength against the constant animal gnawing of the hunger sucking in my guts, and I steadied myself against the shaking, sweating earthquakes that trembled through my body in waves.

Some moments I could almost sleep, others I felt hyperactive, tried to stand, to dance, needing desperately to sweep and clean the apartment, only to feel sick and dizzy when rising to my feet, only to collapse again in a pile writhing on the floor. Nausea would overtake the hunger, I would heave and wretch nothing but spittle 'til I felt I might die. The floor beneath me would roll and wobble and I would cling to the carpet for dear life. I was sick as a dog, out of my mind half the time, but I was alive, and I was as strong as the mad.

I sat and slept in that corner for the next two days and nights, reaching out for the splinters of my mind as they passed by, waiting as my consciousness gradually coalesced. I spent hours trying not to move, practicing how to sit, how to breathe, how to look at an object and actually see it. I was convinced that if I could master all the miniature tasks of life, the micro details of running a functioning body, then every other longer task that was built up out of those small details like so much Lego must come out satisfactorily. I spent hours regulating my breathing and trying not to shake.

Completing these little trials was good. It meant I was staying conscious for whole periods of time. Indeed my concept of time was slowly reasserting itself, and every so often I would have the rising thought that time had passed, *how long has it been? Since I had a thought? How long since I heard this voice?*

Indeed on the second night I was quite conscious, quite well aware of the silent passage of time. My surroundings spoke to me in the silence. My life lay shredded before me, furniture, paintings, tools, everything smashed. I had been rolling in the splinters for days. I peered around, taking in the wrecked kitchen with its doors ripped off, taking in the dents in the plasterboard. The door to the locked room was split and hanging limp. In my madness I had torn the flat apart in the search for blood. I lay on the floor and gazed in stupor across the littered wood and the blood bags to the corner by the door where the rat's cage lay twisted and mangled. The steel bars were bent and the red plastic base lay in pieces. I stumbled over to the corner and started gathering the red shards in my hand. Pressed against the corner on the floor I came across the dry and crushed body of the rat, splayed open like a banana, teeth marks haunting the gauged-out flesh. I knelt, unsure of what I was staring at. A small bundle of fur. The end of a favour. To my side the front door was open, hanging off its hinges with holes kicked through the wood. I'd knocked the door open. Presumably I'd wandered outside.

I managed to find my way over to the French doors and roll the blinds up a little, just enough so that I could see the city beyond the balcony railings. In fact I could see very little, partly because of my low angle on the floor, and partly because the city had grown dark and empty. There were few camps left with their makeshift tents and their oil-drum fires, the city was burnt out. Streets that had once been littered with broken houses and shattered shop fronts were now simply routes between parallel ridges of decaying debris. Stores were burned, their timber beams blackened stumps pointing to the sky. The homes were ransacked and razed to the ground, the people fled and gone. All that remained in the hinterland between the Looter's Causeway and the concentration camps of the Police Zone were roaming family groups, nomads preparing to sail away to the Berkeley hills and the central plains to the east, scrounging whatever they could find to buy passage or build a raft, or to protect them from the harsh icy winter, although in truth there was little left of use in the shadow that was once a city.

I lay on the filthy floor in the dark, peering through the glass and down over the edge of the balcony, unwilling to light a candle, unwilling to roll the blinds any further up. Somewhere in my slow mind squatted the begging notion that I might attract the interest of Cyrus, that he might be able to see me within, that he might be feeling trigger-happy.

It didn't matter that my view of the city was limited to the tilting of flat-roofed buildings and the shattered towers of the Financial District, it took my mind outside of myself and my apartment, it reminded me that there was a world outside and distanced me from the intense, burning hunger that spread from my guts out into my shredding veins, into the stiffness of my hands and the tight inward pull of my fingertips. Knowledge of the huge, endless world outside distracted me from the piercing emptiness in my heart, that need need need. Need of something to fill the hole, fill the empty broken place where my soul should be, where the warmth should be, need chocolate, need sex, need blood to fill the place I leaked from and ran from, to fix me and complete me, however briefly.

It is surely this shuddering, horrifying emptiness that my broken consciousness flees from. It is this that is the needy glint I so dislike when I catch my eye in the mirror. It is this black dog, this bloodhound of emptiness that I know I will never escape in every moment I taste blood on my tongue and every moment I do not. I drink and I am never full. I burn with need and I am never satisfied. It never gets better, drink or not drink, kill or not kill it never gets better, I never get better. I will never escape the endless, desperate, meaningless cycle of blood.

And it was in this state that I was caught, surprised by movement behind me as I stared absently through my faint, dark reflection in the glass.

"Holy Shit!" the girl's voice rang out behind me.

I jumped in shock, instinctively rolling into a ball and turning to face the source of the words from behind my knees. It was Joany of course, hovering on the threshold of the open front door, wide eyed and dirty faced as she surveyed the destruction around her.

"Get out!" I hissed. My heart leapt to attention as the smell of her drifted across the filthy room.

"Get out," I cried again in anguish as her fingertips left the doorframe and she stepped into the room. I shuddered as I sensed her warmth, powerful, magnetic, and my will reached out to her hungrily through the ether.

"What happened here then mister-man?"

Why? Why hadn't I sensed her moving slowly up the building? Gazing out of the window at the empty world beyond, I'd been quite dumb to the strong presence flooding up the stairs, the strong presence flooding my room and my senses unworried and unconcerned of danger.

"You must go!" I said again as she crossed the room towards me, kicking her toes through the broken furniture and papers that scattered the floor.

"What are you doing here? Get out!" I pleaded, but I noticed as I said it that my voice was quieter, less desperate. I saw myself quieten as if from across the room. I watched her step slowly forward. I saw my fingers twitching even as the hunger rose and my face drew still.

She approached me with a crooked smile, "Haven't seen you for a week, so I thought I'd come up."

I remember thinking, I remember thinking in that distant, watching part of me, *ah, she must be out of water – do I have any? Do I have any to spare?*

"Get out, get out, get out!" I whispered, praying the darkness would alert her, that she would recognise the rank smell of blood that laced the air about her, that she would spy the medical blood bags spreading out across the floor from the kitchen like the lava flows of Vesuvius. Dear God, I prayed that some remaining ounce of sense within her would click, that she would glimpse that something wasn't right and she would freak out. Instead she stepped closer. She smiled at me in the unfortunate, knowing way that innocent, ignorant teenagers unknowingly will, and she stepped closer.

There was a blood bag at her toe, the tube protruding. She knocked it away absently with the side of her shoe, she didn't notice. I caught the sound of her breathing, I followed her clumsy, coquettish steps, I heard the pound of her heart and my hunger rose with her musty, six-month sweat. She was warm and fragile and so very, very alive and I wanted her then, oh how I wanted her. My voice said – no, not even that – my words said 'run, run, run' but my heart said 'come, come, come.'

She stepped closer, gazing curiously at the mess before her, and I watched myself from a tinny distance as I clenched my jaw, as my knuckles grew white from grasping the greasy strands of carpet I'd found under my fingertips. She shook her head.

"Man, whatever you're screwed up on, I've seen a lot worse, ok?" She paused and cocked her head, standing over me, standing so close I could count the freckles on her nose, see the dirt under her ragged fingernails in the black and white darkness. I could feel her warmth strike my skin like the glow from a fire, she stood so close I could hear the saliva rolling in her mouth. I squeezed my eyes shut, watching the scene, helpless as the audience in a bad movie. I could have run from her, I could have slapped her face, I could have screamed and shouted and fled. I could have said a thousand things to revolt and disgust her, to scare her away, but I didn't. I just watched myself like it was a movie as she drew nearer and nearer in bloody, predictable teenage stupidity until I could smell the blood running thick and hot through her veins. I watched myself, and then I shut my eyes.

"Joany," I say quietly as I begin to shake bodily.

"So, like, I was kinda wondering," she draws breath, and I glimpse up at her through tightened eyelids, waiting for her to end the longest pause of my life. Only she steps forward. Dear God she steps forward. "If there's anything you need me to do – y'know, jobwise?"

I shake my head gently, pleading with her, with God. "Joany..." My voice cracks, defeated.

Her face crumples into an impatient frown, "What?" she snaps in that patronising tone of voice that teenagers reserve for parents, for people they feel safe to abuse, as I had made her feel safe with me.

"Run." I said softly.

Her frown deepens in confusion, but I have launched

myself upon her before fear has time to cross her face. I fly like a black winged shadow, knocking her to the ground, knocking the air out of her lungs as she begins to scream, but she is smothered by my ragged body and then my arms are around her, holding her vice-like even as she writhes and my teeth are in her neck, oh! Now my teeth are in her neck!

Her gasping scream is a high pitched gurgle, panic stricken as she tries to push me off, push against my shoulders, my chest, but I hold her too close and she can't lever her arms between us, can't get a purchase. She writhes, the blood is flowing into my mouth, rolling over my tongue, hot, metallic, electric as my heart pumps faster with excitement and my veins relax with delight. Joany's thoughts grow loud in my mind, a long, shocked stream of panic and confusion and chatter getting slower and more jumbled. And the fear! How I know her fear, my heart soars as her fear becomes mine, my drug, my black terror. We shudder together – we shake. Our bodies melt into one, my hand slaps vacantly at my chest, flapping weakly, trying to push the monster away. I want to cry. *Are those tears running down my face or hers?* I wonder, as our feet scrabble against the floor. I writhe and feel the pain of teeth tearing the flesh in my neck. Then the pictures come, a house, sunshine, a yellow beach ball, a dolly I loved when I was five and everything seemed not too bad, except I hated school, yes we hated school. I taste her soul, she knows mine, it is delicious, fantastic, the most glorious moment of golden intimacy as the energy flows in ripples across our bodies and bridges the gap between us. We melt into one and it doesn't matter that she is weakening because I have her, yes I have her safe with me forever and that is all that matters.

And then she recoils. I am wrenched bodily as she recoils, as she realises finally that she will not survive this and she recoils in horror. The betrayal, the confusion. *'I trusted him,'* she thinks as the waves of confusion and betrayal burst through her mind. *'I trusted you!'* Oh the regret at that. The regret she feels, the disgust and the betrayal, it hurts us both, swallowing her blood is like swallowing shattered glass, and she tastes it in my mouth and she recoils.

The light opens above. The great white light opens in the ether as her heart slows and her limbs grow floppy, and the part of her that has fled me begins to rise up and lift away and I scream in horror, "NO!" I scream and I struggle to hold on to all of her, but she lifts away, the chatter of laughter echoing in her blind

Samuel Collins

mind, *'Is that all you are?'* echoing in her silent mind, she lifts away and the light shuts off and she is gone, lost to me, part of her is lost to the light and the world that has forsaken me.

I wear her warmth like an overcoat, but the taste in my mouth as I hold her body crushed to me – it's cold and it's bitter. Oh it's bitter. I don't know what to do. For the longest time I don't know what to do. I sit, crouched on the floor clutching the body like a child confronted by death, too little to understand, I sit and I rock while the buzz of the kill hangs about my shoulders like a ghost. She is cold and lifeless and I begin to grow disgusted by her unblinking, glassy stare. The way her head lolls revolts. I throw her off me and back away into the corner by the French doors. Her body lies in an awkward, twisted pile on the carpet, mouth dripping, one eye staring at me lazily. I cry out. I whimper in my shame.

24

There is something broken about a dead body. It sounds trite to say it. Whether it's a goat, or a rat, or a young human girl, the dead body is just so much biological litter, an immensely complex and unique arrangement of molecules that add up to precisely – nothing. The cooling bundle of meat lying crumpled on the floor before me embodied the sheer empty irrelevance of a machine, but it was less than a machine. It was less than the vacated vehicle of a small human existence, less than empty. It had been pillaged. It was the sum of its parts, a collection of aimless, inanimate flesh, and nothing more. The heavenly component that added something essential, that made the arrangement of parts relevant, was gone, missing. What was left was refuse.

You can't place it, the obvious missingness, can't centre it in the heart, or the face, the greyness of the skin or the disturbing stillness of the chest, but they don't look human. They don't look as if they were ever human, the parts attached to one another, the facsimile that never worked. You find it hard to believe they ever walked, laughed, smiled, ever worked in unison as the person you knew. The dead body is the original simulacrum.

You think of the flesh as human, as defining what human is and what its limits are. But the flesh is just so many lamb chops arranged in neat little rows, arranged in clever little orders. The flesh is not the warmth, the wonder, the spontaneity that is a human being. No, those things are kept somewhere else entirely, they define you as a people, and they are untouched by the body, by its ageing, its sickness, its hunger or its joy. They are untouched by death and they are untouchable to me. They are completely independent of the body, and when they go there is nothing left, less than nothing. You are human immortal, more so than I will ever be. Your body is as nothing, a drop in the ocean of now.

I sat staring in shock at the nothingness before me, at the absence of Joany splayed rudely at my feet, wide and loud and angry. Its presence screamed at my mind inescapable, '*Look at me, look at what you've done, you deserve to look at me forever.*' The horror of the body reflected the horror of me. That one glassy eye stared, accusing.

For the longest time I couldn't move, pinned in that corner by the wide black cornea stabbing across the room to me like a laser beam, boring into my skull with horror and disgust with loss and grief but very little guilt. It was as if she were speaking to me in the hours that passed, whispering her anger, her contempt, her sheer bloody outrage at what I had done, I who had saved her only to betray her. I could almost see the finger she pointed. I could almost see the foamy drops of spittle flying from her lips as she talked with cold, icy vehemence.

But none of it was true. She was dead on floor in front of me, stiffening like some demonic statue, and all the disgust, all the recriminations took place within my own head. I wanted to move, oh how I wanted to. I wanted to flee from the horror of that broken empty shell, its inert irrelevance truly shaking me. It was nothing, the body itself meant nothing. I wanted to run from that hollow stare, I wanted to bury my head away from the loathsome evidence of what I'd done and what I was, but I did not. I could not move while the question lay blunt and ugly in a pile on the floor before me. If a body without a soul was nothing, was an irrelevance less than nothing, what was I?

It had been many, many years since I had killed someone I had known. Not out of guilt particularly. No, guilt was one emotion I was still struggling to find amongst the horror of betrayal, the shame and the self-loathing. I was disgusted with myself, outraged. I felt the immense loss, the weeping senseless waste of something unique and precious to the universe, something infinitely important that can never be recovered. I felt great, dogged pain, black and hollow and selfish in the depths of my gut, but guilt? I hadn't chosen my nature, and after millennia trapped in its endless, rapturous, torturous cycle, even when my exaltation in the highs and lows, the uncontrollable addictive indulgences was my own fault, as I liked to blame myself now, even then I found guilt a hard emotion to muster. Indeed, when faced with the questions of my own existence so inescapably as I am when I have killed someone I know, it is hard not to feel the victim of some momentous sick joke. But I'm no victim. Nature has seen to that.

But I didn't need the guilt in order to be pinned down and paralysed on the floor by the object of my torture. The question alone was enough for that. *Dear God, what am I? Why am I here, meant to live by these acts? To live so long that I begin to see your design by such ugly means? Why do you allow me here to see such things when I cannot act? The cycles, the cycles, the cycles...* I was lost among the bloodshed of eons.

I knew there were no answers in my thoughts or in my memories. God was ever silent. It wasn't God that roused me from my torpor, or even the faint perfume of decay that laced its way insidiously across the floor, adding its gentle malaise to the sick stench of the apartment. It was my nature. The sun was coming. The sky beyond the few exposed inches of glass had turned an alarming shade of violet, and I found I must move or face losing my ill-gotten new skin.

I was not about to sleep with the stinking horror in my living room, the idea was repugnant. I paced the room, waiting as the fiery dawn approached, tilting my head to see the light changing under the rolled up shutters. I would not give Cyrus the satisfaction of seeing my weakness or my crime. I waited until it was almost unbearable, until the light was a soggy, powder blue against the peaks across the bay, until I was sure that he would be unable to withstand the terrible illumination, and then I wrapped myself up, donned dark glasses, and rolled up the shutters. The exposed skin of my face immediately prickled and burned. I felt the blisters forming as I threw open the doors. I squinted, my back to the light as I took the body of my friend under the arms and dragged it out onto the balcony. I turned as I heaved the body over the railings, the first rays of a weak autumn dawn catching me with fright as I did so. I wanted to retch as the body slid past my face, as Joany's open eyes slid past my own. I turned towards the doors, and then I heard the thump below, and I did retch – long, thin strings of rust brown blood. Joany's blood. I shut the doors. I drew the curtains. I didn't sleep.

25

Of course, after Joany's murder there was no stopping me. I became the Terror of Russian Hill. I was bodily revived, and mentally – well, I had nothing left to lose – the nights of blood and madness had seen to that. Over the next few nights I grew stronger as the blood seeped into my tissues. Thin, fresh skin toughened, muscle firmed, new teeth pushed through. A thousand little unfinished biological jobs took their turn before the marching restoration of the blood. My nose grew a little, took shape, and found its place in the centre of my face. My eyes took on a piercing grey. My body came back to me as it had been before – a little stronger, a little faster, a lot tougher than a human man. But I didn't wait. I didn't spend those few nights watching my body's miraculous return. I hunted.

At first it was because I couldn't stand to be in the apartment I'd shredded and then defiled. I wasn't hungry so much as anxious, and while I ran to the night and the hunt certainly, I fled the dark stain in the lounge just as fully. The nights grew ever longer but on the occasions when I awoke before sunfall I paced the rooms in rage, unable to escape the hollow space where Joany fell, where no light ever seemed to fall. The darkness hung there in the air like a net of black and I paced, unable to look over to that dark space by the French doors where the shadows hung angry and pregnant. When I felt the sun finally touch the horizon I bolted. I couldn't wait – I knew it would be gone before I reached the bottom of the stairs. I ran down, down, down in circles, running from myself, running to bloody oblivion.

Yet the ground was a spectre I was reluctant to approach – I slowed as the stairwell prepared to give me up and I could no longer hide in its dark maternal folds. I pressed the echoes from my mind. The ground floor was a rude birth into shafts of half-light and dust. I crawled out of the parking garage and left the tower from the rear, avoiding the rotting mound of flesh that was Joany's corpse.

There were three major tribal camps left on the island and a few stragglers. Each group was part way towards evacuating with the great exodus that had taken hold of the city. The people were busy stockpiling the last of their supplies, building rafts or trying to barter passage east across the bay to the central planes, or south along the archipelago to the southern desert and presumably the L.A. Basin. Each group searched desperately through the exhausted remnants of the island, looking through the rubble for wood or anything that would burn, for plastic bottles or containers, bin bags, polystyrene for flotation, anything they could use or barter. Food was most scarce, and the wise ones had taken to eating rats, but even the rats were thin. Each night the fit and able would split up into groups of two or three and scour the island in desperation as the camps competed to get off the sterile island before winter took hold. Each night I threw myself into the hunt.

I lunged after groups of three young men, fighting them, breaking bones, I didn't care. They threw rocks, struck me with bats, I barely noticed. They slashed at me with blunt knives, they could have shot at me had they had bullets for their guns, I didn't care. I would take one down, chase another whilst a third escaped to tell tales of the blood-crazed monster, I didn't care – I had nothing to lose. Part of me expected them to strike back, to form bigger groups, to knock me down, trap me, kill me, or at least try. I wanted them to fight back, I wanted them to catch me, to prise me from my eternal oblivion with their own anger and retribution, but while my legend grew and spread among the camps they did nothing but pack secretly in small groups, flee the island unannounced and unprepared in twos and threes. It was the ones that were abandoned and stranded that I picked off.

It was the chase I loved, the struggle and the madness. I had no patience for finesse, there was no stalking in the shadows, no waiting for the weakest one to be alone. I simply followed my ears till I drew near to a group of scavengers and then I threw myself in. More often than not they ran, and I ran after, gleeful with hungry anticipation. I would wrap my arms around the slowest and bring them down, tear their throat as my legs curled around theirs and we struggled in the dirt like lovers. And then I left their body in the dirt like trash, like an empty snake skin.

I watched myself. I watched with that same poisonous detachment I'd had before, helpless against the responsibility for it to be different somehow, better this time every time I killed a hapless, undeserving stranger. Not 'Why them?' but, 'Why not them?' of course. I watched myself, impotent to prevent their death or to save myself from my endless, meaningless hunger for blood and oblivion. I wasn't hungry, I wasn't in need of sustenance. I was glutted and I gorged myself. I did it anyway, without thought or consideration, or even awareness. It didn't matter if I killed or if I didn't, I didn't need it and I was never satisfied. I did it simply because I could. It seemed all so unnecessary, so irrelevant, and yet there was nothing else to do. I sucked the life out of those unfortunate, irrelevant stragglers and for those few brief, ever less striking moments I forgot the horror of Joany and I forgot the horror of myself as I stole their memories and their lifetimes, and the greatest horror of all was that I took them for granted.

I liked it when they fought back. I liked it when they beat me, when I had to raise my arms for them to break their bats against. I felt something as the pain blazed through my body, something close and also distant. I had a reason to act, to live. The river of blood that flowed down my throat soothed my wounds by day. I liked the risk most of all. I liked the idea that one of those fragile toy men before me might succeed and trade the brief moments of oblivion his death would bring with some more permanent damage, but reckless as I was, I always fought back, I always overwhelmed them. The Terror of Russian Hill always won.

I drank and I drank and I drank. I was never hungry but always in need as my addiction overtook any sense of self I'd had. At first I killed one or two a night, and then three or four, a week later I simply wandered into a camp and chased anyone who cared to run, laughing madly as I did so, lost in a nightmare world where the rubble streets looked like my old neighbourhood, but I was trapped, never able to find my way out. I hid in the tower by day, waiting for the moment I would taste blood again, pacing, tearing my hair. I watched myself kill, unable to prevent it whilst somewhere in the back of my mind I was counting the bodies and doing the math.

There were a finite number of bodies on the island. Everyone that could leave did leave. The blood-induced mindlessness was awful but easy – I had no awareness, no pain, and no sympathy. It was when the river of blood ran dry and my ticket to oblivion expired that the true torture began. Everything I had had run out, I reached the end of the line finally, there was nothing left to buy but my denial. No, oblivion was horror but it was easy. Coming to whilst the teeth of addiction sharpened their grasp on my body and discovering that reality was hell – that was unimaginable torment.

Extinction, like the future, surprises one slowly. I at first had the dim sense that there were a few people on the island, then a few less, and then just one or two hard-to-find souls hiding in the rubble – hiding from me. Then one night I looked down, blinking through the darkness as if I had just woken up, and I found the last body at my feet, crumpled where I had let it fall. I looked around me, bewildered in the chill air, and I knew I was alone, alone and empty. I knew it was over.

I howled. My anger knew no bounds. I screamed with rage on that barren island. Even the rats froze at the sound of it, but there was no one else to hear. I felt it in my bones and saw it in the ether, there was no one left on dry land and I daren't cross the water – I hadn't the wits to make it back in time, nor to let my ferryman live the length of the crossing. You see I was the monster then, those dark nights, I was the mad, deranged hunter and that's all I was, but I was not unconscious in the way that I had been in the apartment. True, my awareness was limited to the smell of warm flesh half a mile downwind, the sounds of whispers over campfire crackling, the glittering dance of torches in the night, but I had awareness, I had intention. My mind contained room only for chases, for strategies, for the hours before dawn and for staying alive, but somewhere inside I knew the risks I could take, I knew what I could get away with without being wholly responsible for my own destruction – and it was responsibility I was running from. Just as ever it was responsibility I couldn't bear. After Joany I had become the monster out of choice, out of abandonment – I had nothing left. I cared for nothing, I valued nothing, there was nothing to prevent me. I picked the road of oblivion and I ran away from myself, ran away from the responsibility of existence. In much the same way if I wanted to find the loving arms of destruction they had to belong to someone else – I couldn't even take responsibility for my own ending.

But now here I was, lost and alone and truly at the end – there was nowhere to go and all my crutches were exhausted, I would have to take a step on my own. I could walk up the steps to an empty, ruined apartment, for no reason but to save myself from the dawn. I could walk into the sunlight. Either way I was responsible, I was making a choice rather than reacting to a situation. So I sat down on the sidewalk by the dead man whose face and life I don't remember – one of many, and I howled and whimpered and raged as the madness enveloped me so lovingly and I tried to give myself over to it, tried to let go, but that sliver of choice infected my mind, illuminated me like the crack of light in a doorway – to live or to die but to unavoidably make the decision. I was angry, mad with rage at being forced into a position, this choice, this position or any position. Yet my anger was useless, impotent, it got me absolutely nowhere, and I was bitterly angry about that too. I saw myself from the outside once again, from across the street, sitting in that light from the doorway. I saw myself screaming and howling and then, like a child who realises his tantrum will get him nowhere I saw myself stop quite abruptly. There was no way to close the door. There was no one to save me. I got up and wandered blindly towards the Tower and my darkened apartment while the dawn light approached. It wasn't so much a decision to live, it was a decision not to die.

The first night of hiding in the apartment was filled with a shocking, pregnant calm, a cold, apprehensive rage that built and built like an ice sheet waiting to crack under its own colossal weight. The horror of it was in living there, in the rooms where I had killed a child. It was in sleeping in the chamber next door, hiding from the light in safety when she'd had no safety. The horror was in the insult. And yet I was trapped, finally, with myself. There was no blood for forgetting. I could sleep my days away at the Leibowitz' place if I cared to, but the dark stain of Joany would still be here, on the carpet, hanging in the air. I could sleep on the Looter's Causeway, or the Police Zone, I could demolish the Tower and travel the world but Joany would still be here in my mind, staring silently.

So I sat, in cold, still silence for nights on end while my anger smouldered and my cravings grew unbearable, content for the hot, guilty pokers to gather around me and pierce my mind. I was not hungry, I was not in need. I was addicted.

I fidgeted as the cravings whispered in my ears, brushing over my skin like slivers of glass until I scratched myself, until I bled. I sucked the blood but it was thin and empty, a pointless, uncomforting substitute. I squinted in the darkness, huddled in the far corner of the room as the shadows danced through the detritus of my life, sipping dregs of stale water from long neglected bottles. My stupor grew as I sat there for days and nights, feeling the dull ache in my belly gather dark, vacuous strength to send tendrils out through my limbs.

Those were the moments where I would snap, where I would whimper at the overwhelming desire for blood, I would tear at my hair and my eyes, clawing at the threads in the carpet and clinging to my knees for fear that I would otherwise get up and fly down the stairs, running out madly into the world in a bid for the Broadway Jetty even though I had not the faintest awareness of whether it was the middle of the day or the end of night.

Sometimes I would scream and rage for endless hours, beating the walls with splintered chair legs and kicking through the empty blood bags and tufts of upholstering foam on the floor. I tore at the kitchen cupboards and threw the carcasses at the French doors, smashing the remaining glass and rattling the blinds so that sunlight rippled through them, a hellish wave of fire. I watched myself do these things. All I had to do was stop, but I could not lift a finger against myself.

Suddenly the rage would be over and I would be left staring at the broken glass, the piles of shredded foam beside me, the evidence of the whirlwind laughing at me in my impotence. I was powerless to stop this process now as ever I was in the times before, but just as then, the blind rage and destruction got me nowhere. It was just another denial, another avoidance of the reality and the responsibility. I looked at my hands and felt foolish.

My body grew lean as the days passed and I bounced between rage and paralysis without sleep nor sustenance. It wasn't hunger yet, if anything I grew stronger not weaker as my body stocked its reserves and steeled itself, becoming wiry and lean for the dry season. I sat, daydreaming and pulling a Japanese silk painting to pieces as the cravings grew stronger, tighter, and I tried to think of other things. I hummed as the black dog came upon me, I whispered jokes to myself as the pain gathered in my guts and my chest, and I tried to stay calm, not let myself get angry at my own denial and stamp my foot like a wet faced toddler. I clung to itchy, jittery calmness like a life preserver, even as the relentless torture of withdrawal marched on and on.

The smell in the flat was obnoxious. I didn't care. The dregs of blood that lingered in the seams of the medical bags, that clung to the tubes like an oil slick began to smell sweet and rancid amidst the perfume of death on the carpet and the mustiness of my furniture. Joany's presence hung over the living room, her grubby odour seemed to take hold, get a little stronger each day as I tried not to cry, tried not to whimper in mad fear. I sat and rotted in the rotten apartment, an easy way to torture myself, and a welcome distraction from the torture my angry body was visiting upon me.

Samuel Collins

But it wasn't the moments of rage and pain, the hours of destructive screaming, or the nights I spent sitting and thinking of blood – only of blood, that brought me progress. It was the moments of clarity, of calmness where I stared down at my hands that had caused such destruction, the moments that I felt foolish and regretful even as the pain writhed within me, even as the addiction tightened its grip. It was those few moments of self-awareness when I understood that the pain would worsen, the cravings would deepen, and there was nothing to do but endure it, accept it, and try to regain control, it was that or lose my mind entirely and wake up outside in the dawn as the first rays of light flayed me alive.

So those moments of clarity grew as I clung to them, often borne out of bursts of rage when I injured myself and the pain awakened me, often out of the intense, whimpering terror I felt when, pressed into the corner of the room I felt the addiction heaving over me, circling my mind as the pressure built and I believed my eyeballs would burst. In those moments when I gasped for air, when I remembered to breathe slowly, to fight and claw for the slowing of my heart, the focus brought that controlling, accepting, never quite serene clarity where I knew, I understood like the hellish times before, that I could ill afford to feed with such indulgence ever, ever.

Gradually those moments of control grew longer and came on closer together as I learned to bear the mad strong cravings that hugged my body like bands of wrought iron. I learned to think as the desire for blood rolled through my mind. I learned to stand, and then to walk as mortar bursts of stolen memories rattled through my thoughts. I learned to cage the anger, the despair, the indignant outrage that I could not have what I wanted. I caught it as it ran into a sacrificial vessel in my mind, as it cooled, solidified, turned to ice. My rage was a hard nugget stuck inside me, offending me like a pearl to an oyster, and it had one focus, one grain of sand about which all else revolved. Cyrus.

I took small steps at first, walking to the end of the corridor outside the apartment, going down and up the stairs one flight at a time. I fought off the tremors as addiction shook me like a rag doll, I fought off the nausea, the vertigo as I stood up. All the while my control hardened with my resolve, my grip on reality grew tighter as Cyrus haunted my bitter thoughts, his lilting voice sliding through my mind, his soft laugh taunting me.

I learned to walk again as the nights came on longer and

346

the weather broke. Autumn arrived abruptly like a ship in harbour, announced by a stiff breeze, something chilled and disappointed in the early evening air. I walked the island as my body grew wiry and taut, learning to trust my will once again as I found the balance between need and addiction, bound together as they are by the thread of hunger. Bound tight to me. I walked the broken streets, listening for life and finding only rats and cats, catching them sometimes, kneeling in the dirt and feeding in the shadow of the Transamerica Pyramid across the floodwater. I was careful. I withheld. I never fed as much as I wanted, and animals are a poor substitute for human lives and souls. I watched myself with distain as I crouched in the rubble and the cracked sidewalks licking the blood from my hands. There was enough here to satisfy the need, not enough to bait the addiction. It's a fine line, no one walks it but me.

I grew confident in my revitalised body, I became familiar with its speed, comfortable with its strength as I chased vermin and trudged up the stairs before dawn. With the absence of blood it had ceased to change, ceased to heal, something about it ceased to flow and it hardened into one steady form that I could get used to, could take for granted. I walked the nights as my being solidified into one controlled, steady mass, until I could ignore the warm brush of a hungry cat about my legs, until I could watch a struggling raft of refugees drift by along the bay without a mad, furious desire. I began to stretch my senses across the water, feeling the few boatmen fighting the waves, feeling the desperation of the stragglers on neighbouring islands. When I could tolerate the sense of closeness, the intimacy of their glittering minds without falling to my knees, without shaking and unravelling in a bitter, addictive rage, without feeling the burning indignant anger at having to deny myself, when I could watch their thoughts and their hopes with detachment and impunity – then I knew I was ready.

I awoke early one evening and scrabbled around in the apartment looking for weapons, tools, anything I could use to wreak revenge against the object of my hatred. I burned to cause pain to such a one who had thrown me to the wolves and expected me to crawl to him.

There were diamonds hidden among the detritus. I found a screwdriver and a hatchet, both hidden under the ruins of kitchen cupboards. All of the guns had spread out in an irregular circle, migrating invisibly under the trash from the point where their cabinet used to be. There were no bullets, I don't know where they went. I sifted carefully through the collapsed shelves, the loose pages of books, torn clothing and splintered wood, I couldn't find them or any sign of their boxes. I have the idea that I threw them over the balcony in my madness, my vague, subconscious sense of self-preservation acting out. If that's all I did with them I am glad.

It was well past the middle of the night when I left the Tower brandishing my tools, a worn-out zippo lighter and a candle in a jar. I left uncomfortably late and made my way down to the jetty, waving my light in the breeze as the air howled over the jar lip. It seemed to take forever to attract a boatman even though I saw several empty taxis slip past in the darkness. The man who approached finally was wide-eyed and cautious but I promised him water and canned fruit as he drew up alongside the sinking, spongy jetty. He looked hungry then, desperate eyes peering from a hollow face as his gaunt, tired body pulled against the oars and the water. He was right to be cautious, I waited until we were out in the deep water and then I killed him, lunging so violently that I thought the boat would capsize.

I was horrified as I punctured his lung with the screwdriver, I can't imagine the pain of it but I needed him to die silently. He struggled as I went for his neck, my new, sharp little teeth making short work of his leathery flesh. I held his mouth closed with one hand, gripping him around the chest with my other arm as he batted against me, his arms flapping weakly as his memories met mine and his life leaked away. Lost in his mind, lost in fascination for his busy little life, his thoughts escaped into me as his body failed. Briefly we were one being until I felt the darkness close around him, sweep up his limbs and surround his brain, and whatever of him was in me could no longer return or escape. He died a pathetic death, flopping about like a bird hit by a car, and I was sorry for that, sorry too that I should murder one in my employ, but I needed the boat and I couldn't take the chance that he would not wait for me where I was heading.

I slipped the body gently into the black waves hoping it would sink but expecting it to float, and then I caught the oars, pulling away from that clothed back, that little mound of death that broke through the peaks and drifted away on invisible currents. I turned the dinghy towards the city, the Financial District, and brought it as close to the sandbanks and rubble as I dared before drawing up silently towards the Transamerica Pyramid.

The little vessel slipped through the water, rocking strongly as I approached the tower and the eddies caught at the hull. I headed straight for the bay doors, catching the sight of the Looter's Causeway in the distance as I turned the hull around the corner of the building. The chain of fairy lights was broken, huge sections of the bridge were dark and derelict, haunted by the whistling wind. The bridge looked sad and abandoned, an illuminated lifeline dying of neglect. I brought the boat around and tied it to the mooring hoop bolted to the concrete before reaching up to press the buzzer on the intercom, and there was nothing. I flushed with impatience, and then a cold shiver of doubt ran through me. I had lost him – they had gone and I would never get satisfaction, I would never get to return the pain. I pressed the buzzer again, viciously, and this time someone replied.

"Get away from the building. You won't be told twice." A female voice snapped.

"Ana."

"Oh. It's you. Top floor. He's at the radio." She didn't sound any more hospitable, but the shutters rolled up, and I stepped out of the boat and into the vast loading bay.

Strip lights flickered on as I crossed to the elevator bank, cutting through the darkness like a lightning strike before settling down. My footsteps echoed across the concrete. I pressed the call button but one of the elevators was already on its way to greet me. I wondered if I was being watched, I wondered where the camera would be. I didn't look around. I looked normal, well even, there was nothing to be suspicious of. I stood there patiently, a man they knew, wearing a sweater, a cloth wrapped bundle under one arm.

The elevator swooshed open, I stepped in as the hairs rose on the back of my neck. This was where I was vulnerable – entering their lair and their machine. I punched the button for the top floor, the doors closed and my stomach sank – the elevator shot upwards.

It was between the tenth and twelfth floors that I pulled the red emergency stop knob. It popped out and the carriage juddered to a halt that made my knees weak. I had to lever the doors open with the screwdriver and the hatchet, breaking them open a crack before I could separate them with my hands. The elevator was between floors, and I ducked down uncomfortably and slipped through the gap, spilling out into the lower corridor. The elevator intercom rattled as I got to my feet, Ana's voice, sharp and concerned warbled through the air.

"Hey, where are you? What's wrong with the elevator? Cancel the stop."

I ignored her and looked about me. I was disorientated, and had no idea what floor I was on, I decided to put some distance between myself and my last known position – they couldn't have cameras everywhere if they had them at all. I found the stairwell to the side of the elevator bank and rushed down a couple of floors. I burst out onto level nine, still no idea where to find what I was looking for, and so I ran along the corridors, opening each door I came to, flicking lights before abandoning a room and moving on. I went by trial and error – I had little time but there was nothing I could do to speed my search. I passed by storerooms full of boxes, rows and rows of shelving, I gazed across empty rooms, cavernous and dead. It wasn't there. I dashed back to the stairs and dropped a floor, terrified I would hear the footfall of Ana and Cyrus before I could locate my prize.

I found myself on another floor of supplies, rooms of tools and copper wire. I passed offices stacked with cleaning fluid and engine oil. Towards the other end of the corridor I came quite suddenly upon the things I was looking for. Fuel tanks. Room after room of fuel tanks, heating oil in large square reservoirs, gasoline in sealed barrels, propane canisters locked in steel cages. There were safety notices everywhere, fire alarms and extinguishers. I set to work, my hands shaking.

There is a room full of gasoline barrels. I strain to rock them through the single doorway, battering the door as the frosted office glass rattles. Once out into the blue-carpeted corridor I roll the barrels to each doorway and place them in the rooms of propane and the rooms of oil. I notice that each of the big, square heating tanks is linked to the others via a series of pumps and pipes that rise away into the ceiling. I want to cut through the copper pipes with my hatchet but I am afraid of sparks. I pray the heat will do the work as I sweat and drag the barrels out one by one and position them along the corridor and through the rooms. It takes me twenty minutes to do this, and I am surprised, overjoyed that I have not been discovered.

Once the barrels are in place I run from room to room, unscrewing the caps and tipping them over. They fall hard on the concrete floor, warbling in strange, fluid whale song as they judder against the carpet. Tipping such a weight is dangerous in itself, and my fingers slip as I grow damp with exertion. The gasoline fills my nostrils and lungs with its obnoxious fragrance, the waves of fumes strike me, threatening to overpower me as the noxious red liquor pools into the carpet, works its way into the cracks between fuel tanks and gas canisters, vaporizes to fill the very air with volatile, explosive vengeance.

I kick an open barrel all the way down the corridor, past the elevator bank to the window in the peculiar sloped concrete wall at the far end. The liquid sloshes out onto my trousers and soaks into my boots, and forms a jagged trail of dark moisture that follows me even as I grow groggy and slow from the fumes. Fumbling for my hatchet I press my forehead to the sealed, double glazed window pane, eager to shatter it and gulp fresh air into my lungs. The bitter tang of gasoline coats my mouth and sticks in my throat, and I am numb as the world outside my mind grows dim and hollow. I must be touching the glass but it seems so very far away.

My first strike of the hatchet glances off the liquid smooth surface but the blade bounces off with barely a scratch and a strange 'tink' sound. I whimper as dizziness and vertigo close in on me, as I feel the strangling fumes gather around my throat, I strike again with what feels as if it should be more force, but the hatchet clatters against the glass and glances off. I gulp a deep, nauseating breath and fall to my knees, grasping the hatchet in both hands to swing again desperately, and finally the first sheet of glass splinters under the corner of the blade, and I twist the hatchet through the laminate, watching dimly as sharp, ugly cracks spread across the pane in lightning flashes. I grin at the destruction, I grin in delight and relief.

I lever gritty, glittering fragments away from the pane, gouging a hole as I shower my knees with the razor shards, and then I strike at the outer layer of glass. With the pressure seal between the panes broken, the outer layer splinters immediately, and bursts open, blossoming with milk white cracks like a perverse flower unfolding at my second blow. Fresh air strikes me hard and cold in the face, gusting up the sides of the Pyramid a hundred feet above sea level. It is like a jet blast of consciousness and I crumple before it, gasping for breath and regaining my grip on the world. I shudder as I suck down air and the strength returns to my inebriated, floppy body. After long, stolen moments I begin to strike at the window again and again, showering my face and hair with fragments as I chop out my escape hole. Eventually the fractures spread across the whole window, milk thistle tendrils dancing into the corners of the glass, and I stand to kick the glass out into the abyss.

Clutching the lighter in my hands, I stare down as the fragments glitter and tumble away from me in seeming slow motion. The wind buffets my face, and it starts to drizzle, a fine, needle sharp moisture biting into my face and hands. Beneath me is only water, but the drop is not vertical. The steeply angled walls of the Pyramid are punctuated by row upon row of angular concrete lintels between each pane of oil-smooth glass. This is my only way out, the only escape route that doesn't depend on the failings of Cyrus and his remotely controlled elevators and doors. I do not know if I can climb down, but I do not jump. I wait.

It isn't long before Cyrus and Ana arrive – erupt, actually, through the stairwell doors. The smell must be rising. Ana steps through first, a pale stiffness on her face, but Cyrus emits a strange, squawking gulp as he steps into the corridor, and I cannot help but smile faintly. Ana stares at me not ten yards away while Cyrus follows the dark trail along the corridor to the barrel discarded at my feet. Our eyes meet but my expression is blank. Time flows between us, the sick knowledge of inevitability, the sheer waste of our mutual journey, and I feel I should say something, I almost feel I should shrug, pat him on the back before wreaking my default vengeance, my arbitrary brand of justice. Almost. It turns out I have nothing for him.

I strike the zippo and time winds down. As I toss it to the puddle at my feet I have in my mind the horrible, ridiculous picture that the trail of flame will run for a few feet and then stop at some gap in the stream of fuel, but this isn't what happens. Cyrus mouths something I cannot hear as the blue light of burning vapour runs jet-fast along the carpet, and then the pool around the barrel erupts in a bright flash, the flames spreading across the corridor so lightning quick it's as if the very air is on fire. Cyrus stares dumbfounded, his head turning as the river of flame speeds past him, and Ana pulls him back into the stairwell, grabbing his arm and shoulder. Then the barrel explodes in my face and I am blown out of the gaping window, smashing my head on the frame and sailing into the night air, tumbling down into darkness.

26

I do not remember hitting the water, I remember the searing pain across my face and body, I remember blindness as I spun through the nothingness of space. I remember hitting concrete. I remember being sucked into icy depths and feeling gently unable to move and unable to care. I did not feel I was moving, but my body drifted upwards, and as my lungs began to scream for air I kicked out, struggling to break the distant surface, fighting the seductive currents and my waterlogged shoes. I emerged into the world, reborn from the dark, silent depths a spluttering, wheezing manchild, and as I squinted through flash-blind eyes and struck out for the walls of the Pyramid that rose out of the waves, the first of many small explosions rang out through the night. It began gently to rain showers of lethal glass slivers.

I clung to the sides of the building like a desperate, waterlogged rat as the waves sucked and pulled me away from the concrete pillars. I dragged myself around three massive sides of the building by my shaking arms, groping semi-blind as I searched for the boat.

The dinghy rocked violently as I heaved myself over the gunwale, water from my sodden clothes pooling in the hull amidst the rain and the sleet. I lay face upwards, watching the Pyramid glow as it was engulfed in a halo of fire, wanting nothing more than to drift off to sleep with the soporific, icy cold that had sunk into my body. It was certain death to fall into sleep as the glass rained down, to lie in a rocking boat as Ana and Cyrus emerged from somewhere above, as I was sure they would. I made myself sit up. With numb hands I fumbled to untie the mooring rope and I began to row clumsily away from the tower, dizzy and numb and not altogether aware of my direction.

The wind bit into my face and stirred me, but its cold teeth sank through my wet clothes and chilled me to the bone. Although there was no hope of drying out as the sleet and the rain wore on, I grew a little warmer as I pulled the boat through the water, squinting as I guided it out into the lake. Pain blossomed over my hands and face as the exertion beat off the numbness, and I found myself covered in a thousand tiny razor cuts, my clothes shredded, my skin was saturated with slivers of glass. Every time I flexed my limbs to row another knife would slide along a wound, but there was nothing I could do as my body wept blood into the rain.

The only thing that saved me from hypothermia was the rowing, and although my agony increased, this knowledge spurred me on. The fire was spreading gloriously around the tower, a ring of light shining out across the bay, its faint heat warm against my rain-beaten face. It was the light of the fire that guided me around the sandbanks of the Financial District, it highlighted the dark shadow of Russian Hill Island against the glittering waves of the bay.

I didn't make it to the jetty. I rowed to the closest point of the island shore and stepped through the murky sludge at the waters edge, struggling and stumbling through the scrap and trash as I fought like mad to drag the boat above the water line. I limped, sodden and shivering through the rubble maze towards my tower, keeping to the shadows and trembling my way uphill to the intersection of my block.

I wailed with relief as the tower loomed large. I didn't need to make it upstairs, I just needed to get out of the rain. Even in my desperation I took the long way round and entered through the parking garage. I gave the front of the building, the place where I imagined Joany's body still lay, a wide berth, despite the feral cats and starving dog packs.

I stopped inside the garage and stripped, wringing my clothes out as my teeth chattered in the dark. I couldn't stand upright, I was so cold, and I huddled over my clothes, clutching them to my chest as I made my way to the stairwell. I climbed the stairs slowly, as the dawn stirred faintly in the east, stopping occasionally to pull the shards from my hands. Explosions thundered in the distance and I smiled despite the deep stiffness that was spreading through my cold body. The music of destruction spurred me on.

Now I stand on my balcony, watching the Transamerica Pyramid burn like a torch across the waters. The flames roar up all sides of the building, a giant roman candle whose light rolls off the waves. I can feel the heat on my face. Wrapped in filthy towels and old blankets I lean on the twisted, heat damaged railings, the burnt-out wreckage of my generator piled crudely at my feet. I have sweet music in my mind as I watch the flames shimmer across the floodplain, a gigantic bonfire born out of vanity and vengeance. The only thing missing to my civilised mind is a glass of blood, but I have fed well enough tonight, I will recover, I will hunt soon.

My eyes gleam as enormous, hundred foot flames lick up the sides of the pyramid. I think of Cyrus, what he will do now that he too has nothing left. I smile at the ruin. Turning my back to the flames I glimpse the wreckage of my apartment through the broken panes of glass. There is nothing left. It's a mass of splintered wood and torn paper, shredded lives and empty sentiments. It is a monument to denial, to waiting patiently for the end, to watching yourself drown.

I do not blame Cyrus for this, I know how little responsibility he bears. The gas was running out, the blood was running out. The era was running out. There is no value any more. The wealth in the room that I keep locked, the room with its door hanging gently from its hinges, it means nothing. For the first time in millennia gold cannot buy water. Three centuries of bonds, deeds and investments are worth only the heat that paper gives up as it burns. I gaze around the apartment unable to recognise the landscape I see before me. Cherished books torn to shreds, silk prints scorched and filthy. I find I am unable to care. Even the old relics, Phoenician beads my mother wore in her hair, Minoan vases, Cretan curse tablets with their words against me scratched into the soft lead. Things I have laboured to save in every age, concessions the modern world can no longer accommodate. These things lie brushed up in corners in the locked room, strewn and broken along with fragments of a mosaic, a portrait of a pale, fair haired woman I believe to be my mother, I like to think is my mother, although I can't be sure. The woman holds the arm of a darker man, but his face is obliterated. I wept when I rediscovered that mosaic two centuries ago, just where I believed it to be. Its presence proved that my past was real, that some of my memories were real. And it means nothing, its value is nothing. I can't cry for it now, and I can't take it with me.

I have outlasted everything I have ever known. I have outlived meaning, and I will continue to do so. We all live because there is nothing else to do – I am fortunate to have such latitude as I do. So it's gone, it's all gone – so what? I glance across the living room at the life I tried to preserve, the straws of a civilised world I tried to cling to as it burned until it damn near took me down in flames with it. I will miss this civilized era, the calm illusion of safety, the lack of true conflict – local wars yes but not the plague of locusts that was Genghis Khan or the Great Alexander. With all of the oil gone this stability will never return. The weather will be violent for centuries to come as nature finds a new balance. For the first time in history man has permanently and radically changed – damaged I should say, his world, and I saw it all for I endure, untouched and unliving. I saw it coming, I saw it play out, I did so very little to prepare for I was fascinated, spellbound by chaos and destruction, the modern replacements for evil, on a scale I could never hope to match in all of eternity. I could never save enough oil nor destroy enough lives. I could never store enough water. I grin faintly. Cyrus couldn't either.

So in reality it's over. I will leave it all behind. I turn away from the empty dwelling, I watch the flames with satisfaction. All around the city people are struggling to leave, to escape, and I will join them. I will seek out the new travellers, the Romany and the displaced, and I will strike a bargain as they travel the vast plains heading northwards to the ice sheets and the frozen water. I'll be a demon, but I'll be their demon, protecting their little ones from the bandits, the pirates and the highwaymen. I will hunt by night on their behalf, the magic man, the cursed one, the one whose spell could be broken by the touch of daylight, and with the currency of stolen life I will make myself invaluable. I will explain to them with a hollow heart and a fearful lump in my throat the things I half believe, that I am a monster, a demon, a non-person, a non-man, scaring them and wooing them and promising them that only I can protect them from the dark hours, if they will only protect me from the light. I will sell them the myth of me and they will be desperate to buy it, they will see the truth amongst the lies as the blood of their would-be murders decorates my hands, asking few questions even as their eyes grow wide in fear and awe, jealousy and hatred. Like the ancient tribes they will turn a blind eye to bargain with a devil, the deal will be struck. I will trade my services with those who can shelter me by day – it's been done before.

So I watch as the tower burns and buckles, I flinch as immense cracking sounds rocket out across the bay and echo off the hills. The concrete is splintering from the heat and pressure. I know how little he has taken from me, that young one. He relieved me of my illusions, and perhaps I should thank him, but I find I am not so generous. He cost me two weeks grace and madness, maybe three if I'd stretched my supplies out. And Joany. He cost me Joany, the shame of Joany. I cannot accept that I would have let myself get so weak, let her wander into danger, if I'd had the time to manage my supplies and my decline, but finally *I* killed her. I took her. He caused me pain and he *embarrassed* me, and like a child I wanted to hurt him back. I took his dreams from him and his smug, self-righteous arrogance. I wanted to see the look on his face as he realised the universe was not a predictable place, that he had not seen yet a hundredth of what's possible, I wanted to show him that he couldn't predict and he couldn't rule. I wanted most to see the look on his face as he stepped out of that stairwell and realised that God has no special plans for him.

He is young, he will learn. He will see the rise and fall as I have and he will grow as bored and weary as me. Trapped in life. Trapped in a cycle no one mind was ever meant to witness so completely. I have seen the ends of eras. I've seen empires dawn and die. I have watched the never-ending peaks and troughs of human life, and I've seen the look of horror dawn across the face of humanity as it realised over and again the price of hubris and the cost of fallacy, as it realised it could indeed descend again into the darkness of ignorance and superstition – that there was no supreme, absolute human world that could not go backwards into the night. I have seen humanity realise, not once, but endlessly, that there is no one there, no one waiting there to save you from your choices or your will. God isn't waiting to save you from yourselves – with love he gives you your mistakes as much as he does your blessings, for your self is the only gift there is.

I have glimpsed the form of God's fractal universe as it folds in on itself. It is a place of endless patterns, of repeating histories, the only factor being scale. I have seen everything come round before, but I continue to watch, to live, for there is nothing else to do. There is no other monster inside, just me – I am responsible, for I am addicted to myself, and I will be standing alone at the end of time when there's no one left to kill. I am the lord of all the nothing I purvey. I am the millionaire who cannot buy water. I am the bringer of death and the custodian of the human procession. I am he whose heart is empty and whose mind is overfull – I dance and laugh and fiddle and weep as God's universe burns through the endless cycle of creation and destruction, as the snake devours its own tail.

I am the endless.

I am the nameless.

I am Nero.

Acknowledgements

This novel is homage to the genius of Richard Matheson.

Thank you to my parents, Bob and Clare Collins, for the amazing life I have led, the things I have been given the opportunity to witness, and for your support during the process of this book. You continue to keep me alive through the bad times. I love you guys.

To my sisters, Louisa and Rebecca, this is what I do. I love you. To the rest of my family, and to Kat Harmon, to Sian Caruth, Karen Glazier, Lana Jackson, Christine Lines, and to my adoptive family in the bay, Chris and Kris and Daniel and Rebecca and the many others – you keep me sane without really trying. I love you too.

Love and thanks to Matthew Govig, Stardust and Stephen Neuburger for reading the draft, without whom this book would not have reached you in its present, vaguely grammatical form – any further mistakes are completely the product of my own literary tyranny.

To everyone who's ever said no to me and told me not to believe in myself: Thank you, I'd never have gotten here without your narrow-mindedness. Now, if only I could remember your names...